The History of Nations

Pakistan

THE HISTORY OF NATIONS

Pakistan

Other books in the History of Nations series:

THE HISTORY OF NATIONS

Pakistan

Jann Einfeld, *Book Editor*

Daniel Leone, *President*
Bonnie Szumski, *Publisher*
Scott Barbour, *Managing Editor*

GREENHAVEN
PRESS®

THOMSON

GALE

San Diego • Detroit • New York • San Francisco • Cleveland
New Haven, Conn. • Waterville, Maine • London • Munich

THOMSON
★
GALE
™

LIBRARY OF CONGRESS CATALOGING-IN-PUBLICATION DATA

Pakistan / Jann Einfeld, book editor.
    p. cm. — (History of nations)
    Includes bibliographical references and index.
    ISBN 0-7377-2044-1 (pbk. : alk. paper) — ISBN 0-7377-2043-3 (lib. : alk. paper)
      1. Pakistan—History. I. Einfeld, Jann. II. History of nations (Greenhaven Press)
    DS376.9.P34   2004
    954.91—dc21   2003048301

Printed in the United States of America

Contents

Chapter 2: Birth and Beginnings of a Nation

Chapter 3: Turbulent Times: The War of Secession and Military Rule

charge to restore law and order, their approaches to
the country's political problems differed substantially.

Chapter 4: Democracy, Disillusionment, and Return of Military Rule

1. New Hope for Democracy
by Benazir Bhutto
When General Zia-ul-Haq called for elections in
1988, Pakistan stood poised at the crossroads of a
continued dictatorship and a new hope for
democracy.

2. The Uncertain Transition to Democracy Under Bhutto and Sharif
by Saeed Shafqat
Under Bhutto and Sharif, Pakistan's history of continual military rule and hostilities among rival political families impeded the development of democratic
institutions.

3. Return to Martial Rule Under General Musharraf
by Rory McCarthy
After a decade of corrupt civil governments, Pakistan
returned to military rule under General Pervez
Musharraf, with his promised "true democracy."

Chapter 5: Current Challenges

1. Pakistan's Economic and Social Agenda for the Twenty-First Century
by Ishrat Husain
The government of Pakistan must restore public confidence in its ability to promote economic and technological change and manage the divisive tendencies
within Pakistani society.

2. Human Rights Abuses in the Name of Islam
by Akbar Ahmed
Under cover of the "blasphemy law," vengeance,
political vendettas, and gross human rights violations

have been perpetrated in the name of Islam.

FOREWORD

I n 1841, the journalist Charles MacKay remarked, "In read-ing the history of nations, we find that, like individuals, they have their whims and peculiarities, their seasons of excite-ment and recklessness." At the time of MacKay's observation, many of the nations explored in the Greenhaven Press History of Nations series did not yet exist in their current form. None-theless, whether it is old or young, every nation is similar to an individual, with its own distinct characteristics and unique story.

The History of Nations series is dedicated to exploring these stories. Each anthology traces the development of one of the world's nations from its earliest days, when it was perhaps no more than a promise on a piece of paper or an idea in the mind of some revolutionary, through to its status in the world today. Topics discussed include the pivotal political events and power struggles that shaped the country as well as important social and cultural movements. Often, certain dramatic themes and events recur, such as the rise and fall of empires, the flowering and de-cay of cultures, or the heroism and treachery of leaders. As well, in the history of most countries war, oppression, revolution, and deep social change feature prominently. Nonetheless, the details of such events vary greatly, as does their impact on the nation concerned. For example, England's "Glorious Revolution" of 1688 was a peaceful transfer of power that set the stage for the emergence of democratic institutions in that nation. On the other hand, in China, the overthrow of dynastic rule in 1912 led to years of chaos, civil war, and the eventual emergence of a Communist regime that used violence as a tool to root out op-position and quell popular protest. Readers of the Greenhaven Press History of Nations series will learn about the common challenges nations face and the different paths they take in re-sponse to such crises. However a nation's story may have devel-oped, the series strives to present a clear and unbiased view of the country at hand.

The structure of each volume in the series is designed to help students deepen their understanding of the events, movements, and persons that define nations. First, a thematic introduction provides critical background material and helps orient the reader. The chapters themselves are designed to provide an accessible and engaging approach to the study of the history of that nation involved and are arranged either thematically or chronologically, as appropriate. The selections include both primary documents, which convey something of the flavor of the time and place concerned, and secondary material, which includes the wisdom of hindsight and scholarship. Finally, each book closes with a detailed chronology, a comprehensive bibliography of suggestions for further research, and a thorough index.

The countries explored within the series are as old as China and as young as Canada, as distinct in character as Spain and India, as large as Russia, and as compact as Japan. Some are based on ethnic nationalism, the belief in an ethnic group as a distinct people sharing a common destiny, whereas others emphasize civic nationalism, in which what defines citizenship is not ethnicity but commitment to a shared constitution and its values. As human societies become increasingly globalized, knowledge of other nations and of the diversity of their cultures, characteristics, and histories becomes ever more important. This series responds to the challenge by furnishing students with a solid and engaging introduction to the history of the world's nations.

INTRODUCTION

One lesson I have learned from the history of Muslims. At critical moments in their history it is Islam that has saved Muslims and not vice versa. If today you focus your vision on Islam and see inspiration from the ever-vitalizing idea embodied in it, you will only be reassembling your scattered forces, regaining your lost integrity, and thereby saving yourself from total destruction.[1]

—Muhammad Iqbal, spiritual founder
of Pakistan, December 29, 1930

Pakistan has a unique place of symbolic and strategic significance in the modern world. As the world's largest Islamic republic, it is a role model for Muslim countries regarding the compatibility of Islam and democracy. It is also one of two nation-states (along with Israel) formed on the basis of religion and thus challenges the Western doctrine of the separation of church and state. Strategically poised at the northwest corner of the Indian subcontinent, Pakistan was a frontline state in the Cold War and remains an important Western ally in the war on terrorism. Finally, Pakistan has the technological capacity to initiate a nuclear war and is embroiled in a decades-long conflict with India that some fear could spark a third world war.

Pakistan was created by the Indian Independence Act on August 14, 1947, so that 70 million Indian Muslims could, in the words of its political founder and first governor-general, Mohammed Ali Jinnah, "live according to the genius of our people."[2] "Pakistan was founded on the basis of a religious aspiration," says British journalist David Loshak. "Its basis, its core, its very being, is Islamic."[3] Yet how this Islamic core based on laws developed in seventh-century Arabia would translate into a modern nation-state was not clear in 1947, and is still under dispute more than fifty years later. Conflict between opposing faces of Islam is a major theme of Pakistan's history and a cause of civil strife and political instability in contemporary times.

This conflict, however, is about more than how to adapt ancient traditions to modern-day life. Pakistanis are heirs of the great Mughal emperors. The Mughal Empire was one of three vast Muslim empires that once dominated the globe before their defeat by the Europeans in the nineteenth and twentieth centuries. Consequently, Pakistan is intimately involved in the larger Muslim drama to regain the lost glory and reassert the supremacy of the Islamic faith. The country's mission, according to its first prime minister, Liaquat Ali Khan, is "to demonstrate to the world that Islam . . . is a progressive force . . . and provides remedies to many of the ills from which humanity has been suffering."[4] Although it is a third world nation of only 150 million people on a landmass the size of Texas and Arizona, Pakistan is a key player in the task of reviving and reinterpreting Islam for modern times.

The Origins of Islam

The origins of Islam, the second largest and fastest growing religion in the twenty-first century, go back to A.D. 610. On the windy peaks of Mount Hira, just outside the Arabic city of Mecca, Muslims believe that God revealed the tenets of a new religion, Islam (which means submission to the will of Allah, or God), to a young Arabic man called Muhammad. Muhammad was the last of a long line of prophets that included Abraham and Jesus of Nazareth.

Islam's message was simple and direct: one God, one book (the Koran, or Muslim holy book), and one Prophet. There was no complicated philosophy, no priestly intermediaries, and no hierarchy based on caste, color, wealth, or social status. All were equal before God and had a direct divine connection by praying five times daily, fasting during the daylight hours of the ninth month of the Islamic calendar (Ramadan), and making a pilgrimage to Mecca once in a lifetime.

Islam promoted a strong sense of community embodied in the notion of *ummah*, Islamic brotherhood that transcended geographic boundaries. It was socially responsible, incorporating *zakat*, or alms for the less fortunate, and rejecting usury, or charging interest, as exploitative of fellow Muslims. According to the Koran, God was forgiving, compassionate, and tolerant of all monotheistic faiths. Islam emphasized the need for the correct proportion between the material plane (*dunya*) and the spiritual

plane (*din*) so that people would lead balanced lives responsive to
the needs and dictates of both worlds.

The life of Muhammad exemplified the Muslim ideal. He was
gentle, kind, and compassionate to the vulnerable groups in society, a spiritual leader as well as a great warrior on the battlefield
in the cause of defending his faith. His mission was to spread the
word of Islam to convert *dar-ul-harb* (infidel lands or lands of
war) to *dar-ul-Islam* (lands of Islam or peace). Armed with the
simple appeal of this new faith and an innate military prowess,
Muhammad began the process that ultimately converted the entire Arabian Peninsula to Islam. Muslim armies went on to establish some of the greatest empires of humankind: the Ottoman
Empire (1300–1922) that sprawled from Eastern Europe to
North Africa; the Safavid Empire (1501–1736) in Persia (Iran),
Turkey, and Afghanistan; and the great Mughal Empire (1526–
1858) in India.

Islam Enters India

Approximately a hundred years after the birth of Islam, in A.D.
711, the Arab general Muhammad bin Qasim led a band of Turkic warriors into India through the Khyber Pass in modern-day
northwest Pakistan. For the next three centuries, wave after wave
of Muslim warriors bent on their divine mission to spread the
faith ventured on repeated raids into India. Mahmud of Ghazni,
for example, led seventeen raids ever deeper into the heartland of
the subcontinent.

These Muslim armies were of a different character than those
of Muhammad the Prophet. Notorious for terrorizing the indigenous communities, they looted and plundered Indian cities
and defiled Hindu temples. Historical accounts of these early
days of Islam in India describe dramatic suicides of Hindu
women plunging into fiery ruins to escape their fate at the hands
of ferocious Muslim soldiers, forced conversions, and subjugation
of the local populace. "The spread of Islam was often accompanied by hatred, oppression, and brutality, the legacy of [which]
remains to haunt Muslims,"[5] notes Islamic scholar Akbar Ahmed.

Not all Muslim leaders, however, were of this ilk. After three
centuries of rule by the Delhi Sultanate, the Turkic leader Babur
arrived in 1526 and began the Mughal Empire, which ruled India for the next three centuries. Babur presented an entirely different face of Islam. The image of the fierce, ruthless warrior was

replaced by that of a man of tolerance and vision. Babur's first act after capturing Delhi was to forbid the killing of cows because that was offensive to his Hindu subjects. Ahmed explains: "Babur arrived from Central Asia not as a barbarian bent on loot and plunder, but with firm ideas about civilization, architecture and administration. He came with a rich cultural tradition, a knowledge of belonging to one of the most resplendent civilizations of the time."[6]

The Mughal Empire unified the entire Indian subcontinent for the first time since the golden age of Hindu empires in the sixth century. Four noted descendants of Babur—Akbar (1556–1605), Jahangir (1605–1627), Shah Jahan (1628–1658), and Aurangzeb (1658–1707)—ruled India at the height of the Mughal Empire, which was eventually superseded by the British Empire in 1858. The Mughal contribution to India included a sophisticated Persian culture, a brilliant administrative structure, elaborate art, and breathtaking architecture. The Taj Mahal, built in honor of Shah Jahan's deceased wife, stands as testimony to these grand days of emperors and sheikhs when Muslims ruled the subcontinent.

Islam and Hinduism

The religion of the Mughals differed radically from the Hindu faith of their subjects. The many gods of Hinduism clashed with Islam's monotheism. The Hindu caste system fixed adherents in a rigid social hierarchy in contrast to the Islamic notion of equality within the world Muslim brotherhood. Hindus venerated cows, while Muslims ate them. Muslims believed in one life that culminated in the final Day of Judgment, while the Hindu faith said that followers were reincarnated across many lifetimes. Austere and self-disciplined, Muslims found the loud music and gaiety at Hindu celebrations grating and offensive. Hinduism's longevity was linked to its capacity to tolerate and absorb what it could not defeat; Islam's success, on the other hand, was attributed to active conversion and militant proselytizing by Muslim zealots.

Through centuries of living side by side, however, Muslims and Hindus began to adopt some of their respective customs, and a process of cultural fusion began. Hindu society adopted certain Muslim fashions, such as the seclusion of women and the wearing of Muslim dress. Muslims wore the Hindu turban. Urdu, a synthesis of Hindi, Persian, and Arabic, became a major literary language. A hybrid indigenous architecture known as Indo-Islamic emerged and produced some of the finest architectural wonders of the world. In the sphere of religion, Sufism, which emerged in reaction to orthodox Islam, emphasized seclusion through meditation as practiced by India's yogis. And Sikhism, which aimed at reconciling the two faiths, incorporated the notions of one God and reincarnation. "Over time the process of cultural accommodation and synthesis—linguistic, artistic, genetic—rubbed off many sharp edges of doctrinal difference between Hindus and Muslims,"[7] notes historian Stanley Wolpert.

Conflicting Models of Mughal Emperors

The Mughal emperors responded differently to this process of cultural synthesis, painting two contrasting prototypes of an Islamic ruler. "Two distinct and opposed political models presented themselves to the Mughals," notes Ahmed. "One was synthesis on the cultural if not religious plane; the other was outright rejection. . . . The choice would resonate in history and into our own times."[8]

Emperor Akbar represented the pinnacle of the syncretic approach. He not only tolerated the Hindu religion but actively encouraged his subjects to accept all faiths. Akbar employed Hindu officials in his court, married Hindu princesses, and built places of worship where people of all faiths could pray. He proclaimed his faith as one compatible with all religions: "Oh God, in every temple I see people that seek Thee . . . if it be mosque . . . if it be a Christian Church . . . it is Thou whom I seek from temple to temple."[9]

Akbar's grandson Aurangzeb, on the other hand, emphasized orthodox Islam; burnt Hindu temples to the ground; discouraged art, music, dancing, and displays of wealth; and reimposed the unpopular *izya* tax on non-Muslims. He appointed censors of public morals to prosecute Muslims who fell below his standards of religious orthodoxy and outlawed Hindu festivals. "[Aurangzeb] inaugurated a reign of unsurpassed religious austerity and doctrinaire orthodoxy," notes Wolpert. "Not since the raids of Mahmud of Ghazni had so many of northern India's temples been razed and replaced by mosques. The jeweled icons of India's holiest places of worship were laid before the mosques of Agra to be stepped upon by Muslims going to their prayers."[10]

Aurangzeb's Hindu subjects rose in revolt against such harsh treatment. Hindu revivalists challenged Muslim dominance in key areas and subjugated the Muslim population. The great Mughal Empire began to shake and tumble. By the eighteenth century it was overstretched, nearly bankrupt, and bereft of leaders of the caliber of Akbar's lineage. Orthodox Muslim scholars expressed their alarm at the condition of their people. In a letter to King Ahmad Shah Abdali of Afghanistan, religious reformer Shah Walliullah (1703–1762) said,

> The Muslim community is in a pitiable condition. . . . Wealth and prosperity is concentrated in [Hindu] hands, while the share of Muslims is nothing but poverty and misery. . . . If, God forbid, domination by infidels continues, Muslims will forget Islam and within a short time there will be nothing left to distinguish them from non-Muslims.[11]

Collision with the West

With the establishment of the British Empire in India in the mid–nineteenth century, the plight of India's Muslims went from bad to worse. British rule sent profound shock waves through India's Muslim community. Christian missionaries and social reformers drawn by the romantic notions of "the white man's burden" (the patronizing view held by the British of that era that it was the West's obligation to "civilize" the people of the East) poured into India as fast as the British fleet would carry them. Christianity, English-language education, Western philosophy, rationality, science, and the new technology of the industrial revolution challenged traditional Muslim society in unprecedented ways. Ahmed notes,

> Colonial rule for Muslims was an unmitigated disaster. . . . No arguments about Europe providing railways and the telegraph, or maintaining law and order, can conceal . . . this fact. Colonization affected the Islamic ideal by contorting and smothering it. . . . During the colonial century, Muslims would wage a desperate battle to save that ideal. The costs would be heavy and Muslims are still paying them.[12]

While Hindus were quick to take advantage of the new opportunities offered by the British (they pressed for political re-

forms, learned English, went to universities in London, and studied English law, European philosophy, and medicine), Muslims
were slow to react. They found they had moved from the top of
the social hierarchy to third place. Themes of despair and lost
glory filtered through nineteenth-century Muslim literature. Ultimately, Muslim leaders responded to the challenge posed by
Westernization and modernization by calling for a return to ancient Islamic practices or by incorporating Western ideas and
technological advances into the faith. Islamic historian Abdur
Rauf explains:

> From the late seventeenth century onwards Muslims
> faced two choices: they could either firmly redraw the
> boundaries around themselves, shutting out the emerg-
> ing realities, or allow the boundaries to become elastic
> and porous thereby effecting synthesis with non-
> Muslim groups. The two alternatives delineated were
> clear: legal orthodox formality, on the one hand and
> eclectic, syncretic, informality on the other.[13]

The conservative orthodox response embodied in the teachings of Shah Walliullah in the eighteenth century, and the Deoband school of Islamic scholars set up in the Indian town of
Deoband in the nineteenth century, called for purification of Islam. They said the Mughal Empire declined because of the di-
lution of Islam after the long cohabitation with Hinduism. The
preeminent position of Muslims in the world, they believed,
would be reinstated by a return to fundamental principles.

Islamic modernists, on the other hand, like Sayyid Ahmad
Khan (1817–1898), embraced Western philosophy and technology and put it into an Islamic framework. Ahmad Khan believed
that the moral and spiritual core of Islam had much in common
with that of Christianity and that the Koran embraced the ra-
tionalist doctrine of Western philosophy. In the first Muslim
Anglo-Oriental College that he founded in Aligarh, Ahmad
Khan taught English and Western academic subjects as well as
Muslim history and theology. He played a major role in boosting
the morale of his people. According to historian John Esposito,

> [Islamic modernists] rekindled the spirit of Muslim
> unity, solidarity, and autonomy, restored Muslims' pride
> in Islam's intellectual and scientific heritage, and gen-

erated modern ideological interpretations of Islam that incorporated modern concepts, disciplines and institutions, from textual criticisms to nationalism, parliamentary government, and democracy.[14]

Call for a Separate Nation

Sayyid Ahmad Khan also played an important role in developing Muslim political consciousness. In 1888 he wrote to the *Times* of London expressing his concern as to who would rule India if the British departed. He concluded that inevitably either the "Mohammedans [Muslims] [or] Hindus [would] conquer the other and thrust it down."[15] Given the numerical supremacy of the Hindu majority (Muslims made up only about 25 percent of the population), the fears of the Muslim community escalated as the concept of representative government took hold.

In 1906 graduates from Ahmad Khan's Aligarh University founded the first political organization for Muslims, the Muslim League, which became the major vehicle to press for the creation of Pakistan. The cry of "Islam in danger," which echoed through Islamic revivalism and modernism of the eighteenth and nineteenth centuries and resulted in the formation of the Muslim League, was taken up by two leading Muslim figures in the twentieth century: Muhammad Iqbal and Mohammed Ali Jinnah, both of whom were instrumental in the creation and the character of the future nation of Pakistan.

Poet/philosopher Muhammad Iqbal (1873–1938), Pakistan's spiritual founder, synthesized modern and orthodox trends in the Muslim intellectual movement and reconciled Islam's conception of God and the Prophet with modern science and technology. Iqbal saw the evils of European society to be a function of the separation of church and state. He contended that because Islam governed all aspects of social and political life, separating the spiritual from the political realm was "unthinkable" to a Muslim; therefore, Muslims needed their own geographic area where they could live according to their religion. In a speech to the Muslim League in 1930, Iqbal said the creation of a self-governing Muslim state comprising the major northern states that had a Muslim majority—the Punjab, Northwest Frontier Province, Sind, and Baluchistan—was "the final destiny of the Muslims."[16]

Western-educated Muslim lawyer Mohammed Ali Jinnah, known as Quaid-i-Azam ("great leader"), carried Iqbal's vision

forward to make it a reality. Though Jinnah had once supported
the concept of a united India, political events of the early twentieth century, particularly the increasing use of Hindu symbols in
the Indian independence movement, caused him to change his
course. Jinnah became for the Muslim community what Mahatma Gandhi was for the Hindus. Like Gandhi, Jinnah united
disparate ethnic and geographic communities from all over India
and turned the vision of a small educated elite into a grassroots
political movement. In his presidential address to the Muslim
League in 1940, Jinnah outlined his two-nation theory that justified the demand for the creation of a separate Muslim nation:

> Islam and Hinduism are not religions in the strict sense
> of the word, but are, in fact, different and distinct social
> orders.... The Hindus and the Muslims belong to two
> different religious philosophies, social customs, and lit-
> eratures.... To yoke together two such nations under
> a single state, one as a numerical minority and the other
> as a majority, must lead to growing discontent and the
> final destruction of any fabric that may be so built up
> for the government of such a state.[17]

Pakistan Emerges

On August 14, 1947, the day before India was freed after nearly
a century of British imperial rule, the Republic of Pakistan was
created. The term *Pakistan*, literally "land of the pure," was
formed from the first letters and last syllable of the names of the
Muslim majority states of north India: the *P*unjab, *A*fghanis
(Northwest Frontier Province), *K*ashmir, *S*ind, and Baluchis*tan*.
Pakistan began its new life beset by many problems, including a
massive influx of Muslim refugees, a disjointed geographical lay-
out, strained relations with India, and unresolved questions of national identity and cohesion.

Violent clashes between Hindu and Muslim refugees vacating
their homes and moving north and south erupted in what became the most bloody mass migration in human history. Eight
million refugees poured into Pakistan, war-weary and trauma-
tized, straining the physical and administrative resources of the
new nation to near breaking point. The *mohajirs* (migrants) were
from diverse ethnic, linguistic, and geographic communities; they
had little in common with their new hosts except their religious

affiliation to Islam. In addition, food shortages were aggravated by disputes with India over access to critical water supplies. The Muslim-dominated state of Kashmir that had been left as part of India was the subject of military conflict with India, as was the slow distribution of British funds to Pakistan's new government.

The shape and composition of the new country proved an immense challenge. Pakistan consisted of two separate territories—an east and west wing—embracing two ethnically diverse Muslim communities divided by a thousand miles of Indian territory. Jinnah called the new nation, which was drawn up in the haste of the British departure, "mutilated, motheaten, truncated Pakistan."[18] The issue of national boundaries was to have serious consequences for national integrity and security for years to come. Even within western Pakistan, the communities in the four major provinces felt very little affiliation with each other, and ethnic conflict strained the viability of the nation. Overriding all these concerns was the question of Pakistan's national identity. Historian Craig Baxter describes the basic dilemma:

> In August 1947, Pakistan was faced with a number of problems. . . . the most important of these concerns was the role played by Islam. Was Pakistan to be a secular state serving as a homeland for Muslims of the subcontinent, or was it to be an Islamic state governed by the Sharia [Islamic law], in which non-Muslims would be second class citizens?[19]

Modern Liberal Vision of an Islamic State: Jinnah and Liaquat Ali Khan

Four distinct interpretations of the role of Islam in the state were to dominate Pakistani politics from 1947 to 1988: Jinnah's modern, liberal Islam (1947–1957), Mohammad Ayub Khan's Western Islam (1958–1969), Zulfikar Ali Bhutto's Islamic socialism (1971–1977), and Zia-ul-Haq's Islamization (1977–1988). Pakistan continues to bear the legacy of all four ideologies.

Mohammed Ali Jinnah became Pakistan's first governor-general in 1947. He had clear views on the role of religion in the new state: Islam was the common cultural heritage and identity of the Muslim majority; however, Pakistan would be run along liberal humanist lines, "without any distinction of cast, creed, or sect."[20] In February 1948 Jinnah categorically stated, "Make no mistake: Pakistan is not a theocracy or anything like it."[21]

Jinnah's liberal humanist orientation was endorsed by the country's first prime minister, Liaquat Ali Khan, who urged that "the principles of democracy, freedom, tolerance and social justice as enunciated by Islam shall be fully observed."[22] In Liaquat Ali Khan's "Objectives Resolution" speech to Pakistan's Constituent Assembly on March 7, 1949, he said, "Sovereignty of the entire universe belongs to Allah Almighty alone . . . [and] the [Pakistani] people are the real recipients of power."[23] Liaquat Ali Khan believed a government led by the religious establishment was "an idea . . . absolutely foreign to Islam . . . and, therefore the question of a theocracy simply does not arise in Islam."[24]

Religious fundamentalists like Mawlana Mawdudi and his Jamaat-i-Islami Party were at odds with Jinnah's vision. Mawdudi pressed for an Islamic state governed by rule of the Sharia. Ongoing disputes over the role of religion in the state dominated constitutional debates, which dragged on for nearly a decade before any national consensus was reached. Ayub Khan, soon to become Pakistan's first military dictator, explained the sentiments of many Pakistanis in these early years: "Most of us within Pakistan . . . were not quite clear how to go about welding our spiritual ideals into the business of statecraft. The result was a great deal of loose groping which infected our politics and our intellect alike."[25]

Ayub Khan's Western Islam

Jinnah died unexpectedly in 1948, and Liaquat Ali Khan was assassinated at a political rally in 1951 by an assailant whose motives remain a mystery to this day. This left the new nation bereft of strong leadership and clear direction. Pakistan's first ten years were marred by corrupt politicians, mismanagement, conflict between the central and provincial governments, ethnic rivalries, and economic hardships. More than five governments formed and crumbled. National elections were promised but never forthcoming.

In 1956, after years of negotiations, the Constituent Assembly ratified the first constitution, in which Pakistan was renamed the "Islamic Republic of Pakistan" in the hopes that this would steer the country on a renewed course of political stability and unity under the common bond of Islam. It failed to do so. The Pakistani people expressed their frustration at their powerlessness in strikes and street demonstrations. By 1958 the situation was out

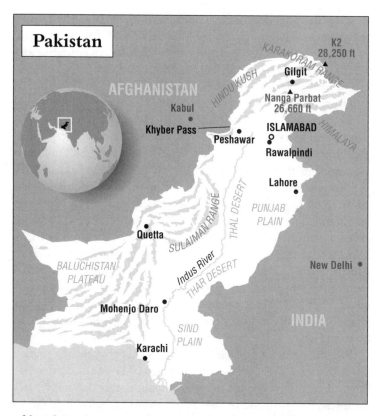

of hand. In response to the growing civil disorder, on October 7, General Ayub Khan staged Pakistan's first military coup, dismissed the National Assembly, dissolved all political parties, and established himself as the chief martial law administrator, thereby setting a precedent that would be repeated many times throughout Pakistan's tumultuous political history.

Ayub Khan believed that his country's failure to evolve a workable democratic system was due to the unsuitability of the Western model of parliamentary democracy to Pakistan's conditions. He reasoned that, because the majority of the people were illiterate, they could not be expected to grasp complex political issues. He devised his own system that he called "basic democracies." Under this system, the country was divided into about one thousand constituencies, and the people voted for a representative at the local level. This formed the base of a multitiered system in which groups of elected representatives voted in the next tier, all the way up to the national level. In practice, this meant that the people's democratic rights were severely curbed, since they did not have any direct say in issues of national significance. Moreover, officials at the national level did not have the backing of the popular vote to challenge General Ayub Khan's authoritarian approach to running the country.

Even though Ayub Khan found Western parliamentary democracy unsuitable to Pakistan's needs, in the spheres of economic and social development policy he followed Western models more closely. Intent on launching the country on a modern trajectory, he promoted rapid industrial growth and launched religious reforms, including family law ordinances giving women more rights in marriage, divorce, and inheritance. Ayub Khan said he intended to "liberate the spirit of religion from the cobwebs of superstition and stagnation which surround it and move forward under the forces of modern science and knowledge."[26] Consistent with this modernist approach, Ayub Khan pushed through a new constitution in 1962 (to replace the 1956 constitution that had been suspended when he declared martial rule) that changed the country's title from the "Islamic Republic of Pakistan" to the "Republic of Pakistan."

Pakistan's religious establishment objected to what they termed Ayub Khan's "Western Islam." Mawlana Mawdudi's Jamaat-i-Islami Party mounted a national campaign against Ayub Khan's family law reforms and succeeded in restoring the term *Islamic* to the country's title. Ayub Khan's critique of traditional Islam, however, did not prevent him from justifying his policies by appealing to the Muslim past. He legitimized his authoritarianism by referring to Mughal rule in India:

> [In Islamic history] the leader, once he is chosen by the community, should have sufficient power to coordinate, supervise and control the activities of government. . . . Muslim rule in the subcontinent started to decline . . . after Mughal Emperor Aurangzeb mainly because of weakening of the central authority.[27]

Ayub Khan's authoritarianism and system of basic democracies frustrated the people's need for a real political voice. Many key decisions that affected people's lives were placed in the hands of inaccessible elected officials who were intimidated by Ayub Khan's increasingly repressive laws and regulations. By the mid-1960s, those who dared to speak out against his policies were thrown in jail. Calling on Islam's doctrine of social justice to legitimize their action, the Pakistani people took to the streets to protest Ayub Khan's repressive regime. "When citizens are disenchanted with their rulers, and have no means of redress, their hearts and minds incline to subversion. And in Islam's insistence on [social] justice they find a powerful weapon,"[28] says journalist Caryle Murphy.

In the face of mounting civil disorder, on March 25, 1969, Ayub Khan resigned his post. In his letter of resignation to the head of the army, General Agha Mohammad Yahya Khan, he urged, "The armed forces must save Pakistan from disintegration."[29]

Islam Fails to Unite the Nation

Yahya Khan's tenure in office was brief (1969–1971) and cataclysmic. Conflict between the ethnically diverse east and west wings of the country had plagued the nation since 1947. East Pakistanis felt the West Pakistan–based government was not giving them their fair share of government resources, and placing a heavy tax burden on the poorer majority of the country. With the huge Indian landmass that separated the east from the west, communication was difficult and strained. After years of mounting civil unrest, in 1970, East Pakistanis led by Sheikh Mujibur Rahman, head of the Awami League, called to secede from the union.

The Pakistani government rushed troops to East Pakistan to quell the rising tide of discontent. Reports of violent slaughter of East Pakistanis by government troops provoked India's military intervention. The stakes were raised. Now Pakistan was engaged in an international conflict with India. The military superiority of the larger country quickly resolved the conflict in favor of the east, and in 1971 East Pakistan became the new nation of Bangladesh.

The loss of more than half of Pakistan's territory and population, combined with the humiliation of the defeat by India, struck what was left of the nation to the core. Yahya Khan was forced to resign. Bangladesh challenged the very basis of Pakistan's Islamic identity and national integrity. The future prime minister Benazir Bhutto wrote in her autobiography,

> The loss of Bangladesh was a terrible blow to Pakistan.
> Our common religion of Islam, which we always believed would transcend the one thousand miles of India which separated East and West Pakistan, failed to

keep us together. Our faith in our very survival as a
country was shaken, the bonds between the four
provinces of West Pakistan strained almost to breaking.
Morale was never lower.[30]

Bhutto's Islamic Socialism

Following Yahya Khan's resignation, Zulfikar Ali Bhutto (1971–
1977), head of the Pakistan People's Party (PPP) and victor in
West Pakistan in the 1970 election, took office. Bhutto believed
that the source of his country's divisiveness lay in the large gap
that existed between the haves and have-nots in Pakistani society. The majority of the nation's poor people had received few
benefits from the economic growth of Ayub Khan's era. So
Bhutto implemented an economic reform program designed to
redistribute wealth by taxing the more privileged social groups
in order to provide basic goods and services for the poor. He
called his socialist program "Islamic socialism," justifying it on the
grounds that it was consistent with Islam's egalitarianism:

> We of the Pakistan People's Party . . . believe that the
> nature of justice in the world demanded by our reli-
> gion is inherent in the concept of a classless society. . . .
> Capitalist society has a class structure which is opposed
> to the equality and brotherhood enjoined upon Mus-
> lims by Islam.[31]

Whereas Ayub Khan had moved Islam to the periphery in his
administration, Bhutto took it to center stage. Bhutto saw Islam
not only as an important vehicle for garnering popular support
for his Islamic socialism program but also as a way to hold the diverse provinces of western Pakistan together following the split
with Bangladesh. He even went so far as to amend the 1962 constitution in 1973 to make Islam the state religion. From then on,
the oath of office for Pakistani presidents and prime ministers involved swearing their allegiance to traditional Islamic principles:

> I am a Muslim and believe in the Unity and Oneness
> of Almighty Allah, the Books of Allah, the Holy
> Quran [Koran] being the last of them, the Prophet-
> hood of Mohammad (peace be upon him) as the last
> of the Prophets and that there be no Prophet after him,
> the Day of Judgment, and all the requirements and

teachings of the Holy Quran and Sunnah [accounts of Mohammad's deeds and sayings].[32]

Bhutto also embraced Islam in his foreign policy, which in turn had implications for his domestic agenda. He sought economic aid from the oil-rich Islamic countries—Saudi Arabia, the United Arab Emirates, and Kuwait—and in return for their support he promoted *ummah* by sponsoring Islamic conferences worldwide. He also introduced Islamic regulations and laws restricting alcohol consumption.

Though Bhutto's Islamic laws met with the approval of the religious establishment, his Islamic socialism met with their harsh criticism. "They found their socialism cannot dance naked," said Mawlana Mawdudi. "After realizing this they started to call socialism 'Islamic.'"[33] The Jamaat-i-Islami Party joined with other religious groups to form the Pakistan National Alliance (PNA) and mounted a campaign to oppose Bhutto's government in the 1977 election. Disgruntled entrepreneurs adversely affected by Bhutto's socialist programs supported the PNA. Official results of the general election accorded a resounding victory to the PPP and humiliating defeat to the PNA. Accusations of foul play in the vote count incited riots. The stage was set for Pakistan's second coup d'etat, known as "Operation Fair Play," under General Zia-ul-Haq.

Zia-ul-Haq's Islamization Program

On July 5, 1977, General Mohammad Zia-ul-Haq declared martial law, suspended the constitution, and placed Bhutto under arrest. Zia pledged to restore unity and national integrity through the common bond of Islam. In his first speech after declaring martial law, Zia praised the "spirit of Islam" that had inspired the opposition movement against the Bhutto government and concluded, "It proves that Pakistan, which was created in the name of Islam, will continue to survive only if it sticks to Islam. That is why I consider the introduction of an Islamic system as an essential prerequisite for the country."[34]

Zia's Islamization program was the most comprehensive attempt to establish Pakistan as an Islamic state that the country had ever experienced. Zia amended the constitution in 1985 to stipulate that all of Pakistan's laws comply with the Koran and rule of the Sharia. He implemented judicial, educational, and economic reforms and adopted the Islamic penal code. Zia justified his authoritarian approach by saying that a presidential style of government that concentrated power in the hands of one man, rather than in the hands of the people as in a true democracy, was more consistent with Islam. "Muslims believe in one God, one prophet and one book [the Koran] and their mentality is such that they should be ruled by one man,"[35] he stated.

Although Zia intended to unify the nation through Islamization, he had the opposite effect. His program fanned sectarian conflict between the two major Islamic sects, the majority Sunnis and minority Shias, who disagreed on how Islamic law should be interpreted. The financial community opposed the introduction of *zakat* (alms), *ushr* (agricultural tax), and interest-free banking. Human rights advocates were horrified by some of the draconian punishments defined under the *hudood* ordinances, which included whip lashing, amputation of hands and limbs, public hanging, and death by stoning for the crimes of adultery, false witness, theft, and alcohol consumption. Muhammad Munir, former Pakistani chief justice, represented the feelings of many Pakistanis when he said, "The order and Ordinances [of Zia's Islamization program] present a grim and dreadful picture of Islam and ignore the forgiving and merciful attributes of God."[36]

Women's groups were formed in Pakistan to challenge new laws that equated the testimony of two women with that of one man in court. Debates on the role of women in Islam were stimulated by the Sharia's assertion that "Men are in charge of women because Allah has made one superior to the other."[37] In addition, Zia's appointment of prayer wardens to enforce the five daily Muslim prayer rituals drew public criticism regarding the invasive nature of the state. Under Zia's blasphemy law, citizens could lay the blasphemy charge against any individual, claiming that he or she made a statement against Islam. If convicted, the punishment was death. This law encouraged personal vendettas and targeted minority groups like Christians and Ahmadis, a breakaway sect of Islam with a history of persecution in Pakistan. Historian John Esposito comments, "Islamization under Zia Ul Haq . . . [became] a source of division, disillusionment, and, at times, oppression."[38]

Ironically, many of the *ulama* (religious leaders) who supported the Islamization program in principle thought Zia's reforms did not go far enough. They became mired in dissension over issues like whether blood transfusions or eye donations were against the teachings of Islam. The result created a distorted public image of

Islam that had lasting repercussions. British historian Ian Talbot says, "To foreigners and Pakistanis alike, Islamization appeared to have reduced a great faith, rich in humanity, culture and a sense of social justice, to a system of punishments and persecution. . . . Zia left behind . . . an atmosphere of bigotry, fanaticism and distorted values."[39]

Zia's Legacy: Pakistan in the 1990s

Zia's legacy lived on long after his death in a freak plane accident. On August 17, 1988, his four-engine Hercules C-130 plummeted to the ground, killing all passengers instantly, including the U.S. ambassador and chief of the U.S. military mission in Pakistan. Shortly afterward, Benazir Bhutto, the former prime minister's daughter, led the PPP to victory in the 1988 general election and became the nation's first female prime minister—and the world's first female leader of a Muslim nation.

Despite campaign promises that Zia's Islamic legacy would be dismantled under the new, more progressive PPP, the Harvard-educated leader of Pakistan found her hands were tied. Pakistan's history of politicizing Islam, under both Zia and her father, had taken its toll. To the majority of the electorate, Pakistan's Islamic identity was primary, regardless of the internal dissension caused by Zia's approach. Thus, rather than dismantling Zia's Islamic legacy, Bhutto found it necessary to strengthen her traditional image. In accordance with Islamic tradition she went on a highly publicized pilgrimage to Mecca, had an arranged marriage, and started a family.

Bhutto's tenure was short-lived. In 1990, amid accusations of corruption and mismanagement, her government was dismissed and replaced by Mian Nawaz Sharif's Islamic Democratic Alliance. Though Nawaz Sharif's focus was on implementing a liberalized economic program to address the stagnant and flailing economy, he could not escape the expectations of Zia's Islamic constituency who supported him. He was forced to endorse a controversial Sharia bill that had been initiated by Zia-ul-Haq but was tabled in Parliament in 1991. Finally, in October 1998, after years of debate, the bill was passed and became the fifteenth amendment to the constitution:

> The Holy Quran and the Sunnah [customs] of the
> Holy Prophet (peace be upon him) shall be the supreme

> law of Pakistan.... The Federal government shall be un-
> der obligation to enforce Shariah, administer zakat, to
> prescribe what is right and forbid what is wrong ... to
> provide substantial socio-economic justice in accordance
> with pure Islam as laid down in the Holy Quran.[40]

With the passing of the Sharia bill into law, Nawaz Sharif congratulated the nation on the "advent of a new Islamic era in the history of Pakistan."[41] Pakistan, a nation founded on religious grounds, has evolved in its more than fifty years to become ever more reliant on Islam as a guiding force in the running of the nation. The result has been deeply divisive. "Government use of Islam has divided more than united, restricted and punished more than guided and liberated, and fostered cynicism rather than pride and respect,"[42] says Esposito.

Disagreements over Islam have led to sectarian-related killings in major Pakistani cities, giving them the reputation of being among the most violent cities in the world. I.A. Rehman, director of Pakistan's independent Human Rights Commission, says the rise in sectarian-related violence is "the inevitable result of Zia's policy ... [whereby] a strong theocratic polity, and the politicization of religion ... [has carried] the most obnoxious intolerance."[43]

Feuds have not been confined to the major sects. Intrasect conflict has led to drive-by shootings, kidnappings, and mosque bombings. Divisions within the Sunni majority (for example the Deobandi, Barelvi, and Wahabi schools clash on different religious interpretations) present an obstacle to a united vision for the state and society. Ethnic-regional cleavages also continue to challenge Pakistan's integrity as a nation. Active regional nationalist movements (in Sind, the Northwest Frontier Province, and Baluchistan) and violent ethnic clashes played a major role in destabilizing democratic administrations in the 1990s. In the Northwest Frontier Province, hundreds of people were slaughtered in confrontations between tribesmen and paramilitary groups over demands to introduce Sharia law.

The Rise of Islamic Fundamentalism

The most potent legacy of Zia's Islamization is the rise of militant Islamic fundamentalism. Adherents to the fundamentalists' literal approach to Islam seek to restore a pure Islamic society, by force if necessary. These groups are transforming their society by developing education models that produce a new breed of Pakistani—young men who are semieducated and motivated to wage jihad, or holy war. Militant-backed *madrassahs* (religious schools) have established a curriculum that combines religious education with commando training, including how to throw bombs, operate rocket launchers, and carry heavy loads through mountainous terrain. According to Islamic historian Saeed Shafqat, the rise of militant Islamic fundamentalist groups has led to "a radical transformation in [the role of religion in] Pakistan."[44]

Extremism is not confined to domestic affairs. Pakistan has been identified as a training center for international terrorists. During the 1980s, the United States trained Pakistani Islamic militants as a force to counter Soviet aggression in Afghanistan. Ironically, these same extremist groups are now infiltrating the Muslim world and plotting assaults against Western targets.

Disillusionment with the country's secular elite after ten years of constant dismissals of democratically elected government (Bhutto and Nawaz Sharif were both elected and dismissed twice in the 1990s) has fueled public receptivity to fundamentalism. "When nations feel something has gone wrong in their midst and citizens feel they have lost control of their lives," says Caryle Murphy, "they take refuge in the familiar and the fundamental."[45] She says Junaid Jamsheed, a major Pakistani pop star, is typical of many young Pakistanis when he says, "I was the West. I knew more about Shakespeare than Iqbal. But now I've discovered Allah."[46]

Return to Military Rule Under Musharraf

The rising tide of Islamic fundamentalism in Pakistan that has erupted in violent sectarian feuds and attacks on foreigners poses a serious threat to the country's internal security. In 1999 General Pervez Musharraf dismissed Nawaz Sharif's government for corruption and mismanagement and returned Pakistan to military rule under circumstances reminiscent of the coup d'etat of Ayub Khan forty years earlier. Despite the backing of the armed forces, Musharraf has been hard-pressed to stem the growth of Islamic fundamentalism. After the September 11, 2001, bombings of the World Trade Center in New York and the Pentagon in Washington, D.C., which were carried out by Islamic terrorists, Musharraf renewed his pledge to outlaw Islamic extremism and cooperate with the United States to hunt down terrorist groups. In a televised speech to the nation on January 12, 2002, he said his government had outlawed key fundamentalist groups and planned to reform the *madrassah* education system to monitor terrorist infiltration. In his national address, Musharraf presented an alternate vision of Islam to that of the extremists:

> Islam teaches tolerance, not hatred; universal brotherhood, not enmity; peace, and not violence.... The extremist minority must realize that Pakistan is not responsible for waging armed Jehad [jihad] in the world. ... In addition to Haqooq Allah [obligations to God], we should also focus on Haqooq-Al-ebad [obligations toward fellow human beings].... There is no room for feuds in Islamic teaching. It is imperative that we teach true Islam i.e. tolerance, forgiveness, compassion, justice, fair play, amity and harmony, which is the true spirit of Islam.[47]

Two Faces of Islam

Ever since Muhammad carried the word of God down from Mount Hira, two conflicting faces of Islam have emerged. One is merciful, egalitarian, bent on social justice and creating a spiritual foundation for daily life. The other face is that of the fierce warrior, offended by difference, self-righteous in its condemnation, and fearful of its own extinction. Pakistani history is the living embodiment of these contradictory impulses. Grappling with the fall from a grand and imperial past, struggling to reassert the foothold of the faithful, the two faces of Islam collide and conflict: Allah as a harsh and punishing God, or one of mercy and compassion. In the first years of the new millennium, this debate is extending its tentacles to the whole world. With trepidation, the world awaits its resolution.

Notes

1. Muhammad Iqbal, "Extract from His Presidential Address to the Muslim League, Allahabad, India, December 29, 1930," quoted in William Theodore de Bary, *Sources of Indian Tradition*. New York: Columbia University Press, 1960, p. 768.
2. Quoted in de Bary, *Sources of Indian Tradition*, p. 838.
3. David Loshak, *Pakistan in Crisis*. New York: McGraw-Hill, 1971, pp. 2–3.
4. Quoted in de Bary, *Sources of Indian Tradition*, p. 848.

5. Akbar S. Ahmed, *Discovering Islam: Making Sense of Muslim History and Society.* New York: Routledge, 1988, p. 10.

6. Akbar Ahmed, *Islam Today: A Short Introduction to the Muslim World.* New York: St. Martin's Press, 1999, p. 88.

7. Stanley Wolpert, *India.* Berkeley and Los Angeles: University of California Press, 1991, p. 41.

8. Ahmed, *Islam Today*, p. 90.

9. Quoted in Steven Warshaw and C. David Bromwell, *India Emerges: A Concise History of India from Its Origin to the Present.* Berkeley, CA: Diablo Press, 1974, p. 60.

10. Wolpert, *India*, p. 60.

11. Quoted in Abdur Rauf, *Renaissance of Islamic Culture and Civilization in Pakistan.* Lahore, Pakistan: Ashraf Press, 1965, pp. 98–99.

12. Ahmed, *Discovering Islam*, p. 79.

13. Rauf, *Renaissance of Islamic Culture and Civilization in Pakistan*, p. 79.

14. John L. Esposito, ed., *The Oxford History of Islam.* New York: Oxford University Press, 1999, p. 650.

15. Quoted in Ahmed, *Discovering Islam*, p. 127.

16. Quoted in de Bary, *Sources of Indian Tradition*, p. 767.

17. Quoted in Christophe Jaffrelot, ed., *Pakistan: Nationalism Without a Nation?* New Delhi, India: Manchar, 2002, p. 12.

18. Quoted in Loshak, *Pakistan in Crisis*, p. 6.

19. Craig Baxter, *Zia's Pakistan: Politics and Stability in a Frontline State.* London: Westview Press, 1985, p. 33.

20. Quoted in Rafi Raza, ed., *Pakistan in Perspective, 1947–1997.* Oxford, England: Oxford University Press, 1997, p. 29.

21. Quoted in Shahid Javed Burki, *Fifty Years of Nationhood.* Boulder, CO: Westview Press, 1999, p. 220.

22. Quoted in de Bary, *Sources of Indian Tradition*, p. 848.

23. Quoted in Raza, *Pakistan in Perspective*, p. 29.

24. Quoted in Raza, *Pakistan in Perspective*, p. 29.

25. Ayub Khan, *Pakistan Perspective: A Collection of Important Articles and Excerpts from Major Addresses by Ayub Khan.* Washington, DC: Embassy of Pakistan, 1965, pp. 3–4.

26. Quoted in John L. Esposito and John O. Voll, *Islam and Democracy.* New York: Oxford University Press, 1996, p. 106.

27. Quoted in Kavita R. Khory, "The Ideology of the Nation State and Nationalism," in Rasul Bakhsh Rais, ed., *State, Society, and Democratic Change in Pakistan.* Karachi, Pakistan: Oxford University Press, 1997, p. 138.

28. Quoted in Akbar Ahmed, "Commentary: The Arabs." Religion News Service, 2002, p. 1.

29. Quoted in Loshak, *Pakistan in Crisis*, p. 32.

30. Benazir Bhutto, *Daughter of Destiny: An Autobiography.* New York: Simon and Schuster, 1989, pp. 68–69.

31. Quoted in Khory, "The Ideology of the Nation State and Nationalism," p. 142.

32. Quoted in Raza, *Pakistan in Perspective*, p. 30.

33. Quoted in Esposito and Voll, *Islam and Democracy*, p. 107.

34. Quoted in Shahid Javed Burki, *Pakistan: A Nation in the Making.* Boulder, CO: Westview Press, 1986, p. 77.

35. Quoted in Omar Noman, *Pakistan: Political and Economic History Since 1947.* New York: KPI, 1988, p. 143.

36. Quoted in Esposito and Voll, *Islam and Democracy*, p. 118.

37. Quoted in Noman, *Pakistan*, p. 142.

38. Esposito and Voll, *Islam and Democracy*, p. 118.

39. Ian Talbot, *Pakistan: A Modern History.* New York: St. Martin's Press, 1998, p. 286.

40. Quoted in Kamal Siddiqi, *1998 Indian Express Newspapers.* (Bombay) Ltd. www.indianexpress.com.

41. Quoted in Siddiqi, *1998 Indian Express Newspapers.* (Bombay) Ltd.

42. Quoted in Esposito and Voll, *Islam and Democracy*, p. 118.

43. Quoted in Esposito and Voll, *Islam and Democracy*, p. 119.

44. Saeed Shafqat, "From Official Islam to Islamism," in Jaffrelot, *Pakistan*, p. 145.

45. Quoted in Ahmed, "Commentary: The Arabs," p. 1.

46. Quoted in Carla Power and Zahid Hussain, "The General and His Plan for Pakistan," *Newsweek International*, February 19, 2001, p. 26.

47. Pervez Musharraf, Address to the Nation, January 12, 2002, reprinted in *Dawn.* January 12, 2002. www.dawn.com.

The Formative Phase

Ancient Origins

By Craig Baxter

In the following extract from Pakistan: A Country Study, *Craig Baxter traces the history of the ancient civilizations that occupied modern-day Pakistan more than four thousand years ago to the advent of Islam in* A.D. 711. *He surveys the major periods, including the sophisticated Harappan civilization, the Aryan invasion, the founding of Buddhism, the imperial age of the early Hindu empires, and the rule of the Turko-Afghan Delhi Sultanate. In 1526 the Muslim leader Babur defeated the last of the sultans and founded the Mughal Empire, which ruled India until Britain's Queen Victoria proclaimed herself empress of the subcontinent in the mid-nineteenth century.*

Craig Baxter, who has written extensively on Pakistan, is professor of politics and history at Juniata College, Huntingdon, Pennsylvania.

When British archaeologist Sir Mortimer Wheeler was commissioned in 1947 by the government of Pakistan to give a historical account of the new country, he entitled his work *Five Thousand Years of Pakistan*. Indeed, Pakistan has a history that can be dated back to the Indus Valley civilization (ca. 2500–1600 B.C.), the principal sites of which lay in present-day Sindh and Punjab provinces. Pakistan was later the entryway for the migrating pastoral tribes known as Indo-Aryans, or simply Aryans, who brought with them and developed the rudiments of the broad and evolutionary religio-philosophical system later recognized as Hinduism. They also brought an early version of Sanskrit, the base of Urdu, Punjabi, and Sindhi, languages that are spoken in much of Pakistan today.

Hindu rulers were eventually displaced by Muslim invaders, who, in the tenth, eleventh, and twelfth centuries, entered northwestern India through the same passes in the mountains used earlier by the Aryans. The culmination of Muslim rule in the Mughal Empire (1526–1858, with effective rule between 1560

Craig Baxter, "Historical Setting," *Pakistan: A Country Study*, edited by Peter R. Blood. Washington, DC: U.S. Government Printing Office, 1995.

and 1707) encompassed much of the area that is today Pakistan. Sikhism, another religious movement that arose partially on the soil of present-day Pakistan, was briefly dominant in the Punjab and in the northwest in the early nineteenth century. These regimes subsequently fell to the expanding power of the British, whose empire lasted from the eighteenth century to the mid-twentieth century, until they too left the scene, yielding power to the successor states of India and Pakistan.

The departure of the British was a goal of the Muslim movement championed by the All-India Muslim League (created in 1906 to counter the Hindu-dominated Indian National Congress), which strove for both political independence and cultural separation from the Hindu-majority regions of British India. These objectives were reached in 1947, when British India received its independence as two new sovereign states. The Muslim-majority areas in northwestern and eastern India were separated and became Pakistan, divided into the West Wing and East Wing, respectively. The placement of two widely separated regions within a single state did not last, and in 1971 the East Wing broke away and achieved independence as Bangladesh.

The pride that Pakistan displayed after independence in its long and multicultural history has disappeared in many of its officially sponsored textbooks and other material used for teaching history (although the Indus Valley sites remain high on the list of the directors of tourism). As noted anthropologist Akbar S. Ahmed has written in *History Today*, "In Pakistan the Hindu past simply does not exist. History only begins in the seventh century after the advent of Islam and the Muslim invasion of Sindh."

Early Civilizations

From the earliest times, the Indus Valley region has been both a transmitter of cultures and a receptacle of different ethnic, linguistic, and religious groups. Indus Valley civilization appeared around 2500 B.C. along the Indus River valley in Punjab and Sindh. This civilization, which had a writing system, urban centers, and a diversified social and economic system, was discovered in the 1920s at its two most important sites [in northeast and central Pakistan]. Mohenjo-daro, in Sindh near Sukkur, and Harappa, in Punjab south of Lahore. A number of other lesser sites stretching from the Himalayan foothills in Indian Punjab to Gujarat east of the Indus River and to Balochistan to the west have also been discovered and studied. How closely these places were connected to Mohenjo-daro and Harappa is not clearly known, but evidence indicates that there was some link and that the people inhabiting these places were probably related.

An abundance of artifacts have been found at Harappa—in fact, the archaeological yield there has been so rich that the name of that city has often been equated with the Indus Valley civilization (Harappan culture) it represents. Yet the site was damaged in the latter part of the nineteenth century when engineers constructing the Lahore-Multan railroad used brick from the ancient city for ballast. Fortunately, the site at Mohenjo-daro has been less disturbed in modern times and shows a well-planned and well-constructed city of brick.

Indus Valley civilization was essentially a city culture sustained by surplus agricultural produce and extensive commerce, which included trade with Sumer in southern Mesopotamia in what is today Iraq. Copper and bronze were in use, but not iron. Mohenjo-daro and Harappa were cities built on similar plans of well-laid-out streets, elaborate drainage systems, public baths, differentiated residential areas, flat-roofed brick houses, and fortified administrative and religious centers enclosing meeting halls and granaries. Weights and measures were standardized. Distinctive engraved stamp seals were used, perhaps to identify property. Cotton was spun, woven, and dyed for clothing. Wheat, rice, and other food crops were cultivated, and a variety of animals were domesticated. Wheel-made pottery—some of it adorned with animal and geometric motifs—has been found in profusion at all the major Indus Valley sites. A centralized administration has been inferred from the cultural uniformity revealed, but it remains uncertain whether authority lay with a priestly or a commercial oligarchy. . . .

Although historians agree that the civilization ceased abruptly, at least in Mohenjo-daro and Harappa, there is disagreement on the possible causes for its end. Conquering hordes of Aryan invaders from central and western Asia have long been thought by historians to have been the "destroyers" of Indus Valley civilization, but this view is increasingly open to scientific scrutiny and reinterpretation. Other, perhaps more plausible explanations include recurrent floods caused by tectonic earth movement, soil salinity, and desertification.

Until the entry of the Europeans by sea in the late fifteenth

century, and with the exception of the Arab conquests of
Muhammad bin Qasim in the early eighth century, the route
taken by peoples who migrated to India has been through the
mountain passes, most notably the Khyber Pass, in northwestern
Pakistan. Although unrecorded migrations may have taken place
earlier, it is certain that migrations increased in the second millennium B.C. The records of these people—who spoke an Indo-
European language—are literary, not archaeological, and were
preserved in the Vedas, collections of orally transmitted hymns.
In the greatest of these, the "Rig Veda," the Aryan speakers appear as a tribally organized, pastoral, and pantheistic people. The
later Vedas and other Sanskritic sources, such as the Puranas (literally, "old writings"—an encyclopedic collection of Hindu leg-
ends, myths, and genealogy), indicate an eastward movement from
the Indus Valley into the Ganges Valley (called Ganga in Asia)
and southward at least as far as the Vindhya Range, in central India. A social and political system evolved in which the Aryans
dominated, but various indigenous peoples and ideas were accommodated and absorbed. The caste system that remained characteristic of Hinduism also evolved. One theory is that the three
highest castes—Brahmins, Kshatriyas, and Vaishyas—were composed of Aryans, while a lower caste—the Sudras—came from
the indigenous peoples.

600 B.C. to A.D. 700

By the sixth century B.C., knowledge of Indian history becomes
more focused because of the available Buddhist and Jain sources
of a later period. Northern India was populated by a number of
small princely states that rose and fell in the sixth century B.C. In
this milieu, a phenomenon arose that affected the history of the
region for several centuries—Buddhism. Siddhartha Gautama,
the Buddha, or "Enlightened One" (ca. 563–483 B.C.), was born
in the Ganges Valley. His teachings were spread in all directions
by monks, missionaries, and merchants. The Buddha's teachings
proved enormously popular when considered against the more
obscure and highly complicated rituals and philosophy of Vedic
Hinduism. The original doctrines of the Buddha also constituted
a protest against the inequities of the caste system, thereby at-
tracting large numbers of followers.

    At about the same time, the semi-independent kingdom of
Gandhara, roughly located in northern Pakistan and centered in

the region of Peshawar, stood between the expanding kingdoms of the Ganges Valley to the east and the Achaemenid Empire of Persia to the west. Gandhara probably came under the influence of Persia during the reign of Cyrus the Great (559–530 B.C.). the Persian Empire fell to Alexander the Great in 330 B.C., and he continued his march eastward through Afghanistan and into India. Alexander defeated Porus, the Gandharan ruler of Taxila, in 326 B.C. and marched on to the Ravi River before turning back. The return march through Sindh and Balochistan ended with Alexander's death at Babylon in 323 B.C.

Greek rule did not survive in northwestern India, although a school of art known as Indo-Greek developed and influenced art as far as Central Asia. The region of Gandhara was conquered by Chandragupta (r. ca. 321–ca. 297 B.C.), the founder of

ISLAMIC CONQUESTS

In the following extract from The Great Moghuls, *author Bamber Gascoigne gives the flavor of Islamic conquests in India with a colorful description of Mongol leader Timur's military cunning in his attack on Delhi in 1398. Timur's incursion was the prologue to the era of the great Moghuls in the subcontinent.*

Timur's preparations for battle were mainly directed against the legendary Indian elephants, the mere prospect of which reduced his army to near panic—several of the learned men whom Timur liked to have around him even went so far as to say that during the battle they would prefer to be near the ladies. He surrounded his position with a stout rampart and ditch, and made ready various devices to cripple the elephants or frighten them into turning and trampling their own army. He planted in the ground stakes armed with three-pronged metal spikes . . . and for good measure he provided his cavalry with caltrops. These were metal objects consisting of four sharp prongs, angled so that at least one of the four must always point upwards; the riders could entice an elephant into pursuing them and then scatter these

the Mauryan Empire, the first universal state of northern India, with its capital at present-day Patna in Bihar. His grandson, Ashoka (r. ca. 274–ca. 236 B.C.), became a Buddhist. Taxila became a leading center of Buddhist learning. Successors to Alexander at times controlled the northwestern region of present-day Pakistan and even the Punjab after Mauryan power waned in the region.

The northern regions of Pakistan came under the rule of the Sakas, who originated in Central Asia in the second century B.C. They were soon driven eastward by Pahlavas (Parthians related to the Scythians), who in turn were displaced by the Kushans (also known as the Yueh-Chih in Chinese chronicles).

The Kushans had earlier moved into territory in the northern part of present-day Afghanistan and had taken control of Bactria.

---

treacherous barbs in its path. Timur's technique for causing the elephants to panic was no less ingenious. Bundles of dried grass were tied to the backs of large numbers of camels and buffaloes, which would be driven towards the advancing elephants. At the last moment the bundles were to be set on fire. The terror of these unfortunate animals would, it was hoped, infect the elephants as they ran blazing and screaming among them.

Both techniques worked. On December 17 the army of Mahmud Shah and Mallu Khan emerged from the gates of Delhi: ten thousand horse, forty thousand foot and a phalanx of the dreaded elephants, clanking forward in their armour and with long swords bound on their tusks. On their backs were fortified turrets bristling with archers and crossbowmen and even specialists using primitive rockets and devices for slinging hot pitch. But this straightforward Indian magnificence was no match for unorthodox cunning. By the end of the day Mahmud and Mallu had fled back into the city and straight out again the other side, and the victorious Timur was pitching his camp by a large reservoir outside the walls.

Bamber Gascoigne, *The Great Moghuls.* New York: Harper and Row, 1971, p. 11.

Kanishka, the greatest of the Kushan rulers (r. ca. A.D. 120–160), extended his empire from Patna in the east to Bukhara in the west and from the Pamirs in the north to central India, with the capital at Peshawar (then Purushapura). Kushan territories were eventually overrun by the Huns in the north and taken over by the Guptas in the east and the Sassanians of Persia in the west.

The age of the imperial Guptas in northern India (fourth to seventh centuries A.D.) is regarded as the classical age of Hindu civilization. Sanskrit literature was of a high standard; extensive knowledge in astronomy, mathematics, and medicine was gained; and artistic expression flowered. Society became more settled and more hierarchical, and rigid social codes emerged that separated castes and occupations. The Guptas maintained loose control over the upper Indus Valley.

Northern India suffered a sharp decline after the seventh century. As a result, Islam came to a disunited India through the same passes that Aryans, Alexander, Kushans, and others had entered.

Islam in India

The initial entry of Islam into India came in the first century after the death of the Prophet Muhammad. The Umayyad caliph in Damascus sent an expedition to Balochistan and Sindh in 711 led by Muhammad bin Qasim (for whom Karachi's second port is named). The expedition went as far north as Multan but was not able to retain that region and was not successful in expanding Islamic rule to other parts of India. Coastal trade and the presence of a Muslim colony in Sindh, however, permitted significant cultural exchanges and the introduction into the subcontinent of saintly teachers. Muslim influence grew with conversions.

Almost three centuries later, the Turks and the Afghans spearheaded the Islamic conquest in India through the traditional invasion routes of the northwest. Mahmud of Ghazni (979–1030) led a series of raids against Rajput kingdoms and rich Hindu temples and established a base in the Punjab for future incursions. Mahmud's tactics originated the legend of idol-smashing Muslims bent on plunder and forced conversions, a reputation that persists in India to the present day.

During the last quarter of the twelfth century, Muhammad of Ghor invaded the Indo-Gangetic Plain, conquering in succession Ghazni, Multan, Sindh, Lahore, and Delhi. His successors established the first dynasty of the Delhi Sultanate, the Mamluk Dynasty (*mamluk* means "slave") in 1211 (however, the Delhi Sultanate is traditionally held to have been founded in 1206). The territory under control of the Muslim rulers in Delhi expanded rapidly. By mid-century, Bengal and much of central India were under the Delhi Sultanate. Several Turko-Afghan dynasties ruled from Delhi: the Mamluk (1211–90), the Khalji (1290–1320), the Tughlaq (1320–1413), the Sayyid (1414–51), and the Lodhi (1451–1526). As Muslims extended their rule into southern India, only the Hindu kingdom of Vijayanagar remained immune, until it too fell in 1565. There were also kingdoms independent of Delhi in the Deccan, Gujarat, Malwa (central India), and Bengal. Nevertheless, almost all of the area in present-day Pakistan remained generally under the rule of Delhi.

The sultans of Delhi enjoyed cordial, if superficial, relations with Muslim rulers in the Near East but owed them no allegiance. The sultans based their laws on the Quran [Muslim holy book] and the sharia [Islamic law] and permitted non-Muslim subjects to practice their religion only if they paid *jizya* [tax on non-Muslims]. The sultans ruled from urban centers—while military camps and trading posts provided the nuclei for towns that sprang up in the countryside. Perhaps the greatest contribution of the sultanate was its temporary success in insulating the subcontinent from the potential devastation of the Mongol invasion from Central Asia in the thirteenth century. The sultanate ushered in a period of Indian cultural renaissance resulting from the stimulation of Islam by Hinduism. The resulting "Indo-Muslim" fusion left lasting monuments in architecture, music, literature, and religion. The sultanate suffered from the sacking of Delhi in 1398 by Timur (Tamerlane) but revived briefly under the Lodhis before it was conquered by the Mughals.

Dawn of the Mughal Period

India in the sixteenth century presented a fragmented picture of rulers, both Muslim and Hindu, who lacked concern for their subjects and who failed to create a common body of laws or institutions. Outside developments also played a role in shaping events. The circumnavigation of Africa by the Portuguese explorer Vasco da Gama in 1498 allowed Europeans to challenge Arab control of the trading routes between Europe and Asia. In Central Asia and Afghanistan, shifts in power pushed Babur of Ferghana (in present-day Uzbekistan) southward, first to Kabul and then to India. The dynasty he founded endured for more than three centuries.

Claiming descent from both Chinggis Khan (Genghis Khan) and Timur, Babur combined strength and courage with a love of beauty, and military ability with cultivation. Babur concentrated on gaining control of northwestern India. He did so in 1526 by defeating the last Lodhi sultan on the field of Panipat, a town just northwest of Delhi. Babur then turned to the tasks of persuading his Central Asian followers to stay on in India and of overcoming other contenders for power, mainly the Rajputs and the Afghans. He succeeded in both tasks but died shortly thereafter in 1530. The Mughal Empire was one of the largest centralized states in premodern history and was the precursor to the British Indian Empire.

The Rise and Fall of the Great Mughal Empire

BY STANLEY WOLPERT

In the following extract from India, *eminent historian Stanley Wolpert emphasizes the enormity of the impact of the Mughal invasion in India, which began in 711. Amid fierce military assaults by Muslim generals dating back to the eighth century A.D., there developed the antipathy between Hindus and Muslims that Wolpert claims is at the root of the historic incompatibility of the two communities. Despite the fact that cultural practices of Muslims and Hindus were intermingled for centuries, and religious tolerance was promoted during Emperor Akbar's reign (1556–1605), orthodox Islam reasserted itself in the later Mughal period and signaled the decline of the Mughal Empire.*

Adherents to the militant brotherhood of *Islam* ("Submission" to the will of Allah) slashed their sharp scimitars through the body politic of South Asia, starting in Sind in A.D. 711. The faith founded by Prophet Muhammad in the sands of Arabia a century earlier thus reached India's shore the same year as it did the Iberian Peninsula, borne with zealous fervor by its galloping legions of true believers in God Almighty and His awesome Last Judgment. Muslim armies were to continue their assault on Indian soil for the next thousand years, during the last 500 of which Muslim monarchs would rule most of India. Not since the Aryan invasions had so powerful, persistent, unyielding a challenge been launched against Indic Civilization and its basic beliefs and values. In many ways, the Islamic impact was more divisive, its legacy more deeply threatening to Indian Civilization, than Aryan rule ever was, for the Aryan–pre-Aryan synthesis gave birth to Hinduism. The only major offspring of Hinduism and Islam has been the Sikh[1] community, which may prove almost as disruptive a challenge to Indian unity as Islam has been.

The Arab conquest of Sind came by sea. The desert sands of that lower Indus province of modern Pakistan proved no springboard, however, for conquering the rest of the subcontinent. Sind remained an isolated Muslim outpost in South Asia for almost three centuries before emerging as a portent of India's "Muslim era." The true dawn of that era came when Mahmud of Ghazni, "Sword of Islam," led his first band of Afghan raiders down the Khyber Pass in A.D. 997 on what would for the next quarter century be an annual hunt. Mahmud's game were Hindus and their temples, whose icons offended his sensibilities as much as their gold and jewels roused his greed. The rapacious Ghaznavid raids were followed by those of their successors to Afghan power, Ghors, whose bloody "holy wars" (jihads) against Hindu India left an equally bitter legacy of communal hatred in the hearts and minds of India's populace. Those early centuries of fierce Muslim assaults upon "infidel" Indians confirmed Hindus in their views of Muslim "foreigners" as polluting "Untouchables," although far more predatory. The gulf of mistrust, fear, and hatred that was soon to divide India's population from its martial Muslim rulers subsequently served to undermine all attempts to reunify the subcontinent, whose political fragmentation since 1947 reflects in part the historic incompatibility of those early centuries of Muslim–Hindu intercourse.

Hindu–Muslim Cultural Synthesis

After 1206, Muslim Sultans of Perso-Afghan-Turkish descent made the rust-colored plains of Delhi their home for three and a quarter centuries. No fewer than thirty-five Muslim Sultans sat on thrones of five successive dynasties at Delhi, ruling over a kingdom aptly called "despotism tempered by assassination." Once Muslim rulers settled permanently on Indian soil, however, they encouraged doctrinal accommodation toward Hindu subjects, no longer given just the extreme options of Islam or "death." Like Christians and Jews, Hindus were permitted to retain their own faith at the price of paying a special head tax for "Peoples of the

1. The Sikh faith, based on a blend of Hindu and Muslim traditions, was founded by Hindu Guru Nanak in the early sixteenth century in present-day Pakistan.

Book," those whose partially revealed Scripture raised them above "infidel" status. Not that Brahmans enjoyed paying for the privilege of remaining second-class subjects in their own land! Still, it was better than forced conversion or death.

Over time the process of cultural accommodation and synthesis, linguistic, artistic, genetic, rubbed off many sharp edges of doctrinal difference between Hindus and Muslims. Most of the Muslims, who represented close to one-fourth the total population of India by the late nineteenth century, were descendants of converts or Hindu mothers. After centuries of residence in India, the "Brotherhood" of Islamic faithful acquired some of the features of Hinduism's "caste" system, particularly with regard to marriage, Sheikhs and Sayyids, Afghans and Muslims, of Persian or Turkish ancestry preferring mates from within their "own" communities. In some circles Muslim eating habits became more restrictive. No "strangers" have ever remained totally aloof from the impact of India. Islamic iconoclastic fervor was also tempered by time and the impossibility of destroying every statue on every Hindu temple in the land. Muslims were soon sated by gestures of symbolic destruction of gods and goddesses, most of whose images, if they date from pre-Muslim times, have a broken nose, arm, or other fractured feature, hacked from their stone body by some angry Muslim sword.

Islam's final wave came out of Central Asia, led by a direct descendant of Ghengiz Khan and Tamerlane named Babur, "the Tiger," founder of the great Mughal Empire. From 1526 to 1530 Babur defeated every Sultanate and Hindu Rajput army that took the field to challenge his relentless march. Born to fight and rule, Babur turned Delhi and Agra into twin capitals of the Empire he bequeathed to his heirs, Great Mughals who ruled India for more than two centuries. The Mughal Empire was the strongest dynasty in all of Indian History, nominally retaining the throne of Delhi until 1858, although for most of its last century the Mughals ruled as puppets of British, Maratha, or Afghan power.

Akbar's Achievements

As had been true of the [Hindu] Mauryan and Guptan dynasties, the third Mughal Emperor proved to be the greatest monarch of his line. Akbar, "the Great," reigned almost half a century (1556–1605), the high point of Mughal "national," enlightened rule, although not of territorial sovereignty. Akbar was the first

Muslim monarch to initiate a general policy of religious tolera-
tion toward Hindus, wooing the Rajputs through marriages that
forged potent "national" alliances, seated on his throne of inlaid

THE LIFE OF A MUGHAL EMPEROR

The Padshahnama (History of the Emperor), *written by
seventeenth-century Persian scholar Abdul Hamid for the Mughal
emperor Shah Jehan, chronicled the first ten years of the emperor's
reign (1628–1638). The following extract describes the demanding
administrative duties and the splendor of the lifestyle of the Mughal
emperors.*

4 A.M. The Emperor rises two hours before sunrise and, after his toilet, says a prayer based upon the *Traditions* of
Muhammad and with his face towards Mecca recites verses
from the Koran. Just before sunrise he repairs to the palace
mosque to make the first obligatory prayers of the day.

6.45 A.M. The Emperor appears at a window of the
palace-fort—called the *jharakha-i-darshan* (the Sanskrit word
darshan means the sight of something high or holy). The
window is in the eastern wall of the Agra fort overlooking
the river Jumna. Crowds of people assemble for the sight
and are permitted direct access to the Emperor in order to
make petitions or complaints. This period lasts about forty-
five minutes. After the public appearance the place is
cleared and elephant fights, a prerogative of the Emperor
alone, take place. Shah Jahan was especially fond of this
'sport'.

7.40 A.M. The Emperor and his suite retire to the *Diwan-
i-am* or 'Hall of Public Audience'. . . . The Emperor entered
the hall through a door at the rear and took his seat on a
cushion in the marble alcove. To his left and right were
placed his sons, and in the hall itself, with their backs to the
open sides, stood the courtiers, nobles, and officers of State.
Those attendants who waited upon the Emperor's person
stood to his right and left close to the alcove. The chief of-

marble as quasidivine monarch of *all* Indians. Some orthodox Mullahs considered Akbar a traitor to Islam, raising battle cries of "Jihad" against him. The Emperor's elephant corps stamped

ficers, in ranks according to their authority, faced the Emperor, and the royal standard-bearers holding their golden banners lined the wall at the Emperor's left hand. The hall, some two hundred feet long by sixty-seven feet wide, was now full, and lesser officials, soldiers, guards, etc. stood in an outside court-yard covered with canopies of velvet embroidered with gold. . . .

According to the amount of business to be transacted, the *durbar* ['audience'] lasted about two hours.

9.40 A.M. After the grand *durbar* is over, the Emperor retires to the *Diwan-i-khas* or 'Hall of Private Audience'. There he writes with his own hand replies to the most important of his letters and gives verbal orders for replies to others. The drafts for these are submitted to the Emperor, revised and corrected by him, and sent to the harem for the affixing of the Great Seal, which is in the charge of the Empress. High revenue matters and the like are discussed here. The ordinary business over, the Emperor examines jewellery and other works of art and consults with architects on the design and placing of new buildings. The business in the *Diwan-i-khas* usually lasts about two hours.

11.40 A.M. The Emperor leaves for the *Shah Burj*, or 'Royal Tower', where secret affairs of State are discussed. Only the princes of the blood and the highest and most trusted officers are allowed in the tower.

12 midday. At this hour the Emperor retires to the harem, makes a prayer, eats, and sleeps for an hour. Afterwards, he hears petitions from widows and orphans, and other women which are submitted to the Empress who in turn reports on them to the Emperor.

Abdul Hamid, "The Padshahnama," quoted in Michael Edwardes, *A History of India from the Earliest Times to the Present Day*. New York: Farrar, Straus, and Cudahy, 1961, pp. 170–71.

out such rebellions with ease. Several of Akbar's leading advisers
were Hindus, the head of his imperial revenue department had
been born a Brahman, his military commander, a Rajput prince.
Akbar chose his leading lieutenants personally, rewarding them
lavishly with lands, whose revenues, generally about one-third of
all crops, sufficed to support from 500 to 50,000 cavalry troops
and their horses, always ready to gallop at the emperor's call. The
system proved effective in securing the borders, expanding them
over the Hindu Kush to incorporate most of what is now Afghanistan within the Delhi-Agra-Fatehpur Sikri imperium.
Fatehpur was Akbar's own new capital, created to celebrate the
birth of his son and heir, although an inadequate water supply
forced its abandonment after little more than a decade. Its haunt-
ing sandstone shell survives on the Jaipur road west of Agra, a
tribute to Akbar's eclectic ingenuity, its ghostly ruins all that remain of his dream of uniting Hindus and Muslims within a
single polity.

    Persian poetry and arts added sophistication and colorful
beauty to the Mughal court and its urbane culture during the ef-
fulgence of its seventeenth-century golden age. Persian became
the official language of the Mughal Empire, rather than Babur's
cruder native Barlas Turkish tongue, and was to remain so until
English deposed it in 1835. Like their Persian neighbors, Indian
monarchs have generally loved beauty, luxury, sensuality,
pageantry, and the trappings of power. The Great Mughals pan-
dered to such indigenous tastes, importing the best Persian artists
and craftsmen to their sumptuous palaces, adding pearl mosques
and peacock thrones encrusted with jewels to marble, fountained
halls, engraved with Persian poetry, such as "If there be Paradise
on earth, it is here, it is here, it is here!" Shah Jahan ("Emperor of
the World") was the most extravagant of Mughal spenders. His
profound remorse, or guilty conscience, following the death of
his beloved wife, Mumtaz, resulted in the construction of the Taj
Mahal, which provides breathtaking proof of the magnificence
of Mughal art at its apogee. Little wonder that centuries later, a
different sort of extravagant empire would dub its early film-
makers "moguls."

Return to Islam

The fatal weakness of later Mughal monarchs was not their
spendthrift waste, however, but their return to narrow-minded

Islamic orthodoxy. India's starving millions could at least derive vicarious pleasure from viewing the Red Fort at Agra or the Taj Mahal, but what joy or satisfaction could Hindu masses feel from Emperor Aurangzeb's (r. 1658–1707) reimposition of the hated head tax on non-Muslims? Or what pleasure could they take from his ban on alcoholic beverages? Or on repairs to Hindu temples? The "prayer-monger" *Padishah* ("Emperor") conquered more real estate than any of his ancestors, yet Aurangzeb did so only after wading to his throne through the blood of his brothers, and stirring up a storm of Hindu hatred throughout the Deccan, Rajasthan, and the Dravidian South. He also unified the Sikhs of the Punjab as no Mughal before or after him did, by torturing and beheading the ninth Guru, for refusing to convert to Islam. The first Guru, Nanak (1469–1538), had founded the Sikh faith, a peaceful blend of his own inherited Hinduism and Islam, which he learned from his dear Muslim friend. Following Aurangzeb's harsh persecution, however, Sikhs fused themselves into an "Army of the Pure" (*Khalsa*), changing their names from passive "Disciples" (*Sikhs*) to martial "Lions" (*Singhs*). Militant Sikhism was thus forged in the furnace of Mughal antipathy, the swords of that mightiest of Punjabi warrior communities initially sharpened against Muslims. After mid-1984, however, when [Indian prime minister Indira] Gandhi ordered the Indian Army to "liberate" Amritsar's Golden Temple, Hindu-Sikh antipathy became modern India's most volatile internal problem.

Maratha opposition to Mughal rule was led by Shivaji (1627–1680), father of the Maratha confederacy, and spread from its Poona (Pune) base within half a century of his death to the environs of Delhi, Calcutta, and Madras. As the founder of Indian guerrilla warfare, Shivaji was reviled by Mughal generals as a "mountain rat," but his shrewd tenacity in battle was matched only by his Hindu faith in his motherland. Shivaji made *Sva-raj* ("Self-rule" or "Freedom") his mantra, launching the first major Hindu revolt against Muslim monarchs and their armies. His successors were so inspired by his fierce "national religious" passion that Pune would remain one of the key cradles of Indian Nationalism in the late nineteenth century. Brahman *Peshwas* ("Prime Ministers") of Pune administered the Maratha confederacy under nominal control of Shivaji's heirs. The singularly astute Peshwas remained a unique secular and religious dynasty rul-

ing the Deccan for almost a century, until the British defeated
their last incumbent in battle in 1818.

Decline of the Mughal Empire

After Aurangzeb's death in 1707, Mughal power started its slow
decline. Court feuds and factional in-fighting at the center coincided with growing provincial autonomy and the emergence of
several regional limbs more robust than the Delhi-Agra head. The
Nizam was the first powerful minister to abandon Delhi and
carve out his own southern kingdom in Hyderabad early in the
eighteenth century. Nawabs of Oudh and Bengal, formerly mere
deputies of the Great Mughal, became virtual kings in their own
wealthy Gangetic domains by midcentury. Simultaneously, Afghanistan became a powerful threat from the west, under its own
Amirs, who embarked on a series of bloody plundering raids into
the Indus Valley, wresting the Punjab as well as the North-West
Frontier from Delhi together with the [lavishly jeweled] peacock
throne [the symbol of the empire's heyday].

As the Great Mughal thus diminished in status, potent new
forces appeared along India's coast, trading quietly, inconspicu-
ously, at first. They came by sea from the West, and for most of
the early eighteenth century were so busy fighting one another
that they seemed uninterested in or incapable of challenging any
Indian rulers, local or regional, not to speak of the awesome
might of that empire, whose twin capitals were remote from the
tiny British and French "factory" towns that dotted the Southern peninsular trunk of the slumbering elephant that was India.

Muslims Under the British Raj

By Ian Stephens

The decline of the Mughal Empire in India coincided with the arrival of Portuguese, French, and British traders eager for valuable Indian spices, silks, and gems. Conflict ensued between the European merchants and Muslim provincial rulers. British military superiority ultimately led to the defeat of their opponents and British control of India. The British ruled India from 1858 until 1947, when India became independent and Pakistan was created.

In the following extract Ian Stephens says that British rule caused tremendous loss of pride and dignity for the Muslims of India: Muslims were displaced from government jobs by British and Hindu officials; Muslim officials were rendered illiterate when English replaced Persian as India's official language; and evangelical Christians incited Muslim fears that Britain intended to make India a Christian nation. Ian Stephens was editor of the Statesman *in Pakistan from 1942 to 1951 and official historian of the Pakistan Army from 1957 to 1960.*

The rise of British power in India is so familiar a tale and so well documented that, though fascinating, and profuse in colourful incident and remarkable men, and very tempting to write about, it needs no detailed describing here. For what concerns us is its effect on the subcontinent's Muslims, the forbears of present-day Pakistanis; and that, within a very short while, became disastrous. A community which, for six centuries, had dominated the country's affairs now found itself shoved down abruptly from first place to third. Admittedly Akbar's secularist policy had put many Hindus in positions of honour and wealth, as supporters of the state; nevertheless throughout his reign, Muslims for traditional reasons had still held most of the big military and civilian administrative jobs, and this remained so during Jahangir's reign and Shah Jahan's. And in Aurangzeb's some pro-Muslim reversal of policy occurred. In any case Muslims knew that the apex of the régime, the final repository of power, namely the emperor himself, was Muslim, or at least Muslim in origin. It gave them reassurance and pride. But now a non-Muslim overseas nation in the guise of a trading company had made itself paramount in the land, and all this privilege was lost and much else too. Naturally the British soon put their own people in the best jobs, formerly enjoyed by Muslims. This became the officially accepted practice during [Charles] Cornwallis's time [as governor-general] (1786–93); moreover such good jobs as remained tended to go to Hindus. And since Hindus outnumbered Muslims by three to one that meant disproportionately grave loss for the latter. Reasons for the British preference for Hindus were several: the chief, simply that Hindus unlike Muslims were not the subcontinent's ex-rulers. Their period of imperial rule was historically so far back as not to matter in British eyes. They had no particular cause to be disloyal, the British felt; no recent privileged past to hanker after. And some of them unmistakably welcomed the change; they saw it as a relief from Muslim supremacy, which gave them fresh opportunities.

Mutual Suspicion

But the Muslims did hanker, and showed it. In general, their cooperation with the newcomers had from the start been less ready than their rivals'. Influential members of the community sulked; withdrew resentfully to their lands; took refuge in Urdu poetry, or meticulous religious observance, or the semi-mystical and perhaps politically subversive doctrines of the Delhi scholar Shah Wali-ullah (1703–62). Understandably, the British viewed all this with suspicion, which state of mind was intensified by revivalist movements on either side: on the Muslims', that of the so-called Wahabis or 'Hindustani fanatics', led by a romantic figure, Syed Ahmad of Rae Bareli (1786–1831), whom Shah Wali-ullah's sons had befriended. Though professedly aimed against Ranjit Singh's Sikh empire in the north-west, this movement was anti-British in implication; and for decades after the Syed's death in battle against the Sikhs his followers caused the British anxiety. There was also a rather similar movement in Bengal, the Faraidis', which was religious and agrarian.

And on the British side there was Evangelicalism. Before,

Christianity had sat rather lightly on most of the East India Company's servants; religious zeal anyway was deprecated on practical grounds. Baptists and other missionaries might find themselves shoo-ed away from Calcutta to the Dutch or Danish settlements nearby, lest their urge to convert the heathen caused riots or other bothers and stood in the way of money-making. But now a strange new note was heard, coming from England; earnest, militant, very self-assured. Evidently to some British minds Westernizing and modernizing the Indians, along the lines advocated so confidently of late by [British author and educator Thomas Babington] Macaulay and others, meant much the same as Christianizing them. In London a director of the Company's court told Parliament that 'Providence has entrusted the extensive empire of Hindustan to England, so that the banner of Christ should wave triumphant from one end to the other'; and eager souls in its employ on Indian soil became imbued with the idea. To Hindus, such extravagances might not much matter; in their broad vague way they can tolerate almost any religious novelty or excess, content in the certainty that, sooner or later, their social system will absorb it, perhaps—in an instance such as this— eventually making Christian zealots into a new Hindu caste. But to Muslims, with their own clear-cut creed to defend, it mattered greatly. So gulfs of antagonism or misunderstanding between them and the British widened.

British Rule Harmful to Muslims

Other things contributed to their decline, unconnected with British suspicions of their imperial past or hostility to their creed. Among these were Cornwallis's 'permanent settlement' of the Bengal land-revenue in 1793 and [William Henry Cavendish] Bentinck's [governor-general, 1834–1835] later reforms of it, both of which, in rather different ways—though this does not seem to have been particularly meant—proved detrimental to Muslims' long-term interests. A weakness among them, which partly explains what happened, was that by comparison with the Hindus their middle class was so small; most Muslims were either landed aristocrats, and high ex-officials, military and civilian, of the Moghul régime—or else mere peasants and artisans. And as regards the last-named, the Bengal weavers, incidentally, were by now in a bad way, owing to competition from imported British manufactures.

Worse however, and quicker in effects, were the Company's decisions in 1835 to displace the Persian used by the Moghuls as the main Government language by English, and, as well, to foster English in education. The former process forthwith deprived many able Muslims of a livelihood, lowering them almost to the status of illiterates. True, this was partly their fault; for unlike the Hindus they had largely, of their own choice, forgone such opportunities for learning English as already existed. But a reason for that lay in their guess, certainly not baseless, that the keener sponsors of the English language sometimes regarded it, not primarily as a means of giving Indians access to modern Western knowledge, but rather as a tool whereby Christian beliefs could be implanted and Muslim ones broken up.

And then on top of all this came, in 1857, the unmitigated disaster of the Sepoy Mutiny. As later evidence has shown, this originated at least as much from annoyed Brahmin troopers of the Oudh army as from Muslims; but that was not what the British thought at the time. They believed it was mainly Muslim-instigated; and the retribution which followed—mixed allegedly with some vile atrocities, undivulged to the British public, such as sewing up Muslim prisoners in pigskins before executing them—bore much more hardly on Muslims than on Hindus, owing to widespread confiscation of lands. The result was that, by 1860 or thereabouts, they had been reduced, as has been vividly said, to 'the lowest depths of broken pride' from which escape seemed impossible. And although sweeping generalizations such as that which now comes should be made only with reservations, and must be cautiously viewed, it is nevertheless in this writer's opinion a fact that, on balance, British rule in India during the first 120 or so of its total of 190 years helped the Hindus and harmed the Muslims.

The Birth of Islamic Nationalism

BY PERCIVAL SPEAR

In the following extract from The Oxford History of Modern India, 1740–1947, *eminent British historian of India Percival Spear describes how the Muslims of British India responded to their confrontation with the West. He traces the growth of Islamic nationalism from the religious revivalist movement of the militant Wahabis in the eighteenth century to Punjabi poet Muhammad Iqbal's twentieth-century vision of a separate Muslim homeland carved out of northwest India. Spear says Muslim leader Mohammed Ali Jinnah then drew the evolving strands of Muslim nationalism together to turn "Pakistan," a term (meaning "land of the pure" in Urdu) invented by Muslim students studying at Cambridge University, into a reality.*

The eighteenth century was a time of stress for [India's Muslim] community. Their political dominion collapsed, and with it went their hold on the chief offices of state. The British monopolized (from the time of [Charles] Cornwallis [governor-general, 1786–1793]) these offices for themselves, leaving the upper classes to jostle for subordinate posts with Hindus, or else to stand aloof in pride and poverty. Soon western education was added as another and unacceptable condition for office. Immigration from the north-west came to an end, except from among the untutored Afghans. The decline of Islam in its homeland reduced the value of such contacts as remained, thus depriving Indian Islam of the spiritual and cultural streams which had so long nourished it. Islam in India was politically depressed and culturally isolated. With the weakening of these Islamic impulses Hindu practices and social customs, like the worship of saints' tombs and caste customs, already well established, became more widespread. It became difficult to tell whether some groups were more Muslim or Hindu in their outlook. The widespread resumption of rent-free lands and the ruin of the Bengal weaving industry further depressed the community.

It was in this condition of political eclipse and cultural depression that Indian Islam was confronted with the challenge of the West. At first bad seemed to grow worse, for while the Muslims stood aloof, the Hindus took advantage of the new western education, thus securing a lead in the new world and the administration which they never lost. The Mutiny made things worse, for in spite of its Hindu origin the Muslims were thought to have revealed their disloyalty to and hatred of the new régime. But the Muslims were too numerous and too vigorous to be absorbed or permanently reduced to insignificance. The first movements of revival came from within and may be described as those of internal renewal or purification. These were amongst the body of the people. Then came a movement among the leaders in tardy response to western influences. It was the Pakistan movement which finally welded these two together into a national movement comparable to that of the Indian Congress.

Origins of the Pakistan Movement

The first of these movements can be traced to Shah Wali-ullah of Delhi (1703–62), described as one of the greatest theologians of Muslim India. He translated the Quran into Persian, while two of his sons added an Urdu version. He began a movement for reform which was carried on by his son Shah Abdul Aziz. In the hands of his disciple Sayyid Ahmad of Bareilly, who was influenced by Wahabi ideas from Arabia, this became the militant 'Wahabi' movement of the early nineteenth century, with its headquarters at Patna. India was regarded as *dar-ul-harb*, or a land of war, since it was under infidel rule. Sayyid Ahmad's efforts, however, were directed against the Sikhs, as being the chief Muslim oppressors of the day. He established himself in the Swat valley where he waged a *jihad* or holy war until his death in battle with the Sikhs in 1831. Two parallel movements in lower India were led by Sheikh Karamat Ali of Jaunpur, another disciple of Shah Abdul Aziz, and Haji Shariat-ullah of Faridpur. The latter [known as the Faraidhi movement] was involved in agrarian agitation, but on the whole the two movements were peaceful.

They were actively propagandist and did much to purify and strengthen east Indian Islam. Karamat Ali's work has been thus described:

> For forty years he moved up and down the elaborate river system of eastern Bengal in a flotilla of small boats, carrying the message of Islamic regeneration and reform from the Nagas of Assam to the inhabitants of Sandip and other islands in the Bay of Bengal. His flotilla of country craft was like a travelling college. One boat was the residence of his family, another was reserved for the students and disciples accompanying him, while the third was for *dars* and lectures and prayers.

Mention should also be made of the Ahmadiya[1] sect founded by Mirza Ghulam Ahmad (1838–1908) with its headquarters at Qadian in the Panjab. It gathered a numerous following in the Panjab and was notable for organization and missionary activity, both in India and abroad, including England. But its founder's claim to prophethood and to the function of completing or adding to the Muslim revelation caused the sect to be considered heretical by the main body of Muslims. It has been notable for the distinction of some of its adherents rather than for its influence on the development of Indian Islam as a whole.

Sayyid Ahmad Khan

The response of Indian Islam to the West came not from the Muslim princes who showed a curious imperviousness to Western thought while they toyed with European trinkets or adopted superficial European manners. Furniture, wines, and uniforms were the limit of their interest. The first concrete move came from Sayyid Ahmad Khan of Delhi. He was born in 1817 and took service under the British in 1837, rising to the rank of subordinate judge. He remained loyal in the Mutiny and published an influential essay on its causes. Sayyid Ahmad came of an aristocratic family of central Asian origin; his combination of oriental with western learning fitted him to be an interpreter between the conservative East and the encroaching West; his forceful character enabled him to impress his ideas on his people

---

1. Persecution of the Ahmadis in contemporary Pakistan by Orthodox Muslims remains a contentious issue.

while his sterling integrity was proof against calumny. He visited England in 1869 and retired from service in 1876. In 1878 he became a member of the Governor-General's Legislative Council and was knighted in 1888. He died in 1898, the acknowledged grand old man of Indian Islam. The Sayyid was convinced that the Indian Muslims must make terms with the West, both politically and culturally. He considered that the tolerance and security of the British régime entitled it to be included in the *Darul-Islam* or region of peace. The British régime having been accepted as in the providence of God, Muslims should win British approval by active loyalty. Otherwise they would be outdistanced in the race for governmental favour by the Hindus, as had already happened in the case of education. A modern education, indeed, was the *sine qua non* of the community's progress, and the Sayyid therefore became a champion of western knowledge, which should not be inconsistent with the tenets of Islam. The fruit of this advocacy was the opening of the Anglo-Oriental College at Aligarh in 1875, with its British principals and staff, its residential system, its mosque and religious instruction, its balance of eastern and western learning. In 1920 the college became the Aligarh Muslim University. Aligarh both enabled the talented young Muslim to compete on terms with the Hindu for government service and in public life, and gave him a dynamic which his community seemed to have lost.

For Sir Sayyid was not concerned with material things only. His movement was one of general reform. It was inspired by the thought that the Muslims of India were a separate people or nation who must not be absorbed within Hinduism, and that the essence of Islam was consistent with the best that the West had to offer. He was, in fact, a Muslim modernist appealing to general principles outside the scope of the four recognized schools of theology. He accepted the mission of the Prophet and God's revelation in the Quran. But he claimed that Reason was also an attribute of God and Nature his handywork. The Quran and Islam might therefore be interpreted on the basis of reason to meet modern needs and problems. The achievements of the West, so far as they rested on reason, might thus be welcomed and assimilated. He laid particular stress upon science, as being the characteristic feature of western progress. His first institution at Aligarh was a scientific society. In pressing this point of view he was much helped by the existence of the strong Greek tradition in

Islamic thought, and by the common Judaic background which
western Christianity shared with Islam. Thus fortified, the Sayyid
conducted a campaign on two fronts, against the isolationist conservative Muslims on the one hand and European critics on the
other. This tended to replace backward-looking by forward-
looking views and to restore the shaken confidence of those in
close contact with western thought.

Aligarh School

These ideas attracted distinguished supporters, who came to be
known collectively as the Aligarh school. Among them may be
mentioned two men nurtured in the pre-Mutiny renaissance at
the Delhi college, Maulvi Nazir Ahmad and Maulvi Zaka-ullah,
the poets Altaf Husain, Hali, and Maulvi Shibli Numani, the
scholar Khuda Baksh, and the educationist Yusuf Ali. The work
of Sayyid Amir Ali though in general accord, had a slant of its
own. His *Spirit of Islam* was the best apologetic of Islam for the
non-Muslim which had appeared, while his *History of the Saracens*
was a tonic for the Muslims themselves. He emphasized the per-
sonality of the Prophet and so introduced what may be described
as prophetic hero-worship. But though emphasizing the value of
tradition, he was also a reformer, advocating women's education.
His insistence on the glories of historical Islam provided a
starting-point for the leaders of the *Khilafat* movement and a link
between them and the westernized liberals.

Sayyid Ahmad's programme was admirably suited to the position of Indian Islam in the Victorian world. It made possible
the assimilation of elements of a culture which then seemed ir-
resistible; it provided for gradual political progress at a time when
that seemed to be the only sort of progress possible. With the advent of the twentieth century conditions changed. Something
more dynamic than reason in the religious sphere was needed,
and something more radical than advisory councils as a political
programme. Europe itself was changing with the development
of industrialism; the old Islamic world was threatened and trying
to save itself by pan-Islamic Caliphate ideas. In India itself came
the first signs of the transfer of power to Indian hands, with the
ultimate prospect of a Hindu government. The collapse of
Turkey before the Balkan states in 1912 and then during the first
World War made Europe appear to many for a time as again the
enemy of Islam. It was this which gave strength to the *Khilafat*

movement in the postwar years. The overriding need, as it
seemed, to defend Islam, justified the Hindu alliance then con-
tracted. The revival of Turkey in 1922 and her emergence as a
secularist state reassured the liberals while removing the whole
basis of the conservative programme. From that time on the
Hindu majority, personified in the enigmatic figure of Gandhi,
seemed to be the main threat to a separate Muslim existence. But

No Separation of Church and State in Islamic Faith

*Muhammad Iqbal (1877–1938) is hailed as Pakistan's national
poet and spiritual founder. In the following extract from his presidential address to the Muslim League delivered in Allahabad on December 29, 1930, he asserts that the European notion of the separation of religion and politics is impossible for Muslims, whose
spiritual ideals must determine how they live on a temporal plane.
This idea became the philosophical rationale for the creation of the
Islamic state of Pakistan.*

It cannot be denied that Islam, regarded as an ethical ideal
plus a certain kind of polity—by which expression I mean
a social structure regulated by a legal system and animated
by a specific ethical ideal—has been the chief formative factor in the life-history of the Muslims of India. It has fur-
nished those basic emotions and loyalties which gradually
unify scattered individuals and groups and finally transform
them into a well-defined people. Indeed it is no exaggera-
tion to say that India is perhaps the only country in the
world where Islam, as a people-building force, has worked at
its best. . . . The ideas set free by European political thinking,
however, are now rapidly changing the outlook of the present generation of Muslims both in India and outside India.
Our younger men, inspired by these ideas, are anxious to see
them as living forces in their own countries, without any
critical appreciation of the facts which have determined their

there could be no return to the days of the Sayyid. Indian Islam needed a more dynamic creed and a larger vision and found it in the writings of Sir Muhammad Iqbal [1876–1938].

Muhammad Iqbal

Iqbal wrote mainly in Persian and only produced one work in English. His theme was the all-embracing sufficiency of Islam as

evolution in Europe. . . . Islam does not bifurcate the unity of man into an irreconcilable duality of spirit and matter. In Islam God and the universe, spirit and matter, Church and State, are organic to each other. Man is not the citizen of a propane world to be renounced in the interest of a world of spirit situated elsewhere. To Islam matter is spirit realizing itself in space and time. . . .

The proposition that religion is a private individual experience is not surprising on the lips of a European. In Europe the conception of Christianity as a monastic order, renouncing the world of matter and fixing its gaze entirely on the world of spirit led, by a logical process of thought, to the view embodied in this proposition. The nature of the Prophet's religious experience, as disclosed in the Qur"an, however, is wholly different. It is not mere experience in the sense of a purely biological event, happening inside the experient and necessitating no reactions on his social environment. It is individual experience creative of a social order. Its immediate outcome is the fundamentals of a polity with implicit legal concepts whose civic significance cannot be belittled merely because their origin is revelational. The religious ideal of Islam, therefore, is organically related to the social order which it has created. The rejection of the one will eventually involve the rejection of the other. Therefore the construction of a polity on national lines, if it means a displacement of the Islamic principle of solidarity, is simply unthinkable to a Muslim.

Muhammad Iqbal, presidential address to the Muslim League, Allahabad, December 29, 1930.

expressing a dynamic spirit of struggle for spiritual freedom. Islam was not merely a valid religion to be compared favourably
with others; it was the root and branch of all religious experience. It was not a fixed and precious deposit to be treasured with
the zeal of the antiquarian, but a living principle of action which
could give purpose and remake worlds. Europe was enmeshed in
its greed for wealth and lust for power. It was for Islam to create
true values and to assert man's mastery of nature by constant
struggle. It was [German philosopher Friedrich] Nietszche in an
Islamic setting. Iqbal's teaching provided the young Muslim generation with a view which out-moderned the moderns, but
which yet seemed distinctive and Islamic. Sayyid Ahmad Khan
gave Indian Islam a sense of separate existence; Iqbal a sense of
separate destiny.

The precipitation of this rich solution of thought and feeling
into the crystals of a political movement required an external cat-
alyst, and this was provided by fear. Sayyid Ahmad Khan gave the
community a new sense of justification and a new line of conduct; he also made possible a new sense of security by pointing
the way to a reconciliation with the ruling power. But the sense
of separateness from others involved an immediate reaction to
any suggestion of commingling or absorption in a plural society.
The British might rule, for they showed no sign of interfering
with Islam; that was the basis of the Sayyid's confidence in them.
But would a hypothetical Hindu government do the same? As
soon as the Congress was formed in 1885 the Sayyid took alarm.
Majority Indian rule for him meant Hindu rule, and Hindu rule
meant the risk of cultural absorption. He had already declined to
support Amir Ali's 'National Muhammadan Association' in Calcutta in 1877 as tending to subversive activity. Only a small group,
particularly in Bombay, supported the Congress to become the
nucleus of the later nationalist Muslims.

The Muslim League

The Muslims in general watched the growth of Congress from
a distance and stood aloof from its controversies with Lord Curzon. But having allowed it to become dominantly Hindu in character through their abstention, they took alarm at the first signs
of concessions to its demands. From this sprang the deputation
to Lord Minto in 1906, led by the Agha Khan, which demanded
separate electorates for Muslims in any representative system

which might be introduced. At the same time they did what the Sayyid had frowned upon during his life by forming the All-India Muslim League. The Morley-Minto reforms with their separate electorates for Muslim landholders, and their retention of irresponsible power by the British, satisfied them for the time so far as India was concerned. But almost immediately the Muslims took alarm at the misfortunes of Turkey and there followed the *Khilafat* movement. Pan-Islamic sentiment overbore the nascent local Muslim nationalism and antipathy to British Turkish policy local fear of Hindu rule. The outward expressions of this emotional upheaval were the Lucknow Pact of 1916 with the Congress which recognized separate electorates, and the alliance with Congress in Gandhi's non-cooperation movement. The passing of this storm left the Muslims as a whole disillusioned and fearful for their future while leaving a fresh sediment of Muslims on the Congress shore. These included many westernized Muslims who took a secularist view on the lines of Ataturk as to the place of Islam in the state. The most distinguished of these was Muhammad Ali Jinnah of Bombay, who had been a member of Congress for many years and now held the balance of power in the Legislative Assembly as leader of the Independent party.

Muhammad Ali Jinnah

The working of the Montford reforms tended to increase these fears. They were expressed in a rising tempo of communal riots and increasingly bitter exchanges between the party leaders. The Ali brothers swung round from the preaching of Hindu fraternalism to the championship of Muslim rights. But the community remained divided and perplexed. In 1927 the League split on the question of the Simon Commission uniting in 1929 in the All-India Muslim Conference. Mr. Jinnah retired in 1931. Only in the Panjab were the Muslims active and confident under the determined leadership of Sir Fazl-i Husain, whose icy and resolute character was reminiscent of the Irish [leader Charles Stuart] Parnell [who opposed the British government by obstructing acts of Parliament]. The constitutional discussions which began with the appointment of the Simon Commission at the end of 1927 increased Muslim fears, for it soon became clear that a further instalment of power would be given to responsible ministers, and that full self-government was now above the horizon of development. Heightened apprehension quickened the urge to unity and also the search for a practical policy. The search for unity led to the reorganization of the League under Mr. Jinnah in 1934, whose emergence from political retirement in this capacity was itself a sign of the times. The search for a positive programme led in two directions. The first was that of safeguards. During the constitutional discussions of the early thirties there was a renewed insistence upon communal representation, not only in the constituencies, but also in the government service. Muslims welcomed federation as giving provinces more freedom and thus tending to safeguard Muslims in their majority areas. They sought to reduce the scope of the Centre as much as possible. The second direction was towards autonomy in the Muslim majority areas. In 1930 Iqbal suggested the union of the Frontier Province, Baluchistan, Sind, and Kashmir as a Muslim state within a federation. This proved to be a creative idea which germinated during the early thirties to burst into vigorous life with the advent of the new reforms. The idealist Choudhri Rahmat Ali developed this conception at Cambridge, where he inspired a group of young Muslims and invented the term Pakistan in 1933. His ideas seemed visionary at the time, but within seven years they had been turned into a practical programme by the future Qaid-i-Azam [great leader] with the new name as its slogan or banner. The ideology of Iqbal, the visions of Rahmat Ali, and the fears of Muslims were thus united by the practical genius of Jinnah to bind Muslims together as never before during the British period and lead to effect an act of political creation.

Call for a Muslim Nation

By Mohammed Ali Jinnah

While the Muslim poet Iqbal provided the spiritual inspiration for a separate Islamic nation on the Indian subcontinent, Western-educated lawyer Mohammed Ali Jinnah made this vision a reality. Following Jinnah's historic presidential address to the Muslim League in March 1940, the party officially adopted the principle of a separate Muslim homeland. In the following extract from his address, Jinnah says that the British solution of a Western-style democracy for India would be disastrous to the Muslim community since more than twelve hundred years of cohabitation had failed to unite their two distinct heritages. In the speech Jinnah outlines his famous "two-nation theory," which remains at the heart of the controversy between Pakistani Muslims and supporters of a united India.

The British government and Parliament, and more so the British nation, have been for many decades past brought up and nurtured with settled notions about India's future, based on developments in their own country which has built up the British constitution, functioning now through the Houses of Parliament and the system of cabinet. Their concept of party government functioning on political planes has become the ideal with them as the best form of government for every country, and the one-sided and powerful propaganda, which naturally appeals to the British, has led them into a serious blunder, in producing the constitution envisaged in the Government of India Act of 1935.[1] We find that the most leading statesmen of Great Britain, saturated with these notions, have in their pronouncements seriously asserted and expressed a hope that the passage of time will

1. The act continued the system of separate electorates for Hindus and Muslims at the central and provincial levels of government established by the British in 1909.

Muhammad Ali Jinnah, "An International Problem," *Sources of Indian Tradition*, edited by William Theodore de Bary. New York: Columbia University Press, 1960.

harmonize the inconsistent elements of India.

A leading journal like the London *Times*, commenting on the Government of India Act of 1935, wrote: "Undoubtedly the differences between the Hindus and Muslims are not of religion in the strict sense of the word but also of law and culture, that they may be said, indeed, to represent two entirely distinct and separate civilizations. However, in the course of time, the superstition will die out and India will be molded into a single nation." So, according to the London *Times*, the only difficulties are superstitions. These fundamental and deep-rooted differences, spiritual, economic, cultural, social, and political, have been euphemized as mere "superstitions." But surely it is a flagrant disregard of the past history of the subcontinent of India as well as the fundamental Islamic conception of society vis-à-vis that of Hinduism to characterize them as mere "superstitions." Notwithstanding a thousand years of close contact, nationalities, which are as divergent today as ever, cannot at any time be expected to transform themselves into one nation merely by means of subjecting them to a democratic constitution and holding them forcibly together by unnatural and artificial methods of British parliamentary statute. What the unitary government of India for one hundred fifty years had failed to achieve cannot be realized by the imposition of a central federal government. It is inconceivable that the fiat or the writ of a government so constituted can ever command a willing and loyal obedience throughout the subcontinent by various nationalities except by means of armed force behind it.

The problem in India is not of an intercommunal character but manifestly of an international one, and it must be treated as such. So long as this basic and fundamental truth is not realized, any constitution that may be built will result in disaster and will prove destructive and harmful not only to the Mussalmans but to the British and Hindus also. If the British government are really in earnest and sincere to secure [the] peace and happiness of the people of this subcontinent, the only course open to us all is to allow the major nations separate homelands by dividing India into "autonomous national states." There is no reason why these states should be antagonistic to each other. On the other hand, the rivalry and the natural desire and efforts on the part of one to dominate the social order and establish political supremacy over the other in the government of the country will disappear. It will lead more towards natural good will by international pacts

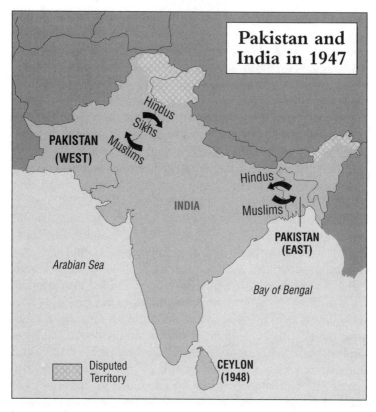

between them, and they can live in complete harmony with their neighbors. This will lead further to a friendly settlement all the more easily with regard to minorities by reciprocal arrangements and adjustments between Muslim India and Hindu India, which will far more adequately and effectively safeguard the rights and interests of Muslims and various other minorities.

Two Distinct Civilizations

It is extremely difficult to appreciate why our Hindu friends fail to understand the real nature of Islam and Hinduism. They are not religions in the strict sense of the word, but are, in fact, different and distinct social orders, and it is a dream that the Hindus and Muslims can ever evolve a common nationality, and this misconception of one Indian nation has gone far beyond the limits and is the cause of most of your troubles and will lead India to destruction if we fail to revise our notions in time. The Hindus and Muslims belong to two different religious philosophies, social customs, literatures. They neither intermarry nor interdine together and, indeed, they belong to two different civilizations which are based mainly on conflicting ideas and conceptions. Their aspects on life and of life are different. It is quite clear that Hindus and Mussalmans derive their inspiration from different sources of history. They have different epics, different heroes, and different episodes. Very often the hero of one is a foe of the other and, likewise, their victories and defeats overlap. To yoke together two such nations under a single state, one as a numerical minority and the other as a majority, must lead to growing discontent and final destruction of any fabric that may be so built up for the government of such a state.

History has presented to us many examples, such as the union of Great Britain and Ireland, Czechoslovakia, and Poland. History has also shown us many geographical tracts, much smaller than the subcontinent of India, which otherwise might have been called one country, but which have been divided into as many states as there are nations inhabiting them. [The] Balkan Peninsula comprises as many as seven or eight sovereign states. Likewise, the Portuguese and the Spanish stand divided in the Iberian Peninsula. Whereas under the plea of the unity of India and one nation, which does not exist, it is sought to pursue here the line of one central government, we know that the history of the last twelve hundred years has failed to achieve unity and has witnessed, during the ages, India always divided into Hindu India and Muslim India. The present artificial unity of India dates back only to the British conquest and is maintained by the British bayonet, but termination of the British regime, which is implicit in the recent declaration of His Majesty's government, will be the herald of the entire break-up with worse disaster than has ever taken place during the last one thousand years under Muslims. Surely that is not the legacy which Britain would bequeath to India after one hundred fifty years of her rule, nor would Hindu and Muslim India risk such a sure catastrophe.

We Must Stand Firm

Muslim India cannot accept any constitution which must necessarily result in a Hindu majority government. Hindus and Muslims brought together under a democratic system forced upon the minorities can only mean Hindu rāj [rule]. Democracy of the kind with which the Congress High Command is enamored would mean the complete destruction of what is most precious in Islam. We have had ample experience of the working of the provincial constitutions during the last two and a half years and any repetition of such a government must lead to civil war and raising of private armies as recommended by Mr. Gandhi to [the] Hindus of Sukkur when he said that they must defend themselves violently or nonviolently, blow for blow, and if they could not, they must emigrate.

Mussalmans are not a minority as it is commonly known and understood. One has only got to look round. Even today, according to the British map of India, four out of eleven provinces, where the Muslims dominate more or less, are functioning notwithstanding the decision of the Hindu Congress High Command to noncooperate and prepare for civil disobedience. Mussalmans are a nation according to any definition of a nation, and they must have their homelands, their territory, and their state. We wish to live in peace and harmony with our neighbors as a free and independent people. We wish our people to develop to the fullest our spiritual, cultural, economic, social, and political life in a way that we think best and in consonance with our own ideals and according to the genius of our people. Honesty demands and the vital interests of millions of our people impose a sacred duty upon us to find an honorable and peaceful solution, which would be just and fair to all. But at the same time we cannot be moved or diverted from our purpose and objective by threats or intimidations. We must be prepared to face all difficulties and consequences, make all the sacrifices that may be required of us to achieve the goal we have set in front of us.

The Genesis of Pakistan

By Rafi Raza

In the following extract from Pakistan in Perspective, 1947–1997, *Rafi Raza traces the key political events that led to the creation of Pakistan on August 14, 1947. He says that Muslims reappraised their role in the Indian subcontinent following the collapse of the Mughal Empire. After a revival of interest in the Muslim faith, the main concern of India's Muslims during the British period was to ensure they had adequate political representation. As the independence struggle gained momentum, Raza says the actions of the Indian National Congress leaders incited Muslim fears that they would be dominated by the majority Hindu community when India became independent. This led their chief spokesman, Mohammed Ali Jinnah, to demand the creation of a separate Islamic nation. Rafi Raza, a Pakistani constitutional lawyer, was special adviser to Pakistan's president Zulfikar Bhutto in 1971 and Minister for Production in the Pakistan government in the 1970s and again in 1990.*

Pakistan came into existence on 14 August 1947—the first State in recent history created on the basis of religion. The founding fathers, fearing Hindu domination, had emphasized the separateness of the Muslims from the Hindus of the subcontinent of India—'Two Nations'—mainly in social and cultural terms. The later stress on Islamic ideology and the assertion that it alone could bind together in nationhood a geographically and ethnically divided Pakistan was undermined by dismemberment and the emergence of an independent Bangladesh in 1971.

To comprehend the motivation for the creation of Pakistan, it is necessary to examine the events leading up to its establishment and the aspirations of the Muslims which it reflected. . . .

Muslims Invade India

The early Muslims in India were conquerors, traders, settlers and converts. The first invasion was of Sindh in 711 by Muhammad Bin Qasim who, after defeating Raja Dahir, captured Multan in 713. The Ghaznavids came from the northwest in 1001, subjugating Multan by 1010; they were followed by the invasion of the Ghors in 1175, again aimed at Multan.

Muslim permanence was eventually established in the thirteenth century by several dynasties of the Sultanate that ruled Delhi. In this period, when India embraced many religions and cultures, of which the principal was Hindu, the Sufis [Islamic mystics] played an important part in spreading Islam through their identification of God with the Universe, a concept which helped accommodate the views of others. The Sultanate of Delhi was succeeded by the Moghul Empire after the invasion of Babar in 1526, and its expansion brought the Muslims into undisputed leadership, particularly in northern India.

The third Moghul Emperor, Akbar, who ruled from 1556 to 1605, adopted an eclectic approach to provide a single framework for his subjects of different faiths and common ground for all religions. The failure of his short-lived policy led to a puritanical reaction, especially under his great-grandson, Aurangzeb, and the movement for orthodox Islam. A rapid decline in Muslim power followed the death of Aurangzeb in 1707; the Empire had suffered as a result of his long and expensive campaigns against the Marathas and others in the Deccan, while his Hindu subjects had been alienated by his intolerance. Even in Bengal, effective Muslim rule was curtailed in 1757. The prevailing disorder and absence of proper central government provided the British East India Company with a ready opportunity to expand and gain control. The failed uprising of 1857 against the British resulted in the final eclipse of the Moghul Empire, and direct British rule in India.

Muslims Under the British

British suspicion of the Muslims, particularly after 1857, was accompanied by increased patronage of the Hindus. The Muslims' sense of exclusion led them to reappraise their role in the subcontinent. From this emerged a Muslim renaissance, whose leading figures included Sir Syed Ahmed Khan. A new political awareness began to grow, and, as a consequence, the Muslim

League was established in Dhaka in 1906. Its aims [included] 'To protect and advance the political rights and interests of the Mussalmans of India, and to respectfully represent their needs and aspirations to the Government.' The same year Mohammad Ali Jinnah joined the Indian National Congress, which had been formed earlier in 1885. He formally enrolled as a member of the Muslim League in 1913.

The main concern of the Muslim League was how to achieve effective political representation when the Hindus outnumbered the Muslims by three to one. The demand for separate electorates for the Muslims was a natural outcome. This was secured under the Indian Councils Act of 1909 through the Minto-Morley Reforms proposed by Lord Minto, the Viceroy of India, and Lord Morley, the Secretary of State for India. However, the Muslims soon received a reversal when, in 1912, the partition of Bengal by [the Viceroy] Lord Curzon in 1906 was set aside. Under this partition, which had been made merely as an administrative convenience, the Muslims had in fact gained; they formed the majority in the newly constituted province of Eastern Bengal and Assam, the latter having been separated from Bengal in 1874.

The outbreak of the First World War gave a new impetus to Indian political aspirations, and soon both Hindus and Muslims participated in the formation of the All-India Home Rule League in August 1916. Later that year, in November, cooperation between the two communities reached a new high in Lucknow where sessions of both the Muslim League and Congress were held. Under the Lucknow Pact, the Muslim League undertook to work with the Hindus to achieve freedom, while Congress accepted the demand for separate electorates and allowed the Muslims weightage in excess of their numbers. This created confidence among the numerically smaller Muslim community, and Mohammad Ali Jinnah was hailed as the 'Ambassador of Hindu-Muslim unity'. The following year he became President of the Bombay branch of the Home Rule League. . . . Jinnah's subsequent disillusionment with Congress led him to leave the Home Rule League at the end of 1920, and subsequently Congress, because, as he correctly predicted, Mahatma Gandhi's efforts 'to generate coercive power in the masses would only promote mass conflict between the two communities' [as stated by K.M. Munshi].

Growth of Self-Government in India

Meanwhile, in response to growing political agitation, on 20 August 1917 the Secretary of State for India announced Britain's new policy 'to provide for the increasing association of Indians in every branch of Indian administration, and for the gradual development of self-governing institutions, with a view to the progressive realization of responsible government in British India as an integral part of the British Empire'. The 'Constitution' that emerged in the form of the Government of India Act, 1919, proved insufficient and did not stem the tide of Indian demands. These came to a climax in 1929 in the call of Congress for independence.

Earlier, in 1927, the British Government had appointed a Commission consisting of British Members of Parliament, led by Sir John Simon, to report on the functioning of the 1919 Act. The Commission included no Indians. In protest, an All-Party Conference was convened which in turn appointed a committee under Motilal Nehru (Jawaharlal's father) to examine various constitutional issues. The Nehru Report, published in August 1928, proved a major turning point for Muslims because it rejected the Muslim League proposals, which had earlier been agreed. Jinnah pleaded in vain for separate electorates to avoid 'civil war'. For him, this became 'the parting of the ways' [according to Henry Hector Bolitho].

The Report of the Simon Commission was published in 1930. Three Round Table Conferences were convened in England between 12 November 1930 and 17 November 1932 to consider proposals for a new Indian Constitution. Congress refused to be represented at the first, and Jinnah was not invited to the third. In fact, in September 1931, he decided to settle in London to pursue his law practice before the Privy Council, returning to India in October 1935 to become President of the Muslim League. By then the British Parliament had passed the Government of India Act, 1935; two of its main features were the introduction of a federal system and a considerable degree of autonomy for the provinces.

The next major development took place after the 1937 elections to the Provincial Assemblies held under the 1935 'Constitution'. The Muslim League remained ill-organized despite Jinnah's recent return. It had only initiated a programme for mass contact from April 1936, and this weakness was reflected in its poor results, securing less than a quarter of the 485 seats reserved for Muslims, of which Congress contested 58 and won 26. Congress, which was in a minority only in Bengal, the Punjab and Sindh, formed ministries in eight provinces, where it decided against coalitions. Instead of minimizing the differences between the two major communities, and providing a propitious beginning to the process of self-rule in India, it only thereby exacerbated the divide. The rift was highlighted by Jawaharlal Nehru's remark in March 1937 that 'There are only two forces in India today, British imperialism, and Indian nationalism as represented by the Congress'; to which Jinnah retorted, 'No, there is a third party, the Mussalmans'.

After its ministries took office in July 1937, the uncompromising attitude of Congress confirmed among Muslims the fear of Hindu domination, and they turned increasingly to the Muslim League. Even earlier, similar concerns had been expressed, most notably by Allama Muhammad Iqbal in his Presidential Address to the All-India Muslim League annual session at Allahabad on 29 December 1930. He referred to Islamic polity as 'a social structure regulated by a legal system and animated by a specific ethical ideal', which had been 'the chief formative factor in the life history of the Muslims of India'. He visualized what eventually became Pakistan:

> I would like to see the *Punjab, the North-West Frontier Province, Sindh and Balochistan amalgamated into a single State* (emphasis added) . . . in the best interests of India and Islam. For India it means security and peace resulting from an internal balance of power; for Islam, an opportunity . . . to mobilize its laws, its education, its culture, and to bring them into closer contact with its own original spirit and with the spirit of modern times.

Iqbal was the poet-philosopher of Pakistan, a name that was coined by Chaudhri Rehmat Ali in England in January 1933. It meant 'Land of the pure'. The letter 'P' stood for the Punjab, 'A' was for the Afghan Frontier, or the North-West Frontier Province, 'K' represented Kashmir, while 'S' symbolized Sindh and 'Tan' Balochistan. Bengal was included by neither Iqbal nor Rehmat Ali.

The post-election period witnessed communal riots and serious efforts to reorganize and reorientate the Muslim League. With the outbreak of the Second World War, there was a swift and dramatic change in the Indian political scene. As a condition for cooperation in the war effort, Congress demanded immediate independence from a beleaguered Britain. Jinnah pressed for the right of self-determination for Muslims, and hailed as deliverance the resignation of the Congress ministries in November 1939. His principled leadership played a major part in making the Muslim League a dominant force in Indian politics, particularly from 1937.

Vision of a Muslim Nation

The next landmark was the Twenty-seventh Session of the All-India Muslim League at Lahore in 1940. In his Presidential Address, Jinnah elaborated on the real nature of Islam and Hinduism:

> They are not religions in the strict sense of the word, but are, in fact, different and distinct social orders.... The Hindus and the Muslims belong to two different social philosophies, social customs, and literature ... and indeed they belong to two different civilizations, which are based mainly on conflicting ideas and conceptions ... and derive their inspiration from different sources of history.... To yoke together two such nations as a single State, one as a numerical minority and the other as a majority, must lead to growing discontent and the final destruction of any fabric that may be so built up for the Government of such a State.

While refering to the Muslims of India as 'a nation by any definition', he cited the Balkan Penninsula and Czechoslovakia as other examples of States incorporating different religions and ethnic groups.

On 23 March 1940, the second day of the session, a resolution was moved which later came to be known as the 'Lahore Resolution' and the 'Pakistan Resolution', although the term Pakistan itself was not mentioned. It affirmed that no constitutional plan for India would be either acceptable or workable unless 'Geographically contiguous units are demarcated into regions ... [so] that the areas in which the Muslims are numerically in a majority, as in the North-Western and Eastern zones of India, should be grouped to constitute Independent States.' Islam itself found no mention, but reference was made to the protection of 'religious, cultural, economic, political, administrative and other rights and interests' of all 'minorities in these units'.

The British Government tried to ensure peace in the subcontinent by sending a mission led by Sir Stafford Cripps, which offered Dominion Status and India's right to secede after the war. This was rejected by Gandhi as a 'post-dated cheque on a tottering bank'. When attempts to find a solution finally failed, Con-

CONFLICTING VIEWS ON THE ORIGINS OF PAKISTAN

In the following extract from Pakistan: The Formative Phase, *Khalid bin Sayeed, assistant professor of political science at the University of New Brunswick, Canada, says that Pakistan was the result of a historic entrenched division between Hindu and Muslim civilizations.*

The origins of Pakistan lie entangled in prejudices. Those of us who have witnessed its gestation and later its final emergence have been brought up to believe passionately in theories which either deride it as the crown and consummation of the British policy of 'divide and rule' in India or in theories which glorify it as the final fulfilment of a clear, uninterrupted and separate stream of Muslim political consciousness in Indian history. . . .

Each view taken by itself is a highly exaggerated account of the origin of Pakistan. Each, perhaps, played its role and Pakistan was brought about by a multiplicity of factors. But perhaps a dominant or decisive cause of Pakistan is that there has never taken place a confluence of the two civilizations in India—the Hindu and the Muslim. They may have meandered towards each other here and there, but on the whole the two have flowed their separate courses—sometimes parallel and sometimes contrary to one another.

Khalid bin Sayeed, *Pakistan: The Formative Phase, 1857–1948.* Karachi: Oxford University Press, 1992, pp. 1, 9.

gress passed the 'Quit India' resolution on 8 August 1942. Instead of the planned mass movement of non-cooperation and non-violence, death and destruction resulted from the arrest of Congress leaders the following day. Jinnah insisted on nonviolent and constitutional procedures, and seized this opportunity to consolidate the League's position.

Further significant developments followed Lord Wavell's installation as Viceroy on 20 October 1943. After nearly two years of frustrating discussions with the British Government, he was finally permitted to announce on 14 June 1945 that he would invite Indian leaders to discuss the establishment of a new Executive Council which, apart from the Viceroy and the Commander-in-Chief, would be entirely Indian, and have equal representation of Muslims and caste Hindus, as distinguished from Scheduled Caste Hindus. The Council would work under the 1935 Act, but would consider framing a new constitution for India. As a consequence, the Simla Conference commenced on 25 June 1945, but it eventually failed because of Jinnah's insistence that only the League could nominate Muslims to the Council. Wavell, however, persisted in his efforts, which were aided by the election in the United Kingdom of a Labour Government favourable to India's independence.

Demand for the Creation of Pakistan

On 21 August 1945, Wavell announced that elections would be held by the end of the year, and, four weeks later, that Britain would allow full self-government in India. The elections to the Central Legislative Assembly foreshadowed the division to come: the goal of Congress was to maintain the unity of India and it won 91.3 per cent of the votes in non-Muslim constituencies; the aim of the League was to achieve the exclusive right to represent the Muslims, and thus create Pakistan, and it secured 86.6 per cent of the votes cast for the Muslim seats. Unlike in 1937, Jinnah and the League were now undisputed leaders of the Muslims in India. They were in a strong position to press their demands before the British Cabinet Mission, and proposed at the League Legislators' Convention in Delhi in April 1946 that the only formula to 'maintain internal peace and tranquility' required

> That the zones comprising Bengal and Assam in the North-East and the Punjab, North-West Frontier

Province, Sindh and Balochistan in the North-West of
India . . . be constituted into a sovereign independent
State and that an unequivocal undertaking be given to
implement the establishment of Pakistan without delay.

It is noteworthy that in the Delhi Resolution the emphasis was
also on Muslims as 'adherents of a faith which regulates every department of their lives (educational, social, economic and political) whose code is not confined merely to spiritual doctrines and
tenets or rituals and ceremonies, and which stands in sharp contrast to the exclusive nature of Hindu Dharma Philosophy'. . . .

This was the first specific demand for the State of Pakistan and
for separate constitution-making bodies, one each for 'the people
of Pakistan and Hindustan for the purpose of framing their respective constitutions'. It was made just prior to the arrival in India of the British Cabinet Mission, comprising Lord Pethwick-
Lawrence, Sir Stafford Cripps and A.V. Alexander, to find agreed
principles for a new constitution on India attaining independence. The Cabinet Mission and Wavell met the Congress and
League leaders on 5 and 6 May, and, ten days later, announced a
plan proposing a federation consisting of (1) north-west regions
with significant Muslim majorities, (2) Bengal and Assam, and (3)
the remaining provinces with Hindu majorities. The Constituent
Assembly was to be elected on a communal basis by the Provincial Legislative Assemblies and the representatives of the Princely
States which joined the federation. Each province could opt out
of this arrangement after the first elections. The Muslim League
accepted but Congress refused to accept parity of representation
either in the Council or the Legislature, claiming that this was
against the principles of democracy. Jawaharlal Nehru also asserted that Congress would have the right to modify the plan after independence. As a result, Jinnab withdrew his acceptance.
With the failure of the Cabinet Mission, Jinnah for the first time
departed from legal methods and called for 'Direct Action'. Massive communal riots followed from 16 August 1946 in Bengal
and other areas, which confirmed the view that the two major
communities of India could not live together.

Prime Minister Clement Attlee sent Lord Mountbatten as
Viceroy in March 1947 with a view to expediting independence.
On 3 June 1947, Mountbatten announced his plan for the parti-
tion of the subcontinent; this conceded Pakistan but excluded

from it East Punjab and West Bengal. In those areas where the will of the people had to be ascertained, as in the NWFP [Northwest Frontier Province] and the district of Sylhet, referenda were held. Mountbatten appointed Boundary Commissions to demarcate the division in Bengal and the Punjab. One result of this was the unfair, if not unscrupulous, provision of a corridor for India to Jammu and Kashmir; the problem of that State has since bedevilled relations between India and Pakistan. Both Congress and the Muslim League accepted the Partition Plan, though neither was satisfied with it.

Pakistan came into existence without receiving its fair share of assets as one of the two successor States that emerged from British India. Unlike India, it lacked a ready-made national government. It also had to cope with a far larger influx of refugees amidst communal rioting and killing that resulted in the death of hundreds of thousands of Muslims. Despite all the difficulties, there was no doubt in the minds of Pakistanis at the time that the country was there to stay, a beacon for Muslims throughout the world.

Birth and Beginnings of a Nation

New Nation in Disarray: Pakistan, 1947–1949

By Ian Talbot

In the following extract, historian Ian Talbot describes the economic, political, geographic, and institutional disadvantages that plagued Pakistan in the two years following its inception in 1947. On top of this shaky foundation, mass migration of refugees and tensions with India over water resources and Kashmir created tremendous stress on the new nation. Talbot says these factors determined the country's future course—the shift from democratic, economic, and social development toward military rule, bureaucratic domination, and diversion of scarce economic resources to national defense.

Ian Talbot was a research fellow at the Institute of Commonwealth Studies in London when he wrote Pakistan: A Modern History, *from which the following is an excerpt.*

Pakistan's birth was a difficult one which involved the immense suffering of thousands of its citizens. Its British midwife had abandoned it to a chaotic environment in which an elder Indian sibling looked on with scarcely disguised hostility. In such circumstances, historians appear slightly perverse in directing more attention to how Pakistan was conceived, rather than to why it was not stillborn. . . . This article describes the features of the new-born state and the traumas which surrounded its arrival into the world.

Economic and Geographical Inheritance

From a political standpoint, the most significant features of Pakistan's geography in 1947 were its relatively small share of the In-

dian subcontinent and the contrasts and distance both within and
between its western and eastern wings. Pakistan was by no means
a small country, with a combined area almost four times that of
the United Kingdom, or equal to that of Texas and Arizona in
the United States, but it was dwarfed by its Indian neighbour. It
had in fact inherited 23 per cent of the landmass of undivided
India and 18 per cent of the population. The disputes over Kashmir, the division of assets and water at the time of Partition, increased anxieties about Pakistan's precarious geopolitical situation
in relation to its much larger neighbour. Furthermore, the Pakistani sense of inferiority and insecurity was psychologically
rooted in the country's status as a seceding state rather than in-
heritor of the Raj. Membership of international organisations
such as the United Nations had devolved upon India, whereas
Pakistan had to go cap-in-hand to apply for membership.

Diplomatic and defence policies have been decisively influenced by the need to counteract this Indian regional preponder-
ance. External alliances with the United States in the [Central
Treaty Organization] CENTO (1955) and [the Southeast Asia
Treaty Organization] SEATO Pacts (1954) and friendship with
China were successively called into play to help offset a strategic
imbalance which worsened dramatically following the secession
of East Pakistan. The emphasis on building an effective army and
bureaucracy rather than representative institutions in the early
years after independence was also rooted in this geopolitical situation. [Political scientists] Wayne Wilcox and Stephen Cohen
have linked the military's central role in the political decision-
making process with Pakistan's unfavourable security environment, which has seen domestic policy much more influenced by
defence and foreign policy than is usual.

No Industrial Base

The Dominion of Pakistan started life not only with a strategic
deficit, but also with an industrial one. At its outset it had an
overwhelmingly agrarian society in which new definitions of
land rights and the needs of imperial rule had strengthened the
existing powers of elite groups. Capitalist farming had been un-
evenly limited to the irrigated areas in Punjab, Sindh and the
Peshawar Valley of the Frontier. Elsewhere age-old nomadism
and subsistence farming remained unaltered.

North-west India's status as what has been termed an 'agrarian appendix' to the subcontinent is revealed in the low rate of urbanisation and industrialisation. The 1931 Frontier Census for example enumerated the urban population at just 16 per cent, a figure which was itself inflated by the listing of large agricultural villages as towns. Sindh recorded an urban population just 2 per cent higher and even the more developed Punjab province remained essentially rural in character.

Colonial industrial development had clustered around Bombay, Ahmedabad, Calcutta and the West Bengal/Bihar coal belt. These areas all formed part of the new Indian dominion leaving Pakistan with just 10 per cent of the subcontinent's industrial base. Significantly, in the areas which went to Pakistan in 1947, there was no equivalent of the giant TATA steelworks at Jameshedpur or of the concentrated industrial belts to the west of Calcutta. Indeed on the eve of partition just one of the top fifty-seven Indian companies was owned by a Muslim. Hindus in fact owned the majority of the industrial enterprises which were in existence in the Muslim majority regions. This, together with the traditional Hindu domination of trade and the professions, explains the disproportionately high non-Muslim urban populations in the future Pakistan areas. The urban imbalance of the Hindus and Sikhs was especially pronounced in the southern towns of the Frontier and in the Thar Parkar and Hyderabad districts of Sindh. Karachi, which was the second largest urban centre in the future West Pakistan with a population just under 400,000, possessed a substantial Hindu population of over 130,000. Cities such as Lahore and Peshawar had always been inhabited by substantial non-Muslim populations, but British rule enhanced the differences between them and their rural hinterland by creating administrative and professional opportunities for employment in addition to the traditional commercial and trading pursuits. Non-Muslims eagerly seized them because of their greater proficiency in English. . . . *Mohajirs* [Muslim migrants from India] mainly took over the running of Hindu-owned shops and businesses after 1947, although in some instances, former artisan employees or local entrepreneurs stepped into the gap.

Cut Off from Markets

Partition not only left most industrial development in India, but separated Pakistani raw materials from their markets. The main cotton producing areas of what became West Pakistan for example had supplied the raw materials to mills in Bombay and Ahmedabad. Just fourteen of the subcontinent's 394 cotton mills were located in Pakistan at the time of partition. It also emphasised the uneven capitalist development between the western and eastern wings of Pakistan. Punjab possessed two-thirds of all the organised industrial units situated in the Pakistan areas. East Pakistan, which produced the bulk of the world's raw jute supply, did not in fact boast a single mill since all the crop was sent in undivided India to Calcutta where it was made into hessian and exported. As British officials acknowledged before the partition of Bengal, East Bengal without Calcutta would be reduced to a 'rural slum'. During the 1950s and '60s East Pakistan was unable to overcome its relative backwardness at the time of Partition—with increasingly dangerous political consequences....

Furthermore, Pakistan received but a meagre share of the Raj's material inheritance. In principle it was entitled to 17.5 per cent of the assets of undivided India, but the growing mistrust between the two governments prevented a smooth division of the spoils. It was not until December 1947 that an agreement was reached on Pakistan's share of the cash balances. The bulk of these (Rs.550 million) were held back by the Government of India as a result of the hostilities in Kashmir, and only paid on 15 January 1948 following Gandhi's intervention and fasting. Pakistan's military equipment was also delivered tardily by the Indians. Just over 23,000 of the 160,000 tons of ordnance stores allotted to Pakistan by the Joint Defence Council were actually delivered. Most of the defence-production facilities and military stores in fact remained on the Indian side of the border.

Strategic and Institutional Inheritance

Strategically and institutionally Pakistan faced harsh challenges from its inception. Its eastern wing was separated from West Pakistan by 1,000 miles of Indian territory. This bred not only a sense of isolation from the centres of power but reinforced the existence of different world outlooks in the two wings with West Pakistan turning its face to the Middle East, East Pakistan to South-east Asia.

Pakistan's north-western borders not only contained potentially troublesome tribal populations but were vulnerable to incursions from an unfriendly Afghan neighbour. The government in Kabul refused to accept nineteenth-century Anglo-Afghan treaties which now demarcated its country's boundaries with Pakistan. It also . . . voted against Pakistan's admission to the United Nations. Armed tribal incursions from Afghanistan into Pakistan's border areas began with the transfer of power and became a continual irritant. Afghan–Pakistan relations were to reach their nadir in 1955 when diplomatic relations were severed following the ransacking of the Pakistan embassy in Kabul, and again in 1961 when the Pakistan Army had to repel major Afghan incursions at Bajaur. By then the army had been greatly expanded, but at the time of partition it was too weak simultaneously to face an Indian and Afghan threat. This reality was immediately brought home by the necessity of employing almost 500 British officers because of the shortfall of qualified Pakistanis in the technical branches and at senior army rank. In the bifurcation of the Indian Army, Pakistan received just six armoured regiments to India's forty, and eight artillery and infantry regiments to India's forty and twenty-one respectively. The Pakistan Army was greatly expanded from its modest beginnings, but only at the cost of dependency on foreign aid and by siphoning funds from development activities.

The organisational atrophy of the Muslim League outside Bengal . . . was a major feature of the freedom struggle. This institutional weakness contrasted with the pyramidal Congress organisation which stretched from New Delhi down to the villages. It was thus better placed to articulate local aspirations and implement policies than its Pakistani counterpart. Most importantly of all, as Ayesha Jalal has pointed out, the League's weakness meant that Pakistani politicians had to concede much 'greater autonomy to the administrative bureaucracy' to consolidate state authority than did their Indian counterparts.

India had inherited both the colonial state's central apparatus in the former imperial capital New Delhi and the Bengal provincial secretariat in Calcutta. Pakistan on the other hand had to improvise its federal government in the provisional capital at Karachi. The Constituent Assembly was housed in the Sindh Assembly building. Far more important than locating officials to Karachi and finding space to house them however, was the shaping of a new federal structure and coordinating the administration of the provinces and princely states. A new provincial government also had to be created at Dhaka in East Pakistan. This task was especially difficult as the majority of the officials were

Hindus and had opted for service in India. Indeed, of the 133 Muslim Indian Civil Service (ICS) and Indian Political Service (IPS) officials who opted for Pakistan at the time of partition, just one came from Bengal. Muslims from other areas of Pakistan were despatched to East Pakistan, although this remedy was to evoke later claims of internal colonisation.

At the same time as establishing a system of government literally from scratch, with ministers using wooden boxes as their tables, the Pakistan authorities were faced with the serious refugee problem which accompanied the partition of Punjab. The two-way mass migrations of August–November 1947 occurred against a background of horrific massacres, administrative chaos and mounting conflict between the two dominions over the division of assets, water ownership and water use and the political future of the northern princely state of Jammu and Kashmir. Most of these problems remained unresolved at the time when Pakistan received the shattering blow of the death of its architect Muhammad Ali Jinnah in September 1948. Indeed as late as May 1960 the joint Indo-Pakistan Punjab Partition Implementation Committee was still grinding its way through various financial disputes, relating to government revenues, pensions of the victims of the 1947 disturbances, third party claims and public investments.

Massacres and Migrations

The magnitude of the refugee problem is brought home by the stark fact that Pakistan's 1951 Census enumerated one in ten of the population, some 7 million people, as of refugee origin. While most refugees went to West Pakistan, the influx into the eastern wing should not be overlooked. At the time of the 1951 Census some 700,000 refugees were reported as residing in East Bengal. Two-thirds of these had originated in West Bengal and Assam, while the remainder were Urdu-speaking migrants from Bihar and UP [Uttar Pradesh]. Most refugees had arrived between August and November 1947; at the same time, an almost equal number of Hindus and Sikhs had departed for India.

In the three and a half months which followed independence, 4.6 million Muslims were evacuated from the East Punjab alone. The migrations were accompanied by horrific massacres which at the most conservative estimate claimed 200,000 lives. The worst violence occurred in Punjab which had been partitioned along a line passing between Lahore and Amritsar. The other disturbed areas were the Punjab princely states and western UP. Bengal remained largely peaceful despite the 'great Calcutta killings' and subsequent rural Noakhali violence and the uncertainties created by its own partition. Even such a prominent Muslim League politician as Hussain Shaheed Suhrawardy continued to reside in Calcutta until 1949. Large minority populations remained in both East and West Bengal. The existence of a considerable Hindu minority in East Pakistan was another factor giving its politics a different flavour from that of West Pakistan. A further important legacy for East Pakistan of the Partition era was the presence of refugees from Bihar and UP who had fled the communal violence in their Indian homeland. Their attachment to North Indian culture led to increasing conflict with the indigenous Bengali elite. Those who were able, embarked on the second migration of their life in 1971. Many remained 'stranded' in refugee camps and the issue of their repatriation emerged as a major demand of the *mohajir* movement in Sindh in the late 1980s. . . .

The new Pakistan government was totally unprepared for the mass migrations and had not anticipated the violence which precipitated the flood of refugees. The demand for a separate Muslim homeland had not been linked with a call for movements of population. This was discouraged by the uncertainties over the exact boundary demarcation. Moreover, the so-called 'hostage' theory propounded the benefits of large minority populations in both India and Pakistan as a guarantee of communal stability. The only anticipatory migration which Jinnah had encouraged was the establishment of some 'nation-building' enterprises in the Pakistan areas. The future problems might however have been forseen from the stockpiling of weapons in Punjab and its surrounding princely states from the spring of 1947 onwards. Private Sikh armies had sprung up often under the leadership of ex-INA (Indian National Army) soldiers in the wake of the attacks on the scattered Sikh communities of north-west Punjab in March 1947. During the final days before the publication of the Radcliffe Boundary Award, Sikh raiding parties launched heavy attacks on Muslim villages in disputed 'border' areas of Punjab. Shortly before independence, 5,000 Muslim refugees reached Lahore from the disturbed Amritsar district. They arrived in a city already abandoned by its Hindu and Sikh inhabitants following weeks of communal disturbances. . . .

Poor Condition of Refugees

The poor physical state of many of the migrants added to the Pakistan Government's problems of resettlement. In the confusion, families had been split up, their womenfolk kidnapped and disgraced. Many refugees had been robbed of all their possessions by the East Punjab police. The Sub-Inspector of Police at Sarhali, for example, extorted Rs. 10,000 from the villagers of Kot Muhammad Khan as the price for a military escort. The police looted trains to such an extent that the East Punjab Governor, Sir Chandulal Trivedi, exclaimed at a conference on 17 September that he would 'not be sorry if the army shot . . . those [police] . . . including their officers.'

The squalid conditions in the refugee transit camps resulted in the spread of cholera and other diseases. The smell emanating from one of the biggest of these just outside Ludhiana was so bad 'that it continued for almost a mile down the road'. According to K.C. Neogy, the Indian Minister for Relief and Rehabilitation, there were between 100 and 250 deaths from cholera in one Muslim foot convoy from Rohtak alone, besides another 200 serious cases. When the Pakistan Government complained about the lack of sanitation and low rations in such camps, Nehru was forced to concede privately that these criticisms were justified.

The dramatic displacement of population in north-west India and the tensions generated by the Kashmir dispute should not be allowed to obscure the much slower but continuous migration in the north-east. A close reading of the British Deputy High Commissioner's reports for East Bengal during 1948 immediately dispels the view that problems were non-existent in this region. In addition to surges of Hindu migration despite repeated reassurances to the minorities, there were serious tensions between the West Bengal and East Bengal governments. Sporadic armed clashes erupted in the riveraine area between Rajshahi and Murshidabad throughout October and November 1948, and the Pakistan border with Tripura was another flashpoint area. . . .

Crisis in Indo-Pakistan Relations

The refugee situation formed part of a wider deterioration in Indo-Pakistan relations. Indeed, it played an important role— many Pakistani officials were convinced that the Indians were intent on making things impossible for them by pushing as many Muslims out of their country as possible. Certainly, Pakistani at-

titudes towards the increasingly serious situation in the princely
state of Jammu and Kashmir were influenced by the migration
issue. Before turning to Kashmir we must refer to another area of
Indo-Pakistan conflict, the Indus Waters dispute.

The dispute over water management and water-sharing between the two dominions reveals both the insecurity of Pakistan
and the importance of administrative as opposed to political initiatives in solving its post-Partition problems. The British had
never anticipated that it would be necessary to disentangle the
intensive network of canals which drew water from Punjab's famous five rivers (Sutlej, Beas, Ravi, Chenab, Jhelum) and also
from the Indus. The massive irrigation schemes which they had
constructed from the end of the nineteenth century had trans-
formed the desert of the West Punjab into one of the most prosperous farming regions in Asia. Pakistan's economic survival depended on the continued availability of water from these
irrigation systems.

The Punjab Partition Council which met in Lahore from the
end of June 1947 agreed that the existing apportionment of water resources from the canal systems should be maintained intact
after independence. However, the Radcliffe Boundary Award
which was not announced until 17 August placed the Madhopur
and Ferozepur control points of the Upper Bari Doab canals, the
Pipalpur canal and the Eastern Grey canal—all vital for Pakistan—on the Indian side of the border. . . .

On 1 April 1948 the East Punjab Government shut off water
supplies to the Dipalpur canal from the Ferozepur headworks.
This not only deprived Lahore of its main water supply, but put
at risk 5.5 per cent of the sown area of West Pakistan at a crucial time in the agricultural year—the sowing of the *kharif* (au-
tumn harvest crop). The Indian action was based on the claim
that Pakistan had no right to the waters and would have to pay a
seigniorage charge if the canals were to be reopened. Direct negotiations between the two dominions in May 1948 led to the
restoration of the flow of water to the Dipalpur but not to the
Bahawalpur canals. Supplies to Pakistan's canals were increasingly
reduced by Indian construction of new canals and the raising of
the capacity of the Bhakra dam. Moreover, it proved impossible
to resolve the impasse created by the contention that proprietary
rights in the waters of the East Punjab rivers were vested wholly
in the East Punjab Government. India refused Pakistan's offer to

refer the legal dispute to the International Court of Justice.

The tension between India and Pakistan over the Kashmir issue prevented a political breakthrough over the legal arguments
concerning water ownership. The initiative thus fell to administrators such as Muhammad Ali and S.S. Kirmani to find a technical solution to provide insurance against the cessation of supplies from India. This both proved to be costly and marked a
further shift towards Pakistan's transformation into an 'administrative state'. The Balloki-Suleimanki, Bambanwali Ravi-Bedian
and Marala-Ravi link canals were sanctioned as was the Mangla
Dam on which preliminary access work began in 1959. By the
time of its completion it was the longest (11,000 feet) earth-filled
dam in the world.

The Indus Waters dispute was only finally resolved in September 1960 partly as a result of the initiative taken by the World
Bank. The Indus Waters Treaty created a permanent Indus Waters Commission and assigned the waters of the Indus, Jhelum
and Chenab to Pakistan. Internationally-financed link canals
nearly 400 miles long transferred water from the above three
rivers to areas previously irrigated by the water supplied from India by the eastern Ravi, Sutlej and Beas rivers. . . .

Kashmir Conflict

Indo-Pakistan relations during the fifty years since independence
have been dominated by the dispute over Kashmir. This has provoked . . . wars [in] 1948 and 1965, threatened war in 1987 and
led to sporadic fighting from 1984 onwards on the Siachen gla-
cier in northern Kashmir. The danger of nuclear conflict as a result of an escalation of hostilities over Kashmir existed throughout the 1990s. [Editor's note: India and Pakistan came to the
brink of a third war over Kashmir during a ten-week confrontation in 1999 (the Kargil conflict).] Almost as damaging to the Indian subcontinent's future is the threat to its material well-being
arising from the dispute. The distrust this has generated continues to fuel a regional arms race which diverts scarce resources
from infrastructural investment and human development. Furthermore the hindrance it provides to Indo-Pakistan economic
cooperation seems likely to marginalise the region in a world
dominated by trading blocs.

Vital strategic interests were at stake in Kashmir in 1947.
Moreover, their continued presence helps in part to explain the

conflict's bitterness and longevity. The headwaters of the Indus, Jhelum and Chenab rivers which were crucial to West Pakistan's agriculture were all situated in Kashmir. Its borders met with Tibet and China and were only a few miles distant from the Soviet Union. Control of Kashmir was thus of exceptional economic and military importance.

In addition the fate of Kashmir in 1947 was (and indeed remains) symbolically significant for both Pakistan and India. Kashmir formed the 'K' in the term 'Pakistan' which was first coined by Chaudhri Rahmat Ali in 1933. As a Muslim majority princely state it was expected, in keeping with the two-nation theory, to form part of Pakistan on the lapse of British paramountcy. Indeed its non-inclusion was a threat to the ideological basis of Pakistan's existence. However, the decision concerning accession in 1947 lay with the ruler and not the subjects of a princely state although, as Pakistanis noted, this did not seem to be the case in circumstances where Indian interests were threatened, as in the Kathiawar state of Junagadh.

For Nehru, whose family originally hailed from Kashmir, and for the Indian National Congress the accession of Kashmir was of course symbolically important as a guarantor of the ideals of a 'secular' composite Indian nationalism. The self-identity of both India and Pakistan thus became linked with Kashmir. In such circumstances, conciliation and compromise have been almost impossible. It is indeed very difficult for the 'outsider' to appreciate the emotions aroused in Pakistan by the Kashmiri cause....

Events in Kashmir in 1947–9 provided a defining moment both in Indo-Pakistan relations and for Pakistan's domestic priorities. Any lingering hopes of the two dominions' economic or military interdependence were snuffed out in Jammu's killing fields. Although the military conflict between the two dominions was confined to Kashmir, it brought home the strategic dangers facing Pakistan, the weaker of the protagonists. The priority of building up the armed forces was spelled out by Liaquat Ali Khan in a broadcast to the nation on 8 October 1948: 'The defence of the State is our foremost consideration ... and has dominated all other governmental activities. We will not grudge any amount on the defence of our country.'

Pakistan thus embarked on the establishment of a 'political economy of defence'. The years 1947–50 saw up to 70 per cent of the national budget being allocated for defence. This sum could only be made available by diverting resources from 'nation-building' activities and expanding the state's administrative machinery to ensure the centre's control over the provinces' finances. The long-term repercussions were a strengthening of the un-elected institutions of the state—the bureaucracy and the Army—at the expense of political accountability. This process contributed incalculably to the sense of alienation in East Pakistan, where priorities were of a different order and did not involve sacrificing democratic politics on the altar of the Kashmiri Muslim cause. Moreover, the Army increasingly acquired an almost insatiable appetite for new technology, and which became ever more expensive. By 1958 an American intelligence report

IDEOLOGICAL AND EMOTIONAL STRAINS

In an article that first appeared in Foreign Affairs *in 1960, Ayub Khan, Pakistan's first military ruler, explains some of the emotional and ideological strains the new country was under in 1947.*

I am not sure if the peculiar strains which confronted Pakistan immediately on its emergence as a free state are adequately understood.

The first strain was ideological. . . . [Muhammad] Iqbal's thesis that in their free state the Muslims were to practice their own way of life posed an ideological problem which was not easy to handle. On the one hand, there were many outside Pakistan who charged us with planning to establish an obdurate theocracy in the mediæval sense of the term. On the other, most of us within Pakistan itself were not quite clear how to go about welding our spiritual ideals into the business of statecraft. The result was a great deal of loose groping which infected our politics and our intellect alike. Pakistan was thus involved in the paradox of almost losing its ideology in the very act of trying to fulfill it. . . .

Then there is the emotional factor. Till the advent of Pakistan, none of us was in fact a Pakistani, for the simple reason that there was no territorial entity bearing that name.

attested that the 'Pakistani army had developed as a pressure group' and would 'continue to have priority over economic development for appropriations', irrespective of the Indian factor.

Dependence on US Aid

However much Pakistan skewed its economy and politics to meet its strategic defence requirements, it could not match unaided the resources of its Indian neighbour. This fact was recognised from the outset. Indeed as early as October 1947 Pakistan unsuccessfully requested a $2 billion loan from the United States. Britain lacked the financial resources to provide major assistance and also needed to appear even-handed in its dealings with the Indians

Actually, the boundaries of Pakistan were still being drawn and re-drawn secretly in the Viceregal Lodge at New Delhi when independence was proclaimed. Never had the destiny of so many millions depended so helplessly on the arbitrary strokes of one man's pencil. It was because [British Administrator Cyril] Radcliffe happened to make a small dent on the wrong side of the line that over 4,000,000 inhabitants of Jammu and Kashmir have been locked in a life-and-death struggle for self-determination for 13 long and dreadful years.

So, prior to 1947, our nationalism was based more on an idea than on any territorial definition. Till then, ideologically we were Muslims; territorially we happened to be Indians; and parochially we were a conglomeration of at least eleven smaller, provincial loyalties. But when suddenly Pakistan emerged as a reality, we who had got together from every nook and corner of the vast sub-continent were faced with the task of transforming all our traditional, territorial and parochial loyalties into one great loyalty for the new state of Pakistan. This process of metamorphism was naturally attended by difficult psychological and emotional strains which we have borne in full measure—and are still bearing.

Ayub Khan, *Pakistan Perspective: A Collection of Important Articles and Excerpts from Major Addresses.* Washington, DC: Embassy of Pakistan, 1965, pp. 3–6.

and Pakistanis. The Americans thus appeared a better bet especially in the light of their requirement for regional Cold War allies as part of their policy of containment towards the Soviet
Union and China. When external US military and economic assistance eventually arrived in 1954, it inevitably came with the
strings of membership of SEATO and the Baghdad Pact at-
tached. In the wake of the Kashmir conflict, the Pakistan authorities thus eschewed ties with the Muslim world which would
have commanded popular support and became increasingly
locked into a dependent relationship with the United States. It
provided the bureaucrats and their military allies at the centre
with both the motives—the exclusion of political interference
on foreign policy issues and increasing resources—to tilt the balance of power away from representative parties and politicians.
A full five years before the military takeover of October 1958,
the Governor-General had appointed a political nonentity,
Muhammad Ali Bogra, as Prime Minister because of his pro-
American stance.

Role of the People

How did Pakistan survive the social turmoil, economic disloca-
tion and hostility with India which accompanied its birth? The
answer lies as much in the courage and resilience of the ordinary
people as in government initiatives. Standard 'top-down' accounts
of Pakistan's politics have ignored this dimension, as have subsequent prognostications concerning the collapse of the Pakistan
state. In an earlier study the present author discussed the way in
which many of the refugees regarded their journey to Pakistan as
a true *hijrat*, an opportunity for a renewal of their faith. Individual acts of heroism and sacrifice amid the sadism and inhuman-
ity of the Partition-related massacres have also been pointed out.

Some politicians and officials got rich on the pickings of evacuee property or through the exploitation of refugees themselves.
Amir Abdullah Khan Rokri in his autobiographical account even
recalls one incident in the main Muslim transit camp in Pathankot
in which Muslim officers in connivance with local Muslim and
Hindu businessmen sold on to the black market rationed goods
which had been provided by the Indians for the refugees. But
many ordinary Muslims acted as true *ansars* [saviors] feeding and
clothing the *mohajirs* [refugees] and taking them into their own
homes. They acted in this way, as [Muslim writer A.A.K.] Rokri

records for the Mianwali district, 'because they knew that these people were being driven out of India simply because they were Muslims'. The author moved his entire family to one small room to accommodate refugees and paid for their needs out of his own pocket. A similar idealism was displayed by the women who came out of *purdah* to work for the Red Crescent or who pawned their jewellery for the emergency loan raised to cover Pakistan's 'missing' share of the cash balances.

Those who have grown cynical over the passage of time in Pakistan will be surprised by the widespread manifestations of social solidarity and improvisation, reminiscent of Britain during the Blitz in the Second World War, which marked the early days of the state's existence. Auxiliary nurses worked in the hospitals, and bank clerks were trained in evening classes to fill the gaps left by the Hindu clerks and accountants. In the countryside, cooperative societies provided the credit formerly supplied by the departed moneylenders. They also opened stores, handled the distribution of essential commodities, and ran abandoned cotton ginning mills. The cooperative banks initially replaced the joint stock banks and acted as treasuries for the Government. . . .

Survival of Pakistan

An important key to understanding both the survival of the infant Pakistan state and its democratic growing pains can be found in its early months of existence. On the face of it, those members of the Indian National Congress who expected Pakistan to be still-born had good cause. Few states have sprung into existence with as many material disadvantages, institutional weaknesses and uncertain national loyalty. The refugee problem alone could have suffocated Pakistan at birth. This fate was avoided thanks to both the resilience of innumerable ordinary men and women and to the organisational capabilities of the civil bureaucracy. Herein however lay the seeds of future problems.

If Pakistan meant anything at all to the masses during the freedom struggle, it had been understood in terms of social and economic transformation and a diffusion of political power. In order for the state to survive its painful delivery its rulers had to draw on another tradition inherited from the colonial era. This emphasised bureaucratic control and the maintenance of the local elites' power, which was seen most clearly in the great missed opportunity for land reform at the time of refugee rehabilitation in West Punjab, an episode which has, remarkably, been over-looked in most standard histories.

The immediate post-Partition era also provides an important key to the future course of Indo-Pakistan relations and the sub-continent's international links. Negative stereotypes of Muslim 'fanaticism' and Hindu 'chauvinism' which developed during the freedom struggle appeared to be borne out to Pakistani and Indian elites during the traumas of 1947–8. The refugee crisis and disputes over the division of assets and the Indus Waters con-firmed the view soon to be expressed by Liaquat Ali Khan that the Government of India had never 'wholeheartedly accepted the Partition scheme' and 'was out to destroy' the Pakistan state.

The Kashmir conflict and war with India in 1948–9 provided the defining moment. The armed conflict coming in the wake of Indian military intervention in Junagadh (later confirmed by intervention in Hyderabad and Goa) established an apprehension of an Indian security threat to the Pakistan state which subse-quently coloured not only its foreign but domestic policy. Pak-istan sought to counterbalance India's greater material resources first by calling on British and later American assistance. But the latter possessed its own agenda for intervention in the South Asia region, leading to eventual strains in its relationship with Pakistan.

Domestically, Pakistan's suspicions of India supported the need for a strong central authority even if this flew in the face of the loose federal structure envisaged by the Lahore Resolution. This in itself took the country further away from the direction of democracy, given the likely effects of centralisation on an ethni-cally plural society. Moreover, Pakistan was set on the course of dependence on foreign aid and of the diversion of scarce re-sources to military expenditure in order to overcome its strategic weakness. The growing ascendancy of the civil bureaucracy and the Army over the elected representatives during the 1950s ac-companied this course of action.

The Refugee Crisis

By Chaudhri Muhammad Ali

*In 1947 Chaudhri Muhammad Ali was the Pakistani representative on
the Partition Council established to administer the settlement of millions
of refugees moving between India and Pakistan. He went on to become
secretary general to the government of Pakistan and cabinet secretary. He
wrote about his experiences in* The Emergence of Pakistan.

*In the following extract, the author paints a graphic portrait of the
plight of more than seven million Muslim refugees who poured into the
new nation of Pakistan in the final months of 1947. He describes the legal, economic, political, and social problems that arose and concludes it
was the sheer determination of the people that defied the predictions that
Pakistan would not survive the economic and administrative burden imposed by the massive influx of refugees.*

The greatest mass migration in history was under way [in
the closing months of 1947]. Within a matter of weeks
over twelve million people had left their homes and gone
forth on foot, by bullock-cart, by railway, by car, and by plane to
seek shelter and safety in the other Dominion. The London *Times*
of September 4, 1947, reported a column of Muslim refugees 20
miles long, and estimated the number at twenty thousand; most
of them were on foot, moving toward Pakistan. Footsore and
weary, ill-nourished and exhausted, seven million refugees stag-
gered across to Pakistan. They had no earthly possessions save the
clothes they wore and, more often than not, these were in tatters.
They had tasted misery to the dregs. They had seen babies killed,
corpses mutilated, and women dishonored. Death had stalked
them on the way. Tens of thousands had died on the road, of star-
vation and disease, or had been killed by Sikh murder gangs. Many
others died as soon as they touched the frontier post.

During the four months up to December 10, 1947, 4.68 million refugees had arrived in West Punjab. Of these 3.92 millions

were moved by the Military Evacuee Organization (MEO), which had been set up in Lahore on August 28. A similar organization was set up by India. To ensure close cooperation between the two MEO's, the Indian organization set up its tactical headquarters in Lahore alongside the Pakistan MEO; and the latter established its tactical headquarters in Jullundur.

Administrative Challenges

Purely in administrative terms, the task of feeding, clothing, settling, and rehabilitating these millions was impossibly difficult. The violent upheavals that had taken place had shattered the economy, strained a yet hardly formed administration beyond breaking point, and disrupted communications. The Hindus who formed the bulk of the trading class had left. Shops lay empty. The Sikhs in their organized withdrawal had taken away cattle and grain. Fields and crops were untended. Chaos reigned supreme. What saved the situation was the spirit of the people and their faith in the leadership of the Quaid-i-Azam [Mohammad Ali Jinnah].

As refugees poured into Lahore and other places in West Punjab, the local residents went forth to share food and clothing with them, to render them assistance, and to alleviate their sufferings. They willingly made sacrifices and readily underwent hardships for the sake of rehabilitating refugees. There were, it is true, some selfish and hardhearted inhabitants who took advantage of the prevailing conditions to misappropriate evacuee property for themselves. But by and large these were the exception in the first phase, when a generous impulse to help the refugees still pervaded all classes. Later there was a deterioration in public morals. The Quaid-i-Azam opened a relief fund which was liberally subscribed to, and which provided much needed succor for the refugees.

In the beginning of September, the Ministry of Refugees and Rehabilitation was formed in the Pakistan government and an emergency committee of the cabinet was set up. The following month, the Prime Minister shifted his headquarters to Lahore temporarily to help and supervise the provincial administration in the immense task of settling refugees. The Quaid-i-Azam himself paid frequent visits to Lahore. The strain and stress of the tragic events of those days, the colossal problems, and the ceaseless work impaired the health of both the Quaid-i-Azam and the

Prime Minister [Liaquat Ali Khan]. But with a grim determination which knew no relaxation they battled valiantly with every adverse circumstance.

By the middle of October the need was felt for a joint organization of the central government and West Punjab, the province most concerned with the refugee problem. The Pakistan Punjab Refugee Council was formed. It was presided over by the Prime Minister and included the Governor and Chief Minister of West Punjab and the central and provincial Refugee ministers. In the earlier stages I attended many meetings of the Council, which did extremely useful work in formulating the policy and coordinating the activities of the central and provincial governments. Later, similar joint refugee councils were set up for the North-West Frontier Province and for Sind.

The work of the Pakistan Punjab Refugee Council, which was served by a joint secretariat, covered a wide variety of subjects. Legislative measures had to be taken for the protection of evacuee property. Custodians of evacuee property and rehabilitation commissioners had to be appointed. Arrangements for the administration of camps and the evacuation, dispersal, and rehabilitation of refugees had to be made and supervised. Principles for the allocation of land, industries, shops, cinemas, houses, and for the fixation of rent had to be laid down. Measures for the restoration of the economic life of the province through the provision of consumer goods, normal functioning of rail and road services, revival of banking, trade, and agriculture had to be taken. Arrangements in concert with India had to be made for the recovery of abducted women and converts, for the transfer of prisoners, safe deposits, and provident funds, for the protection of sacred places, and for innumerable other matters incidental to the vast unplanned and involuntary exchange of populations that was taking place.

Government Shortcomings

The Governor of West Punjab, Sir Francis Mudie, was an administrator of great experience. He worked devotedly day and night, and so did government servants of all ranks. But there were serious shortages in almost every department. Hindu officials had left. Their replacement by Muslims who had opted for Pakistan or refugees was not a mechanical task but required a thorough reorganization for which there was no time. The West Punjab ministry from the beginning showed signs of disunity and lack of cohesion. There were disputes regarding the delimitation of functions between the various ministers. The Minister in charge of Industries insisted upon dealing with everything that was connected with abandoned industrial undertakings. The Revenue Minister had to be consulted on all questions of abandoned land, and in many matters proposals for rehabilitation were initiated and final decisions were taken by him. The West Punjab Premier controlled the administrative machinery for the allocation of houses and shops. To complicate matters, abandoned evacuee property offered a temptation to which many of the leading figures in the districts succumbed, and these usurpers looked to one minister or another for political protection. . . . The confusion regarding the functions of the various ministers had the disastrous result of making each deputy commissioner a law unto himself in his district. The Pakistan Punjab Refugee Council had to exert itself a great deal to bring order out of the administrative chaos produced by divided authority.

Camps were organized in a number of places to receive, feed, and clothe the refugees as they came in, and to nurse the sick and the wounded. Local volunteers as well as those sent from abroad by missionary societies, particularly from the United Kingdom and the United States of America, performed services of great value in these camps. Originally, the camps were regarded as transit camps only. The bulk of the refugees were agriculturists. By far the most pressing task was to allot them lands vacated by Hindu and Sikh refugees so that standing crops could be harvested in time and preparation made for sowing wheat.

More People than Land

However, the number of refugees West Punjab had to accommodate exceeded by some 1.7 million the number of evacuees who had left. As time passed, lands, factories, and shops available to new arrivals began to diminish. The great food shortage after January, 1948, which affected towns and villages alike, hampered efforts at resettlement. Thus the camps became more or less permanent with a population of about three quarters of a million in April, 1948. With strenuous efforts this number was brought down to half a million some months later. The prolonged stay in camps had a demoralizing effect on the people and bred a beggar's mentality. Special efforts had to be made to keep up the morale of the refugees. Schools for children and adults were opened and facilities for vocational training were provided. Nevertheless, it was essential to speed up the work of resettlement. Many of the refugees were keenly interested in being settled according to the district they came from, so that the social life and economic cooperation of village communities in East Punjab could be preserved intact. But this demanded resources in camps and organization far beyond the capacity of the West Punjab administration to provide. There was nothing for it but to settle the refugees as they came in.

There is a great divergence in the productivity of farm land in the various parts of West Punjab. Colony areas in Lyallpur and Montgomery, which are irrigated by canals, are far more productive than rainfed lands further to the west. Everyone wanted an allotment in the colony districts, but there was not enough land to go round. In Montgomery there was a serious clash between the police and a section of the refugees who wanted to settle forcibly on lands already allotted to earlier arrivals.

Economic Challenges

Trade in wheat, cotton, and other commodities had been almost entirely in the hands of Hindus, who had also provided the bulk of rural credit. Except for cooperative credit societies in Muslim villages and some cooperative banks, all other credit institutions, such as commercial banks, had been controlled and run by Hindus. Ginning factories and other industrial units were mostly owned by Hindus and Sikhs. When they left, there was a serious danger that the economy of West Pakistan might collapse. Before partition, when the whole subcontinent formed a single market, the channels of trade from West Punjab ran mostly in an eastern direction. Amritsar was a big commercial center. Wheat and cotton were the two main crops. Wheat was exported to East Punjab, Delhi, and other areas further south. Cotton went to the textile mills of Bombay and Allahabad by rail. In return, cloth and other manufactured goods flowed from these industrial centers to West Punjab. The upheavals in the Punjab disrupted these channels.

Karachi was the only major port of West Pakistan; and all exports and imports had now to be reoriented toward Karachi. The Karachi market was mostly in the hands of the Hindu merchants of Sind, who are noted for their business acumen. But for a few sporadic incidents here and there, which were quickly put down, nothing had happened to mar the peace of Sind. However, in a deliberate effort to paralyze the economy of Pakistan, the Hindus of Sind were prevailed upon to leave Pakistan. Hopes were held out that within a few months Pakistan would collapse and they could return to their homes. Acharya Kripalani, who was the Congress President at this time, originated from Sind and had considerable influence there. He was a strong believer in an Akhand Bharat, or undivided India. When the Congress accepted the partition plan, he called on the Congress party to make India a strong, happy, democratic, and socialist state, and declared, "Such an India can win back the seceding children to its lap . . . for the freedom we have achieved cannot be complete without the unity of India." He came to Karachi in the third week of September, 1947, and saw the Quaid-i-Azam who assured him of the Pakistan government's firm intention to maintain peace and to give full protection and equal rights to the minorities. Nevertheless, Kripalani persisted in his efforts to spread panic among the Hindu community by painting a highly colored picture of their present hardships and making gloomy predictions about the future unless they pulled out of Pakistan soon. Despite the prevalence of peaceful conditions, and despite the Quaid-i-Azam's repeated assurances of equal rights and security for the minorities, an exodus of Hindus started which hurt both the migrants and Pakistan.

These designs against Pakistan were defeated by the indomitable will of the people to build a strong and prosperous Pakistan. Except for a few business communities of Muslim converts from Hinduism, the Hindus had from time immemorial a monopoly of trade in the subcontinent. For the Muslims in general, business was a closed field; and it was the common belief among Hindus and Muslims alike that Muslims lacked an aptitude for business. Now, with the departure of Hindus, these false inhibitions were swept away. With a display of enterprise that astonished even themselves, Muslims stepped forth into the field and filled the gap left by the exodus of Hindus. What might have been a crippling blow turned out to be a blessing in disguise. The spell of Muslim incompetence in trade and industry was broken forever, and the hold Hindus would have had over the economy of Pakistan was destroyed by their own miscalculations. . . .

Abducted Women and Children

An important part of the work of rehabilitation related to the recovery, restoration, and care of abducted women and children. An Indo-Pakistan agreement, reached in November, 1948, recognized the need for special legislation in both countries. The laws enacted under this agreement were so devised that by taking the victims away from the influence of their abductors, fear was eliminated, and by allowing them to resume contacts with their relatives and community they could make their own free decision regarding their future. Recovery offices and transit camps were set up in both India and Pakistan. Dedicated social workers helped greatly not only in the recovery but in the mental rehabilitation of abducted persons. By October, 1952, the number of non-Muslim women and children recovered from Pakistan was 8,326 and that of Muslim women and children recovered from India was 16,919.

Pakistan's Achievements

The total number of refugees in West Pakistan ultimately rose to nearly nine million or one fourth of the population. Most of them have been rehabilitated, but the process of their integration into the social and economic life of the country is by no means complete. For a number of reasons the process of settlement and rehabilitation has been unduly slow and marred by inefficiency and corruption. Perhaps the main cause is to be found in the policy of staffing the organization almost wholly with temporary government employees whose personal interest is to prolong the period of their employment. Delay in the final settlement of claims has led to neglect of houses and factories allotted on a temporary basis, as well as to the sale of stocks of raw materials and spare parts to make a quick profit. It has provided greater opportunity for political pressures and for false claims and litigation. Yet the magnitude of the task performed must not be minimized. The problem was colossal and it threw, proportionately, a far greater burden on Pakistan than on India. Many predicted at the time that it would be beyond the economic and administrative resources of Pakistan to solve it and that Pakistan would be engulfed by the refugees. However, Pakistan not only surmounted these difficulties, but emerged stronger and more unified from this forced exchange of populations.

A Constitutional Framework for an Islamic Nation

By LIAQUAT ALI KHAN

Historians give Pakistan's first prime minister, Liaquat Ali Khan, credit for creating the government of Pakistan out of the chaos following the partition of India in 1947. After Mohammed Ali Jinnah's untimely death, Khan carried the vision of the nation's founder forward until his assassination in 1951. In the following extract from his "Objectives Resolution" speech delivered to the Constituent Assembly on May 7, 1949, Khan outlines the principles of a proposed democratic constitution based on the tenets of Islam. Khan says that Islam, with its fundamental belief in democracy and tolerance of all faiths, offers a panacea to the world's problems.

Following Khan's death a period of political instability ensued during which there was no consensus on the provisions of a constitution for the new nation. Finally, in 1956, Pakistan adopted its first constitution that included a parliamentary form of government with limited powers given to the head of state. This constitution lasted only two years before it was abrogated by General Ayub Khan when he declared martial rule. In 1962, Khan passed Pakistan's second constitution, which gave Pakistan a presidential form of government. A third formal constitution that heralded the return to a modified parliamentary system was ratified in 1973 during Zulfikar Ali Bhutto's tenure. Since 1973, Pakistan's constitution has been amended several times. While Pakistan has failed to institute a coherent and enduring constitution, Liaquat Ali Khan's speech remains a reference point for ongoing constitutional debates.

S ir, I beg to move the following Objectives Resolution embodying the main principles on which the constitution of Pakistan is to be based:

Liaquat Ali Khan, "Pakistan as an Islamic State," *Sources of Indian Tradition*, edited by William Theodore de Bary. New York: Columbia University Press, 1960. Copyright © 1958 by Columbia University Press. All rights reserved. Reproduced by permission.

"In the name of Allāh, the Beneficent, the Merciful;

WHEREAS sovereignty over the entire universe belongs to God Almighty alone and the authority which He has delegated to the State of Pakistan through its people for being exercised within the limits prescribed by Him is a sacred trust;

This Constituent Assembly representing the people of Pakistan resolves to frame a constitution for the sovereign independent State of Pakistan;

WHEREIN the State shall exercise its powers and authority through the chosen representatives of the people;

WHEREIN the principles of democracy, freedom, equality, tolerance, and social justice, as enunciated by Islam, shall be fully observed;

WHEREIN the Muslims shall be enabled to order their lives in the individual and collective spheres in accord with the teachings and requirements of Islam as set out in the Holy Qur'ān and the Sunna;

WHEREIN adequate provision shall be made for the minorities freely to profess and practice their religions and develop their cultures;

WHEREBY the territories now included in or in accession with Pakistan and such other territories as may hereafter be included in or accede to Pakistan shall form a Federation wherein the units will be autonomous with such boundaries and limitations on their powers and authority as may be prescribed;

WHEREIN shall be guaranteed fundamental rights including equality of status, of opportunity, and before law, social, economic, and political justice and freedom of thought, expression, belief, faith, worship and association, subject to law and public morality.

WHEREIN adequate provision shall be made to safeguard the legitimate interests of minorities and backward and depressed classes;

WHEREIN the independence of the judiciary shall be fully secured;

WHEREIN the integrity of the territories of the Federation, its independence and all its rights including its sovereign rights on land, sea and air shall be safeguarded;

So that the people of Pakistan may prosper and attain their rightful and honored place amongst the nations of the world and make their full contribution towards international peace and progress and happiness of humanity."

Commentary on the Resolution

Sir, I consider this to be a most important occasion in the life of
this country, next in importance only to the achievement of independence, because by achieving independence we only won
an opportunity of building up a country and its polity in accordance with our ideals. I would like to remind the House that the
Father of the Nation, Qaid-i-azam, gave expression to his feelings on this matter on many an occasion, and his views were endorsed by the nation in unmistakable terms. Pakistan was founded
because the Muslims of this subcontinent wanted to build up
their lives in accordance with the teachings and traditions of Islam, because they wanted to demonstrate to the world that Islam
provides a panacea to the many diseases which have crept into
the life of humanity today. It is universally recognized that the
source of these evils is that humanity has not been able to keep
pace with its material development, that the Frankenstein mon-
ster which human genius has produced in the form of scientific
inventions, now threatens to destroy not only the fabric of human society but its material environment as well, the very habi-
tat in which it dwells. It is universally recognized that if man had
not chosen to ignore the spiritual values of life and if his faith in
God had not been weakened, this scientific development would
not have endangered his very existence. It is God-consciousness
alone which can save humanity, which means that all power that
humanity possesses must be used in accordance with ethical standards which have been laid down by inspired teachers known to
us as the great Prophets of different religions.

We, as Pakistanis, are not ashamed of the fact that we are overwhelmingly Muslims and we believe that it is by adhering to our
faith and ideals that we can make a genuine contribution to the
welfare of the world. Therefore, Sir, you would notice that the
Preamble of the Resolution deals with a frank and unequivocal
recognition of the fact that all authority must be subservient to
God. It is quite true that this is in direct contradiction to the
Machiavellian ideas regarding a polity where spiritual and ethical
values should play no part in the governance of the people and,
therefore, it is also perhaps a little out of fashion to remind ourselves of the fact that the State should be an instrument of benef-
icence and not of evil. But we, the people of Pakistan, have the
courage to believe firmly that all authority should be exercised
in accordance with the standards laid down by Islam so that it

may not be misused. All authority is a sacred trust, entrusted to us by God for the purpose of being exercised in the service of man, so that it does not become an agency for tyranny or self-ishness. I would, however, point out that this is not a resuscitation of the dead theory of divine right of kings or rulers, because, in accordance with the spirit of Islam, the Preamble fully recognizes the truth that authority has been delegated to the people, and to none else, and that it is for the people to decide who will exercise that authority.

Power to the People

For this reason it has been made clear in the Resolution that the State shall exercise all its powers and authority through the chosen representatives of the people. This is the very essence of democracy, because the people have been recognized as the recipients of all authority and it is in them that the power to wield it has been vested.

Sir, I just now said that the people are the real recipients of power. This naturally eliminates any danger of the establishment of a theocracy. It is true that in its literal sense, theocracy means the Government of God; in this sense, however, it is patent that the entire universe is a theocracy, for is there any corner in the entire creation where His authority does not exist? But in the technical sense, theocracy has come to mean a government by ordained priests, who wield authority as being specially appointed by those who claim to derive their rights from their sacerdotal position. I cannot overemphasize the fact that such an idea is absolutely foreign to Islam. Islam does not recognize either priesthood or any sacerdotal authority; and, therefore, the question of a theocracy simply does not arise in Islam. If there are any who still use the word theocracy in the same breath as the polity of Pakistan, they are either laboring under a grave misapprehension, or indulging in mischievous propaganda.

You would notice, Sir, that the Objectives Resolution lays emphasis on the principles of democracy, freedom, equality, tolerance, and social justice, and further defines them by saying that these principles should be observed in the constitution as they have been enunciated by Islam. It has been necessary to qualify these terms because they are generally used in a loose sense. For instance, the Western Powers and Soviet Russia alike claim that their systems are based upon democracy, and, yet, it is common

LIAQUAT ALI KHAN: ARCHITECT OF PAKISTAN

Muslim historian I.H. Qureshi describes Liaquat Ali Khan's life and personal attributes.

The credit for creating a government in Pakistan out of the chaos which followed Partition goes mainly to Liāquat Alī Khān (1895–1951). Jinnāh was the founder of Pakistan, Liāquat its chief architect.

Born to a rich and noble family which had extensive landed property in the Punjab and the United Provinces, Liāquat was educated at Alīgarh and Oxford and, having been called to the bar from the Inner Temple, he entered politics as a Muslim Leaguer. He was a member of the United Provinces Legislative Council from 1926 to 1940, when he was elected to the central legislature. From 1936 to 1947 he was the general secretary of the Muslim League and Jinnāh's right-hand man. On the establishment of Pakistan in August, 1947, he became its first prime minister until his death in 1951. Despite his wealthy origins and success in public life, Liāquat died a poor man.

During Liāquat's tenure, the reputation of Pakistan as a progressive and stable state increased steadily. A powerful speaker, whose addresses thrilled and inspired the masses, Liāquat still was no demagogue but a coolheaded statesman dedicated to the service of his country. Though he fully shared his people's love for Islam, there was no narrowness or bigotry in his soul; he judged issues on their merits and combined breadth of outlook with regard for detail. When finally struck down by the bullets of an assassin, the only words he muttered were the Muslim formula of faith and the prayer, "May God protect Pakistan."

I.H. Qureshi, "Pakistan: Its Founding and Future," in William Theodore de Bary, ed., *Sources of Indian Tradition*. New York: Columbia University Press, 1958, pp. 841–42.

knowledge that their polities are inherently different. . . . When we use the word democracy in the Islamic sense, it pervades all aspects of our life; it relates to our system of government and to our society with equal validity, because one of the greatest contributions of Islam has been the idea of the equality of all men.

Tolerance of Islam

Islam recognizes no distinctions based upon race, color, or birth. Even in the days of its decadence, Islamic society has been remarkably free from the prejudices which vitiated human relations in many other parts of the world. Similarly, we have a great record in tolerance, for under no system of government, even in the Middle Ages, have the minorities received the same consideration and freedom as they did in Muslim countries. When Christian dissentients and Muslims were being tortured and driven out of their homes, when they were being hunted as animals and burnt as criminals—even criminals have never been burnt in Islamic society—Islam provided a haven for all who were persecuted and who fled from tyranny. It is a well-known fact of history that, when anti-Semitism turned the Jews out of many a European country, it was the Ottoman empire which gave them shelter. The greatest proof of the tolerance of Muslim peoples lies in the fact that there is no Muslim country where strong minorities do not exist, and where they have not been able to preserve their religion and culture. Most of all, in this subcontinent of India, where the Muslims wielded unlimited authority, the rights of non-Muslims were cherished and protected. I may point out, Sir, that it was under Muslim patronage that many an indigenous language developed in India. My friends from Bengal would remember that it was under the encouragement of Muslim rulers that the first translations of the Hindu scriptures were made from Sanskrit into Bengali. It is this tolerance which is envisaged by Islam, wherein a minority does not live on sufferance, but is respected and given every opportunity to develop its own thought and culture, so that it may contribute to the greater glory of the entire nation. In the matter of social justice as well, Sir, I would point out that Islam has a distinct contribution to make. Islam envisages society in which social justice means neither charity nor regimentation. Islamic social justice is based upon fundamental laws and concepts which guarantee to man a life free from want and rich in freedom. It is for this reason that the principles of democracy, freedom, equality, tolerance and social justice have been further defined by giving to them a meaning which, in our view, is deeper and wider than the usual connotation of these words.

Islam and the State

The next clause of the Resolution lays down that Muslims shall be enabled to order their lives in the individual and collective spheres in accord with the teachings and requirements of Islam as set out in the Holy Qur'ān and the Sunna. It is quite obvious that no non-Muslim should have any objection if the Muslims are enabled to order their lives in accordance with the dictates of their religion. You would also notice, Sir, that the State is not to play the part of a neutral observer wherein the Muslims may be merely free to profess and practice their religion, because such an attitude on the part of the State would be the very negation of the ideals which prompted the demand of Pakistan, and it is these ideals which should be the cornerstone of the State which we want to build. The State will create such conditions as are conducive to the building up of a truly Islamic society, which means that the State will have to play a positive part in this effort. You would remember, Sir, that the Qaid-i-azam and other leaders of the Muslim league always made unequivocal declarations that the Muslim demand for Pakistan was based upon the fact that the Muslims had a way of life and a code of conduct. They also reiterated the fact that Islam is not merely a relationship between the individual and his God, which should not, in any way, affect the working of the State. Indeed, Islam lays down specific directions for social behavior, and seeks to guide society in its attitude towards the problems which confront it from day to day. Islam is not just a matter of private beliefs and conduct. It expects its followers to build up a society for the purpose of good life—as the Greeks would have called it, with this difference, that Islamic "good life" is essentially based upon spiritual values. For the purpose of emphasizing these values and to give them validity, it will be necessary for the State to direct and guide the activities of the Muslims in such a manner as to bring about a new social order based upon the essential principles of Islam, including the principles of democracy, freedom, tolerance, and social justice. These I mention merely by way of illustration; because they do not exhaust the teaching of Islam as embodied in the Qur'ān and the Sunna.

Tolerance of Differences Within the Faith

There can be no Muslim who does not believe that the word of God and the life of the Prophet are the basic sources of his inspiration. In these there is no difference of opinion amongst the Muslims and there is no sect in Islam which does not believe in their validity. Therefore, there should be no misconception in the mind of any sect which may be in a minority in Pakistan about the intentions of the State. The State will seek to create an Islamic society free from dimensions, but this does not mean that it would curb the freedom of any section of the Muslims in the matter of their beliefs. No sect, whether the majority or a minority, will be permitted to dictate to the others and, in their own internal matters and sectional beliefs, all sects shall be given the fullest possible latitude and freedom. Actually we hope that the various sects will act in accordance with the desire of the Prophet who said that the differences of opinion amongst his followers are a blessing. It is for us to make our differences a source of strength to Islam and Pakistan, not to exploit them for narrow interests which will weaken both Pakistan and Islam. Differences of opinion very often lead to cogent thinking and progress, but this happens only when they are not permitted to obscure our vision of the real goal, which is the service of Islam and the furtherance of its objects. It is, therefore, clear that this clause seeks to give the Muslims the opportunity that they have been seeking, throughout these long decades of decadence and subjection, of finding freedom to set up a polity, which may prove to be a laboratory for the purpose of demonstrating to the world that Islam is not only a progressive force in the world, but it also provide remedies for many of the ills from which humanity has been suffering.

Pakistan's First Ten Years Lacked Democracy

By Mazhar Ali Khan

The death of Mohammed Ali Jinnah in 1948 and the assassination of Pakistan's first prime minister, Liaquat Ali Khan, in 1951, left a vacuum in political leadership that plunged the new country into a period of political instability. More than five governments formed and crumbled in Pakistan's first ten years. National elections were promised but never forthcoming. Popular sentiment in the country is described in the following extract from the Pakistan Times *on August 14, 1957, the tenth anniversary of Pakistan's founding. In the editorial, Mazhar Ali Khan reviews his country's record with dismay. He asserts that greed, corruption, and political wrangling held his people hostage for their first decade, and he calls for free and democratic elections to place power in the hands of the Pakistani people. Mazhar Ali Khan was associate editor and then editor of the* Pakistan Times *from its inception in 1946 until he resigned in 1959 to protest Ayub Khan's censure of the free press. He was arrested in 1978 during General Zia-ul-Haq's regime for his outspoken commentary.*

We celebrate today the tenth anniversary of the dawn of freedom. Whatever changes fortune may bring us and whatever occasions, happy or sad, may in future befall, the fourteenth day of August will forever remain the most important date in our national history. This day, therefore, should be a day of rejoicing, not regret, of hope, not despair, of looking forward to the happiness of unborn tomorrows, not of looking back on the heartache and the pain of unhappy yesterdays. And yet it is not so with us, and rarely has been. Year after year on this day, the shadow of uncertainties, the memory of wrongs endured and hardships gone through, the deadweight of a seemingly changeless polity, inhibits the joy and obstructs the song, and although we still devoutly greet the day, the sight is clouded with anxieties and the heart yearns for a fuller and a more carefree hour. Why should it be so? It is not because the country has made no material progress during the last ten years. It has. We have set up many new light industries, even though their products are neither cheap nor plentiful enough to lighten the daily cares of the great majority of our people. We have built dams and barrages and brought vast new areas under cultivation, even though our daily bread has become more scarce than ever. The defences of the country have been consolidated and we face no immediate threat of aggression, even though some very grave disputes with our closest neighbours are still unresolved. Above all, we have, at long last, obtained a Constitution for the land, even though its most important provisions still await the birth of popularly elected legislatures.

Depriving the People of Their Rights

This record, however inadequate, should yet have provided the common man with material enough for national self-confidence and hopeful resolve. It has done nothing of the kind. In public and in privacy, inside homes and out in the market place, the speech of the people is sick with disgust and frustration, streaked with impotent anger. There are many reasons for this, but there is one basic cause which enters into them all. And this basic cause is the complete exclusion of the people from the power which should have devolved on them with the coming of independence, the power which has been rightfully theirs ever since this day ten years ago, but has been withheld from them by a succession of self-appointed coteries. For ten years, one person (or group of persons) after another, with the help of a few cronies and camp-followers, has set himself up as the custodian of the people's political belongings, and each such regime has been speedily undone by the jealousies, intrigues, and machinations of rival pretenders. With the passage of time these conflicts in the ruling camp have sharpened, the methods of attaining or retaining power have become more ruthless and more corrupt, the contact between the rulers and the ruled become steadily more remote. Crises, emergencies, deadlocks, enthronements and dethronements, squabbles and hand-clasps, attachments and defections, are all enacted within this same small group which changes shape and colour with every change of season and ever remains the same. In none of these transactions have the people ever had a hand and in many of them even the present hand-picked legislatures are allowed little voice.

And this is the cause—this arrogation of power by an apparently irremovable few, this forcible suspension of the people's right to choose their own government and call them to account through popular institutions—for all our ills, political, economic, moral, and psychological. It is because of this that 'politics' and 'politician' have become terms of abuse and political organisation has become practically extinct. Because of it, the wealth of the land has become fair spoil for anyone who has some political capital to sell; because of it normal commercial routines have given place to smash and grab methods for permits and licences, and the black market is the only market for many goods. This is the cause of corruption in high places and low, the cause of the prevailing mentality to make speedily what you can, for tomorrow your Ministry or the Ministry of your friends might die. Because of it honest praise has been replaced by grovelling and flattery, honest criticism supplanted by slander and blackmail.

Call for Elections

And yet these abuses, and the state of mind they have engendered among our people, are by no means native to our national genius or national temperament, as many prophets of doom would have us believe. They are as artificial and as hand-made as the arbitrary political structure which has given them birth. They will endure as long as the present irreparable political structure endures. It is foolish to hope or pretend that any coalitions, combinations, or permutations can give to this structure either strength or stability. Under the present circumstances all parliamentary coalitions will be coalitions of the same few people whom no political ideal holds together, all combinations will be the combinations of the same irreconcilable personal interests. One hears some talk these days of a 'National Government' composed of the present parliamentary Parties. Nothing could be more unrealistic. How can you have a 'national' Government in whose composition the nation has had no voice? When not a couple of these groups have been able to keep house together, how will half a dozen of them live happily ever after? There is, therefore, only one remedy to the situation: the reversion of power into the hands of the people. And there is only one method whereby it can be done—free, impartial General Elections, the setting up of genuinely representative parliamentary institutions and the total enforcement of the constitution.

Declaration of Martial Law

By Ayub Khan

To stem the rising tide of chaos and civil disorder that arose from years of political instability, on October 7, 1958, the Pakistan Army under General Ayub Khan staged the first of a series of military coups d'etat that have since become part of the fabric of Pakistani politics. In the following extract from Ayub Khan's first broadcast to the nation on October 8, 1958, he describes the chaotic political, economic, administrative, and moral condition of the country and says that while the armed forces ultimately intend to reestablish democracy, in the short-term they must restore law and order. Ayub Khan, Pakistan's first military dictator, ruled the country until 1969, when renewed civil strife led him to resign his post and pass the government over to another military ruler, Yahya Khan.

I am going to address you on matters which are both solemn and serious. It is vital that you should listen to them carefully, understand them correctly, so as to be able to act constructively—as in correct action lies the salvation of us all and our future generations.

You should have heard by now the declaration by the President abrogating the Constitution and imposing Martial Law throughout Pakistan. He has appointed me as the Chief Martial Law Administrator and all the Armed Forces of Pakistan, including the civil armed forces, have been put under my command. This is a drastic and extreme step taken with great reluctance, but with the fullest conviction that there was no alternative to it except the disintegration and complete ruination of the country. History would never have forgiven us if the present chaotic conditions were allowed to go on any further.

These chaotic conditions, as you know, have been brought about by self-seekers who, in the garb of political leaders, have ravaged the country or tried to barter it away for personal gains. Some have done it as a matter of right because they professed to have created Pakistan, and others who were against the very idea of Pakistan openly worked for its dissolution or in any case did all they could to aggravate its problems. Their aim is nothing but self-aggrandizement or thirst for power. Meanwhile, weak and ir-resolute governments looked on with masterly inactivity and cowardice and allowed things to drift and deteriorate, and disci-pline to go to pieces.

Our People Betrayed

Ever since the death of the Quaid-i-Azam [the great leader, Mo-hammed Ali Jinnah] and [Pakistan's first prime minister] Mr. Li-aquat Ali Khan, politicians started a free-for-all type of fighting in which no holds were barred. They waged ceaseless and bitter war against each other, regardless of the ill-effect on the country, just to whet their appetites and satisfy their base motive. There has been no limit to the depth of their baseness, chicanery, de-ceit and degradation. Having nothing constructive to offer, they used provincial feelings, sectarian, religious and racial differences to set a Pakistani against a Pakistani. They could see no good in anybody else. In this mad rush for power and acquisition all that mattered was self-interest. The country and people could go to the dogs as far as they were concerned. There were a few hon-ourable exceptions but their conscience was dead and they were rendered ineffective by hordes of their supporters in the Assem-blies changing party affiliations from day to day.

There are two things a man—a man of any conscience—finds it very difficult to do: change his religion, change party affiliations. But our so-called representatives in the Assemblies shifted from one party to the other without turning a hair or feeling any pangs of conscience. This is the basis on which democracy has been run in Pakistan and in the sacred name of Islam. In the process, all ideals and the high sense of values inherent in our religion and culture have been destroyed. The result is total administrative, eco-nomic, political and moral chaos in the country, which cannot be tolerated in these dangerous times. Pakistan certainly cannot af-ford this luxury. It has far too many internal problems to solve and external dangers to guard against—to solution of which the pre-requisite is a secure and stable base within the country.

Our people are by nature patriotic and good people. They are

tolerant, patient and can rise to great heights when well led. They
are also intelligent and could see all this happening in front of
their eyes. But they found themselves helpless as they did not
wish to aggravate the problems facing the country or perhaps did
not wish to hurt the feelings of the Army which in the final
analysis, is responsible for law and order and which had served
them so well with loyalty and devotion. But lately I could see that
they were beginning to lose faith even in us for not saving them
from the tyranny and mental and spiritual torture. I am sure they
are sick and tired of the unscrupulous type of politicians who
were busy tearing their dear country into pieces. The Army too
felt the same and much more, but held their patience for reasons
which I will just now explain.

Role of the Armed Forces

This is the occasion on which I feel I should take my countrymen and women into confidence as to the Army's attitude and
behaviour. Ever since the inception of Pakistan we in the
Armed Forces saw very clearly the internal problems facing the
country and the external dangers to which it was exposed. We
were also conscious of our limited means. We solemnly decided
to build a true national army free from politics, a model of devotion to duty and integrity imbued with the spirit of service
to the people and capable of effectively defending the country.
Further, I always told my people that our major task is to give
cover to the country behind which it could build a sound democratic system and lay the foundation of a stable future. We kept
severely aloof from politics.

You may not know, but I refused on several occasions the late
[president] Mr. Ghulam Mohammad's offer to take over the country. I did so in the belief that I could serve the cause of Pakistan
better from the place where I was, and also had a faint hope that
some politicians would rise to the occasion and lead the country
to a better future. Events have falsified those hopes and we have
come to the present pass. A perfectly sound country has been
turned into a laughing stock. This is sad, but the situation has to
be faced and remedies found, as God willing they are going to be.

Let me announce in unequivocal terms that our ultimate aim
is to restore democracy but of the type that people can understand and work. When the time comes your opinion will be freely
asked. But when that will, events alone can tell. Meanwhile, we

have to put this mess right and put the country on an even keel.

There are certain problems which need immediate solution, yet there are others which are of a long-term nature. We shall do our utmost to solve them and eradicate evils. But in all this, I must demand your wholehearted understanding, co-operation and patience. I must also ask you to work hard and put in your best effort. This is the period when our State has to be built and this can only happen if people work. Slogan-mongering can never take the place of hard sweat. Remember that there are certain things which it should be in our power to put right. We shall see that is done. But there are others, solutions to which are beyond, leaving result to God. So, when judging our performance, do keep these hard realities of life in mind.

Administration of Martial Law

As to the operation of Martial Law, I propose to use the civilian agencies to the maximum. The Armed Forces will be utilised as little as possible. In the main, they will continue to attend to their prime role of external defence. Martial Law Regulations will be produced which will tighten up the existing laws on matters like malingering or inefficiency amongst officials, any form of bribery or corruption, hoarding, smuggling or black-marketing, or any other type of anti-social or anti-State activity. Such matters will be dealt with ruthlessly and expeditiously. In other words the nefarious activities of the bad characters of all description shall be firmly curbed in order that Pakistan is made safe for the law-abiding citizens.

Since Martial Law will, in the main, be operated by the civilian agencies I must ask them to discharge this onerous and perhaps unpleasant duty honestly, justly and faithfully. Here is an opportunity for you to show your mettle. Go to it and show us what sort of stuff you are made of! Your Services have tremendous traditions. Do not miss this opportunity to revive them and in doing so you can be assured of the Armed Forces' faithful support. At this critical juncture it is more than ever necessary for the Armed Forces to be prepared at all times to face external aggression. But they are fully aware that internal stability is absolutely essential if they are to successfully repel aggression from outside.

Some of them may have to be called upon to perform duties in connection with Martial Law. Whatever these duties may be, I expect them to do them loyally, efficiently, and unhesitatingly.

Their behaviour at all times must be correct, disciplined and impartial. I have every confidence in their ability to face any challenge, however difficult it may be.

A word for the disruptionists, political opportunists, smugglers, black-marketeers and other such social vermin, sharks and leeches. The soldiers and the people are sick of the sight of you. So it will be good for your health to turn a new leaf and begin to behave, otherwise retribution will be swift and sure. At any rate, they have no cause to feel neglected. We shall be making desperate efforts to catch up with them as soon as possible.

I have spoken to you, my fellow citizens, at some length to put you in the picture and remove doubts and misgivings and to convince you that this extreme step has been taken in your interest and in the interest of the stability of Pakistan. Now let us all bow before Almighty God in all humility to guide us to a better future, so that we may emerge from this hour of trial as a sound, solid and strong nation! Amen! Pakistan Paindabad [Long Live Pakistan]!

Ayub Khan's Unbenevolent Dictatorship

By David Loshak

Ayub Khan ruled Pakistan as chief martial law administrator and then self-appointed president from 1958 to 1969. In the following extract from the book Pakistan Crisis, *British journalist David Loshak says Ayub Khan's presidency initially signaled many welcome changes—the removal of corrupt politicians, the resettlement of refugees, and the implementation of agricultural reforms. His "basic democracies" program sought to revamp the Westminster parliamentary system to suit local conditions. Loshak asserts that Khan's downfall came because he deprived the people of their legitimate political rights and freedoms following the 1965 war with India over Kashmir. The national revolt that arose in response to this repression led to his resignation on March 24, 1969. Loshak was the foreign correspondent for the* London Daily Telegraph *and* Sun Telegraph *in India and Pakistan from March 1969 to the early 1970s.*

T he years of Ayub Khan's presidency were Pakistan's heyday. The takeover by the top corps of [British Military Academy] Sandhurst-trained officers was engineered with great intelligence, with no bloodshed and the very minimum of disruption. The new regime stamped down on corruption in government and business, rigorously weeding out venal civil servants and sending the discredited politicians into deserved obscurity. The highly able hard core of the civil service was able to get on with the task of administering the country without the incubus of incompetent and self-interested ministers. The threads of the economy were firmly pulled together again. Tens of thousands of urban refugees who had been living in appalling squalor ever since partition were resettled with impressive speed and vigor. One of the worst of the many pullulating shanty colonies which disfigured the towns was on the road from Karachi airport to the city center, giving Pakistan a deplorable image in the eyes of almost all visiting foreigners: it was quickly bulldozed away under military direction and 500,000 people in Karachi were re-housed in satellite townships. President Ayub's brisk new government also tackled Pakistan's backward agriculture, where still feudal tenurial systems impeded the development of improved techniques and made it necessary to continue the expensive import of food from abroad. The purge of corrupt politicians and officials was followed by moves aimed at stripping excess land-holdings from feudal landlords. The reforms, even though they never worked out to the extent intended and largely failed to curb the political power of the landed aristocracy, were never-theless an index of the new government's zeal and intentions and, with its other moves, confirmed the view of many in Pakistan that the army knew how to get things done and had its priori-ties right. Side by side with this, Pakistan's international stature was steadily enhanced and President Ayub flowered, if briefly, into a statesman of international significance.

With notable boldness, Ayub confronted the basic problem of Pakistan's inability to evolve a democratic system suited to its par-ticular needs and difficulties. Parliamentary democracy had patently failed: at any rate, Pakistan's politicians had patently failed democracy. And, to the army's leadership, it was equally patent nonsense to expect a largely illiterate population to be able to grasp complex political issues sufficiently to participate in a Western-style parliamentary process: they took a classically elitist view. This led Ayub to formulate his electoral system of "basic democracies." The entire country was broken up into thousands of tiny constituencies, containing only about 1,000 people, and voters elected representatives from each of these areas. Repre-sentatives from each group of ten constituencies formed a "union council" and this indirect elective system proceeded upwards tier by tier, with nominated members being added to councils at each ascending stage, up to the national assembly itself, which was cho-sen by an electoral college distilled from the basic democratic process. Under a constitution promulgated in 1962, the President retained considerable executive powers. By these means it proved possible, later that year, to lift martial law.

And yet, it all went wrong and came to naught. Why?

The War in Kashmir

It was, first, that bane of Pakistan's sad history, the problem of Kashmir, which started the rot. Over the years, it had proved as intractable as ever. The Indian attitude hardened with steps to bring the part of Kashmir that it held into the Indian union as a constituent state, in apparent defiance of undertaking given earlier. In 1965, after a series of incidents along the cease-fire line, full-scale war broke out. It lasted three weeks before petering out under the weight of heavy losses. Although Pakistan was not seriously worsted in the encounter, the war, concluded in an aura of spurious good will with a treaty signed under Russian auspices at Tashkent, was the death knell of the reign of Ayub Khan.

At the outbreak of fighting, the government imposed a series of emergency regulations, including indefinite detention without trial. Many of these were not rescinded when fighting stopped. Three years later, hundreds still languished, untried, in the jails. The regime had become increasingly harsh in its treatment not merely of critics but even of basically sympathetic (and certainly patriotic) critics. The war also aroused deep disquiet in East Pakistan. For the Kashmir issue meant very little to the Bengalis—they neither felt involved in it, or concerned about it, nor felt they had anything to gain from Kashmir's accession, if it could be achieved, to Pakistan. Yet East Pakistan had, willy-nilly, become involved in the war. It had been a heavy contributor toward the costs, though it could ill afford it. And, even more crucially, the war against India had left the east wing cut off from the west and undefended for seventeen days by anything more than one army division. The feeling that East Pakistan's security had been jeopardized for the sake of West Pakistan acutely vexed Bengali sentiment. It seriously intensified anti-West wing opinion already hardening in East Pakistan, for a complex of reasons.

The Facade of Freedom

But it was not only the Kashmir war and its consequences that brought Ayub down. For those realities of military dictatorship lying hidden behind the façade which Pakistan's leaders skillfully presented to the world—and, for a time, to their own people— eventually came, in all their ugliness, to the surface. From 1962 the government, ostensibly civilian, in fact continued as a catspaw of the military circles surrounding Ayub—a reality symbolized by the removal of the national capital from commercial Karachi

THE DEFENSE FORCES MUST RESTORE ORDER

In the following extract from his letter of resignation of March 25, 1969, to General Yahya Khan, Ayub Khan describes his government's impotence in response to the deteriorating condition of the country and calls for military intervention to restore law and order.

My dear General Yahya,

It is with profound regret that I have come to the conclusion that all civil administration and constitutional authority in the country has become ineffective. If the situation continues to deteriorate at the present alarming rate, all economic life, indeed, civilized existence will become impossible.

I am left with no option but to step aside and leave it to the Defence Forces of Pakistan, which today represent the only effective and legal instrument, to take full control of the affairs of the country. They are by the grace of God in a position to retrieve the situation and to save the country from utter chaos and total destruction. They alone can restore sanity and put the country back on the road to progress in a civil and constitutional manner.

The restoration and maintenance of full democracy according to the fundamental principles of our faith and the needs of our people must remain our ultimate goal. In that lies the salvation of our people who are blessed with the highest qualities of dedication and vision and who are destined to play a glorious role in the world. It is most tragic that while we were well on our way to a happy and prosperous future, we were plunged into an abyss of senseless agitation. Whatever may have been used to glorify it, time will show that this turmoil was deliberately created by well-tutored and well-backed elements. They made it impossible for the government to maintain any semblance of law and order or to protect the civil liberties, life and property of the people. Every single instrument of administration and every medium of expression of saner public opinion was subjected to inhuman pressure. Dedicated but defenceless government functionaries were subjected to ruthless public criticism or blackmail. The result is that all social and ethical norms have been destroyed and instruments of government have become inoperative and ineffective.

The economic life of the country has all but collapsed. Workers and labourers are being incited and urged to commit acts of lawlessness and brutality. While demands for higher wages, salaries and amenities are being extracted under threat of violence, production is going down. There has been a serious fall in exports and I am afraid the country may soon find itself in the grip of serious inflation. All this is the result of the reckless conduct of those who, acting under the cover of a mass movement, struck blow after blow at the very root of the country during the last few months. The pity is that a large number of innocent but gullible people became victims of their evil designs. . . .

I have exhausted all possible civil and constitutional means to resolve the present crisis. . . .

It is beyond the capacity of the civil government to deal with the present complex situation and the Defence forces must step in. It is your legal and constitutional responsibility to defend the country not only against external aggression but also to save it from internal disorder and chaos. The nation expects you to discharge this responsibility to preserve the security and integrity of the country and to restore normal social, economic and administrative life. Let peace and happiness be brought back to this anguished land of 120 million people. . . .

Yours sincerely,
M. Ayub Khan

Ayub Khan, quoted in Altaf Gauhar, *Ayub Khan: Pakistan's First Military Ruler.* Karachi, Pakistan: Oxford University Press, 1996, pp. 342–44.

to Rawalpindi, the seat of the army's general headquarters. And this reality was not merely a military government, but a dictatorial one at that. There was never the freedom of expression enjoyed in most Western democracies or, more pointedly, in neighboring India.

Military rule might have seemed fine at first—efficient, disciplined, incorrupt, honorable, purposive. But the actuality was otherwise. Ayub Khan's constructive, reformist, even progressive social policies, aimed at giving a modern shape to this still new nation, eventually turned sour because they gave the semblance of political freedom without its substance. Bitter experience taught that the system of "basic democracy" did not work: the elected representatives were too easily cowed or corrupted by the regime. Land reforms were circumvented by the landlords. Corruption was stamped down but not stamped out: in the last years of Ayub's presidency, it was more rampant than ever, pervading the civil service, commerce, business, even the army, even the president's own family—and on a blatant scale. The government's only answer to increasing restiveness was increasing repression. By late 1968 this had built up a head of steam which blew the lid off the pressure cooker and overthrew what had by then become a hated, feared regime.

This parlous situation was well described by Air Marshal Asghar Khan, former chief of the Pakistan air force, a widely respected, courageous and selfless figure. In November 1968 he announced his entry into politics as an opponent of Ayub. "Graft nepotism, corruption, and administrative incompetence are affecting the lives and happiness of millions. Social inequality and economic disparity are increasing. Telephones are tapped, opinion is shackled, the Opposition is shadowed and jailed, no one can express his views fully."

Riots and Civil Disorder

The students were the first to revolt. They had become increasingly restive under curbs on their political activity, including laws which went so far as to provide for the forfeiture of degrees by graduates deemed to be "subversive." In November 1968 they launched an agitation for educational reform. This developed into widespread rioting after police killed a student at a demonstration. A young man came near to assassinating President Ayub at Peshawar, which was followed by the internment of Ayub's former foreign minister, the mercurial [Zulfiqar Ali] Bhutto, on charges of inciting the students. The rioting spread, and took on a more general political character. Within days it broke out also in East Pakistan. Although Ayub now backtracked rapidly in a bid to save his position, it was too late. Faced with growing disorder, he offered in February 1969 to negotiate with Opposition leaders over their program for thoroughgoing constitutional and economic reform. He ordered the release of Mr. Bhutto and other political prisoners, including the East Pakistan leader, Sheikh Mujibur Rahman, facing trial on a trumped-up conspiracy charge. Ayub further announced that he would not seek a further term of office. But it was no use. The masses of Pakistan's disparate wings had found common cause and were making sweeping demands: direct elections and full democracy, ending of press censorship and similar curbs, abrogation of the emergency regulations, wide-scale nationalization, and, above all, a large measure of autonomy for the East wing. And this was the "crunch." For although Ayub conceded two fundamental demands, for parliamentary government and direct elections, he stalled on the others. A massive wave of strikes in West Pakistan, which brought immense disorder, was magnified in the East wing, where unrest spilled over into violence and the breakdown of authority. On March 24, 1969, President Ayub resigned. Martial law was reimposed. The army's commander-in-chief, General Yahya Khan, took over the reins.

Turbulent Times: The War of Secession and Military Rule

The Yahya Khan Interlude

By Omar Noman

By 1969 Ayub Khan's limited democracy, political repression, and economic policies that failed to benefit the poor majority left Pakistan divided and in turmoil. When he could no longer contain the regional, ethnic, and class cleavages that threatened to tear the nation apart, Ayub Khan resigned his post. On March 24, 1969, he called on General Yahya Khan, chief of the armed forces, to restore law and order in Pakistan.

Yahya Khan inherited a difficult situation. The division of Pakistan into east and west wings, separated by a thousand miles of potentially hostile Indian territory, had posed political strains on the country from its inception. By the late 1960s violent protests had erupted in east Pakistan over the government's failure to allocate a fair share of resources to the poorer state. To quell the increase in public protests, leaders of the Awami League, who represented east Pakistan, proposed a six point plan. Under this plan the eastern state would have separate budgets, currencies, and armies from those of West Pakistan. Yahya Khan proved incapable of defusing the growing discontent. The subsequent intervention by the military to restore order in East Pakistan led to a civil war, which in turn provoked an Indian military assault. The short war with India led to the partition of the country and the establishment of Bangladesh. In 1971 Yahya Khan was forced to resign to avert further civil strife.

In the following extract from The Political Economy of Pakistan, 1947–85, *Oxford University economist Omar Noman says Yahya Khan's misplaced confidence in his ability to mediate between the rival politicians of east and west Pakistan and his failure to anticipate the consequences of Indian military intervention in the conflict account for his failure to resolve Pakistan's political crisis.*

The national revolt against military rule had forced Ayub Khan to concede, on 21 February 1969, to the demand for parliamentary elections. Next month he transferred power to General Yahya Khan, who began his constitutional quest for a settlement to Pakistan's political crisis. Yahya announced a Legal Framework Order under which elections were to be held in December 1970. Yahya earned the respect of all the participants by adhering to his promise of impartiality and honesty. The 1970 national elections . . . [were the first instance] of a free, untampered exercise of democratic rights in Pakistan.

The results of the national and provincial elections . . . [were as follows:] In East Pakistan, the Awami League won all but two of the 153 seats to the National Assembly. The League's victory was never in doubt, although its overwhelming magnitude came as a surprise. The result in West Pakistan was far more complex. [Zulfiqar Ali] Bhutto's PPP [Pakistan People's Party] emerged as the major party, winning eighty-one out of the 148 seats. The PPP's significance far exceeded the 54% of seats captured by it. The other parties in West Pakistan were in total disarray with the Qayyum Muslim League [a breakaway party from the Muslim League led by Abdul Qayyum Khan] emerging as the second largest party, with just nine seats. . . . Although other parties received 46% of the votes, compared with the PPP's 41%, this support was split among ten parties. No party, other than the PPP, managed to get into double figures in either [the two major provinces of] Punjab or Sind. . . . The main feature of the election result was the mutually exclusive regional base of the two major parties. [Sheikh Mujibur Rahman] Mujib's Awami League won 151 seats in East Pakistan. Bhutto's PPP had support only in West Pakistan. In fact, no political party was able to win a National Assembly seat in both the regions. Only the relatively minor parties . . . were able to win a few provincial assembly seats in both regions.

Yahya Khan's Strategy

Controversy still surrounds the army's motives in holding these elections. One common view holds that Yahya had no intention of surrendering complete power to civilians, hoping to retain a permanent role for the army in a new constitutional structure. The hypothesis that the army hoped to control the victors, rather than fix the ballot, only partially explains the untampered freedom of choice permitted in 1970. Indeed, if one wishes to manipulate the outcome of the electoral process, one does not do so by allowing a free and fair ballot. The conventional, and well tried, method is to ensure the desired result. It would not have been too difficult for the army to bend the electoral mechanism. Further, contrary to popular belief that the army was surprised by the Awami League's victory, official intelligence reports had predicted a large majority for Mujib. Accordingly, in determining the army's motives for holding an unrestricted election, particular emphasis needs to be placed on the sequence of events to which the army was responding. In the wake of the mass revolt against Ayub, the army appeared to have resigned itself to the inevitability of transferring power to civilians. At this stage, the army expected the polls to produce a splintered outcome, with no single party able to command an absolute majority. None the less, the army's primary focus of concern was Mujib's Awami League. Consequently, the Legal Framework Order (LFO), under which the 1970 elections were held, provided a *conditional* framework for the transfer of power. The elected National Assembly had to frame a constitution within 120 days of its first meeting. This constitution required the approval of the President, i.e. the army. This measure was designed to give the army the leverage to exercise a veto over the Awami League's six points being incorporated into a constitution. . . . The six points, which included a proposal for two separate currencies, would have created a confederation.

As the polling day approached, the army was aware of the likelihood of an overwhelming victory for the Awami League. However, by this stage it was too late to tamper with the electoral mechanism to prevent such an outcome. Once the elections were held Yahya, armed with the LFO, appeared to be confident of his ability to mediate successfully as far as the Awami League's six points were concerned. Mujib's meetings with Yahya's aides had assured the general that the Awami League leader would modify the six-point demand to the extent that Pakistan would be a federal state, and not a confederation between two regions. The cordiality of Yahya's initial contacts with Mujib suggested his confidence in having reached an understanding for a federal Pakistan. Indeed, Yahya referred to Mujib as Pakistan's next prime minister, whereas the latter is reported to have offered Yahya the post of constitutional head of state.

Negotiations Break Down

However, as the time approached for the transfer of power, the divergent pressures on the participants became apparent. Yahya saw his role of arbiter as involving commitments from the Awami League to tone down the six points. Pressed by factions within the army, he sought reassurance for this by demanding to see a draft constitution before transferring power to the Awami League. Mujib became wary of Yahya's conditions, demanding that an immediate announcement be made to call a session of the newly elected National Assembly. Mujib had previously voiced public concern at factions in the army who were conspiring to undo the election results and prevent a transfer of power. The strain between Yahya and Mujib was seized upon by the more hawkish figures in the army. They were not convinced about Mujib's ability to tone down the Awami League's platform for a confederation, especially in view of such an overwhelming mandate for the six points. The position of the hawks was strengthened by the posture adopted by Z. A. Bhutto. The PPP manifesto had criticised the Awami League's demands for a separate currency and a separate militia on the grounds that this implied an effective partition into two nation-states. The PPP's emergence as the main party in West Pakistan, particulary Punjab, lent greater authority to their criticisms. Bhutto took a strident view of the importance of his party, declaring that the question of the six points had to be settled before the convening of the National Assembly. Since the Awami League had a majority in the legislature, Bhutto sought a constitutional accord prior to a meeting of the National Assembly. To this end, he allied himself with the hawks in the army, threatening to 'break the legs' of party members who dared to attend the inaugural session of the National Assembly, scheduled for 3 March 1971. The failure of the Mujib-Bhutto talks to thrash out a broad consensus on the future constitution, had convinced Bhutto that Mujib could not back down from implementing a confederation. Confident of support from within the army, Bhutto pressed Yahya for a postponement of the National Assembly.

Failure of Yahya's Constitutional Quest

Two days before the scheduled inaugural session, the convening of the National Assembly was postponed indefinitely. Yahya did not personally announce the postponement, a distance which has been interpreted as demonstrating his reluctance to follow this course. In any case, Yahya's constitutional quest had failed, as the junta prepared for a military crackdown. In East Pakistan, there was little illusion regarding Yahya's appeals for further talks with the Awami League to resolve the deadlock. . . . The military offensive led to the creation of a new nation-state, Bangladesh. Perhaps this is the only instance in which the majority of the population had broken away to form a new country.

Conflict between the centre and regional units is inherent in the structure of post colonial nation-states; several of these countries have been carved out of artificial and arbitrary boundaries. Separatist movements are therefore not uncommon. What is universal, however, is their lack of success in meeting their objectives. Modern armies have proved themselves to be quite capable of forcing reluctant regional groups to stay within national boundaries. This supremacy of military power has been evident in separatist movements in Asia, Latin America and Africa. The only factor which seems capable of ensuring success for a regional movement is military assistance and intervention by a foreign power. It is self-evident that Bangladesh could not have been created without Indian military intervention. What is surprising, however, is not the fact that India meddled, but the failure of the Pakistan army to anticipate the consequences of Indian military intervention. On the one hand, Pakistan's entire foreign policy was determined by the fear of India. On the other, insufficient measures were taken to protect the most vulnerable region of Pakistan, perhaps under the delusion that China and/or the United States would prevent an Indian military offensive on East Pakistan. In the event, when the carnage was over, the Muslims of the Indian subcontinent were spread across three nation-states.

Civil War, the Indo-Pakistan War, and the Birth of Bangladesh

By Keesing's Research Report

Tension between the ethnically diverse east and west wings of Pakistan had plagued the nation since its beginning in 1947. The seat of government, the military, and the country's major politicians came from the smaller western portion, which received a disproportionate share of government resources. By the 1960s the eastern Pakistanis conducted mass demonstrations to demand control over their own resources, budgets, and currency. West Pakistan politicians resisted these demands, which would have made Pakistan a confederation.

The east-west conflict became more intense following the 1970 national election. East Pakistan's Awami League, under Sheikh Mujibur Rahman, garnered the greatest share of the votes and was entitled by law to form the government. Zulfikar Ali Bhutto, leader of the western Pakistan's People's Party (PPP), refused to attend the inaugural session of the National Assembly, claiming that his party would have no say in government policy. Despite efforts by General Yahya Khan to arbitrate between the leaders, negotiations broke down and renewed riots in east Pakistan led to a military crackdown. A full-scale civil war ensued, which provoked Indian intervention on behalf of east Pakistan. Indian troops scored a quick military victory, and in December of 1971 the Independent People's Republic of Bangladesh was established.

The events of the civil war, which escalated into an international conflict with India, are described in the following extract from Keesing's Research Report, Pakistan: From 1947 to the Creation of Bangladesh. The report details the events of the civil war and international conflict, the recognition of Bangladesh by India, and the defeat of Pak-

Keesing's Research Report, *Pakistan: From 1947 to the Creation of Bangladesh*. New York: Charles Scribner's Sons, 1973. Copyright © 1973 by Keesing's Publications. All rights reserved. Reproduced by permission.

istan's army. Keesing's is an international research service that distills world political, economic, and social events from major press sources.

Full-scale civil war erupted in East Pakistan on March 26, 1971, when a clandestine radio broadcast announced the proclamation by Sheikh Mujibur Rahman and the Awami League of the "sovereign independent people's republic of Bangladesh". The broadcast, which was monitored in India, said that heavy fighting was in progress at Chittagong, Comilla, Sylhet, Jessore, Barisal and Khulna, where West Pakistan forces were claimed to be surrounded by troops of the East Bengal Regiment, the East Pakistan Rifles and the "entire" police force. Calls were made to the people of Bangladesh ("Bengal Nation") to continue the struggle for independence "until the last enemy soldier had vanished", and Sheikh Mujibur—who was said to have gone underground—was described as "the only leader of independent Bangladesh", whose orders should be obeyed to save the country from "the ruthless dictatorship of the West Pakistanis". Another clandestine broadcast said that Bangladesh had appealed to the United Nations and to the Afro-Asian countries for help in its "struggle for freedom".

On the same day President Yahya Khan outlawed the Awami League, placed a ban on political activity throughout Pakistan, and imposed complete press censorship.

With official communications between East Pakistan and the rest of the world cut, and a rigorous press censorship in force, the only news of the civil war in the province came from clandestine radio broadcasts, from refugees crossing into India, from statements by foreign press correspondents after they had left East Pakistan for the outside world, and from Indian newspapers. Completely contradictory reports about the fighting, moreover, were given on the one hand by official Pakistani statements and broadcasts and on the other by clandestine broadcasts monitored in India and by the Indian Press. Reports reaching Calcutta on March 28–29, however, spoke of fierce fighting in Dacca, Rangpur, Comilla and other centres in East Pakistan; the clandestine Bangladesh radio said on March 27 that the Pakistan Air Force had bombed Dacca, Comilla and Khulna and alleged that Dacca University—an Awami League stronghold—had been destroyed by shelling by Pakistan Army tanks, with heavy casualties among students.

Press Reports on the War

Two journalists, Mr. Simon Dring of *The Daily Telegraph* and Mr. Michel Laurent, an Associated Press photographer, both of whom had evaded the round-up and deportation of press correspondents in the province, made an extensive tour of Dacca, describing it later as "a crushed and frightened city" after "24 hours of shelling by the Pakistan Army", and saying that as many as 7,000 were dead and that large areas had been levelled.

Despite official Pakistani statements to the contrary, it appeared that, at least during the first ten days of April, the Bangladesh forces were continuing to put up a stubborn resistance in a number of centres; all the main towns of East Pakistan, however, were in the hands of the Army within a relatively short time, and the secessionist forces, lightly armed in comparison with the regular troops, were being driven more and more into the remoter rural areas.

By April 12–13, press correspondents' reports from the Indo-Pakistan frontier area indicated that the Pakistan Army was everywhere on the offensive and fanning out in all directions north and west of Dacca, and that the resistance of the Bangladesh "liberation forces" was everywhere crumbling despite bitter last-ditch opposition in some areas.

Those towns—among them Jessore, Sylhet and Khulna—which for a time had been partially or wholly under secessionist control were firmly in the hands of the Regular Army, which also controlled all main roads and waterways, and to all intents and purposes the civil war ended on April 18 with the capture by the Pakistan Army of the village of Chuadanga, 300 yards from the Indian border, which had been proclaimed the provisional capital of Bangladesh.

With the Pakistan Army in complete control of the western frontier area bordering on India, all effective resistance by the Bangladesh "liberation army" had virtually ceased by April 18–19.

Republic of Bangladesh Proclaimed

A clandestine radio broadcast on April 11 had announced the formation "somewhere in Bangladesh" of a six-member Cabinet of the "independent sovereign republic of Bangladesh", with Sheikh Mujibur Rahman as President.

The Bangladesh "Government" had set up its headquarters in the village of Chuadanga, only a few hundred yards from the Indian frontier, where on April 17, 1972, the "Democratic Republic of Bangladesh" was formally proclaimed. On the following day, however, when Chuadanga was occupied by the Pakistan Army, no trace was found of any of the members of the Cabinet.

The Government of India announced on April 2, 1971, that more than a quarter of a million refugees from East Pakistan had crossed into India since the civil war broke out.

Deterioration of Relations Between India and Pakistan

Relations between India and Pakistan, already tense, deteriorated sharply in 1971 as a result of the civil war in East Pakistan, leading to acrimonious exchanges of Notes between the two countries and to numerous charges and countercharges by each side.

Mr. Swaran Singh, the Indian Minister of External Affairs, accused the Pakistan Army of "suppressing the people of East Pakistan" and said that "the Government of India cannot but be gravely concerned at events taking place so close to our borders", and on March 31, 1971, both Houses of the Indian Parliament passed a resolution, moved by the Prime Minister, Mrs. [Indira] Gandhi, expressing "wholehearted sympathy and support" for the people of Bengal.

The acute friction between India and Pakistan was heightened by alleged incidents on the border of India and East Pakistan, and by the defection of the Pakistan Deputy High Commissioner in Calcutta, which was followed by the closing of the Pakistan Deputy High Commission in that city and of the Indian Deputy High Commission in Dacca (the staffs being later repatriated in August). At the same time vast numbers of refugees passed into India from East Pakistan on a scale unprecedented in any part of the world since World War II. By mid-June 1971 some 5,500,000–6,000,000 people had crossed the border. . . .

President Yahya Khan issued a statement on May 21 urging *bona fide* Pakistani citizens who had "left their homes owing to disturbed conditions and for other reasons" to return to East Pakistan, and on June 10 offered a general amnesty.

Mrs. Gandhi said on June 17 that the refugees were "certainly not going to stay there in India permanently", and that the Government were "determined to send them back". Planes on June 15 began flying refugees from the border areas to 50 large camps in Madhya Pradesh, Orissa, Uttar Pradesh and Bihar, with the help of Soviet, British, Australian and U.S. aircraft.

Meanwhile, acute tension continued to exist on the border between India and East Pakistan, many charges being made by both sides during the months from April to July alleging border violations and acts of aggression by the other.

The Indian Defence Minister, Mr. Jagjivan Ram, told Indian Army units at Jullunder (Punjab) on June 20 that they should be prepared "to meet any eventuality that might arise because of the desperate acts" of Pakistan's military rulers. Alleging that Pakistan had been violating India's eastern borders, Mr. Ram declared: "We are a peace-loving country and we want to avoid war, but Pakistan is creating a situation where war may be thrust on us". . . .

Both India and Pakistan made repeated allegations in September and October that their territory had been shelled from the other side of the East Pakistan border, and during October the Indian Press claimed that the Pakistan Army was concentrated near the West Pakistan frontier; that new defence lines were being constructed on the border; and that the civilian population had been evacuated from a 500-mile stretch of the frontier opposite the Indian State of Rajasthan. President Yahya Khan, on the other hand, stated on Oct. 12 that a large number of Indian Air Force units and Army formations had been brought forward towards the West Pakistan border, and it was confirmed on Oct. 24 that the Army had taken over defence duties in the Rann of Kutch from the Border Security Force. Violations of the cease-fire line in Kashmir were also alleged. . . .

Finally, Indian troops were officially stated to have entered East Pakistan on Nov. 27, after Pakistani artillery had heavily shelled the Indian frontier towns of Hilli and Balurghat, the Indian Defence Minister giving the explanation that it was more effective to silence the guns from Pakistani territory.

President Yahya Khan proclaimed a state of emergency on Nov. 23, declaring that "a most critical situation has been created because Pakistan is faced with external aggression"; the practical implications of this proclamation were not clear, however, as the country had been under martial law since 1969. Mrs. Gandhi described the President's declaration as "the climax of his efforts to divert the attention of the world from Bangladesh and to put the blame on us for the situation which he himself has created", and said: "We shall refrain from taking a similar step, unless further aggression by Pakistan compels us to do so."

The Indo-Pakistan War

The clashes between the Indian and Pakistani forces finally developed into open war on Dec. 3, 1971, when the Pakistan Air Force made a surprise attack on military airfields in western India. The main aims of the attack, it was believed, were to reduce the pressure on the forces in East Pakistan by creating a diversion in the west; to occupy territory in Kashmir and Rajasthan which could be used as a bargaining counter in negotiating a settlement in East Pakistan; and to secure the intervention of the great Powers or the U.N. Security Council.

Two hours before the Pakistani air raids in the west, Pakistani aircraft attacked the airfield at Agartala (Tripura) on Dec. 3 for the second consecutive day. Indian troops which had crossed the border on Dec. 2 forced the Pakistanis to withdraw artillery which had been shelling the town for the past three days, and took up positions just inside Pakistani territory.

On Dec. 4 India launched an integrated ground, air and naval offensive against East Pakistan. The Army, linking up with the *Mukti Bahini* [East Bengal Liberation Army], entered East Pakistan from five main directions, the aim being to divide the Pakistani units stationed round the border and to prevent them from uniting in defence of Dacca, which occupies a strong strategic position protected by the complex river system at the mouth of the Ganges and the Brahmaputra.

India announced on Dec. 6 that she had recognized the Provisional Government of Bangladesh, whereupon the Pakistan Government broke off diplomatic relations with India.

On Dec. 7 the advancing Indian troops achieved two major successes, capturing Sylhet and then Jessore.

Western journalists who visited Jessore described the tumultuous welcome which the Indian forces received from the Bengali population, and gave details of the ordeal to which the civilian population in the town had been subjected since April. An Italian missionary told reporters that during the week April 4–10 the streets and houses had been full of bodies of residents executed in batches by the soldiers and *Razakars* [civilian collaborators], and estimated that 10,000 people had been executed in and around Jessore, which normally has a population of about 60,000. Over half the population, including almost all the women, had fled to the countryside or to India during the occupation by the Pakistan Army; the Hindu community had disappeared, and many of the houses in the empty Hindu quarter had been demolished.

General Sam Manekshaw, the Indian Army Chief of Staff, broadcast on Dec. 7 an appeal to the Pakistan Army in East Pakistan to surrender "before it is too late", promising them good treatment. Pointing out that their Air Force was destroyed and the ports blocked, he warned them that "the *Mukti Bahini* and the people fighting for liberation have encircled you, and are all

MY COUNTRY TORN ASUNDER

Benazir Bhutto, the future prime minister of Pakistan, was studying at Harvard University during the 1971 war. In the following extract from her autobiography, Daughter of Destiny, *she writes of the sorrow and humiliation of her people in response to the defeat by India and the secession of East Pakistan.*

The loss of Bangladesh was a terrible blow to Pakistan. Our common religion of Islam, which we always believed would transcend the one thousand miles of India which separated East and West Pakistan, failed to keep us together. Our faith in our very survival as a country was shaken, the bonds between the four provinces of West Pakistan strained almost to breaking. Morale was never lower, compounded by Pakistan's actual surrender to India.

As television cameras focused in, General [Amin Abdullah Khan] Niazi [Pakistani military commander] approached his Indian counterpart, General [Jagjit Singh] Aurora [commander-in-chief, Indian Eastern Command], on the race course at Dacca. I couldn't believe my eyes when I saw General Niazi exchange swords with the conqueror of Dacca, an old classmate from Sandhurst, and embrace him. Embrace him! Even the Nazis did not surrender in such a humiliating manner. As commander of a defeated army, Niazi would have acted far more honorably if he had shot himself.

When my father landed in Islamabad, the city was in flames. Angry mobs were even torching the liquor stores that

prepared to take revenge for the atrocities and cruelties you have committed".

The Indian Army continued to advance on all fronts in East Pakistan during the period Dec. 8–14, converging on Dacca towards the end of this period. The Army began shelling the city on Dec. 14, while aircraft attacked with rockets, meeting with virtually no resistance.

had supposedly supplied Yahya Khan and the members of his regime. Watching Pakistan's surrender to India on TV after weeks of the regime's claims that Pakistan was winning the war sent huge crowds in Karachi to storm the television station and try to burn it down. And bellicose editorials in the Indian press threatened further devastation to Pakistan, claiming our country was "an artificial nation which should never have come into being."

On December 20, 1971, four days after the fall of Dacca, the people's fury forced Yahya Khan to step down. And my father, being the elected leader of the largest parliamentary group in Pakistan, became the new president. Ironically, since there was no Constitution, he had to be sworn in as the first civilian in history to ever head a Martial Law administration.

At Harvard I was no longer known as Pinkie from Pakistan, but as Pinkie Bhutto, the daughter of the president of Pakistan. But my pride at Papa's accomplishments was compromised by the shame of our surrender and the price Pakistan had paid. In the two weeks of the war, one-quarter of our air force had been downed. Half our navy had been sunk. Our treasury was empty. Not only was East Pakistan gone, but the Indian army had captured 5,000 square miles of our land in the West and taken 93,000 of our men prisoners of war. Pakistan could not last, many were predicting. The united Pakistan that Mohammed Ali Jinnah had founded after the partition of India in 1947 died with the emergence of Bangladesh.

Benazir Bhutto, *Daughter of Destiny: An Autobiography.* New York: Simon and Schuster, 1989, pp. 68–69.

After long discussions with his Ministers the Governor of East Pakistan, Dr. A. M. Malik, wrote a letter tendering his resignation to President Yahya Khan in the afternoon of Dec. 14 in an air-raid shelter in his garden; his official residence had been destroyed in an air raid shortly before. He then took refuge with his family and his Ministers in the Intercontinental Hotel, which had been declared a neutral zone for foreigners, wounded soldiers and other non-combatants and was administered by the Red Cross. 16 senior officials, including the Inspector-General of Police, had already sought refuge in the hotel.

Demand for Unconditional Surrender

On Dec. 15 the Indian forces closed in on Dacca from all sides, and in the afternoon of that day General Amin Abdullah Khan Niazi, the Pakistani military commander, sent a message to General Manekshaw through the U.S. Consulate in Dacca and the U.S. Embassy in New Delhi proposing a cease-fire; in it he asked for facilities for regrouping his forces with their weapons in designated areas pending their repatriation to West Pakistan, a guarantee of safety for the paramilitary forces and for all those who had settled in East Pakistan since 1947, and an assurance that there would be no reprisals against those who had collaborated with the martial law authorities. In his reply, however, General Manekshaw insisted on the unconditional surrender of the Pakistani forces.

On the morning of Dec. 16 General Niazi was unable to inform General Manekshaw of his acceptance of these terms because communications at his headquarters had been put out of action by Indian bombing. A message was therefore sent to New Delhi through U.N. radio facilities, 10 minutes before General Manekshaw's ultimatum was due to expire, asking for a six-hour extension of the bombing pause and for an Indian staff officer to negotiate terms of surrender.

Major-General J.F.R. Jacob, Chief of Staff of the Eastern Command of the Indian Army, arrived by air, and discussions began at once. The surrender terms agreed upon between General Niazi and General Jacob provided that all Pakistani regular, paramilitary and civilian armed forces would lay down their arms, and guaranteed that they would be treated in accordance with the Geneva Conventions and that foreign nationals, ethnic minorities and personnel of West Pakistani origin would be protected.

An Indian battalion had already entered Dacca unopposed during the morning, and was joined in the afternoon by four more, including two battalions of the *Mukti Bahini;* they were greeted in the streets by thousands of jubilant Bengalis, who hugged and kissed the soldiers and garlanded them with flowers.

The signed surrender documents were presented to General Jagjit Singh Aurora (C.-in-C., Indian Eastern Command) on Dacca race-course, while Indian troops held back cheering crowds. . . .

Cease-Fire Agreement: Yahya Khan Resigns

In a broadcast on Dec. 16 President Yahya Khan admitted defeat in East Pakistan, though without mentioning that the Army had surrendered, and declared that the war would go on: "We will continue to fight the enemy on every front, and also continue our efforts to form a representative Government in the country, which the enemy, by launching an attack, tried to set aside. According to the programme, the Constitution will be announced on Dec. 20. This guarantees the maximum autonomy to East Pakistan on the basis of one Pakistan, for whose establishment and protection the people of both Wings of the country sacrificed so much. A Central Government will be formed after this, and subsequently Provincial Governments will come into being . . .".

Mrs. Gandhi shortly afterwards announced that she had ordered a unilateral cease-fire on the western front from 8 p.m. on Dec. 17, declaring that "India has no territorial ambitions" and that, Pakistani forces having surrendered and Bangladesh being free, "it is pointless in our view to continue the present conflict". After this decision had been communicated to President Yahya Khan through the Swiss Embassy, he subsequently announced that he had also ordered a cease-fire to come into force at the same time.

Following the President's decision, the U.N. Security Council suspended its discussions about the war (previous attempts by the U.N. to bring about a cease-fire had resulted in failure), and after consultations met again on Dec. 22, when a compromise resolution was put forward by Argentina, Burundi, Japan, Nicaragua, Sierra Leone and Somalia. . . .

The resolution was adopted by 13 votes to none, with Poland and the Soviet Union abstaining. The Chinese delegation, while voting for the resolution, expressed dissatisfaction with it.

Meanwhile, however, violent demonstrations against the military regime in West Pakistan, beginning on Dec. 18, had led to the resignation of President Yahya Khan, in succession to whom Mr. Bhutto was sworn in as Pakistan's new President on Dec. 20.

The Zulfikar Ali Bhutto Era

By Shahid Javed Burki

The war of secession was the death knell for Yahya Khan's administration. On December 20, 1971, the military high command handed power to Zulfikar Ali Bhutto and his Pakistan People's Party (PPP), which had won the 1970 election in West Pakistan. In the following extract from Pakistan: Fifty Years of Nationhood, *Shahid Javed Burki says that though Bhutto succeeded in reforming the economy and gaining a political consensus for the 1973 constitution, his mistreatment of the political opposition caused his downfall. This opposition rallied into a national alliance to challenge Bhutto in the 1977 election. When they failed to garner many votes in the election, accusations of foul play led to violent public protests. General Zia-ul-Haq staged the country's third military takeover to restore law and order and forced Bhutto from office in July 1977. Bhutto was sentenced to death by hanging in April 1979 for his alleged role in a conspiracy to murder a political opponent.*

World Bank economist and author Shahid Javed Burki became finance minister for the caretaker administration in Pakistan following the dismissal of Prime Minister Benazir Bhutto, Zulfikar Ali Bhutto's daughter, on corruption charges in 1996. He has written many books on Pakistan, including Pakistan Under Bhutto.

The Bhutto era lasted for five and a half years, during which the economy was restructured, the public sector was given a great deal of prominence, Pakistan's approach to the outside world was redefined on the basis of a relationship with India that no longer sought equality with it, and a new consensus was developed on constitutional issues among different political players. It was a period, therefore, of remarkable dynamism—a period during which a great deal was accomplished. It might have lasted much longer than it did but for the serious flaws in the character of the man who guided the country during this period of adjustment and change. On July 5, 1977, Bhutto was ousted from power by the military, which took control once again not out of political ambition but because of the tensions generated by Bhutto's treatment of other political leaders, their parties, and their platforms. For instance, Asghar Khan, one of the prominent opposition politicians, actually invited the military to intervene and restore a democratic order to the country. . . . This [viewpoint] reveals the nature and scope of the political consensus that formed the basis of his constitution—the constitution of 1973, the third in Pakistan's history.

Regional Diversity

The principle of parity between two wings of roughly equal size was the basis of the constitutions of 1956 and 1962. With Pakistan now divided into four very unequal parts, there was no easy solution to the problem of power sharing between the center and the provinces. The domination of Punjab was feared by the smaller provinces. Punjab had nearly 60 percent of the population and a large representation in the armed forces; it also produced well over one-half of the GNP [Gross National Product]. Sindh, second to Punjab in size and wealth, had an enormous untapped agricultural potential; although irrigation had arrived in Punjab in the early decades of the twentieth century, Sindh's virgin soil was still in the process of being "colonized" by farmers, many of whom were either immigrants from Punjab or retired army officers. Sindh had also accommodated another set of migrants— namely, those who had come to Pakistan from the cities of India in the aftermath of the partition. These migrants—the *muhajirs*— settled in the major cities of Sindh (in Karachi, Hyderabad, Sukkur, and Khairpur) and had little contact with the political culture of rural Sindh. That culture was dominated by large landlords—the *weidaras*—one of whom was Zulfikar Ali Bhutto himself. The Northwest Frontier Province was as heterogeneous as Sindh; within its borders lived Pathans as well as Punjabis. The Pathans were divided into two groups—those of the "settled districts" (the districts that had accepted the British *raj* and its laws) and those of the tribal areas in which *pukhtunwali* (the local Pathan law) was still followed. The Punjabis had an important economic presence in the cities of Peshawar and Abbotabad. Finally, there was the province of Balochistan, which, though smallest in size in terms of population, had a landmass twice the size of Punjab. Balochistan was the poorest of the four provinces, but it had potential riches—some known, some still unknown. It was certainly rich in natural gas and had vast deposits of coal and marble in addition, perhaps, to iron, gold, and copper. The Balochis, not unlike the Pathans, were a fiercely independent people. They, too, had rejected the "civilizing" influence of the British *raj*, preferring to live under their own code. But there was one important difference of great political significance between the Pathans and the Balochis: The tribal Pathans lived in small independent communities that were highly egalitarian, whereas the Balochis were divided into tribes, each under the control of the powerful *sirdar* (chief).

The Pakistan that emerged in 1971, therefore, was a colorful mosaic of many different peoples. They spoke a number of dif-

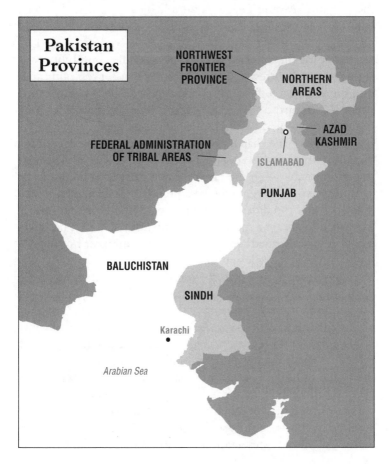

ferent languages—Punjabi, Sindhi, Baruhi, Pushto, Balochi, Urdu, Saraiki, and so on—and belonged to many different cultures. These differences had remained submerged for as long as Bengal was a part of Pakistan; then the question of finding a viable solution to the sharing of power between the two wings had occupied all political attention. With Bengal now gone, the focus shifted to West Pakistan's internal differences.

1973 Constitution

The trauma of defeat in East Pakistan may have made it possible for the politicians of West Pakistan to agree to a new constitution. Bhutto convened the National Assembly to meet in Islamabad on April 4, 1972. The Assembly was made up of 139 members—138 elected from West Pakistan and Nurul Amin, one of the two non-Awami Leaguers who had been returned in East Pakistan. On October 20, 1972, only six months after the first meeting of the Assembly, a constitutional accord was signed by the leaders of the different political parties. The constitution was authenticated by President Bhutto on April 12, 1973, and came into force on August 14 of the same year. Thus Pakistan, on its twenty-sixth birthday, acquired its third constitution. The constitution represented a consensus on three matters: the role of Islam in politics, the sharing of power between the federal government and the federating provinces, and the division of responsibility between the president and the prime minister.

Bhutto would have preferred a presidential form of government, one not too different from that of Ayub Khan, but he was persuaded to accept a modified parliamentary system. The modification was intended to protect the prime minister from frivolous changes in party loyalty of the type that had paralyzed governments in the period before Ayub Khan. Under the procedures of the new constitution, the exercise of considerable political will was required in order to remove the prime minister. A vote of no-confidence against the prime minister was made virtually impossible, at least for ten years. Once the constitution had been put into force, Bhutto stepped down from the presidency and became the prime minister. Fazal Elahi Chaudhury, a small town politician from Punjab of no great standing, was appointed president.

The fears of smaller provinces about Punjab domination were assuaged by the creation of a bicameral legislature—a Senate with equal provincial representation and an Assembly with seats distributed according to population—as well as by Bhutto's solemn word that he would not interfere with the workings of the provincial governments in which his Pakistan People's Party (PPP) did not have a majority. Accordingly, when the constitution came into force, two non-PPP governments were put into place—one in Peshawar, the capital of the Northwest Frontier Province, and the other in Quetta, the capital of Balochistan.

The third consensus—the one concerning the role of Islam in government and in politics—took Pakistan much beyond the intent embodied in the constitutions of 1956 and 1962. "Islam shall be the State religion of Pakistan," declared the new constitution, using a phrase that had not occurred in the previous constitutions and one that was to have a profound impact in the future. The new constitution also laid down the course of action to be followed by the country in its relations with the outside world. This was an unusual area to be covered in a constitution, and the need for incorporating it was not clear. In particular, the constitution required that the state "shall endeavour to preserve and strengthen fraternal relations among the Muslim countries based on Islamic unity."

Bhutto's Political Repression

Soon after the adoption of the constitution, it became clear to the opposition that Bhutto did not really intend to abide by the consensus he had reached with them. The opposition governments in Balochistan and the Northwest Frontier Province were openly discriminated against; their leaders were frequently criticized for being unpatriotic; and, finally, on February 12, 1974, the government of Balochistan was dismissed on charges of having incited the people of that province to rebel against central authority. The government in the Northwest Frontier Province resigned in sympathy with its counterpart in Balochistan.

On May 24, an amendment in the constitution gave the executive the authority to declare illegal any political party found "operating in a manner prejudicial to the sovereignty or integrity of the country." This power was to be exercised with the approval of the Supreme Court, and, as demonstrated by later events, the court was ready to oblige. This power was used to ban the National Awami Party, by now the only effective opposition to the People's Party, and one other step was taken toward Bhutto's unstated but by now obvious objective of turning Pakistan into a one-party state. The final step toward this ultimate goal would be another general election, which would put the People's Party in total command of the National Assembly. The election for the National Assembly was slated for March 7, 1977, and that for the four provincial assemblies was slated for March 10.

The Elections of 1977

Opposition was fragmented and in retreat when, on January 7, 1977, Zulfikar Ali Bhutto announced the intention of his government to hold general elections for the national as well as the provincial assemblies. But the remarkable speed with which the opposition was able to organize itself into a fairly cohesive force—a force that was given the name of Pakistan National Alliance (PNA) for the purpose of contesting the elections—must have surprised Bhutto. The PNA, launched on January 11, 1977, was a collection of nine political parties ranging from Jamaat-i-Islami on the right to the National Democratic Party (previously called the National Awami Party) on the left. The opposition was able to put together a program that seemed attractive to many; it also campaigned hard, drew very large crowds to its public meetings, and, on the eve of the elections, seemed in a position to capture a significant number of seats in both the national and the provincial assemblies. Nobody expected the PNA to win, not even its leaders, but most political observers expected it to improve its position in the legislatures. It was therefore with surprise and dismay that the PNA and its supporters heard the results on the morning of March 8. Of the 192 seats contested, only 36 (or 18.8 percent) went to the PNA. The Punjab result seemed most surprising of all, in that the opposition won only 8 out of 116 seats.

The opposition cried foul and took to the streets. Once again, elections had generated tensions that the politicians found impossible to cope with; demonstrations occurred daily, fired upon first by the police and then, when the law-and-order situation deteriorated further, by the armed forces. Bhutto now faced a situation not too dissimilar from the one Ayub had confronted in 1969. In fact, he adopted the same approach. Opposition leaders were summoned and talks were begun, but, once again, the army intervened. The army took Bhutto and the leaders of the PNA into custody, and General Zia ul-Haq announced that fresh elections would be held within ninety days. The army's operation was called "fair play."

The Fall of Bhutto

Although forced out of power on July 5, 1977, Bhutto continued to dominate Pakistan's politics for another twenty-one
months. During most of this time, he remained in prison. His
first incarceration was in the nature of "protective custody," having been ordered by General Zia ul-Haq to save Bhutto from the
people's wrath "in a political climate which is distinctly hostile
to the former Prime Minister." But the political climate began to
improve; on July 17, less than two weeks after the coup d'état,
Bhutto addressed a large meeting of his followers on the lawn of
his improvised prison. The time for launching movements such
as the one that had removed him was over, he declared: "The
time had come for a revolution." Released from custody soon afterward, he hesitated only for a moment before advising his supporters that he would participate vigorously in the elections
promised for October 1977 by the military regime.

According to a Pakistani journalist who closely followed the
course of events that occurred after the assumption of power by
the military, Bhutto's visits to Karachi and Lahore, the two principal cities of Pakistan, attracted large crowds; but "irrespective of
the continuing popularity . . . the local press, including some newspapers that used to be almost lyrical in his praise, are daily discovering two or more of his misdeeds." Freed from the shackles of
government control, the press displayed considerable enthusiasm
in investigating abuses of power during the Bhutto years. These
investigations resulted in a clamor for "accountability," a process
that began with a case lodged in Lahore's High Court that accused
Bhutto of participating in a conspiracy to murder a political opponent. The court proceedings not only focused on the criminal
charge brought against the former prime minister but also dwelt
at length on the way Bhutto had administered Pakistan during his
years of stewardship. To help the debate along, the government
published a number of white papers detailing his administration's
misdeeds. These investigations and the people's reaction to them
demonstrated vividly how polarized Pakistan's society had become. General Zia articulated the middle-class response: "I said to
him 'Sir'—I still called him that—'Sir, why have you done all
these things, you whom I respected so, you who had so much' and
he only said that I should wait and he would be cleared. It was
very disappointing." Bhutto's followers labeled the campaign
against the deposed prime minister a vendetta of the social classes

that had suffered under him and promised that "nothing could avert their skinning." This was a reference to the PPP's manifesto for the October elections, which resolved to "skin alive the capitalists and other property owners."

Bhutto's judgment that time would clear his name proved wrong. The Lahore Court announced its verdict on March 19, 1978, finding him to be an "arch culprit" in the ambush of November 1974. The purpose of that ambush had been to kill Ahmad Raza Kasuri, a one-time political protégé turned opponent. The court then ordered Bhutto's execution.

The execution was delayed for more than a year while Bhutto's lawyers explored all possible legal avenues to save their client's life. The final legal pronouncement came on March 31, 1979, when the country's Supreme Court refused to review their earlier verdict. On April 4, 1979, Zulfikar Ali Bhutto was hanged at the Rawalpindi jail.

"Islamization" Under General Zia

By Mohammad Waseem

Amid renewed political chaos and violent clashes among rival economic and ethnic groups under Zulfikar Ali Bhutto, in 1977, General Zia-ul-Haq led Pakistan's third coup d'etat. General Zia became president of Pakistan and ruled until he was killed in a plane crash on August 17, 1988. In the following extract from Politics and the State in Pakistan, *Pakistani political scientist Mohammad Waseem describes the social, economic, punitive, and educational measures implemented under Zia-ul-Haq's "Islamization" program, which was a major pillar of his administration. Waseem says that both the program and the timing of its implementation were based on astute political calculations by Zia in his efforts to legitimize his authoritarian regime. Each successive leader of Pakistan has used certain aspects of the Islamic tradition to pursue their own political agenda.*

Almost from the beginning, the Zia regime recognised the tremendous potential of Islamic idiom as a political resource.... The ulema [Muslim religious leaders] emerged as a political force for the first time in Pakistan's history during the 1970 election campaign. Even though they had been defeated in the elections, they used this opportunity for formulating and expressing their views on the country's economic and constitutional problems. Prominent ulema from East and West Pakistan proposed a 23-point formula to establish an Islamic economic system in Pakistan, which included the elimination of interest, gambling, speculation and business monopolies, a wage-raise for the industrial labour and its share in the ownership of factories. ... During the 1977 anti-Bhutto agitation, the ulema and a vast number of religious-minded people acquired a heightened political consciousness which the Zia regime considered mandatory

upon itself to address. The CMLA [chief martial law adminis-
trator] decided to adopt Islam as the political programme of his
regime. . . . [Zia called up the] emerging economic wizard of the
regime, Ghulam Ishaque Khan, [who] declared that Islam enjoins
man to make economic gains in a righteous way as against the
modern view in which the 'economic man' supersedes, and even
defines, other aspects of social life. Khan claimed that after the
great depression of 1931 [economist John] Keynes had argued
in favour of lowering the rate of interest and increasing the official intervention for alleviation of poverty and unemployment;
thus, he claimed, the followers of the capitalist system after blun-
dering through a maze of economic depressions reached the
same conclusions which Islam had posited 1300 years ago.

Zia's "Islamization" Program

We can divide President Zia's Islamization programme into three
categories: (1) punitive measures, (2) reconstruction of economic
system, and (3) general Islamization of morals, education and science. First, in February 1979, the president announced the
Hadood Ordinance which contained severe punishments for
theft, adultery and drinking, such as the amputation of hands,
stoning and flogging. Subsequently, in a unique decision of the
Shariat Court, stoning for adultery was announced to be against
Islam. The Sharia Courts were barred from reviewing the Martial Law ordinances, family law and fiscal law. The final authority in appointing the members of these courts and giving assent
to their decisions continued to be in the hands of the president.
. . . The Hadood Ordinance of 1979 attracted strong criticism
from the domestic and foreign media. As against the widespread
condemnation of its punitive measures by world opinion, the
negative reaction at home focused on provisions directly affecting women in cases of adultery. Indeed, rape was hardly distin-
guishable from adultery as far as the punishment for a woman was
concerned.

> As the law stands, it protects rapists, prevents women
> from testifying and confuses the issue of rape with
> adultery. As a result, a woman who registers a case of
> rape can by her own admission be prosecuted for adul-
> tery while the rapist goes free for lack of evidence.

That is what happened in the case of an 18-year-old blind

girl, Safia Bibi, whose father registered a case of rape leading to pregnancy against her employers, father and son, who were finally acquitted while she herself was sentenced to 15 lashes in public, 3 years imprisonment and fine. In view of the international embarrassment faced by the government, the Federal Sharia Court had the case transferred to itself for review and rescinded the judgement. While a woman could be thus medically examined following rape, or get pregnant, a man could not be found guilty, 'for what *salah* [God-fearing] Muslim men would stand by and let a women be raped'. The Ordinance, however, continued to be in existence in the face of strong protest from various human rights groups, especially the women's organisations. Educated women from urban centres were alerted to the growing threat to their position vis-a-vis men represented by various cases tried under the Hadood Ordinance and the demand for the repeal of the Muslim Family Laws Ordinance [of] 1961 [which gave women basic legal protection, including the right to divorce, support, and inheritance] initiated by religious circles. It was against the background of this trend of legally reducing women's status as well as the overall conservative atmosphere sponsored by the regime that women's action groups started to mobilize public opinion.

On 26 April 1984, President Zia issued Ordinance No. 20, which held liable to punishment by imprisonment for up to three years and by fine, any Qadiani [an Islamic sect who broke away from the Ahmadis, a Muslim sect, in 1914] who 'refers to or names, or calls, his place of worship as "Masjid", 'recites Azanas used by the Muslims', or 'directly or indirectly, passes himself as a Muslim or calls, or refers to, his faith as Islam'. There followed international condemnation of the Ordinance by various human rights groups. As to the enquiry of the Subcommittee on Human Rights and International Organisations of the U.S. House of Representatives into this matter, with its implications for the U.S. aid to Pakistan, the Reagan administration interpreted the Ordinance as an attempt to defuse the immediate threat of violence by anti-Ahmadi[1] elements. Later, the Sub-Commission on Prevention of Discrimination and Projection of Minorities of the United Nations Commission on Human

1. Ahmadis are an Islamic sect with beliefs considered heretical by some orthodox Muslims.

Rights passed a resolution in August 1985 demanding repeal of the Ordinance. On 17 July 1986, the U.S. House of Representatives passed a resolution demanding that the Government of Pakistan should repeal the Ordinance, that it should stop persecution of and discrimination against Ahmadis, and that it should restore internationally recognised human rights. A UN consultative body, the Human Rights Advocates, observed that this ordinance '*prima facie* contravenes international law standards of freedom of religion, the right to non-discrimination'. Meanwhile, cases of attacking Ahmadis' places of worship continued to make headlines in Pakistan. In one instance, the Ahmadiya *Baitul Hamd* in Quetta was attacked by an angry crowd mobilized by ulema, which led to its take-over by the district authorities, and the arrest of 85 Ahmadis. Two Ahmadis were killed in Sukhur on 11 May 1986, bringing to 6 the number of Ahmadis killed since the promulgation of the presidential ordinance. At the same time, the liberal sections of the intelligentsia and politically active groups condemned such activities and demanded the withdrawal of the Ordinance. It is clear from these observations that President Zia's promulgation of Islam's punitive measures led to a heated controversy both at the national and international levels. The initial impetus for these policies seems to have come from political considerations relating to the crisis of legitimacy. The regime took a calculated risk of alienating world opinion and deflecting Pakistan's image as a modern nation, in order to build up a constituency at home. The multiplication of judicial systems seemed to dilute the institutional profundity and spread confusion. Among the expected gains of the regime were perhaps the postponement of the pressing need to resolve the legitimacy crisis, the relatively free exercise of the government's authority and the integration of Pakistan into the Islamic world in terms of co-operation on such issues as Palestine, Afghanistan and the projection of Islam in general.

Islam and the Economy

The second major area of Islamic legislation related to economic affairs. . . . The Martial Law government . . . levied zakat [taxes] on all bank accounts except for current accounts at the rate of 2.5%. There was to be one zakat fund at each village/locality and province, and one in the Centre; after deducting 25%, the rest of the collected fund was to be spent on deserving candidates from amongst the poor; a provincial zakat council under a High Court judge or an equally qualified person would be run by the chief administrator; the Central Zakat Council would be formed on similar lines; Zakat collections were to be audited annually and it was to be levied in addition to income tax. . . .

Unlike zakat and ushr [agricultural tax], which were operated on an individual basis, interest free banking involved an incremental change in institutional practices. First, a few public corporations such as the House Building Finance Corporation and the Investment Corporation of Pakistan started interest free operations. Then small farmers were issued interest free loans. The government promulgated the Modarba Companies and Modarba (Floatations and Control) Ordinance 1980, whereby *Modarba* as a business partnership scheme based on participation of modarba certificate holders was to raise risk capital on the basis of profit and loss sharing. Participation Term Certificates (PTC) were issued for a fixed period not exceeding ten years for financing the medium and long term requirements of the corporate sector; profits out of the PTC were to be treated as a deductible expense for income tax purposes. However, out of the $8–10 billion which were deposited on an interest free profit and loss basis, $3–4 billion reportedly lay unused. In view of the procedure of selling goods back to their clients, thus indicating that a transaction had taken place, the whole exercise was criticized as a cosmetic measure. The opinion on the left saw in interest free banking a futile effort to legitimize capitalism with a change of nomenclature, and found the pre-Quranic concept of modarba as being implemented to maximize profits under that system. Even the protagonists of Islamic economics feared that the replacement of interest by profit sharing system might increase the level of exploitation of the poor by the rich, in the absence of a policy of regulating profits, which would then make it a subterfuge for reinstating capitalism in the name of Islam.

Religion, Science, and Public Behavior

The third aspect of Islamization includes a plethora of suggestions flowing from institutes and commissions sponsored by the government, individuals seeking to develop Islamic models of various branches of knowledge as well as presidential orders relating to specific modes of behaviour. As a general policy, the government exercised its patronage in favour of the explicitly conservative elements in the educational institutions and information infrastructure. President Zia deplored the existing dichotomy between science and religion, and asked scholars to work with a spirit of jihad [holy war in defense of the Islamic faith] on the model of Al-Azhar University. Some scientists seeking the regime's patronage produced exotic theories under the rubrics of Islamic science. For example, they claimed that heaven is running away from the the earth at a speed of one centimeter per second less than the speed of light; that the seven heavens are like quantum levels of an atom; and that the services of *jinns* (genies) as fiery beings, commanding vast energy, can be utilized to offset the energy crisis of Pakistan. . . . Such views were consid-

PAKISTANI WOMEN'S MOVEMENT

Pakistan's women's movement arose principally in response to Zia's "Islamization" program, which was highly discriminatory against women. Anita M. Weiss, American professor of international studies, describes the role and activities of the Women's Action Forum, a group formed by urban women to protect their rights, in the following extract from Pakistan: A Country Study, *edited by Peter R. Blood.*

The Women's Action Forum was formed in 1981 to respond to the implementation of the [Islamic] penal code [under General Zia,] and to strengthen women's position in society generally. The women in the forum, most of whom came from elite families, perceived that many of the laws proposed by the Zia government were discriminatory and would compromise their civil status. In Karachi, Lahore, and Islamabad the group agreed on collective leadership and formulated policy statements and engaged in political action to safeguard women's legal position.

The Women's Action Forum has played a central role in heightening the controversy regarding various interpretations of Islamic law and its role in a modern state, and in publiciz-

ered irrational by the 'modern' scientists who felt insecure with the prospects of government patronage flowing in that direction.

Islamization of science had its parallel in the realm of social sciences, such as Islamic economics and Islamic anthropology. Attempts were made to develop an Islamic theory of knowledge. According to this approach, Islam sees man as essentially an ethical being required to use his judgement to differentiate between good and evil, which should thus be the basis of all social science. It was suggested that Islam stands for social justice, not in terms of equality or collective good, but on an ethical and moral basis. These developments influenced the educational system in as much as a process of ideologisation of social sciences was set in motion. The new approach led to the task of re-writing the his-

ing ways in which women can play a more active role in politics. Its members led public protests in the mid-1980s against the promulgation of the Law of Evidence. Although the final version was substantially modified, the Women's Action Forum objected to the legislation because it gave unequal weight to testimony by men and women in financial cases. Fundamentally, they objected to the assertion that women and men cannot participate as legal equals in economic affairs.

Beginning in August 1986, the Women's Action Forum members and their supporters led a debate over passage of the Shariat Bill, which decreed that all laws in Pakistan should conform to Islamic law. They argued that the law would undermine the principles of justice, democracy, and fundamental rights of citizens, and they pointed out that Islamic law would become identified solely with the conservative interpretation supported by Zia's government. Most activists felt that the Shariat Bill had the potential to negate many of the rights women had won. In May 1991, a compromise version of the Shariat Bill was adopted, but the debate over whether civil law or Islamic law should prevail in the country continues to this day.

Anita M. Weiss, in Peter R. Blood, ed., *Pakistan: A Country Study.* Washington, DC: Government Printing Office, 1995, pp. 3–4.

tory of Pakistan in order to highlight the vanguard role of Islamic ideology and ulema in the struggle for independence. In
view of these observations on the legal, constitutional, economic,
educational and cultural aspects of Islamization under the Martial Law regime, we can now look at the underlying forces directing the ideological currents in a variety of fields. In the following pages, we plan to bring out the essentially political nature
of these forces.

Politics of Islam

Each successive Pakistani government saw it to its advantage to
invoke the Islamic nature of Pakistan as a residual source of legitimacy. An Islamic stance was projected to counter a wide range
of political developments such as a perceived communist influence from the North, the ethnic nationalisms of provinces other
than Punjab, the widely perceived threat from 'Hindu' India and
the constant public pressure for holding elections and establishing a representative government in the country. . . . The fall of
[Zulfikar Ali Bhutto's] PPP [Pakistan People's Party] regime in
1977 'testified' to the tremendous mobilizing capacity of Islam.
General Zia considered it almost mandatory to assume a public
profile conforming to religious injunctions. Indeed, in view of
repeated postponements of elections and arbitrary constitutional
amendments which cost it in terms of 'political credibility', the
Martial Law government tried to enhance its 'religious credibility' through a comprehensive programme of Islamization. It was
hoped that an earnest effort in this regard would expand the
regime's support base. . . .

A more tangible benefit could perhaps accrue from denying
legitimacy to parliamentary politics, which was after all based on
the Western and therefore non-Islamic model. The 1983 Ansari
Commission[2] Report brought out its recommendations couched
in these terms. The Report recommended that the head of state
should also be the head of government, which was a clear indi-
cator of the presidential system. Following the recommendations
of the Council of Islamic Ideology, it observed that elections on
a party basis were against Quran and Sunna. . . . The president's
own vision of an Islamic order was close to the Commission's

2. Headed by Islamic religious leader Mavlana Zafar Ahmed Ansari, the commission
made recommendations to General Zia on the political directives of Islamic laws.

Report. [Political scientist] Lawrence Ziring sees the whole process of Islamization in terms of a transition from an Islamic republic, with its secular features enshrined in the three constitutions of 1956, 1962 and 1973 to an Islamic state as portrayal of authoritarian government. . . .

Manipulation of Islamic Principles

It is clear that Islam operated as a manifestation of the power struggle in order to decide who would rule, rather than as a determining factor in political change. Islam is not a monolithic belief system. Instead, there is a variety of notions within its conceptual framework, which are available for political uses by leaders. The structure of the state finally lends a meaning to such activities. On the one hand, it is an institutional framework barring the entry of the non-bureaucratic elite as far as possible, wielding immense powers and legitimate authority which enabled it to perform its functions. On the other hand, it maintains itself as a complex entity along with its vast network of institutional and group relationships. After the Muslim League ascended to power in post-independence Pakistan on the basis of its victory in the 1946 elections, it tried to close the doors on others seeking entry into the state system, by putting electoral politics in abeyance on various pretexts. As its political support shrank in the following years, it increasingly projected Islamic ideology as an alternative source of legitimacy. Under the Ayub system, this process was taken further. Public representatives at the local level were subordinated to bureaucratic tutelage under the Basic Democracies, while legislatures at the national and provincial levels became redundant in the face of the patriarchal rule of the president. During the anti-Ayub movement and the subsequent election campaign of the PPP, the new ideological formulation of Islamic Socialism became the rallying ground for political participation. After it rose to power, however, the PPP adopted ways and means to bar the political opposition from making a serious bid for power. It used public meetings, legal suits and constitutional amendments to contain the opposition. . . . It was, however, the relatively open-ended and less specifically defined Nizam-e-Mustafa which carried the day, essentially because it was backed and financed by big business and the middle class in general, which sought entry into the system. The Zia regime, in turn, sought to close the doors on public representatives. It borrowed the 'Islamic' idiom from the PNA [Pakistan National Alliance, a coalition of right-wing Islamic parties] movement and used it both to project the 'un-Islamic' character, of [Bhutto's] PPP and to make it the basis of its own legitimacy. Politics of Islamization can thus be considered a function of entry into, and the subsequent closing of, the administrative state in Pakistan.

Pakistan's Military Presidents: A Comparative Analysis

By Shahid Javed Burki

In the following extract, Shahid Javed Burki compares the first three military rulers in Pakistan, contrasting the well-defined, but unsuccessful, "basic democracies" policies of Ayub Khan (1958–1969) with the uncertainty and rigidity of Yahya Khan's (1969–1971) term leading to the 1971 war. Burki elaborates on the series of creative experiments conducted by Zia-ul-Haq (1977–1988) designed to legitimize his authority. Shahid Javed Burki is a Rhodes scholar who has written many books on Pakistan, including Pakistan: Fifty Years of Nationhood, *from which the following piece has been extracted.*

Pakistan's three military presidents, General (later Field Marshal) Ayub Khan (1958–1969), General Yahya Khan (1969–1971), and General Zia ul-Haq (1977–1988), attempted to find a workable solution for Pakistan's political problems. Their approaches differed considerably. Ayub had well-developed ideas about the type of political system that could be made to work in Pakistan: He was convinced that Western political ideas could not take root in the political soil of Pakistan. He experimented with his system of Basic Democracies in which the people were allowed only a limited amount of participation. But the system did not work, and his willingness to tinker with what he had created only encouraged his political opposition to ask for more changes. Ultimately, they sought the resurrection of the par-

Shahid Javed Burki, *Pakistan: Fifty Years of Nationhood.* Boulder, CO: Westview Press, 1999.

liamentary system that Ayub Khan had dispensed with in 1958. But this outcome was not acceptable to the armed forces and their partners in the powerful civil bureaucracy. They responded with another coup d'état, the second in the series.

General Yahya Khan, unlike his predecessor, became a political leader by accident, inasmuch as he happened to be commander in chief of the armed forces at the time of the collapse of Ayub Khan's government. Since the aim of the anti-Ayub movement was the resignation of the president, it must have been clear to the movement's leaders that the military would not accept a constitutional transfer of power in case the president agreed to resign. If the provisions regarding succession in the constitution of 1962 had been followed, the speaker of the National Assembly would have succeeded the president in case of the president's resignation. In 1962, Abdul Jabbar Khan—a Bengali politician of little significance—was the speaker. The politicians seemed quite content with another martial law, which is why they called off the movement the moment that martial law was declared. It would appear that General Yahya Khan's decision to put the country under martial law had little to do with personal ambition; any other general in his position would probably have behaved in much the same way.

Yahya Khan came into office without any political program. His first impulse was to entirely dismantle the system erected by Ayub Khan; after all, that was the demand of the politicians. His second impulse was to resist with all his might the workings of the political dynamic released by his earlier actions. Yahya Khan went from one crisis to another, becoming more and more inflexible along the way. By the time he left the presidency, Pakistan was in political shambles, its "eastern wing" having finally left the union.

Zulfikar Ali Bhutto, Yahya Khan's successor, was a civilian politician who moved into the President's House in Rawalpindi on the basis of an unambiguous mandate that he had earned from the people in the election of 1970. During the Bhutto years, Pakistan's political development moved in a direction opposite to the one taken during the Ayub period. Ayub Khan, having used the military to assume power, tried very hard to gain legitimacy. Bhutto was able to displace the military because he had been elected by the people, but his particular way of managing the political system lost him all his legitimacy. By the spring of 1977,

Bhutto had also lost the support of a large part of his original constituency and had totally alienated his opposition. The result was a political movement even more violent than the one that had dislodged Ayub Khan eight years earlier. As had happened before, the commander of the armed forces stepped in to remove a discredited system and an unpopular politician. General Zia ul-Haq's coup d'état—much like those of General Ayub Khan and General Yahya Khan—was seen then not as the product of personal ambition but as a political imperative. Although General Zia was politically as ill-prepared as General Yahya had been, he was willing to experiment and innovate. Like Yahya Khan, he went from one political crisis to another, but, unlike his predecessor, he managed not to be overwhelmed by them.

Zia's Evolving Strategies

General Zia ul-Haq's approach to Pakistan's political problem was much different from those of his two military predecessors. Ayub Khan had behaved like a master architect with a carefully worked out design before the first shovel of political dirt was removed from the ground. In 1954, he worked out the system that was put into effect between 1958 and 1962. When the ground began to shake under the structure, General Ayub's approach was to strengthen what he thought were its weak points. But the structure continued to crack; it was wobbling by the time General Yahya Khan moved in to take command of it. General Khan decided to pull it down altogether without any idea as to what could be erected in its place. Within a few weeks of assuming control, he found himself without a political shelter. It was Yahya Khan's civilian successor, Zulfikar Ali Bhutto, who took up the task of putting up another political structure in the place that had been left devastated by General Yahya Khan.

Metaphorically speaking, General Zia ul-Haq did not immediately move into the house his civilian predecessor, Prime Minister Zulfikar Ali Bhutto, had built. Instead, he was content to stay in the Army House, even after assuming the presidency many months after the coup d'état of July 5, 1977. During his sojourn in the Army House, he continued to remodel the structure he had inherited from Bhutto. By the time he had inducted civilians back into the government, Pakistan had acquired a political system that was considerably different from the one Bhutto had fashioned in 1973. The changes were brought in gradually and involved a great deal of experimentation. But the structure that finally emerged in the summer of 1985 in which the politicians were prepared to accept a political role for the military might survive longer than any of those Pakistan has tried during the course of its turbulent political history.

There are four discernible periods in the political maturation of Pakistan's third military president. The first ranged from 1977 to 1979, during which time the objective seems to have been to use existing political institutions to transfer power to civilian leadership. The process was complicated by the remarkable resilience exhibited by Zulfikar Ali Bhutto and the persistence of the political phenomenon that can only be described as Bhuttoism. To deal with this problem, General Zia adopted a risky solution, but one that, in his mind, was really the only viable one: physical elimination of Zulfikar Ali Bhutto.

The second period started after Bhutto's execution in April 1979 and lasted until the summer of 1983, during which time Zia, not unlike Ayub Khan before him, began to seek ways to legitimize his military government. He tried a number of methods, including incorporation of some of the anti-Bhutto forces in a civilian-cum-military government; rule by diktat, with the civilian bureaucracy playing the role of a surrogate political party; Islamization of the economy and the society in the belief that faith would provide the glue to hold together a country that had been created on the basis of religion in the first place; a limited amount of popular participation through the establishment of a system—or, rather, four systems, one for each of the four provinces—of local government; and, finally, an emphasis on improving economic management, as if to suggest that the legitimate purpose of the government in a developing nation is not necessarily to administer in accordance with the wishes of the people (no matter how these wishes are articulated) but to improve the people's economic well-being.

Problems and Pitfalls

Experience proved all of these methods to be seriously flawed. The anti-Bhutto forces, especially those that were willing to work with the government, represented a small section of the population. The close proximity of a few politicians to the military served only to diminish their appeal—a fact that weighed heavily in the elections of 1985, when a number of government supporters failed to win seats in the national legislature. The resurrection of the military-civilian bureaucratic model pursued by Ayub Khan during the first half of his tenure (1958–1962) also proved to be a nonviable solution, even though the military in the late 1970s was much more broad-based in its social composition than it had been during that early period. Islamization was a move that proved popular with some segments of the society, but these segments would have supported the military anyway. Indeed, the national and provincial elections of February 1985 demonstrated that the government's relentless drive toward Islamization only caused the Islamic parties to fare even less well than they had in the previous elections. The establishment of local governments was a move in the right direction but only a small step toward the creation of a *reasonably* representative form of government. Economic development, especially when it produced benefits for all segments of the population (as it did during much of Zia ul-Haq's political stewardship), was again welcome to the people. As Ayub Khan was to discover after his own very successful experiment with economic development, however, an increase in GDP [Gross Domestic Product] satisfies the people but does not substitute for political development. An average rate of growth of more than 7 percent per annum from 1958 to 1966 did indeed keep people reasonably satisfied; but they became restive when the growth rate dropped below 5 percent in the 1966–1969 period. A remarkable rate of economic growth was also experienced during the first six years of the Zia presidency, but in the seventh and eighth years the economy began to falter. It was either by design—following a lesson learned from history—or purely by chance that Zia began to civilianize his regime during this period.

An Astute Politician

The fact that General Zia ul-Haq did not persevere with any of these indirect methods for gaining political legitimacy for his regime attests to his astuteness as a politician. From 1982 on, his cabinet had mostly military officers, retired civil servants, and technocrats. The few politicians who remained were included not so much to bring legitimacy as to ensure that the regime did not lose total contact with the established political groups. The government continued its efforts to evolve a viable system of local government and to Islamize the economy, but, once again, the motives for doing all this were not necessarily political.

The lesson that General Zia learned from these experiments was that he had to organize a system in which people could directly participate in order to ensure a degree of political tranquility. Indeed, the launching of the Movement for the Restoration of Democracy in 1981 had sent a strong signal to the president that the political opposition now considered itself strong enough to challenge him directly. The movement's initial success, particularly in the province of Sindh, appears to have convinced the president and his military colleagues that they had to seek a political solution to Pakistan's persistent constitutional problems.

The third phase in Zia's political evolution began with the president's speech of August 12, 1983, in which he presented a blueprint for the restoration of constitutional government. This blueprint was very rough in that the only item spelled out clearly was that the president expected the process to be completed by March 23, 1985—namely, the forty-fifth anniversary of the adoption by the Muslim League of the "Lahore Resolution" asking for the establishment of a separate homeland for the Muslims of British India. During this period General Zia ul-Haq, by taking a number of steps (many of which were not contemplated in advance), was to bring Pakistan to the threshold of another constitutional experiment. The fourth phase began in the summer of 1987 when Zia realized that a parliamentary system could not accommodate a strong president. His dismissal of [Prime Minster Mohammad Khan] Junejo on May 29, 1988, was the first step toward the establishment of a presidential form of government, which he would have introduced had he lived.

THE HISTORY OF NATIONS
Chapter 4

Democracy, Disillusionment, and Return of Military Rule

New Hope for Democracy

By Benazir Bhutto

Groomed by her father, former prime minister Zulfikar Ali Bhutto, for a political career, Benazir Bhutto led the Pakistan People's Party (PPP) to victory in the 1988 election following the sudden death of General Zia-ul-Haq. In the following extract from her autobiography, Daughter of Destiny *(1989), Benazir Bhutto describes the events leading up to the November 1988 election in Pakistan; her distrust of General Zia, her father's executioner; the challenge of campaigning while pregnant with her first child; and Zia's delaying tactics in response to her evident popularity. The extract concludes days before Zia's sudden death in a plane crash on August 17, 1988.*

On May 29, 1988, General Zia abruptly dissolved Parliament, dismissed his own handpicked Prime Minister, and called for elections. I was in a meeting at 70 Clifton [Pakistan People's Party headquarters] with party members from Larkana when the startling message was passed to me. "You must be mistaken," I said to the party official who had sent in the note. "General Zia avoids elections. He doesn't hold them." Even when he assured me that Zia had just made the announcement on radio and television, I still couldn't believe it. "You must have confused the call for elections with some other country," I said.

The congratulatory phone calls flooding into 70 Clifton and the clamoring of reporters at the gate confirmed Zia's totally unexpected move. Many were suspicious of the timing. Four days before, a Karachi newspaper had announced I was to become a mother. "I told you if you started a family Zia would hold elections," Samiya [friend and confidante] said triumphantly. "He thinks you won't be able to campaign." I didn't know whether Zia's announcement was influenced by my condition, but it did follow the confirmation that I was expecting. Though [her hus-band] Asif and I had wanted to wait before starting a family, we had been delighted with the unexpected news. Now with Zia's melodramatic announcement, 1988 promised to be a year for un-expected happenings all around.

No one had known of Zia's intentions beforehand, including Prime Minister Junejo, who had just returned from a trip to the Far East and had held a press conference at 6 P.M. An hour later, one of his aides who had heard Zia's broadcast informed Junejo that he was fired. Zia gave four reasons for the dissolution of the government: the failure of Junejo's administration to introduce Islamic law quickly enough; the mishandling of the investigation into the devastating Ojri munitions depot explosion in April which had launched missiles and bombs into the civilian popu-lation; corruption in the administration; and the breakdown of law and order throughout the country.

Though I had little trust with Junejo, I felt sorry for him as he was dismissed so peremptorily. Junejo had served Zia well, rubber-stamping Zia's constitution, indemnifying all actions of Martial Law, confirming Zia as President and Chief of Army Staff until 1990. But I quickly found that there was no echo of sympathy for Junejo. "When you lie with dogs, you get bitten," some people said, while others suggested that Junejo's epitaph should read: "The man who tumbled into history and tumbled out of it."

Suspicious of Zia's Motive

Regardless, the mood throughout the country was ebullient. Zia's own constitution called for elections within ninety days of the dissolution of the government, and to many it seemed that vic-tory was within reach. "No one can stop the PPP now," said one supporter after another. I tried, unsuccessfully, to plead caution. Though publicly I issued a conditional positive response to the promise of elections—"If fair, free and impartial party-based elections are held within ninety days, we will welcome it"—pri-vately I had my doubts.

Free, fair elections meant the return of the PPP and the Bhuttos. Zia was already on record as saying he would "not re-turn power to those he had taken it from." If he found it diffi-cult to coexist with Mr. Junejo, his own creation, how could he accept as Prime Minister the daughter of the man he had ordered executed? "Zia hasn't dismissed Junejo to permit the PPP to capture Parliament," I said, trying to temper the enthusiasm of our exultant supporters. Zia's subsequent actions were to confirm my suspicions.

On June 15th, Zia announced the installation of *Shariah*, or Islamic law, as the supreme law of the land. Because he did not define what it was or was not in his television address, nobody was sure what it meant. Would currency notes with representations of Mohammad Ali Jinnah, the founder of Pakistan, be withdrawn because some Islamic scholars consider the portrayal of the human face un-Islamic? Would government bonds, which carry a fixed rate of interest, be declared usurious? What it boiled down to was that any citizen could now challenge an existing law before the High Courts as "un-Islamic." If the court found the law to be contrary to Islam, the judges could strike it down. But why had Zia waited until 1988 to implement *Shariah*?

Many thought that the timing of Zia's latest exploitation of Islam was directed at me. The Urdu press was speculating that he could use the interpretation of the law by Islamic bigots to try to prevent me, a woman, from standing for election. Or perhaps he would try to use it after the elections to try to disqualify me as the leader of the victorious party in the National Assembly. I doubted that he would succeed. The Constitution of 1973, approved by the country's religious parties, declared women eligible to become heads of government. So did Zia's own Constitution of 1985.

More than ever we doubted that the elections would be fair and impartial. In spite of Zia's declared intention to announce an election date after Islamic law was installed, no date was announced. Nor did we know whether political parties would be allowed to field candidates. Zia was up to his old tricks to avoid meeting the PPP at the polls. But this time we had ammunition of our own.

Supreme Court Challenge

In February we had gone to the Supreme Court to challenge Zia's 1985 Voter's Registration clause, which required all political parties to register with the regime. Under Zia's rules, all political parties that wished to take part in elections had to submit their accounts as well as their list of officeholders to the administration's chosen Election Commissioner. Armed with that information, the Election Commissioner could then disallow participation in elections of any political party on such vague grounds as the party's being against the ideology of Islam, regardless of the fact that the "ideology" was not defined. Just as incredibly, the Commissioner could also preclude the office bearers from standing for election for fourteen years and even impose seven-year jail sentences!

Blatantly designed to keep the PPP out of the electoral field, the law violated not only the fundamental right of freedom of association, but gave Zia's nominee the right to recognize which parties could participate and which could not. Fortunately for us, Mr. Yahya Bakhtiar, the former Attorney General of Pakistan, who had headed my father's appeal team, consented to argue the case before the Supreme Court. Eleven judges heard the case, the largest bench ever convened in the court's history. The unanimous decision, handed down on June 20, 1988, constituted a moral and legal victory for the people of Pakistan. Zia's registration clause was struck down as "void in its entirety."

"Parliamentary government is a government of the party and a party government is a vital principle of a representative government," the Chief Justice wrote in his statement. ". . . At a minimum an election provides a legal means for validating a claim to govern. It is a party system that converts the results of a parliamentary election into a government." Agreeing with the Chief Justice, another Supreme Court judge observed: "Persons elected to the legislature in their personal capacities have hardly any importance. They just toss around on the political scene, rudderless and without a destination. It is only when they band themselves into a group as a party that they become a force exercising some influence by their activities. Only as members of a political party and not as individual members of the legislature can they achieve their objectives."

The intent of the Supreme Court in striking down Zia's registration clause was clear: no party, registered or unregistered, could be prevented from participating in elections. The court's verdict was also clear. Every citizen had the fundamental right to participate in elections through a political party of his or her choice. Elections had to be held on the basis of political parties. There was no other constitutional option, even under Zia's own constitution. But Zia, we all knew, was not one to hold himself accountable to the laws of Pakistan.

Zia Tries to Make a Deal

I was touring the country, traveling from Larkana to an enthusiastic welcome in Jacobabad, then on to Nawabshah, where former members of the Muslim League joined ranks with the PPP. Momentum was building in favor of the PPP, starting a bandwagon effect. When I returned to Karachi, more Muslim League parliamentarians joined us. Potential candidates were all seeking the heavy party support that the PPP's symbol on the ballot would bring.

There was increasing evidence that Zia's rash move was backfiring. Reports were coming in to us that Zia, who had always been known to be cool and calm, was losing his composure. "General Zia is acting in a very erratic and unstable fashion," one political analyst reported to me. A retired army officer told me, "Zia has always taken calculated risks but now he's acting like a gambler. There is no logic to his actions."

Zia's sense of insecurity must have deepened when, in spite of the searing heat and the summer rains, the numbers of people attending PPP public meetings throughout the country swelled to many thousands. In Lahore, in July, the press compared the crowd that came to hear me speak to the multitudes that had welcomed me home from exile in 1986. Zia's nerves cracked. At a reception that followed, a PPP loyalist conveyed a message to me from someone close to Zia. "General Zia is said to be depressed, demoralized, and confused," he said. "He is clutching at straws and is not sure what road to follow. My contact says he advised Zia to hold the elections, accept the verdict of the people, and then to leave the country. The contact wants to know your response."

This approach from Zia, later confirmed by others, was an effort to make a deal with the PPP. The details, which soon followed, proposed a trade-off: Zia would hold elections in return for immunity from any legal action against him and his family. Certain countries would act as guarantors.

I refused. Not only did I doubt the sincerity of his offer, but I didn't see the rationale in it. "Zia is trying to tarnish my image by seeking a deal," I told the emissary. "Besides, I don't understand what he is afraid of. If he does hold elections, what cause would there be for anger and therefore the need for guarantors of his safety? The people are only going to be angry if he does not hold elections." The discussion ended there, and there was no follow-up. I continued to tour the country.

By the grace of God, I felt fit and filled with energy. "I didn't know you were really having a baby," a woman doctor said to me while I was on the road. "We all thought it was a political trick to get Zia to hold elections." I was surprised to hear that many shared the skepticism all over the country. "People keep asking me how you can keep up such a hectic travel schedule if you're really in the family way," Fakhri [Bhutto's aide] said to me in exasperation. But there was too much at stake to rest. If Zia upheld his own constitution, elections would be held by the end of August.

Zia's Tactics

At a breakfast meeting with the Australian ambassador at 70 Clifton on July 20th, another note was handed to me. The elections, Zia had just announced, were to be held on November 16th. While he admitted that the Constitution provided that elections should have been held within ninety days of the dissolution of the National Assembly, Zia said he was delaying the date because of the coming monsoons, the Muslim month of mourning (Muharram), and the month of pilgrimage (the Haj). The tension that develops during Muharram, Zia maintained, would make elections impossible. Ninety thousand Pakistani pilgrims on Haj would be deprived of their right to vote if the elections were held during the constitutional period. The rains had already caused flooding in many parts of the country. I took his excuses with a grain of salt. His real reasons, I felt, had more to do with my physical condition. Zia could not afford to have me on the campaign trail.

But at least a date had been set, and we felt a measure of relief. We still had no assurance that Zia wouldn't cancel the elections, or as to whether he would hold the elections on a party or nonparty basis. The signs, however, pointed to panic in the Zia camp. The Muslim League had disintegrated following Zia's abrupt dismissal in May of Junejo and the National Assembly. He had to woo back the very ministers he had accused of being corrupt and inept, including his own Prime Minister, if he were to reunite the party against the PPP challenge. . . .

Zia's fear of the PPP was demonstrated clearly on July 21st. Claiming that party-based elections violated the spirit of Islam (though he had included them in his own 1985 Constitution), Zia announced that the polls would be held on a nonparty basis and the candidates would not be allowed to have political party symbols on the ballot. Once again, the vast majority of the population would be unable to identify those they wished to vote for. Instead, Zia's system would promote influential individuals at the cost of dedicated political cadres who could only win through party support.

Once more Zia had flouted the Constitution as well as the sentiments of the highest court in the land. A newspaper report on July 31st clarified his decision. Shortly before his latest announcement, Zia had summoned to Islamabad the provincial secretaries from all four provinces as well as other senior officials to discuss the polls. Because of the infighting in the Muslim League, the paper reported, the leaders from Baluchistan, Sindh, Punjab and the Northwest Frontier Province all felt that the PPP would have little difficulty in sweeping the polls. The divided party, the leader of the NWFP reportedly said, "will make it comfortable for Ms. Benazir Bhutto to earn enough seats to emerge as the single majority group." Three days later, Zia announced the nonparty elections.

Once again we turned to the courts. We filed a petition before the Supreme Court in early August challenging the constitutionality of Zia's partyless elections. But would a victory at the Supreme Court really help us, considering that Zia had held the court's earlier judgment in contempt? As a dictator, Zia held vast powers. Even if the Supreme Court decided in our favor, Zia could simply issue a decree changing the Parties Act, or declare a state of emergency, thereby nullifying the decision. He was thought to be setting the stage for the latter already. On August 4th, the eve of the Muslim month of mourning, a Shiite leader was shot dead in Peshawar. In the opposition we speculated whether the regime, hoping to create the strife necessary for a declaration of emergency, was behind the assassination.

As further protection for a Zia win, it was also being widely rumored that new election laws were on the anvil whereby successful candidates could be disqualified on the pretext of having any support from political parties. Sources told us that the law would be enacted during the first week of October, leaving Zia's opposition too short a time to challenge the law in court before the elections. It was clear that the dictator had every intention of manipulating the election results through partyless polls, intimidation, and stacked election laws.

The Conscience of the Country

As we approached the November elections, Pakistan hovered at the crossroads of democracy and continued dictatorship. The people of Pakistan were crying out for self-determination. Their voice was the Pakistan People's Party. And Zia knew it. After eleven and a half years, he was still unable to hold free and impartial elections for fear that the PPP would sweep them.

Facing the probability of partyless elections, we needed every solid and well-known candidate possible. I was hopeful that my mother would return to Pakistan to stand for a seat and that even my sister Sanam might be persuaded to run. Regardless of the odds, the PPP was determined to challenge Zia through peaceful democratic means, using the legal framework that is the backbone of any civilized country. Bludgeoning the population into acquiescence with guns and tear gas might win capitulation and resignation, but not the soul. Zia knew he had never been able to win the hearts or the support of the people. Instead he had ruled by terror and threat.

Just as a flower rarely blooms in the desert, so political parties cannot flourish in a dictatorship. That the political parties managed to survive and flourish for eleven years despite the draconian measures taken against them was a tribute to those who gave their lives for democracy, and to the people of Pakistan who realized that their rights could be restored and protected only if they banded together in a national party. We were, and are, the conscience of the country, the future and the hope. Our day, I know, will come.

Karachi,
August, 1988

The Uncertain Transition to Democracy Under Bhutto and Sharif

BY SAEED SHAFQAT

In the following extract, Saeed Shafqat describes Pakistan's experience in the transition to democracy in the late 1980s and 1990s under Benazir Bhutto and Nawaz Sharif. He says the country's democratization process has been hampered by powerful interest groups promoted under recurring military regimes who have violated democratic principles and practices; the inexperience of and dissension among the political elite; the manipulation of Islam for political purposes that encouraged religious intolerance and sectional cleavages; and the conflict among ethnic groups for a greater share of economic resources.

Saeed Shafqat is a political scientist who has taught for more than twenty years in major universities in Lahore, Pakistan. The following extract is an updated version of his paper, "Transition to Democracy: An Uncertain Path," presented at a conference on political development and democracy in Pakistan held at Columbia University in 1992.

In 1985, the Martial Law regime (1977 to 1985) of General Ziaul Haq, under increasing pressure from the opposition, conceded to allow limited political participation. The military did not disengage itself from politics, it only encouraged controlled and guided political participation of those groups who were willing to operate under its hegemony. Thus the 1985 elections provided the framework for sharing power with those groups whom the military had guided into the political arena. It was, however, the accidental death of General Ziaul Haq on 17 August 1988 that

Saeed Shafqat, "Transition to Democracy: An Uncertain Path," *State, Society, and Democratic Change in Pakistan*, edited by Rasul Baksh Rais. Karachi, Pakistan: Oxford University Press, 1997. Copyright © 1997 by Oxford University Press, Pakistan. All rights reserved. Reproduced by permission.

put Pakistan on the path to re-democratization. After his death the military opted to distance itself from politics and decided to hold elections. It broadened the base of electoral competition and encouraged the political participation of those groups, leaders, and political parties which had hitherto been excluded. It reassured the electorate that they would share power with the elected representatives of the people. From a distance it also continued to guide the direction of electoral competition. There were reports to the effect that Inter Services Intelligence (ISI), an integral component of the military, played an important role in unifying political forces that were opposed to the Pakistan People's Party (PPP). Irrespective of these reports, there are political parties and interest groups which were not comfortable with the PPP and had identified themselves with the ideological legacy of General Ziaul Haq. As a result, the Islami Jamhoori Ittehad (IJI) came into being. In the November 1988 elections, the IJI was routed in Sindh and marginalized in Balochistan, although it emerged as the dominant force in Punjab and did well in the NWFP [Northwest Frontier Province]. The PPP returned with a simple majority in the Centre. It did exceedingly well in Sindh, especially in the rural areas. The elections brought to the fore the political and social groups that had been excluded from the political process for over a decade. Thus the 1988 election paved the way for the transition to democracy. The PPP assumed power at the centre, and Benazir Bhutto took office as prime minister of the country on 2 December 1988.

Bhutto's Pragmatism

On assuming power, Benazir Bhutto was quick to concede that on the Pakistani political scene she had not emerged as a 'free agent.' She had to make major compromises to form a government. She showed pragmatism and flexibility when she accepted the office of prime minister. She gave the impression that she understood that politics entails bargaining, compromise, and consensus building, and not confrontation alone. Appeasing the military, she agreed to let General Aslam Beg continue as Chief of the Army Staff (COAS). She agreed to give the military a direct role in foreign policy by retaining Sahibzada Yaqub Ali Khan as foreign minister, who had been elected a Senator on the IJI ticket. She agreed to remain the nominal head of the Defence Committee, not to interfere in the internal affairs of the military, and to retain a large budget for the armed forces. She agreed to let the military handle Pakistan's Afghan policy. She also agreed to support the candidature of Ghulam Ishaq Khan for the presidency. Furthermore, she agreed to abide by the agreements with the IMF [International Monetary Fund] that had been signed, in an ill-conceived manner, by the interim government.

The PPP leadership developed an expectation that the military would in return withdraw from politics and transfer power, while the military elites had accepted Benazir Bhutto's installation in power with reluctance and expected to continue sharing power. These diverging expectations about the nature of each other's role produced tensions in the structure and caused uncertainties along the path of democratization. In addition, the PPP leadership revealed an inadequacy in the political skills needed to translate popular support into effective policy choices. Thus, during its twenty-month rule, the PPP under Benazir Bhutto portrayed the image of an inefficient, indecisive, policy deficient, and administratively inexperienced regime. This image ultimately led to the removal of the regime and the dissolution of the assemblies by the president on 6 August 1990.

Bhutto Assessed

A brief analysis of the PPP's regime (December 1988 to August 1990) reveals that, at the global level, the coalition under Benazir Bhutto continued to align itself with the US. It also secured the re-entry of Pakistan into the British Commonwealth. In general, the world responded favourably towards the democratic transition in Pakistan. As a woman leader, Bhutto did earn global respect. She was skilful in the conduct of foreign relations. In the regional context, the Benazir government took some bold initiatives in pursuing the policy of accommodation towards India. The January 1991 exchange of letters between Pakistan and India agreeing not to strike each other's nuclear facilities emanated during her government, in December 1988.

Internally the regime was faced with a number of challenges. Firstly, the IJI opposition had been consistent in criticizing the Benazir government's policy of accommodation towards India. It propagated the view that Benazir had accepted India's hegemony and alleged that she had compromised Pakistan's national interests. The PPP government was ineffective in dispelling these allegations and criticism. Secondly, during its twenty-month rule the regime's performance in dealing with the nature of centre-province relations was inept to a large extent, if not dismal. In both constitutional and political terms, the Benazir government was unable to deal effectively with the issue. The attitude of the IJI opposition, spearheaded by Nawaz Sharif, was also not conducive to democratic transition, but the stalemate had to be resolved in the larger national interest.

Meanwhile in Sindh, the ethnic issue [conflict between indigenous Sindh groups and "muhajirs," migrants from India] persisted and there was a need to evolve a serious national dialogue on ways and means to promote reconciliation among the various warring communities. Thirdly, the law and order situation continued to deteriorate, which suggested that the effectiveness of governmental authority was weak, and the PPP's struggle to establish its authority proved inefficient. The primary concern of the government was to improve the law and order situation. Fourthly, the PPP was caught between the economic realities and the political imperatives. Unemployment, inflation, and the paralysis of the industrial sector demanded immediate attention. However, the PPP government concentrated on the politics of patronage only. There were reports to the effect that large-scale inductions were being made in the financial, administrative, and public sectors to accommodate PPP sympathizers. This led to further inefficiency and dissatisfaction in these sectors. There grew a public perception that the PPP was perpetuating an environment of corruption. The PPP government failed to devise long-term economic policies to give relief to the common person and to restore the confidence of commercial-industrial groups.

Finally, the PPP as a party in government was faced with a serious predicament. On the one hand it suffered from organizational weakness and ideological incoherence, as a result of which factionalism was brewing in the party. Factionalism was on the increase because, as a government, the PPP was under tremendous pressure to accommodate interests and provide jobs to party affiliates, supporters, and sympathizers; hence the government began to indulge in the politics of patronage, dispensing jobs and rewards to its supporters. On the other hand, the bureaucracy was getting restive, nervous about the revival of the lateral-entry system and large-scale inductions of party affiliates into bureaucratic positions. Scepticism between the PPP government and the bureaucracy was on the rise. It must be recognized that bureaucracies take pride in and thrive on principles of merit, selection, and promo-

PERSISTENT POLITICAL INSTABILITY

In the following extract from Pakistan: Fifty Years of Nationhood, *Pakistan economist Shahid Javed Burki says that
the landed aristocracy's continued domination of Pakistan's political system played a major role in creating political instability in the 1990s.*

The fact that Pakistan had held five general elections in
eight years (1990–1998); had six administrations take office, three of which were caretakers; witnessed the dismissal of three prime ministers on grounds of corruption and incompetence; and continued to turn to the
military for resolving disputes among politicians are some
of the many indicators of persistent political instability.
Clearly, the country had failed to bridge the great divide
that separated the structure of the society from the structure of the political system. The society had evolved
rapidly since independence. A number of new socio-
economic groups had emerged that wanted a place for
themselves in the political structure but were unable to
find one because the political system remained dominated by one socioeconomic group: the landed aristocracy. This group, although powerful, was insecure about
the future. It realized that if the political system were allowed to evolve as envisaged in the constitution, it would
lose a great deal of power to the new groups. The constitution of 1973 had provided for the reapportionment
of seats in the National Assembly on the basis of population distribution, which was to be determined by cen-
suses held every ten years. This was not done; the landed
interests were able to prevent a census from being held
for seventeen years. Thus groups that lacked representation in this system had no choice but to resort to extra-
constitutional means. The pressure that they exerted contributed to the periodic dismissals of prime ministers.

Shahid Javed Burki, *Pakistan: Fifty Years of Nationhood.* Boulder, CO:
Westview Press, 1999, pp. 92–93.

tion, while political parties invariably indulge in dispensing patronage. This is considered part of the political process in most democratic systems. However, in the Pakistani context, merit and patronage were in conflict. The PPP needed to evolve a policy choice to co-opt the bureaucracy, appease its institutional needs, and restore confidence in party government as the protector of its interests. In addition, the regime, without mustering sufficient organizational strength and support, made futile attempts to weaken the military's hegemony. It presumed that power had been *transferred* to a civilian leadership, while the military had conceded only *sharing* of power. This conflict of perceptions and policy choices aggravated the nature of adversarial relations.

Bhutto's Dismissal

These tenuous conditions prompted the president to dissolve the Benazir government, and the national and provincial assemblies, on the charges of corruption, inefficiency, and misuse of state power. The president's action, while legitimate, strengthened the military's hegemony. The removal of the Benazir government paved the way for yet another election in November 1990. Ghulam Mustafa Jatoi, the opposition leader in the national assembly, was installed as the interim prime minister. His appointment and subsequent hostile policies towards Benazir Bhutto and the PPP considerably tarnished the non-partisan image of the interim government. Therefore, when elections were held, the announcement of the results immediately aroused suspicions of rigging. During the elections the IJI launched a particularly nasty character-assassination campaign against the person of Benazir Bhutto. Whether or not the elections were rigged, they demonstrated one point effectively: that Punjab was no longer the bastion of the PPP. The Pakistan Democratic Alliance (PDA) could secure only 44 seats in the national assembly, while the IJI under the leadership of Nawaz Sharif scored a landslide victory, obtaining 106 out of 207 seats in the national assembly.

New Leadership Under Sharif

Nawaz Sharif and his associates (the Elahis of Gujrat, Chaudhry Nisar Ali, Sheikh Rashid, the Saifullahs of NWFP, etc.) were initiated into politics under Ziaul Haq. The military provided them political patronage. In return, they were quick to establish close links with the military-bureaucratic elites and institutions. This new

leadership had an urban social base. Their primary business interests were in trade, commerce, steel, rerolling, real-estate, and some
agricultural farming. They were shrewd enough to recognize how
access to government could enhance their business interests. During the Zia years this new breed of leaders built government connections, entered into inter-family marriages to extend their family ties, and developed into formidable business and political groups.
These new leaders grew and gained strength as collaborators, sharing power with the military. They were not public advocates in the
sense of espousing popular causes or sentiments. They represented
particular interests and advocated and protected these interests.
Thus, in 1990, Nawaz Sharif was installed as prime minister as a
leader and representative of these groups. The IJI ruling coalition
that took power under his leadership had been the primary bene-
ficiary under the Zia regime. This leadership was groomed in the
process of power sharing. Under ordinary circumstances they
would have little difficulty in accepting the military's hegemony.
However, internal contradictions within the ruling coalition, divergent interests of opposition political parties, the spill-over effects of the Gulf War, and the sudden death of Chief of Army
Staff General Asif Nawaz Janjua in January 1993, disrupted this
power-sharing pattern of civil-military relations in the country.
The president and prime minister ran into conflict on the selection of the next COAS; eventually the president had his way, and
appointed General Abdul Waheed Kakar. However, the tension between president and prime minister continued to persist. Finally,
in April 1993, the president dismissed the government of Prime
Minister Nawaz Sharif on charges similar to those that had been
levelled earlier against the government of Benazir Bhutto.

Obstacles in the Transition to Democracy

The foregoing analysis suggests that the uncertain development
of democracy in Pakistan is rooted in the country's peculiar
socio-political conditions, and complicated by divisions among
the elite and by strife. Consequently, a combination of historical
circumstances and the policy choices exercised by the elite has
produced what can be described as obstacles to democratic transformation in Pakistan.

Pakistan's legacy from a history of persistent military rule has
undermined democratic values, norms, and institutions that promote democracy, i.e., political parties, autonomous groups, and a

free and responsible Press. Uneven economic development under the first military regime (that of President Ayub Khan, 1958–69) enhanced state power and weakened democratic norms and institutions; indeed, each military intervention met the needs of particular interest groups at a given moment (under Ayub big business, the military, and the bureaucracy gained strength, while under General Ziaul Haq in the 1980s trader-merchants and religious groups gained momentum). In return, over the long run, these particular interests spawned powerful groups within the government that threatened democratic norms and values and violated the legal and constitutional procedures.

Political Obstacles

(a) There is a general lack of consensus among the elite groups on how to promote the democratic process. Since independence, divisions among the elite have increased, regional and ethnic conflicts have intensified, partisan antagonism is also on the upswing, and in recent years hostilities between rival political families have also risen. Even processes of state building, national consolidation, and industrialization have not fostered elite cohesion. Thus, division among the elite continues to hamper the process of democratic consolidation.

(b) Weak political parties and dynastic, personality-centric parties have either developed or grown as opposition movements to the government. Consequently, the political parties have a mobilization character, but find it difficult to act as channels of interest representation. Most political parties are non-democratic in their structure, character, and outlook. There is no process for leadership selection—it is not by election, but rather by nomination, that party leaders are chosen within the political parties. Religious or ethnic parties are closed groups. In such groups, ideology or ethnic factors determine the leadership selection process. Political parties have no links with policy process. Personalities rather than issues matter.

(c) Since military rule has been persistent, and democratic government has remained an illusion, the political elites have little experience with democratic rule. In the 1970s, although Bhutto assumed power through the electoral process and framed a constitution, he found it difficult to rule through democratic means. Even the Mohammad Khan Junejo, Benazir Bhutto, and Nawaz Sharif governments, and current ex-

perience, reveal unfamiliarity with democratic norms.
(d) Political leaders are not only inexperienced in the democratic tradition, but also find it difficult to hold democratic values. Tolerance, compromise, and bargaining are absent. Vendetta and suppression of opponents is the norm rather than the exception.

Cultural Obstacles

Is Islam hostile to democracy? The experience of Pakistan reveals that Islam has been used as an instrument of centralization and social control by elites in power or otherwise. Consequently, the politics of Islamization have promoted intolerance, rather than the politics of bargain and compromise with other groups. On the other hand, religious groups have become influential—quite disproportionately to the size of their real support base. The politics of Islamization has given new life to various Islamic sects. Sectarian politics are undermining the spirit of Muslim brotherhood, in turn promoting intolerance and weakening the politics of accommodation and consensus. Thus, state-sponsored Islamization is hampering democratization.

However, the biggest challenge to democratization is the rising demands of ethnic groups. The demands of the ethnic groups for greater political participation, autonomy, and sharing of economic resources are causing tensions between the elites, who are well entrenched in the power structure, and aspiring ethnic elites. The revival of religious sects and increased ethnic assertion have thus become a serious challenge to the smooth transition to a democratic order.

It cannot be denied that cultural and structural constraints exist in Pakistan that make this transition difficult. It needs to be recognized that trying to reform the culture of society is like addressing the wrong question. There is need to encourage the establishment of those rules, procedures, and laws under which democracy flourishes. It is not merely the political culture of a society that hampers or promotes the growth of democracy; appropriate rules, judicious decisions, and elite accommodation also facilitate the creation of democratic order. Formulation, acceptance, and implementation of rules and laws that popularize the principles of democracy need to be devised. It is through public education that democracy can be consolidated.

Return to Martial Rule Under General Musharraf

By Rory McCarthy

In October 1999, Pakistan army chief General Pervez Musharraf dismissed Prime Minister Nawaz Sharif and his cabinet in a swift and bloodless coup. This was the fourth dismissal of an elected government in Pakistan on charges of corruption since the last martial rule in Pakistan ended in 1988 with Zia-ul-Haq's death. General Musharraf's actions met with public approval as did his commitment to implement "real" instead of "sham" democracy and hold national parliamentary elections by October 2002.

In the following extract, Guardian journalist Rory McCarthy says that by July 2002, the initial credibility given to General Musharraf had been seriously challenged. He says Pakistanis were disillusioned with his mishandling of corruption, of the economy, and with his constitutional amendments designed to limit the power of elected politicians while giving a near dictatorial role to his own office, the presidency. McCarthy's prediction that public skepticism would be reflected in the 2002 election results has proved correct. Pakistan's Muslim League, the party most closely allied with the general, failed to obtain a majority in the October election. While no political party won enough votes to form a government, the success of a number of minority parties hostile to General Musharraf was viewed as evidence of public disapproval of his regime.

In 1999, Pakistan's army chief General Pervez Musharraf led a strangely popular coup. There were no tanks on the streets, not a single shot was fired and no blood was spilt. Most Pakistanis applauded the arrival of the military after a decade of corrupt civilian governments. Gen Musharraf, a straight-talking for-

mer commando, promised a bright future. Corruption would be
eliminated, the economy would be rebuilt, the rule of law would
be ensured and, perhaps most importantly, a decent democratic
system would be restored. "Our people were never emancipated
from the yoke of despotism," the general said. "I shall not allow
the people to be taken back to the era of sham democracy but
to a true one."

Many people gave him the benefit of the doubt. The American ambassador in Islamabad at the time praised him as a "moderate man who is acting out of patriotic motivation". Pakistan's
supreme court gave him three years to prepare for general elections. The west turned a blind eye as a court convicted the
friendless former prime minister, Nawaz Sharif, of hijacking and
terrorism in connection with the night of the coup. Now those
three years are almost up and Gen Musharraf has committed
himself to holding parliamentary elections in October [2002].
But is he really emancipating Pakistan from the "yoke of despotism"? Many think not.

If the general gets his way, he will end up with unprecedented
power as a president who is able to dismiss at will his unfortunate
puppet prime minister. For the first time the military, through a
new national security council, will have an institutionalised role
in forming policy, particularly on sensitive issues such as Kashmir,
Afghanistan and nuclear deterrence. At the heart of the problem
is the poorly disguised contempt with which Gen Musharraf regards the politicians who have ruled Pakistan in the short breaths
between military dictatorships. He reserves special opprobrium
for Mr Sharif, the last prime minister, and Benazir Bhutto, who
took turns in running the country during what the general calls
a "decade of disaster".

A Free Hand

To keep the legislators in check, Gen Musharraf is putting the
finishing touches to a list of constitutional amendments which
do as much as possible to constrain future politicians. In a country where a third of the population is illiterate, he has ordered
that only graduates may stand for election. As president, he will
be free to appoint any elected politician as prime minister,
whether or not they lead the largest party in parliament. Anyone
who has already served two terms as either prime minister or a
provincial chief minister will not be able to hold those posts

again—a move which, unsurprisingly, rules out Mr Sharif and Ms Bhutto.

Most importantly, the general is giving himself blanket powers as president to dismiss any prime minister, cabinet or parliament that he does not like. In short, it amounts to what Gen

KEEPING A TIGHT REIN ON THE POLITICIANS

In the following extract from journalist Isabel Hilton's interview with Pakistan's president, General Musharraf, published in the August 12, 2002, edition of the New Yorker, *Musharraf responds to public criticism of his constitutional amendments giving his office more power by saying that these amendments were required to keep a check on the corruption and nepotism of elected officials.*

When I suggested that the constitutional proposals had been widely criticized for giving [General Musharraf] too much power, he grew animated. Far from increasing his powers, he insisted, he planned to shed them. "Right now, I am Chief of Army Staff, Chief Executive, and President. What is power? Power is being Chief Executive. Taking decisions, running the government, undertaking development, running the economy, finance, developing the coastal highway, education. I am making these decisions. I am going to shed that power to the Prime Minister. So what's left? I have to make sure that Pakistan is governed well. Is that unrealistic? I give him full authority. If he does not do well, I will check him." He went on, "In our political setup, if you give a free ticket to the Prime Minister the government and the Cabinet are looting and plundering. So you have to contain it. Elected governments played merry hell here."

Pervez Musharraf, interview by Isabel Hilton, "The General and His Labyrinth," *New Yorker*, August 12, 2002, p. 14.

Musharraf describes in his trenchant soldier-speak as "unity of command". In a chilling warning, he said in a speech in April [2002] that future prime ministers "would not dare" reverse these reforms. "I do not believe in power sharing," he brazenly admitted. "There has to be one authority for good government."

In his defence, the general has made no secret of these plans, which he insists provide the only "checks and balances" that will prevent corruption and misrule. The reforms have been floated and debated for months. Pakistan's politicians, lawyers, journalists, clerics, academics and human rights experts have been scathing in their condemnation. Yet there has not been a single word of criticism from the west. Instead, London and Washington have quietly backed away from any disapproval of the regime.

West Turns a Blind Eye

In the months after the coup, the British and American governments at first turned on the pressure for a return to democracy. Robin Cook, the then foreign secretary, said that Britain would "strongly condemn any unconstitutional actions". Gen Musharraf quickly promised elections within three years and his critics appeared mollified. And so there was little complaint [in 2001] when, in a clearly unconstitutional action, he appointed himself president. When [in 2002] he decided to hold a heavily rigged referendum to endorse his presidency for another five years, the US administration dismissed it as an "internal matter". Britain said nothing.

Since September 11, 2001, Gen Musharraf has been expediently promoted from troublesome dictator to crucial ally in the war against terror. Overnight, the little remaining pressure from abroad for reform disappeared. When [British Foreign Secretary] Jack Straw visited Islamabad [in July 2002] to discuss peace in Kashmir and war in Afghanistan, he did not think to question the stark military vision of "true democracy" which Gen Musharraf is slowly imposing on Pakistan.

Achievements and Shortcomings

However, while the general is for now a friend of the west, he is facing dissent at home from a growing number of Pakistanis who resent the idea that their country is soon to be run like an army by a general. Looking back at the promises made three years ago, it is difficult to see what he has achieved. The general appears to have slowed the infiltration of Islamist militants into Kashmir, something a political leader may have found difficult. He has also created a system of new local councils which have challenged the colonial-era dominance of bureaucrats and have given a rare voice to women.

Yet in many other areas he has fallen short. Too many people convicted of corruption have paid their way out of jail, the economy is still struggling and the rule of law is all too frequently overwhelmed by terrorist attacks, sectarian killings or brutal and misogynistic tribal customs. ([In July 2002], village leaders allowed four death-row convicts to sell their daughters as brides to the elderly relatives of their victims in an attempt [to] escape the gallows.)

This discontent is likely to rear its head in the October elections, and the general and his entourage are said to be increasingly anxious about what the vote might bring. The supreme court rulings, which have allowed Gen Musharraf to run the country untroubled thus far, insist that every reform he has introduced and every amendment he has added to the constitution must be ratified by a parliamentary vote. If, as appears increasingly likely, the majority elected in the October parliament opposes the general, he will find himself in a sticky position. Perhaps one day, his critics say, he may even stand trial for treason.

For months, politicians have feared that he may delay the inevitable by postponing the elections. Now there are rumours of unhappiness among senior army officers, who feel the military's image is being sullied. Gen Musharraf may be about to discover that seizing power in a bloodless coup was easy compared with imposing himself as the unassailable commander of his own "true democracy".

THE HISTORY OF NATIONS
Chapter 5

Current Challenges

Pakistan's Economic and Social Agenda for the Twenty-First Century

BY ISHRAT HUSAIN

Despite impressive economic growth rates, Pakistan's human development indicators (adult literacy, life expectancy, and infant mortality) lag behind other Asian countries. Physical infrastructure has not been maintained to support increased economic activity, and excluding nuclear technology, technological and scientific progress has been slow. In the following extract from Pakistan: The Economy of an Elitist State, *Pakistani economist Ishrat Husain identifies several major issues that confront Pakistan in the new millennium: the decline of public confidence in the government, the judiciary and the educational establishment; the collapse of law and order; poor physical infrastructure; an unskilled workforce; limited access by the poor to basic amenities; regional, ethnic, and religious conflict; suspension of civil rights; and the country's failure to take advantage of the technological revolution. Husain says the government must improve its policy formulation, interdepartmental coordination, and program evaluation skills. Its main goals should be to restore public confidence in the major institutions, to promote social harmony, and to bring Pakistan into the modern world economy.*

Pakistan's economic and social record for the last fifty years has been mixed. While its achievements in income, employment, and living standards are by no means modest,

Ishrat Husain, *Pakistan: The Economy of an Elitist State*. Karachi, Pakistan: Oxford University Press, 1999. Copyright © 1999 by Oxford University Press, Pakistan. All rights reserved. Reproduced by permission.

the opportunities missed in social progress, equitable income distribution, and regional integration are too numerous to count. . . .

The problems facing Pakistan at present are no different from those facing other developing countries at a similar juncture in their historical evolution. There is broad agreement as to what the real issues and problems are.

First, there has been a complete breakdown of trust and confidence in the major institutions governing the country. Law and order has broken down and the inability to protect personal life and property has become a recurring nightmare, both among the poor rural areas of the country and the highly advanced metropolitan centres. The judicial system is not only slow, complex, time consuming, and cumbersome, but it has lost the aura of neutrality and impartiality on which it thrived during the early period of the country's history. The common perception that the police and judiciary can be manipulated by those who enjoy power or material wealth at the expense of the ordinary citizenry is getting stronger every day. Drug money, Klashnikovs [assault rifles] and private armies have contributed significantly to this state of near anarchy.

Second, the future of the country is being gradually devastated through neglect of the physical infrastructure, and, more importantly, through the decapitalization of the country's human resources. The accumulation of human capital that takes place through the educational institutions and research bodies in any civilized country has been put into reverse gear in this country. The law of the jungle, i.e., 'unfair practices' at examinations, favouritism, nepotism by the teachers, and free use of arms and intimidation have replaced the normal and decent standards of instruction, curriculum development, hard work by students and teachers, inquisitiveness, and search for knowledge. The future generation is not equipped with the skills that are normally demanded by a country in transition to a modern path. Empirically, it has been established that this failure of investment in and nurturing of human resources is the most debilitating factor in the way of economic and social progress.

Third, access by the common citizen to the basic amenities of life—water, power, health services, transport, and communications—has been severely curtailed by a syndrome of short supply, discretionary subsidized prices that benefit the fortunate few, inadequate financing for investment, and further reduction in the supply of output. Many public services are in theory provided free or subsidized on the premise that the poor can have access to them. In practice, because of budget constraints, public services must often be rationed, and the poor people, who have no connection with the administrators of these services, are the ones who fail to get them.

Revolt Against Inequities

In general, discretionary powers in the hands of regulators and controllers create sources of power and patronage, and an enormous scope for corruption, alienating the general public who derive little or no benefits. A political government that is sensitive to general public opinion and keen to be returned to power would soon discover that the benefit of these discretionary powers for the benefit of the chosen few is likely to be more harmful to their interests. It is true that these controls confer enormous benefits to some powerful members of the society, but the common voter in Pakistan is no longer oblivious to these inequities. The defeat of many of these power brokers at the [1999] elections was the manifestation of this revolt. The society of Pakistan in the next century is not going to be driven by the whims and caprices, orders, or sanctions of a handful of feudal landlords, industrial tycoons, ambitious bureaucrats, or unscrupulous politicians, as in the 1950s or 1960s. The broadening of the middle class and its disproportionately large influence on political events and outcomes in Pakistan, as evidenced by the last four general elections, calls for a different strategy of political survival than the exclusive dependence on traditional power brokers and their machinations. The dismantling of controls and the fostering of competitive forces in the provision of these services have a greater probability of success in the Pakistan of the twenty-first century.

Fourth, the last decade or so has witnessed a dehumanizing intensification of centrifugal and divisive forces in the country. Every conceivable cleavage or difference—Sindhi vs Punjabi, *Mohajirs* [migrant] vs [indigenous] Pathans, Islam vs secularism, Shias vs Sunnis, Deobandies vs Barelvis [schools of Islamic interpretation] literates vs illiterates, Woman vs Man, Urban vs Rural—has been exploited to magnify dissensions, giving rise to heinous blood baths, accentuated hatred, and intolerance. A religion that prides itself on its message of peace and harmony and tolerance finds itself exploited by a few individuals or groups. A country that was created in the name of Unity, Faith, and Discipline is the epitome of a highly divided, despondent, and indisciplined nation. Ethnic and linguistic jingoism is fast permeating the fabric of the society and corroding the foundations upon which the country was built. The solid pillars of a harmonious multicultural society are in danger of developing cracks.

Conspiracies and Intrigue

Fifth, the rights of freedom of expression, dissent, and difference of opinion have been curbed for such a long time that ill-founded rumours, speculations, and half-truths have become the handtools of conspirators and vested interests to perpetuate their game. Their favourite pastime of nurturing sectional and parochial suspicions, arousing unnecessary emotions of violence and vengeance, and evoking sympathy for 'oppression and denials of rights' sooner or later becomes a self-fulfilling prophecy. The example of a group of Bangladesh nationalists of the 1960s is still vivid in our memory. They sparked the emotions of the ordinary peace-loving inhabitants of East Pakistan through rumours and whisper-mongering that the export earnings of jute were being used to pave the streets of West Pakistan with gold, and that without access to these earnings West Pakistan would collapse economically. The fact that realities proved different from their rhetoric and that West Pakistan has done economically better during the past twenty-five years is rebutted by the same group arguing that it is drug money which is fuelling the economy of Pakistan.

Sixth, while other countries in Asia have performed economic miracles in recent years with an economic base and endowment much smaller, Pakistan is still struggling to find a few niches here and there. The 'impressive' growth rates so blatantly publicized by every succeeding government have led to an illusion in the national psyche. By consuming 95 per cent of national output and then borrowing from outsiders for a little investment, the nation is clearly living beyond its means, and this situation is not likely to be tenable in the long run. In addition, despite such foreign borrowing the investment level is low in relation to the requirements or in relation to other countries at the same income level, and the composition and pattern of investment are also well behind the times. The technological revolution that is sweeping the frontiers of production in microelectronics, defence, telecommunications, genetic engineering, etc., has hardly touched the fringes of Pakistan's production structure. The increasing dependence on a limited set of agriculturally-based commodities for the manufacturing and export sectors is a cause for serious concern. The managerial revolution that is introducing new techniques and tools of industrial and financial management in other parts of the world seems to be bypassing Pakistan. The intensity of knowledge and skills in the country's output of goods and services is rudimentary. The 'negative equity' and 'negative value-added' type of industrialization has brought about few social gains but enormous private benefits to a handful of families who have been the beneficiaries of the largess made available by successive governments.

Future Policy Directions

The three imperatives that should influence the governance of this country are:

- Restore confidence in the country's institutions—government, legislature, judiciary, universities, etc.
- Initiate and sustain technological change and manage the transition to a modern economy and society.
- Foster stability and trust in social and cultural relationships between various segments of the population.

The implementation of the above goals is intertwined and should be looked at collectively rather than individually or sequentially. Ethnic and cultural cleavages arise primarily because the younger generation graduating from colleges and universities see no hope of employment or a stable career ahead. This is interpreted as a denial of opportunities, discrimination against their particular ethnic group, and usurpation of their rights by other groups. The collapse and paralysis of institutions also implies that only those with connections or riches can have access to public services or the basic amenities of life. The protection and near monopoly provided by the government to a few industrialists and the absence of a technological base in the country means inefficiency, high-cost production, and lack of opportunity for further expansion or job creation. An attack on each of these problems simultaneously is therefore a prerequisite for the achievement of these goals.

The credibility of government policy-making in achieving the goals it sets for itself needs to be restored so that it is taken seriously by everyone concerned. It must be recognized that the administrative division of functional responsibility is not necessarily co-terminous with the sphere of substantive policy changes required. The complex web of interrelationships between the various sectors and policies makes it essential that changes that take place in one particular sector under the control of one ministry are followed up by necessary changes in other affected sectors. Failing this, even the originally initiated changes will not be able to survive in the long run. The problem in Pakistan, unfortunately, has been that policy is designed for each sector separately at different points of time in complete isolation of others. Policies and plans abound in Pakistan. Enormous resources of time and effort have been spent at regular intervals in formulating the industrial policy, agricultural policy, education policy, health policy, science policy etc. These policies have sounded very convincing on paper, but scant regard has been given either to the trade-offs involved among various competing goals, or their resource implications or implementation constraints. In many cases, before the policy could ever be put to serious test, the government of the day has changed or the minister responsible for the original policy has been reshuffled, or some crisis has erupted that has led to a practical abandonment of the policy, so that the credibility of these policies has eroded more quickly than it takes to print the policy papers. There is too much fanfare in announcing the policies and too little monitoring or evaluation of their success or failure, or of their impact on the majority of the population.

No Intergovernment Coordination

In those instances where a policy did survive or made some faltering progress, its life span was short because the complementary policies were never in place. Take, for example, the education policy that aimed to redirect and reorient education towards vocational and technical training. For this objective to be successful, complementary industrial and labour policies are needed that assure the creation of jobs for those who complete such education. As industrial and labour policies remained unaltered, the abundant supply of unemployed technical and vocational graduates produced as a result of the new education policy soon put a damper on the new policy, which soon receded into oblivion and we were back to the *status quo ante*. As a result of this sort of thinking, the policy makers lose credibility and, when a new government or new minister proposes to initiate yet another education policy, there is widespread cynicism and scepticism. Although the bureaucrats and others involved go through the motions and rituals of writing a policy document, there is only a half-hearted or indifferent response as far as implementation is concerned. As results are hard to come by, the political leaders become wary and disenchanted with the civil servants, who they blame for the sabotage of their ideas and initiatives and non-cooperation. The civil servants, on their part, assume a more defensive, unmotivated, and uninspired posture, hoping that the minister or the government will wither away. There is very little thought given to an objective analysis of the factors that led to unsatisfactory results or the failure of a policy. The cycle of policy pronouncements with a big bang and policy failures with a senile shrug has been the history of policymaking in Pakistan.

Need for Realistic and Sustainable Policies

To give some semblance of respectability to policy formulation, it is essential that sectoral changes are not made in sequence or isolation, but are followed through with the necessary action in other related or affected sectors or fields. It is prudent to initiate only a few strategic policy changes and follow them to their logical conclusion rather than announce a new policy every day of the year which no one takes seriously. Equally important is to ensure that the policy itself is internally consistent and to design its implementation in a realistic way. The tendency of political leaders and ministers to make tall promises and initiate radical changes overnight should be avoided at all costs. In the ultimate analysis, it is the results, i.e., the extent of changes brought about, that counts, not the promises made.

Pakistan inherited and subsequently established a number of solid institutions at various levels in diverse areas of economic policy. However, with the passage of time, the tendencies towards overcentralization, excessive control, increased government interference, and arbitrary instructions from the top made most of them ineffective and impotent, rendering them unable to perform the tasks for which they were set up. The basic configurations which underpin most of these institutions have become fragile. The top-down nature of the administrative fabric, the control mind set of the decisionmakers, and the centrally-commanded ways of doing things are major factors accentuating this fragility.

The agenda for institutional reform is both broad and deep-seated, as decades of neglect and disrepair have done almost irreparable damage. Implementation might be manageable. A real start can be made if a broad political consensus is reached on reforming three key institutions: judicial, educational, and financial. What should be the nature of this consensus? An agreement must be reached between the two major political parties that these three areas—the judiciary and educational and financial institutions—will be completely insulated from the intrusion of political interference and will remain out of bounds as far as the exercise of political patronage is concerned. This should not be interpreted to mean that setting sound objectives, policies, and performance standards and enforcing practices of supervision and accountability should be abandoned, either by the legislature or the ministries concerned, but the areas of discretion should be limited and clearly defined.

Human Rights Abuses in the Name of Islam

BY AKBAR AHMED

In the following article Akbar Ahmed, who holds the Ibn Khaldun Chair of Islamic Studies at American University, criticizes human rights abuses perpetuated under Pakistan's "blasphemy law." Under the law, any remarks that could be considered derogatory to Muhammad are punishable by the death sentence. Ahmed says the number of people on death row stands as testimony to the growing power of intolerant religious fundamentalists and is an example of the blatant abuse of laws promulgated in the name of Islam that have targeted religious minorities. Ahmed asserts this law violates true Islamic law, which advocates tolerance of other religious views.

I t is not every day that I get a letter from the Death Cell, Central Jail, Rawalpindi in Pakistan. As any Pakistani would be, I was aware that Central Jail was where the country's most popular democratic leader, Zulfiqar Ali Bhutto, was executed more than two decades ago.

The letter was dated April 15 [2002] and addressed to me and to a Pakistani colleague here in Washington. Written in a clear and neat hand, the sender's name made me sit up: Mohammad Younas Sheikh, who teaches at the homeopathic medical college in Islamabad. He is one of perhaps dozens of educators accused by their students of a crime that doesn't exist in many countries: blasphemy. Sheikh has been convicted and awaits execution, which is mandatory under the blasphemy law. Many other Pakistanis, particularly minorities, also have been charged. These cases offer an alarming glimpse into the machinery of state under Pakistan's president, Gen. Pervez Musharraf, Washington's partner in the "war on terror."

Sheikh's problems began in October 2000 when he made some innocuous remarks about the origins of Islam. Muslims believe that the Koran came to the prophet Muhammad as a revelation when he was 40. In response to a student's question, Sheikh said that before he was 40, Muhammad was neither a prophet nor a Muslim, as there was no Islam. For those Muslims who believe his prophethood was divinely preordained, this was blasphemous. The students took the matter to some local mullahs, who in their role as religious leaders registered a case with the police. Matters then moved rapidly and, as in such cases, with a certain inexorability.

But Sheikh was not ridiculing or rejecting the prophet. On the contrary, like many Muslims grappling with issues of modernity, he raised questions of interpretation. Although partly educated in Ireland, Sheikh was born and raised in Pakistan and is a devout Muslim who has said that one of the books that most inspires him is the Koran. He is the founder of the Enlightenment, a society of like-minded Pakistanis who discuss Islam in a modern context. His father is recognized as having memorized the Koran.

In his letter, Sheikh called the blasphemy law "wide open to abuse, through and by the miscreant mullahs for political, repressive and vindictive purposes. . . ." The law's abuse is part of "a rising wave of aggressive ignorance, incivility and intolerance as well as the medieval theocratic darkness," he wrote. I must say I agree.

Dangers of "Challenging Islam"

His trial was held in closed session, inside the Central Jail. "Even my solicitors were harassed with a fatwa [religious proclamation] of apostasy and they were threatened with the lives of their children," he wrote. He asked us to bring the case to the notice of Musharraf so that the president could "repeal this notorious and fascist blasphemy law."

By writing this, I do indeed hope to focus attention on the law. In the meantime, I am aware that by raising the issue I become a bit player in the drama.

Several Pakistani friends have warned me to say nothing about this out of concern for my safety. Anyone who questions the blasphemy law's power may be seen as challenging Islam—and therefore suspect under the very law he or she questions. But as a Sunni Muslim from a mainstream, orthodox family, I feel compelled to speak, in part because of the emphasis that Islam places on peace and compassion. And as a former governmental administrator in my native country, I know how intimidating majority views can be for religious minorities. About 95 percent of Pakistan's 145 million people are Muslims.

Need for Law Reform

In the 1970s and '80s, when I was a district officer in charge of law and order in two Pakistani provinces, a reform of the nation's legal and administrative system was long overdue. Those who turned to the law for recourse found themselves involved in exhausting and expensive cases that could last decades. Individuals had few rights, and the system favored the rich and powerful. There was a disastrous mismatch between aspects of the remnants of British colonial law and the contemporary needs of society.

Then, as now, there are four distinct sets of laws that sometimes overlap: British colonial law, which by and large was the basis in 1947 for Pakistan's penal code and criminal procedure code; Islamic *sharia* law; tribal law, which applies to certain areas of the country; and state law, which is codified by each state's local ruler. The application of the law has never been fully resolved.

Amid this confusion, Gen. Mohammed Zia ul-Haq, as president, added new laws to the penal code, including 295-B in 1982, which made desecrating the Koran or making a derogatory remark about it punishable by life imprisonment—though, in yet a further nod toward confusion, judges sometimes reduce the term. Two years ago, for instance, Naseem Ghani and Mohammed Shafiq were sentenced to seven years for allegedly burning a Koran.

The Blasphemy Law

In 1984 came the 295-C clause, usually referred to as the blasphemy law. It rather sweepingly stipulates that "derogatory remarks, etc., in respect of the Holy Prophet . . . either spoken or written, or by visible representation, or by any imputation, innuendo, or insinuation, directly or indirectly . . . shall be punished with death, or imprisonment for life, and shall also be liable to fine." Six years later, the stakes were raised when the Federal Sharia Court, where cases having to do with Islamic issues tend to be heard, ruled, "The penalty for contempt of the Holy Prophet . . . is death and nothing else."

In the application of the blasphemy law, intolerance has fed on intolerance. So far, none of the convicted has been executed, in part because scheduling an execution can take years. But lynch mobs have killed several of the accused.

Over the years I began to see the blasphemy law used more and more for cases of political vendetta, land disputes or political rivalry. The law became a way to challenge someone's identity, a powerful tool to intimidate anyone, Muslim or non-Muslim.

The targets of this law have largely been minorities, such as members of the Ahmadi sect (who consider themselves Muslims) and Christians, though the latest anecdotal evidence suggests that

RETROGRESSIVE INTERPRETATIONS OF ISLAM PERSECUTE PAKISTANI WOMEN

Pakistani author Neshay Najam writes of human rights abuses against Pakistani women based on retrogressive readings of Islamic law.

Our women still seem to be living in the dark ages. It is a matter of deep sorrow that being Muslims we have completely forgotten the status of women given by Islam. Annie Bessant in her book, 'The Life and Teachings of Mohammad (P.B.U.H)' says, "I often think that women are more free in Islam than in Christianity. Women are more respected by Islam than by the faith which preaches monogamy."

Islam was the first religion to recognize the equality of sexes and granted women rights unheard of 1400 years ago. Their other tragedy lies in the fact that what was highly progressive in those early days of Islam and which ought to have been kept in step with the changing of the realities of life, ... was frozen in that position through retrogressive interpretation of religious edicts. In addition to that, male chauvinism and cultural taboos, some of them derived from the Hindu society, have combined to keep our women down.

the pendulum is now swinging toward Muslims. In the past decade or so, perhaps 2,000 Ahmadis have been charged under the blasphemy law, according to that community. The Ahmadis were declared non-Muslims by Prime Minister Bhutto in 1974. Ten years later, they were denied the right to practice their faith.

The Pakistani government says it does not have exact figures for the number of people charged under the blasphemy law. But the State Department report, "International Religious Freedom 2001," offers some clues. Over the past three or four years, 55 to 60 Christians a year have been charged. That figure probably hasn't changed much since the law was enacted. And as evidence

---

In Pakistan the story of a woman's deprivations start even before her birth, because the girl-child is not a particularly 'wanted' child. Her life is a journey of subordination. When she is young her father decides for her on matters ranging from whether she will get any education, to the all important matters of whom she would marry. After marriage, her husband and her in-laws get hold of her reins and decide matters on her behalf; like shall she or shall she not have a child every year, or whether she would produce only boys, or whether she can seek independent employment and so on. Finally when she becomes old and her husband gets weak or may have gone already, it is her son or sons who decide her fate in the declining years of her life. As if this is not enough, the whole society acts as an oppressor, browbeating her in to obedience. Thus, the word 'woman' in Pakistan is synonymous with 'endurance'. She is simply forced to accept certain bare facts of life once she grows up to be a woman. Be it on streets, or for that matter in restaurants, a woman is first and foremost required to be alert. It is best to try and not notice, women are told. According to Hina Jilani, Lawyer and Human Rights Activist, "the right to life of women in Pakistan is conditional on their obeying social norms and traditions."

Neshay Najam, "The Status of Women in Pakistan: A Muslim Majority State and the 21st Century," www.crescentlife.com/articles, n.d.

of that possible shift in who is targeted, the report says that three-quarters of those on trial for blasphemy in 2001 were Muslims.

Human Rights Abuses

Bail is usually denied for those charged with blasphemy. Trials are expensive and can last for years. Worse: They can take years to begin. For example, Riaz Ahmad, his son and two nephews, all Ahmadis, have been imprisoned since their arrest in November 1993. They were detained on the vague allegation that they had "said something derogatory." Local people in Piplan, Mianwali District, say that rivalry over Ahmad's position as village head-man is the real motivation for the complaint against him. Their trial has yet to begin.

Anwar Masih, a Christian from Samundri in Punjab, has been in detention since February 1993 when a Muslim shopkeeper alleged that Masih insulted the prophet during an argument over money.

Roman Catholic Bishop John Joseph, a Pakistani human rights campaigner, had been leading a campaign against the blasphemy law and said he felt he was getting nowhere when he took his own life on May 6, 1998. He had failed to find a lawyer willing to take the case of convicted blasphemer Ayub Massih, a Christian. Massih's family had applied to a government program that gives housing plots to landless people. The local landlords, who brought the allegations against him, resented this because landless Christians work in their fields in exchange for a place to live. By getting a plot of land Massih would have escaped his bondage.

"Most of these cases," concludes Amnesty International in its latest report on Pakistan, "are motivated not by the blasphemous actions of the accused, but by hostility toward members of minority communities, compounded by personal enmity, professional jealousy or economic rivalry."

The bishop's suicide put international pressure on Pakistan's rulers. Benazir Bhutto, who was then prime minister, approved two amendments to the penal code designed to reduce the abuses of Section 295. The number of arrests has dropped, but the law remains intact. When Musharraf seized power in October 1999, he talked about wanting to move Pakistan toward progress and tolerance. He suggested mild changes to the blasphemy law in April 2000, but withdrew them under pressure from religious elements the following month. That is where the matter rests.

Islam Demands Compassion

Musharraf recently ratified his presidency for five more years with his "landslide victory" in a widely questioned referendum. Both commander in chief of the army and president, he is the most powerful man in Pakistan. He can cause meaningful change. Islam expects the ruler to show high moral authority, but no ruler has dared to reexamine the blasphemy law in the light of Islamic law itself. Musharraf should consider the Koranic verse that says, "There is no compulsion in religion."

If he is to move his country toward the tolerant and modern Muslim nation envisioned by Pakistan's founder, Musharraf must begin by taking this important first step: reopening the case of Sheikh and other alleged blasphemers who await death and showing the justice, compassion and mercy that Islam requires.

Confronting the Legacies of the Afghan–Soviet War: Radical Islam, Sectarian Violence, and Terrorism

BY MANDAVI MEHTA AND TERESITA C. SCHAEFFER

In the following extract, Mandavi Mehta and Teresita C. Schaeffer say that involvement in the war in Afghanistan between 1979 and 1989 had serious consequences for Pakistan that continue to the present. These challenges include the radicalization of Islam, growth in sectarian violence, and an increase in domestic terrorism. They assert that these problems pose a serious threat to the country's internal security and have proved difficult to resolve because of the public perception that government intervention in disputes about Islam represents an attack on the religion itself.

Mandavi Mehta is a CSIS research affiliate. Teresita C. Schaeffer is the Director of South Asia Programs at the Center for Strategic and International Studies (CSIS) in Washington, D.C., and former U.S. ambassador to Pakistan.

M any of the acute problems for which Pakistan has taken center-stage today have their genesis in the Afghan war and its equally turbulent aftermath. Pakistan became the frontier state from which the United States waged a proxy war against the Soviets, which invaded Afghanistan in 1979. US arms and money were funneled to militants fighting in Afghanistan through the Pakistani army, particularly the Pakistani intelligence service, the Inter-Services Intelligence (ISI). Many Pakistanis went to join the Afghan jihad [Muslim holy war], and Pakistani army officers and soldiers stationed along the border and in constant contact with mujahideen (freedom fighters), grew to have a deep admiration for them.

In addition, Pakistan and the United States embraced the term 'jihad' and built up the mujahideen, to mobilize and unite the Afghan anti-occupation forces. They also set up an infrastructure to support the 'jihad', encouraging other Arab nations, such as Saudi Arabia, to donate money directly towards the jihad and also to support religious centers, madrassahs [Islamic schools] and clergy, both Deobandi[1] and Ahle Hadith,[2] who supported the jihad. The Iranian Revolution of 1979 meanwhile had had a profound influence on the Muslim world, and Sunni states like Saudi Arabia were particularly keen to give material support to these groups. Madrassahs started to grow rapidly, vying with one another to attract valuable Saudi money.

General Zia-ul Haq benefited from this interaction, which gave his authoritarian rule legitimacy through Islam. In 1979, for example, Zia supplemented his policy of building a 'military-mosque' alliance by administering a formal Zakat (religious tithe), whereby money was automatically deducted from bank balances and disbursed to institutions that were seen as worthy by influential religious leaders, who were predominantly Deobandi or Ahle Hadith. Zia was personally a devout Muslim, and under his leadership, religious practice became more prevalent in the Pakistan army as well. A corollary to Zia's policy of using the state to privilege particular groups (both religious and ethnic, such as the Mohajir MQM [a coalition of religious parties that fared well in the October 2002 Election]) was that it made it more difficult for a unified opposition to his rule to emerge. Meanwhile the lack of democracy and channels for political participation created a vacuum in public life that was increasingly filled by ethnic or sectarian groups as a medium for voicing dissent.

1. The Deoband School of Islamic interpretation originated in the late nineteenth century in the Indian town of Deoband. It calls for the purification of Islam and advocates an Islamic state in Pakistan governed by its interpretation of Islamic law. 2. Ahle Hadith is the most orthodox school of Islamic interpretation in Pakistan and follows the lead of religious leaders in Saudi Arabia.

The Pursuit of "Strategic Depth"

After the Soviet withdrawal and the victory of the Afghan ji-hadis, peace did not come to Afghanistan, which descended into an equally destructive civil war between mujahideen leaders who were vying for power and were armed to the teeth with Soviet and American weapons. The war had displaced millions of Afghans internally and sent millions of others as refugees to Pakistan, as well as to Iran and India. The civil war continued this trend, straining Pakistan's economy and social services. The warlords and their armies in Afghanistan were ethnically divided between Pashtuns, Tajiks, Uzbeks and Hazaras.

Making a reliable friend out of Afghanistan and giving Pakistan "strategic depth" on its northern front in the eventuality of an Indian invasion, had been longstanding strategic goals for Pakistan. During the Afghan civil war Pakistan decided to pursue its policy of "strategic depth" in Afghanistan by supporting leaders who would be sympathetic to its interests. This led the government of Benazir Bhutto, which was allied with the religious party Jamiat-e-Ulema Islami (JUI), to throw in its lot with the Pashtun-majority Taliban when they first rose to prominence. The Taliban had a shared ethnicity with the Pashtuns of the NWFP [Northwest Frontier Province] in Pakistan, they were Sunnis, and many of their leaders had studied in Deoband madrassahs in Pakistan (most notably the Dar-ul-Uloom Haqqania in Akora Khattak), and hence had close links to the country, unlike the Northern Alliance leaders (who were in turn supported by Iran, India, Russia and some Central Asian republics). Indeed, both Nawaz Sharif and Benazir Bhutto, during their prime ministerships, maintained close ties to the Taliban and worked to support them in the civil war, a policy continued by General Musharraf when he came to power in 1999.

Sectarian Violence Escalates

Perhaps the most significant domestic consequence of Pakistan's policies in Afghanistan is the dramatic rise in sectarian violence in the last two decades. This dimension of the growth of radical Islam has been as threatening to Pakistan's internal cohesion and survival as developments in Afghanistan or Pakistan's deteriorating relationship with India. While sectarianism is not a new phenomenon in Pakistan, Zia's policies and his alliance with particular interpretations of Pakistani Islam (Deobandi and Ahle

Hadith), started a phenomenal growth in sectarian organizations in Pakistan, be they Barelvi, Ahmadi or Shia. Deobandi and Ahle Hadith organizations also mushroomed after the institution of the compulsory collection of Zakat and the beginning of the jihad in Afghanistan. Jihadis, as well as jihad-oriented madrassahs, were strongly influenced by Deobandism and Wahhabism, and both schools of interpretation grew rapidly in strength in this period. Moreover, mujahideen who were returning from Afghanistan were becoming an economic and social challenge for the state domestically, and were fuelling the rise of sectarian violence against Barelvis and Shias within Pakistan, as well as feuding amongst themselves. While this has predominantly characterized the public face of Islam (in the private or non-political sphere, the Sunni-Shia divide is not nearly so sharp), the lawlessness of militant groups and the rise of an intolerant redefinition of Islam was leading to mounting tensions in society. Their fight against Barelvis, Ahmadis and Shias was a fight to 'purify' the practice of Islam, much as the Taliban had done in Afghanistan. Sectarian violence, fuelled by readily available weapons from the jihad, mushroomed.

The impact of sectarian violence in Karachi is worth singling out because of the tremendous economic cost it has had to Pakistan's economy. The port city of Karachi is Pakistan's largest city and commercial heart, a big, busy metropolis with a hectic mix of ethnic and sectarian communities from all over the country, including a large number of rootless elements who have migrated there in search of jobs. The sectarian killings between Sunnis and Shias, and between Deobandis and Barelvis, that started in the 1980s has descended into a vicious cycle of violence, whose horror is encapsulated in the murder of Shia doctors in the city and in regular attacks on people praying in mosques. Since 1998, more than 70 physicians have been murdered and in 1995, 1,742 people were killed in Karachi at the height of the violence.

Madrassah Education

The radicalization of a section of the madrassah system is another profoundly destabilizing phenomenon with its roots in the Afghan jihad. A millennia old system of education designed to educate the intellectual elite in Muslim societies, the madrassah system in Pakistan has changed drastically in substance and context in the past two decades. Madrassahs in Pakistan are estimated to have more than doubled between 1988 and 2000 due to a host of complex internal and external factors. They have stepped in to take up the vacuum left by the Pakistani state's failed educational system (Pakistan spends a mere 2 percent of its GNP [Gross National Product] on education), but the vast majority remain entirely free of government control. The Musharraf government's attempts to regulate madrassahs have become a divisive issue in Pakistan, and it has already had to compromise on its Madaris Ordinance[3] 2002, which remains unenforceable. According to varying estimates, there are currently anywhere from 10,000 to 40,000 madrassahs in Pakistan, educating up to 3 million students.

The 'problem' of madrassah education has two distinct aspects—the first is the quality of madrassah education in equipping students with basic tools to earn a living, and the second is the relationship between certain madrassahs and radical militant groups that recruit them to fight internationally, or in sectarian struggles. These are two distinct problems with different solutions. Nothing in the institution of madrassahs is inherently prone to militancy. While the curriculum in madrassahs is overwhelmingly outdated, madrassahs are often the only schooling option for poorer Pakistanis. The madrassah system today provides a vital social service, not only teaching basic reading and writing, but providing food, shelter and other basic services. In addition, madrassahs are seen as repositories of religious and cultural values that are important to Pakistanis. Admission to these institutions is highly competitive and madrassahs and mosques collect over 1.1 billion dollars in charitable donations from Pakistani residents every year. The vast majority of madrassahs are dedicated to religious education and are not involved in politics. While they are stumbling blocks to progress and need to be reformed, they are not a vital security threat.

Madrassahs and Radical Militant Groups

Though it is hard to get concrete data, most estimates indicate that only about 10–15 percent of Pakistan's madrassahs are affiliated with radical militant groups. These extremist madrassahs propagate a culture of violence and disaffection, both domesti-

---

3. Under the Madaris Ordinance the government developed a new curriculum for madrassahs that includes Mathematics, Science, English, and Pakistan Studies in addition to religious subjects.

cally and internationally, and dealing with them (as distinct from non-violent madrassahs) is one of the most intractable problems facing Pakistan today. The Madaris Ordinance 2002, which attempts to regulate madrassahs by getting them to register with the education board, is particularly ineffective when it comes to dealing with extremist madrassahs as it relies overwhelmingly on the voluntary submission of data. The Musharraf government has had a little more success in dealing with militant groups involved with militant madrassahs, and it needs to intensify its efforts. Madrassah militancy is a tremendously complex subject and different factors promote militancy from region to region, depending on socio-economic, ethnic and sectarian patterns and local power structures.

Madrassah reform has become a very tough issue for Musharraf because a general attack on the institutions that promote the study of Islam is perceived to be an attack on Islam. It is an issue that unites religious parties and extremist groups, who in turn can manipulate the rhetoric of religion to win popular support. To deal with the issue effectively, the government needs to refine its approach and try to build genuine consensus for reform. But at this point, it remains unclear if the Pakistani state even has the organizational capacity to regulate madrassahs effectively, given its poor track record with public education.

Violence, Terrorism, and Gangs Threaten Internal Security

Islam has become the banner of groups that now pose a serious challenge to the Pakistani state and its leadership. President Musharraf's efforts to reassert state authority over militant groups has in the short run produced an increase in violence. This became especially apparent after the attack on the Indian parliament in December 2001. A militant backlash against the Pakistan government's decision to ban several extremist groups the following month, coupled with the apparent presence of al-Qaida elements in certain militant circles in Pakistan, has created a new and much more dangerous internal security situation. Its impact is enhanced by the waning of Musharraf's popularity following the April 2002 referendum.[4] Sectarian violence in Pakistan has been high

4. The referendum sought public endorsement for Musharraf's presidency for the next five years. Voter turnout was low. Despite the widely held view that the referendum was "rigged," Musharraf took the results to mean he had the people's backing.

in the months since September 11, 2001, as has militant violence in Kashmir.

The new element is the anti-foreign focus of violence. Since the beginning of 2002, there has been a series of attacks aimed at foreigners: the murder of [kidnapped *Wall Street Journal* reporter] Daniel Pearl, the bombing of a protestant church in Islamabad attended chiefly by foreigners, the bombing outside the US consulate in Karachi, the attack on French naval construction engineers in Karachi, and the attacks on a Christian missionary school in the Murree hill station and a foreign-supported eye hospital in Taxila. These incidents have to be seen as an effort not only to hurt foreign and Christian interests but also to damage Musharraf. They have coincided with persistent and plausible reports of assassination attempts on Musharraf himself. They have also coincided with increasingly brazen attacks on Indian interests, including the December 2001 bombing of the Indian Parliament, and the attack on the Indian army camp at Kaluchak in Kashmir.

While the terrorist attacks of September 11 [2001] and the US war on terrorism have ended the association between Pakistan and the Taliban, other elements of the catastrophic association with the Afghan jihad and civil war remain. These include an entrenched drug network, and a widespread gun and gang culture that the state has been unsuccessful in curbing. The fight against terrorism is taking place on Pakistan's own soil, as coalition troops fight to track down the large numbers of Taliban and soldiers who are believed to be hiding in Pakistan's northern territories. This action has a political price for President Musharraf. Inaction would be at least as dangerous, however, as it could lead the militant groups to overplay their hand against a government they regard as weak. It would also add to the erosion of Musharraf's support among Pakistan's "silent majority," which has broadly supported the state's efforts to reassert control over the militants.

The Threat of Nuclear War with India over Kashmir

By Sharif Shuja

The political status of the Jammu and Kashmir region in northern India has caused conflict between Pakistan and India ever since the British decided to keep the region part of India during the partition of the country in 1947. Pakistanis believe that the Muslim majority state should be in Pakistan, while Indians see symbolic significance in the state remaining part of India to show that Hindus and Muslims can coexist in peace. The Kashmiri demand for an independent state is opposed by Pakistan and India. Tensions escalated in 2002 with the development of nuclear bombs by India and Pakistan, the buildup of troops along the border in Kashmir, and provocative statements by Indian and Pakistani leaders.

In the following article from Contemporary Review *published in October 2002, political analyst Sharif Shuja says that fears generated by the western press about the likelihood of a nuclear holocaust in the region are misplaced. He says that leaders on both sides understand the conflict in Kashmir requires a political, not military, solution and do not want war. Shuja asserts that prospects for peace in the region have improved, yet tensions sparked by violent acts of Hindu and Muslim extremists remain a possible trigger for further conflict.*

The Himalayan region of Jammu and Kashmir has been a flashpoint for hostility between India and Pakistan for more than half a century. The former princely state includes the Hindu-majority plains of Jammu, the mainly Muslim Kashmir Valley and the mainly Buddhist Ladakh area. About 12 million people live in Kashmir, of whom about 70 per cent are Muslims and the rest Hindus, Sikhs and Buddhists.

Sharif Shuja, "The Conflict in Kashmir," *Contemporary Review*, vol. 281, October 2002, pp. 220–27. Copyright © 2002 by Contemporary Review Company, Ltd. Reproduced by permission.

After the subcontinent was partitioned in August 1947, the Hindu ruler of Kashmir, facing a pro-Pakistan revolt in parts of the state, acceded to secular India rather than to Islamic Pakistan. The two nations then started their first war over Kashmir, which lasted until December 1948, and ended with a UN-mediated ceasefire. India controls 45 per cent of Kashmir, Pakistan about 35 per cent and China the rest. Indian- and Pakistan-ruled areas are separated by a ceasefire line known as the Line of Control (LOC).

In 1965, Kashmir was the arena for a second Indo-Pakistan war that ended with a UN-mediated ceasefire. The two countries again fought in Kashmir in December 1971, but that war was mainly over Bangladesh, formerly East Pakistan. India and Pakistan agreed to respect the Line of Control under the Shimla Agreement in 1972, 'without prejudice to the recognised position of either side'. This accord said 'both sides further undertake to refrain from threat or the use of force in violation of this line'.

The two countries came to the brink of a fourth war during a 10-week confrontation in 1999 (the Kargil conflict) along the Line of Control. Since 1990, the Kashmir Valley, which is under Indian control, has been the hub of a revolt by Muslim separatist militants who, India says, are trained and armed in Pakistan. Pakistan denies this accusation, saying it only offers political and diplomatic support to what it calls a legitimate struggle for self-determination by the mostly Muslim people of Kashmir. [In 2002] the two countries were again close to war, if not nuclear conflict. At least 35,000 people have been killed in Kashmir. Separatists put the death toll at more than 80,000.

Rival Claims

India claims the whole of Kashmir. Pakistan wants the predominantly Muslim Kashmiris to decide in a plebiscite whether to join Islamic Pakistan or secular but Hindu-majority India. The Kashmiris want to reunite Kashmir as an independent state. Being mostly Muslims does not make them Pakistanis. Their separate identity is based on place, kinship and culture as much as on religion. This idea of an independent state has been rejected by both India and Pakistan.

In India's view, Kashmiris would become loyal citizens again if only Pakistan would stop interfering. It sees the insurgency as a proxy war, which would end as soon as Pakistan stopped giving militants arms and letting them infiltrate Kashmir across the

Line of Control. Most militants, India claims, are foreign zealots imported from other 'holy wars', such as that in Afghanistan. Pakistan continues to deny giving them anything other than moral and diplomatic support. It claims to have limited power to curb them.

The leaders of India and Pakistan since 1947 were desperate to acquire Kashmir to bolster their respective visions of nationhood. India's first Prime Minister, Jawaharlal Nehru, who originally came from Kashmir, wanted to demonstrate that an Islamic population could coexist with the Hindu majority. Mohammad Ali Jinnah, Pakistan's 'Father of the Nation', insisted that Pakistan would be incomplete without the Muslim enclave. After all, the sole raison d'etre of Pakistan's creation was the idea that religion was the basis of a nation state. Moreover, Pakistan depends on rivers flowing out of Kashmir—the Jhelum, the Chenab, and the Indus—to irrigate fields and generate electricity.

Renewed Violence, Post–September 11, 2001

In the troubled year that has followed since the events of September 11 [2001] there has been an increase of violent attacks in Kashmir. There was firstly a suicide attack on the Kashmir Assembly. This was followed by a similar attack on the Indian Parliament on December 13. There was yet another incident of killing innocent bus passengers and civilians in a cantonment in Kashmir. The Indian government took an aggressive posture and massed troops on the Indo-Pakistan border. Pakistan also responded by doing the same.

India said Pakistan has a connection with the terrorists who attacked the Parliament, and it wants an end to all sorts of 'cross border terrorism'. Pakistan denies any connection. Under such grim circumstances, India deployed more than a million troops, backed by heavy artillery and a formidable array of air power, along the 2880 kilometre Line of Control. As India threatened war, Pakistan declared its readiness to retaliate.

India has declared a nuclear 'no–first–use' policy, but Pakistan has indicated it is prepared to use nuclear weapons to defend its territory. In other words, the message clearly indicates that if Pakistan's existence is threatened, it is likely to use nuclear weapons. Neither nation has a well-developed nuclear doctrine; neither knows what would provoke a nuclear response from the other.

On a recent visit to Indian troops deployed a few miles from the Line of Control, the Indian Prime Minister, Atal Behari Vajpayee, said: 'Our goal is victory. It is time to wage a decisive battle. India is forced to fight a war thrust on it and we will emerge victorious. Let there be no doubt about it: a challenge has been thrown to India, and we accept it.'

In reply, Pakistani President Pervez Musharraf vowed to use 'full force' if it were attacked by India. 'If war is forced on Pakistan, the enemy will find us fully prepared', he said, adding that Pakistan's strategy was 'basically one of deterrence'.

At the time of writing, both countries have recalled their High Commissioners, and all road and rail links have been cut. More than 25,000 villagers have fled their homes on the Pakistani side in anticipation of fighting. This is potentially the most serious conflict the world could face at the moment. Alarmed by the rapid escalation in tensions, the United States has called for restraint on both sides. The British Foreign Minister, Jack Straw, recently visited India and Pakistan and held talks with the leaders of these countries. His mission was part of intense international efforts to calm tensions between India and Pakistan. . . .

Western Media Overreacts

The frightening military situation along the Line of Control, together with India's ongoing military modernisation programme, has put the international community on alert. Under such grim circumstances, the Western media has been telling us for days that there are 'real' fears of a nuclear war between India and Pakistan over Kashmir. CNN and the BBC, along with most of the other world media, predicted that if nuclear war were to start, over 12 million Indians and Pakistanis would die; nearly as many would be injured and the radioactive fallout would bring in famine and disease and generations of cancer. There have been editorials, front-page stories and innumerable comment and opinion pieces on the situation.

The coverage of military details such as the exact numbers of warheads owned by each of the nations, the debate whether India has 60 warheads or more and whether Pakistan has other secret arsenals, has been widely debated recently by the international media. This media blitzkrieg is enough to convince anyone that the threat of nuclear war is very real and imminent.

All this was exacerbated by the Embassies and High Commissions of the United States, the United Kingdom and Australia, along with the United Nations, urging their non-essential staff to leave the subcontinent. The Department of Foreign Affairs and Trade asked Australians to defer all travel to India and Pakistan, and for those in the subcontinent to leave those places as soon as possible. And the Australian government chose to close their Mumbai Deputy High Commission just a few days before US Special Envoy Richard Armitage's visit to India and Pakistan. Pakistan also tested three nuclear missiles, just at a time when the whole world was asking the two nations to stay calm. All of these incidents demonstrate that the situation was deteriorating.

Yet, this scare was misplaced, according to many Indians living in India, who were more interested in World Cup soccer at the moment than any possibility of nuclear attacks from Pakistan. 'There is so much exciting football on television—why waste time over and over again on the same India-Pakistan drill?' they asked. No one believes that Indian leaders would be stupid enough to let a nuclear war occur. India's Minister for Women and Children, Mrs Sumitra Mahajan, who was in Sydney recently, urged Indians in Australia to remain calm and not believe the nuclear war hype created by the Western media.

Threat of Accidental War Is Groundless

Yet there are some factors which could lead to a nuclear war. One of these is the use of nuclear weapons through 'miscommunication or misperception' according to Ben Shappard, a defence analyst in London. In an interview with the American Broadcasting Corporation recently, Mr Shappard said Pakistan's control structure was especially weak, creating the theoretical risk that army central command could circumvent the political leadership if it came to a nuclear launch. As evidence, Mr Shappard cited reports that Pakistan's army, during a previous border crisis in 1999 (Kargil), had prepared to fit nuclear warheads to missiles without the knowledge of then Prime Minister Nawaz Sharif.

However, one could dismiss the fears of accidental war by rejecting the often-quoted assertion that 'there are no strict control structures in operation'. In fact, there are very good command and control structures in place in both India and Pakistan. So, the fears of an accidental war on that count are baseless.

In India, the civilian leadership is well aware of the awesome nature of the problem, and does not take it lightly. In Pakistan, nuclear weapons have always been under military command, and generals in the armies of the subcontinent are extremely capable men—indeed, no one rises to the rank of general in these militaries without having the credentials for it. Besides, contrary to

PUBLIC EUPHORIA OVER THE NUCLEAR BOMB

In the following extract from "Islamabad Dispatch: Trigger Happy" published in the New Republic *in June 2002, journalist Eric Weiner points to the tremendous public support in South Asia for nuclear weapons along with general ignorance as to their real dangers.*

When it comes to nuclear weapons, South Asians display an odd mix of bravado and ignorance. They love the bomb yet know little of its destructive power. Many people I spoke with believe a nuclear bomb is exactly like a conventional bomb, only a bit bigger. The Indian and Pakistani governments seem content to keep their citizens in the dark about the terrifying realities of nuclear war. They rarely hold civil-defense drills; offer no pamphlets on radioactive contamination; and, in Pakistan at least, prevent the broadcast of anti-nuclear materials. . . . And so it's not surprising that ordinary Indians and Pakistanis rode out this latest crisis while hardly missing a beat. While the world fretted about the prospect of nuclear Armageddon, people in Islamabad quietly went about their business, more concerned about the arrival of the summer monsoon than about finding the nearest fallout shelter. (There aren't any.) Unlike Americans during the height of the cold war, South Asians don't even pretend to prepare for nuclear war. Islamabad's civil-defense budget is a whopping $40,000.

Eric Weiner, "Islamabad Dispatch: Trigger Happy," *The New Republic*, June 24, 2002, p. 19.

popular belief, the Indian and Pakistani military are in constant touch and exchange information regularly, including information about nuclear weapons. So, the fear in the West that things 'could get out of hand' in the event of a conflict is quite misplaced. Besides, the subcontinent is inhabited by ancient civilizations, fully aware of the enormous responsibilities wrought by these weapons of mass destruction.

Need for a Political Solution

The causes of the underlying hostility between India and Pakistan are political, not military or nuclear. Military and nuclear preparations add to the existing political hostility. They can never be the methods or mechanisms for the resolution of such political tensions. To put it in the form of an historical analogy—the Cold War arms race between two politically hostile countries, the US and the USSR, was not reversed because of nuclear weapons. Nuclear weapons preparations did not lead to a reduction, but an increase, in Cold War political tensions. It was only Gorbachev's determination and effort to end the political Cold War that led to reductions in nuclear arms and a reversal of that arms race. South Asia is a region that has had a continuous hot-cold war for fifty years. Only by first shifting the political foundations of this situation can we hope to decrease nuclear tensions, not the other way round.

Despite fears of a war, many observers believe, however, that a concerted Indian attack on Pakistan is unlikely. Any pre-emptive move by India would draw an international backlash that would damage both its standing and its efforts to paint Pakistan as the 'aggressor' and to blame it for the continuing turmoil in Kashmir. Furthermore, it would also strengthen the resolve of the Kashmiri militants while undermining any effort by Pakistan to curtail their lines of support in Pakistan. President Musharraf would find great difficulty in curbing religious extremism and control militants, because conflicts with India tend to unite Pakistanis. But there is also 'politics' behind the war cry.

Domestic Pressures from Fundamentalists

Mr Vajpayee's Bharatiya Janata Party (BJP) government is under mounting threat after losing a series of state elections to the opposition Congress Party, and is also under attack for its poor economic management. The BJP now relies more heavily on its core support base among fundamentalist and militant Hindus—some of the most strident advocates of a tough line on Kashmir and a show of force against Pakistan. There are repeated calls by BJP leaders to teach Pakistan a lesson. This means war with Pakistan.

The BJP wants to project itself as a true nationalist force. The probable aim behind this war cry is to exercise maximum pressure on Pakistan and take maximum concessions. Many observers believe that the BJP wants a war with Pakistan, but the BJP-led government does not want a war. It is quite understandable. Rhetoric and reality are two different things.

President Musharraf is also under pressure from fundamentalists angered by his backing for the US-led war in Afghanistan and his efforts already to crack down on extremists. Recent violence and bombings, such as: the kidnapping and murder of Wall Street journalist Daniel Pearl; the murders of French engineers at the Sheraton Hotel, Karachi; a bombing of a church in a secure diplomatic outlet in Islamabad; a suicide bomb/car blast near the US Consulate in Karachi; and most recently the shooting of seven men at the offices of a Christian charity in the centre of Karachi have pointed to Pakistan's own continuing vulnerability to terrorism. Any sign of weakness in his response to India on Kashmir could further threaten Musharraf's position. In this context, it is fair to say that the US relies now on Pakistan's help in the 'war on terrorism'. That strengthens Pakistan's hand in its dealings with India.

Thus, the Kashmir problem is deeply rooted in the histories and national identities of India and Pakistan. The question is, will a war solve the issues relating to Kashmir and Indo-Pakistan relations?

A full-scale war could lead to the use of nuclear weapons, and that would not settle the Kashmir issue but would certainly settle India and Pakistan because of the results of the catastrophe. What would a war achieve? The only thing the Indians could do in a war would be to destroy the Pakistani state as it exists now. In order to preserve that state, the Pakistani military will use nuclear weapons; they have made that very clear. If we take them at their word, the war is not going to solve the Kashmir issue.

Dialogue Is the Key

The conflicts in Kashmir are political in nature. Military response, however, is not a solution. Devising appropriate mechanisms for their resolution continues to require the application of scientific method, rational inquiry and balanced argument. Because you dislike war does not mean you should not study it. And because we don't like the behaviour of politicians does not mean we can ignore them.

The Kashmir issue is still unresolvable. Of course, it is impossible to foresee the future turn of events. In politics and history, perhaps in everything, that unknown power the ancients called 'fate' is always at work. Without forgetting this, I must add that, in politics as well as in private life, the surest method for resolving conflicts, however slowly, is dialogue. Talking with our adversary, we become our own interlocutor. This is the essence of democracy. It is a task that demands realism and imagination and, at the same time, a certain virtue. There is a terrible law: all great historical creation has been built upon sacrifice. In the case of Indian democracy, the blood of Mahatma Gandhi, and also that of Indira Gandhi, her son Rajiv Gandhi and countless innocent victims—all of them died so that one day Hindus, Muslims, Sikhs and the others could talk in peace.

The Kashmir issue appears to be unresolvable at the moment. The manoeuvre, I think, should not be to try to resolve the issue, but to leave it unresolved and negotiate around it. This is what the Indians and the Chinese have done quite successfully about the border conflict, which led to a war between them in 1962 and is still officially unresolved.

Tariq Ali, the Pakistani writer and analyst, while promoting his latest book *The Clash of Fundamentalism*, talked recently in Melbourne about Musharraf's Pakistan and on the current situation in the subcontinent. He said:

The only way of settling the Kashmir issue is peace, and that means an overall deal on a South Asian level. I have been calling for a European Union type structure within South Asia, which includes India, Pakistan, Sri Lanka, Bangladesh and Nepal. Within this structure then, many regional problems could be solved—the Tamil problem in Sri Lanka and the Kashmir problem.

He further said that 'Kashmir should become an autonomous republic, which shares sovereignty with both India and Pakistan, and China, if China is willing, and its autonomy should be guaranteed by all these three states. It won't have a standing army, but it should have the right to govern itself'.

Easy solutions to this Kashmir problem are not to be expected.

But there are at least two hopeful signs:

The first is the new and unique position of the United States in this confrontation. For fifty years, US relationships with India and Pakistan have been a seesaw—as one goes up, the other goes down. But over the past few years, India and the US have been getting on better than ever. And since September 11, US relations with Pakistan have blossomed too. So, for the first time, America's relationship with both sides is on the upswing at the same time, and this gives Washington real leverage.

For the first time in history, both India and Pakistan are US allies in the 'war on terrorism'. As a frontline state with Afghanistan, the US cannot abandon Pakistan. Millions of dollars have been pumped into Pakistan as a gift for its support of the US attacks on Afghanistan. There are US Special Forces in Pakistan still hunting for Al Qaeda militants. President Musharraf has already cracked down on madrassas (religious schools) and changed the country's election system. Washington hopes that Pakistan under Musharraf will not only help its war effort, but will also back away from being a centre of militant and political Islam.

Nor can America ignore India, the world's biggest democracy. There have been joint exercises between the US and Indian forces near Agra recently. The US has also indicated it will supply modern military wares to India.

And secondly, both countries have something to hope for. Musharraf is pulling Pakistan back from the brink of state failure. India is aiming to be a major economic force and key global power. The time may have come for both to realise that they have bigger fish to catch than Kashmir.

Tensions between Pakistan and India have now subsided a bit. Yet the danger of war still remains high as Islamist militants in Kashmir have the potential and reasons to re-ignite hostilities between New Delhi and Islamabad, as evidenced in the Kashmir State Assembly pre-poll violence.

On September 11, 2002 militants in Kashmir killed Mr. Mushtag Ahmed Lone, Kashmir's junior minister for law and parliamentary affairs campaigning for re-election, signalling an increase in violence as elections approach. Three of his bodyguards were also killed. The killing was followed by an attack on a bus-stop in which at least seven people were killed. Militants have vowed to disrupt the elections by killing anyone who participates.

How India will respond to the attack is not yet clear. The Indian government, under pressure from US officials, has been working towards a credible result in the Kashmir election. The immediate problem is how to persuade Pakistan, which naturally sympathises with Muslims across the Line of Control in India, to neutralise extremists totally, so that all Kashmiris can live in peace. US Secretary of State Colin Powell said, 'We have spoken with the Pakistanis about not interfering in any way with those elections, which we expect to be free and fair'.

The governments of India and Pakistan have no intention of fighting any war, let alone a nuclear war. India has shown remarkable restraint in the face of provocation, and Mr. Musharraf is trying his best on the Pakistani side. But the pot is still being heated by many fires, and, as the latest massacre in Gujarat shows, it is the extremists on both sides who usually end up calling the shots.

Pakistan Allies with the United States in the War on Terrorism

By Pervez Musharraf

Following the terrorist attacks on the World Trade Center and the Pentagon on September 11, 2001, President Pervez Musharraf pledged Pakistan's support for the U.S.-led war on terrorism. On the eve of the U.S. attack on Afghanistan, Pakistan provided intelligence, air space, and a ground force for U.S. operations to dislodge the Taliban and attempt to capture Osama bin Laden, who the United States believed masterminded the attack in New York. Despite international support for Mussharaf's actions, within Pakistan he met with opposition. The Pushtan minority in the northwest identified strongly with Afghanistan, and its religious fundamentalists viewed the Taliban as Islamic heroes. In October 2001, as the American bombing began, street demonstrations incited by the religious extremists erupted in major Pakistani cities.

On January 12, 2002, President Musharraf delivered a strong rebuke to the fundamentalists in a national televised speech, extracted below, in which he rejected terrorism and theocracy and said the fight against extremism was in Pakistan's interest. He announced the banning of five of the most radical Islamic groups and warned that his government would not tolerate activities that incite terrorist acts in mosques or other religious institutions. In addition, madrassahs—religious schools, a small proportion of which had become training grounds for Islamic militants—would be regulated to bring the schools more in line with the secular education system.

*P*akistani Brothers and Sisters!
     As you would remember, ever since I assumed office, I launched a campaign to rid the society of extremism, violence and terrorism and strived to project Islam in its true perspective. In my first speech on October 17, 1999, I had said and

Pervez Musharraf, address to the nation of Pakistan, January 12, 2002.

I quote; "Islam teaches tolerance, not hatred; universal brother-hood, not enmity; peace, and not violence. I have a great respect for the Ulema [Muslim religious leaders] and expect them to come forward and present Islam in its true light. I urge them to curb elements which are exploiting religion for vested interests and bringing a bad name to our faith". . . .

In the National Interest

The campaign against extremism undertaken by us from the very beginning is in our own national interest.

We are not doing this under advice or pressure from anyone. Rather, we are conscious that it is in our national interest. We are conscious that we need to rid society of extremism and this is being done right from the beginning.

This domestic reforms process was underway when a terror-ist attack took place against the United States on the 11th of Sep-tember. This terrorist act led to momentous changes all over the world. We decided to join the international coalition against ter-rorism and in this regard I have already spoken to you on a num-ber of occasions. We took this decision on principles and in our national interest.

By the grace of God Almighty our decision was absolutely correct. Our intentions were noble and God Almighty helped us. I am happy to say that the vast majority of Pakistanis stood by this decision and supported our decision. I am proud of the re-alistic decision of our nation. What really pains me is that some religious extremist parties and groups opposed this decision. What hurts more was that their opposition was not based on principles. At a critical juncture in our history, they preferred their personal and party interests over national interests.

They tried their utmost to mislead the nation, took out pro-cessions and resorted to agitation. But their entire efforts failed. The people of Pakistan frustrated their designs. As I have said, I am proud of the people of Pakistan who support correct deci-sions and do not pay heed to those who try to mislead them.

Religious Extremists

I have interacted with the religious scholars on a number of oc-casions and exchanged views with them. I am happy to say that our discussions have been very fruitful. A majority of them are blessed with wisdom and vision and they do not mix religion with politics. Some extremists, who were engaged in protests, are people who try to monopolise and attempt to propagate their own brand of religion.

They think as if others are not Muslims. These are the people who considered the Taliban to be a symbol of Islam and that the Taliban were bringing Islamic rennaissance or were practising the purest form of Islam. They behaved as if the Northern Alliance [an Afghan Islamic rebel faction that opposed the country's Taliban regime], against whom the Taliban were fighting, were non-Muslims! Whereas, in fact, both were Muslims and believers. These extremists were those people who do not talk of "Haqooq-ul-ibad" (obligations towards fellow human beings). They do not talk of these obligations because practising them demands self-sacrifice. How will they justify their Pajeros [imported Jeeps] and expensive vehicles? . . .

We must ask what direction are we being led into by these extremists?

The writ of the government is being challenged. Pakistan has been made a soft state where the supremacy of law is questioned. This situation can not be tolerated any more. The question is what is the correct path?

Government Strategy

First of all, we must rid the society of sectarian hatred and terrorism, promote mutual harmony. Remember that mindsets can not be changed through force and coercion. No idea can ever be forcibly thrust upon any one. Maybe the person changes outwardly but minds and hearts can never be converted by force. Real change can be brought about through personal example, exemplary character and superior intellect. It can be brought about by Haqooq-ul-ibad (Obligations towards fellow human beings). Have we forgotten the example of the Holy Prophet (Peace Be Upon Him) where Islam was spread by virtue of his personal conduct, true leadership and that is how changes in the world took place at that time. . . .

The second thing I want to talk about is the concept of Jehad [holy war] in its totality. I want to [expand] upon it because it is a contentious issue, requiring complete comprehension and understanding. In Islam, Jehad is not confined to armed struggles only. Have we ever thought of waging Jehad against illiteracy, poverty, backwardness and hunger? This is the larger Jehad.

Pakistan, in my opinion, needs to wage Jehad against these evils. After the battle of Khyber [in the eighth century], the Prophet (Peace Be Upon Him) stated that Jehad-e-Asghar (Smaller Jehad) is over but Jehad-e-Akbar (Greater Jehad) has begun. This meant that armed Jehad i.e. the smaller Jehad was now over and the greater Jehad against backwardness and illiteracy had started. Pakistan needs Jehad-e-Akbar at this juncture. By the way we must remember that only the government of the day and not every individual can proclaim armed Jehad.

The extremist minority must realise that Pakistan is not responsible for waging armed Jehad in the world. I feel that in addition to Haqooq Allah (Obligations to God), we should also focus on Haqooq-al-ibad (Obligations towards fellow human beings). At Schools, Colleges and Madaris, Obligations towards fellow beings should be preached. We know that we have totally ignored the importance of correct dealings with fellow humans beings. There is no room for feuds in Islamic teachings. It is imperative that we teach true Islam i.e. tolerance, forgiveness, compassion, justice, fair play, amity and harmony, which is the true spirit of Islam. We must adopt this. We must shun negative thinking.

Policy on Madrassahs

We have formulated a new strategy for Madaris [religious schools] and there is need to implement it so as to galvanize their good aspects and remove their drawbacks. We have developed new syllabi for them providing for teaching of Pakistan studies, Mathematics, Science and English along with religious subjects. Even if we want these Madaris to produce religious leaders they should be educated along these lines. Such people will command more respect in the society because they will be better qualified. To me, students of religious schools should be brought in to the mainstream of society. If any one of them opts to join college or university, he would have the option of being equipped with the modern education. If a child studying at a madrasa does not wish to be a prayer leader and he wants to be a bank official or seek employment elsewhere, he should be facilitated.

It would mean that the students of Madaris should be brought to the mainstream through a better system of education. This is the crux of the Madrasa strategy. This by no means is an attempt to bring religious educational institutions under Govt control nor do we want to spoil the excellent attributes of these institutions.

My only aim is to help these institutions in overcoming their weaknesses and providing them with better facilities and more avenues to the poor children at these institutions.

We must check abuse of mosques and madaris and they must not be used for spreading political and sectarian prejudices. We want to ensure that mosques enjoy freedom and we are here to maintain it. At the same time we expect a display of responsibility along with freedom. If the Imams [religious leaders] of mosques fail to display responsibility, curbs would have to be placed on them. After this analysis, now, I come to some conclusions and decisions:

First, we have to establish the writ of the Government. All organizations in Pakistan will function in a regulated manner. No individual, organization or Party will be allowed to break [the] law of the land. The internal environment has to be improved. Maturity and equilibrium have to be established in the society.

We have to promote an environment of tolerance, maturity, responsibility, patience and understanding. We have to check extremism, militancy, violence and fundamentalism. We will have to forsake the atmosphere of hatred and anger. We have to stop exploitation of simple poor people of the country and not to incite them to feuds and violence. We must concern ourselves with our own country.

Pakistan comes first. We do not need to interfere and concern ourselves with others. There is no need to interfere in other countries.

Now I turn to other important issues. In my view there are three problems causing conflict and agitation in our minds. They include; first the Kashmir Cause, secondly all political disputes at the international level concerning Muslims and thirdly internal sectarian disputes and differences.

These are the three problems which create confusion in our minds. I want to lay down rules of behaviour concerning all the three.

Kashmir

Let us take the Kashmir Cause[1] first. Kashmir runs in our blood. No Pakistani can afford to sever links with Kashmir. The entire

---

1. Pakistan supports the Muslim groups in the Indian state of Kashmir who wish to secede and become part of Pakistan.

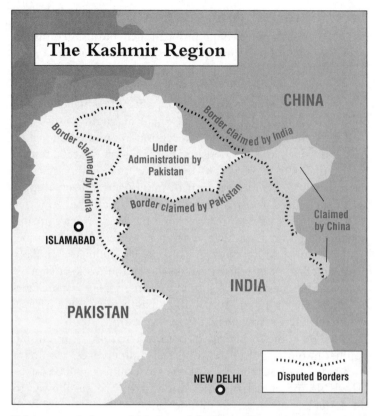

The Kashmir Region

CHINA

Border claimed by India

Under
Administration by
Pakistan

Border claimed by India

Border claimed by Pakistan

Claimed
by China

ISLAMABAD

INDIA

PAKISTAN

NEW DELHI

Disputed Borders

Pakistan and the world knows this. We will continue to extend our moral, political and diplomatic support to Kashmiris. We will never budge an inch from our principle stand on Kashmir. The Kashmir problem needs to be resolved by dialogue and peaceful means in accordance with the wishes of the Kashmiri people and the United Nations resolutions. We have to find the solution of this dispute. No organization will be allowed to indulge in terrorism in the name of Kashmir. We condemn the terrorist acts of September 11, October 1 and December 13.[2] Anyone found involved in any terrorist act would be dealt with sternly.

Strict action will be taken against any Pakistani individual, group or organization found involved in terrorism within or outside the country. Our behaviour must always be in accordance with international norms.

2. Bombs were exploded by terrorist groups in Kashmir and at the Indian parliament building in Delhi.

Stop External Interference

Now we come to the second problem, which causes confusion in our minds and is of our particular concern. It relates to conflicts involving Muslims. Our religious leaders involve themselves in such conflicts without giving serious thought to them [referring to their support for Muslim groups in Afghanistan, Kashmir, and the Middle East]. I don't want to talk at length on this.

It is for the government to take a position on international issues. Individuals, organizations and political parties should restrict their activities to expression of their views. I request them to express their views on international issues in an intellectual spirit and in a civilized manner through force of argument.

Views expressed with maturity and moderation have greater convincing power. Expressing views in a threatening manner does not create any positive effect and anyone who indulges in hollow threats is taken as an unbalanced person by the world at large.

I would request that we should stop interfering in the affairs of others. First, we should attain the strength and the importance where our views carry weight when we express them.

Now we come to internal decisions. The third issue causing conflict in our minds relates to sectarian differences.[3] As I have already pointed out that writ of the Government will be established. No individual, organization or party will be allowed to break the law of the land. All functioning will be in a regulated manner and within rules.

Now I come to the extremist organizations. Terrorism and sectarianism must come to an end. I had announced a ban on [the extremist groups] Lashkar-e-Jhangvi and Sipah-e-Mohammad on 14 August last year [2001]. On that occasion, I had pointed out that [the Islamic militant group] Sipah-e-Sahabaand TJP would be kept under observation.

I am sorry to say that there is not much improvement in the situation. Sectarian violence continues unabated. We have busted several gangs involved in sectarian killings. You would be astonished to know that in year 2001 about 400 innocent people fell victim to sectarian and other killings.

Many of the gangs apprehended include people mostly belonging to Sipah-e-Sahaba and some to TJP. This situation can-

3. In the 1990's clashes between rival Islamic sects erupted into violent confrontations in the major Pakistani cities endangering the lives and safety of the people.

not be tolerated any more. I, therefore, announce banning of both Sipah-e-Sahaba and TJP. In addition to these, TNSM (Tehrik-e-Nifaz-e-Shariat Mohammadi) being responsible for misleading thousands of simple poor people into Afghanistan also stands banned. This organization is responsible for their massacre in Afghanistan. The Government has also decided to put the Sunni Tehreek under observation. No organization is allowed to form Lashkar, Sipah or Jaish. The Government has banned Jaishe-Mohammad and Lashkar-e-Taiba.

Any organization or individual would face strict punitive measures if found inciting the people to violence in internal or external contexts. Our mosques are sacred places where we seek the blessings of God Almighty. Let them remain sacred. We will not allow the misuse of mosques. All mosques will be registered and no new mosques will be built without permission. The use of loudspeakers will be limited only to call for prayers, and Friday Sermon and Vaaz [sermon]. However, I would like to emphasise that special permission is being given for "Vaaz". If this is misused the permission will be cancelled.

If there is any political activity, inciting of sectarian hatred or propagation of extremism in any mosque, the management would be held responsible and proceeded against according to law.

I appeal to all Pesh Imams [head religious scholars] to project the qualities of Islam in the mosques and invite the people to piety. Talk of obligations towards fellow beings, exhort them to abstain from negative thoughts and promote positive thinking. . . .

On Madaris, a detailed policy will be issued through a new Madressa Ordinance. The Ordinance will be issued in a few days. I feel happy that the Madressa policy has been finalized in consultation with religious scholars and Mashaikh [eminent religious authorities]. I have touched on the merits and shortcomings prevailing in the Madaris. Merits have to be reinforced while shortcomings have to be rooted out.

Under the Madressa policy, their functioning will be regulated. These Madaris will be governed by the same rules and regulations applicable to other schools, colleges and universities. All Madaris will be registered by 23rd March 2002 and no new Madressa will be opened without permission of the Government.

If any Madressa (religious school) is found indulging in extremism, subversion, militant activity or possessing any types of weapons, it will be closed. All Madaris will have to adopt the new syllabi by the end of this year. Those Madaris which are already following such syllabi are welcome to continue. The Government has decided to provide financial assistance to such Madaris. The government will also help the Madaris in the training of their teachers. The Ministry of Education has been instructed to review courses of Islamic education in all schools and colleges also with a view to improving them. . . .

My brothers & Sisters,

Pakistan is an Islamic Republic. There are 98 percent Muslims living in this country. We should live like brothers and form an example for rest of the Islamic countries. We should strive to emerge as a responsible and progressive member of the comity of nations.

We have to make Pakistan into a powerful and strong country. We have resources and potential. We are capable of meeting external danger. We have to safeguard ourselves against internal dangers. I have always been saying that internal strife is eating us like termites. Don't forget that Pakistan is the citadel of Islam and if we want to serve Islam well we will first have to make Pakistan strong and powerful. There is a race for progress among all nations. We cannot achieve progress through a policy of confrontation and feuds.

We can achieve progress through human resource development, mental enlightenment, high moral character and technological development. I appeal to all my countrymen to rise to the occasion. We should get rid of intolerance and hatred and instead promote tolerance and harmony.

May God guide us to act upon the true teachings of Islam. May He help us to follow the Quaid-e-Azam's [The great leader and founder of Pakistan, Mohammed Ali Jinnah] motto: "Unity, Faith and Discipline". This should always be remembered. We will be a non-entity without unity.

The Influence of Religious Parties on Pakistan's Government

In October 2002, Pakistan's first general election since the 1999 military coup led by General Musharraf produced surprising results. With Benazir Bhutto and Nawaz Sharif, the leaders of the two main opposition parties, in exile, and maneuvers by Musharraf to ensure his party's victory, all looked on with shock at the electoral success of the MMA, a coalition of Islamic right-wing religious parties. No one party captured enough seats to declare victory, however, and leaders of Pakistan's political parties were forced to negotiate with other parties to form a coalition government. Given the divergence of the parties' views in any coalition government, commentators forecast the country is in for another period of political instability.

In the following article, the editors of the Economist *analyze the likely implications of this unforeseen success of the religious right, which include virulent opposition to the antiterrorist alliance with the United States, a reversal of Musharraf's moves to liberalize Islamic laws, and a departure from the country's modernization path. Some commentators suggest the result should not be interpreted as a vote for Islamic fundamentalism, but rather as a defense of the Islamic faith, which is perceived to be under assault by a U.S. policy of global recrimination toward Muslims.*

"Americans are the killers, the butchers, the murderers," observes the mild mannered but plain speaking secretary-general of Pakistan's Jamaat-i-Islami party, Syed Munawar Hassan. The views of Mr Hassan and his party

"Oh, What a Lovely Ally; Pakistan's Election," *The Economist*, vol. 365, October 19, 2002. Copyright © 2002 by The Economist Newspaper Group. Reproduced by permission.

are not new. Like much of the Muslim world they are convinced that the United States and Israel have formed a tag team for the purpose of oppressing Muslims, a belief fanned into fury by the American bombing of Afghanistan [in October 2001], Israel's assaults on Palestinians and now the threat of war against Iraq.

Until now, such views could be treated as dissent, blasting Pakistan's pro-western policies without injuring them. Pakistan has been among the most valuable members of the American-led coalition against terrorism. [The October 2002] general election may have changed that. The MMA grouping of religious parties, including Jamaat-i-Islami, stormed from the fringes of Pakistani politics into the centre, positioning themselves to govern two of Pakistan's four provinces and winning more seats in the national parliament than they have ever done. There is a chance that this group will be part of the coalition in charge of the central government.

Opposition to Pakistan's anti-terrorist alliance with the United States was the centrepiece of their campaign and will be their top priority in government, says Mr Hassan. The two provinces they look set to govern, North West Frontier Province and Balochistan, blur into Afghanistan. They are prime hunting grounds for refugee members of al-Qaeda, including, perhaps, Osama bin Laden. George [W.] Bush and Pakistan's president, Pervez Musharraf, must now be wondering what the religious parties can do to sabotage the hunt. They are not the only ones in shock. The days of freedom of expression in parliament are behind us, laments Aitzaz Ahsan, a leader of the centrist Pakistan People's Party. He recalls that in 1999 a handful of fundamentalist senators so intimidated their colleagues that only four voted for a resolution condemning honour killings of women who had eloped. Will tradition now smother modernity?

India Concerned

India, Pakistan's perennial enemy, is also worried. Its foreign minister, Yashwant Sinha, called the gains of the religious parties a bad signal. How much closer will fundamentalists get to controlling Pakistan's arsenal of nuclear weapons? The rise of the religious parties is the sum of some fears, not all of them. It brings an illiberal, anti-American element to the centre of Pakistan's political arena, which cannot but complicate the war on terrorism. General Musharraf, who tried, though not very consistently, to curb the influence of religion in public life in the three years since seizing power in a coup, will probably stop trying.

Concessions to India over the disputed state of Kashmir, never imminent, are even less likely. But there is little danger of Pakistan becoming a rogue Islamist state, an Iraq with a hankering for martyrdom. Some of the religious parties are pro-Taliban, but are more worldly and pragmatic than their defeated Afghan brothers. Access to political power will make them more so. They must contend with many other forces, including rivals in the fragmented parliament, the armed forces, which can veto almost anything politicians do, pressures from the United States and divisions within their own ranks. Pakistan is in for a period of uncertainty, perhaps even instability, but not revolution.

The elections knocked Pakistan askew. The idea had been to restore democracy after three years of military rule without bringing back the habitual sins of corruption, political vendettas, masochistic economic policies and clashes between civilian and military authorities, which often ended with the army taking over. To this end, General Musharraf first secured his own position as president by holding a referendum in April [2002], which almost no one but he regards as legitimate. He then amended the constitution to give the president the power to dismiss parliament and to give the armed forces a permanent role in government through a National Security Council, headed by the president and including the top generals and elected officials. Finally, he tried to engineer the election so that the parliament it produced would acquiesce in all of this.

Success of Religious Parties

Criminal proceedings against Pakistan's two pre-eminent politicians, Benazir Bhutto and Nawaz Sharif, both former prime ministers, kept them out of the country. A split was arranged in Mr Sharif's Pakistan Muslim League; PML(Q), the bit friendly to General Musharraf, got extra help from the administration and won more seats than any other party. The election had serious flaws, said observers from the European Union. Not serious enough, though, to deliver a comfortable result for General Musharraf. The religious parties were supposed to do well (a decent showing would make the general look all the more indispensable to the West as a bulwark against extremism), but not too well. As things turned out, the Muttahida Majlis-i-Amal (MMA),

PAKISTANI PEOPLE PROTEST U.S. MILITARY OPERATIONS

Author Navnita Chadha Behera points to the divergence between government policy and popular sentiment regarding the U.S. military operations in Afghanistan in October 2001.

There is a growing "disconnect" between the people and the government. While the Musharaf regime has offered unstinted support to the US including the use of its air bases for its military operations, the anger against the air strikes and Islamabad's support to Washington, has singed all the four provinces of the country. Pakistan is simmering and the ranks of anti–US demonstrations continue to swell. At the popular level, this may not be for any ingrained support for the Taliban but because of the emotional sympathy for the plight of fellow Muslims although some religious leaders have issued fatwas asking their followers to wage jihad against the US. Nearly ten thousand tribesmen are reported to have gathered in the Bajaur Agency, located around 145 kms from Peshawar, to enlist their services for jihad. Officially, no Pakistani is allowed to cross the border. But the border crossing on top of the hill, Ghaki, has seen thousands cross into Afghanistan. The response to Mullah Sufi Mohammad, the leader of the Tehrik-e-Nifaz-e-Shariat-e-Muhammadi (TNSM) call for help has been massive also in terms of collection of funds for the Taliban war effort: hundreds of kgs of gold, other jewelry, blankets, quilts, warm clothes and even antique guns have landed at TNSM-run seminaries. The divide between the political choices of the government and the society is indeed sharp.

Navnita Chadha Behera, "Pakistani Choices," *Middle East Insight*, January/February 2002. www.brook.edu.

the six-party religious alliance, won enough seats in parliament to deny the general's allies, PML(Q) plus assorted others, a reliable majority.

General Musharraf's other potential partner is the People's Party of Miss Bhutto, which agrees with him about fighting terrorism but, like the MMA, rejects the constitutional innovations that place him above parliament. He seems to face a choice between a party with a hostile ideology and one that is merely hostile to his ambitions. Just what will emerge from the parliamentary scrum is uncertain. The price the People's Party will set for joining the government, which may include dropping cases against Miss Bhutto and her husband, who is in jail, may be too high for General Musharraf to meet. Other coalitions are quite possible. A friends-of-Pervez government, including everyone but the MMA, the People's Party and Mr Sharif's faction of the Muslim League, might eke out a majority, though it would be too slender to last.

The current parliament, however, is unlikely to deliver stable government. Avowed foes of military rule have about half the seats. Even seemingly compliant civilian prime ministers have a way of turning on the generals once they sniff power. The current political line-up seems doomed to constant bickering over position and policy, which may end with the president dismissing parliament or even with the politicians getting rid of the president. None of this would be new for Pakistan. What is new is that the religious right will have a big say in what happens.

The official line, from the government, headed by General Musharraf until he gives way to a prime minister, from the religious parties themselves and from potential coalition partners, is that the MMA will use power responsibly. It is not fundamentalist or militant, merely religious, says Pakistan's information minister. Some Pakistanis compare it to the Bharatiya Janata Party, the Hindu-nationalist party that rules India. The MMA downplays its radicalism, eager to be seen as a savvy player in the give and take of parliamentary politics. Even on its top priority, ridding Pakistan of American terrorist-hunters, the party sounds reasonable. It's a process, says Mr Hassan of Jamaat-i-Islami, not a switch button.

MMA Personality Profiles

Parliamentary polish does not quite obscure the MMA's rough pedigree. Some of its constituent parties have a soft spot for the

Taliban. One leader said that if the United States molested Mr
bin Laden Americans in Pakistan would be attacked. Largely
non-violent themselves, their advocacy of jihad has underwrit-
ten violence in Afghanistan, against Indian rule in Kashmir and
even against other Islamic sects within Pakistan. In their commingling of violence and respectability they are typical of Pakistani institutions, including the army. Fazlur Rahman, issuer of
the threat to kill Americans, heads the most powerful faction of
the Jamiatul Ulema-i-Islam (JUI). Its madrassas (religious schools)
educated the Taliban and supplied legions for its army. Its fierce
creed, a puritanical brand of Sunni Islam, developed during the
19th century in the Indian town of Deoband, spawned even
fiercer groups.

Sipah-i-Sahaba, a Punjab-based group started by former JUI
men in 1985, has a record of killing Shia Muslims. It spun off an
even more violent group, called Lashkar-i-Jhangvi, which is sus-
pected of involvement in recent attacks on westerners and foreigners. Sipah-i-Sahaba is banned, and too disreputable for the
MMA, but its leader, Azam Tariq, won a parliamentary seat in the
southern Punjabi city of Jhang, boasting in a campaign brochure
of loving the great soldier, Osama bin Laden. Mr Rahman is
more politician than warrior. He was chairman of the foreign-
affairs committee of parliament and an ally of Miss Bhutto, and
has been named by his party as a candidate for prime minister.

His nickname, Maulana Diesel, testifies to a reputation for
commercial acumen, which some suggest can be exploited in the
cause of moderation. Like many stalwarts of the religious right,
he is thought to be partly beholden to the armed forces, which,
through its Inter Services Intelligence agency (ISI), has used religious parties for tasks as diverse as promoting Pakistani influence in Afghanistan, fighting Indian rule in Kashmir and clipping
the wings of political parties at home.

Jamaat-i-Islami, the driving force behind the MMA, has had
nothing to do with the narrow ideologies that spawn violence
among Islamic sects; though it was a pioneer of promoting jihad
in Afghanistan and in Indian-administered Kashmir. Qazi Hussain Ahmad, its leader, is more moderate than Mr Rahman, but
perhaps less yielding. He is generally considered the MMA's
weightiest leader.

Its other constituents make strange bedfellows. Shias and
Barelvis, an easier-going sort of Muslim, have both been victims

of savage Deobandi attacks and answered in kind. Yet they have shown up in the MMA. The fusion of these and other groups is something of a miracle, brought about, some say, by the army, which wanted a counterweight to the mainstream political parties besides PML(Q). It betokens moderation. Or maybe, its adversaries hope, an eventual falling out. Their rising stake in democratic politics could tame them further.

This is what General Musharraf counts on when he declares that Pakistan will remain a key member of the coalition against terror. If the United States attacks Iraq, the MMA can express Pakistan's rage from the podium, making it less likely that people will do so with guns. Despite the brave face some Pakistanis are putting on it, the MMA's success has put it in a position to slow down, if not derail, the initiatives that have made General Musharraf a popular figure in Washington.

Political Wrangling

By just how much depends on the outcome of the multi-sided tussle now taking place in Islamabad, the capital. Fighting al-Qaeda is mainly the job of the central government. The brunt is borne by such agencies as the ISI, by the army and by centrally run militias such as the Frontier Constabulary. Some 60,000 Pakistani troops and a handful of Americans are ranged along the border with Afghanistan, most in the federally administered tribal areas of North West Frontier Province, which are governed by the centre to the extent they are governed at all. If the MMA tries to undermine the fight against terrorism, the government has hinted that General Musharraf's National Security Council will block it. One message this sends out is that Americans ought to love the council, even though most Pakistani parties want to dismantle it. But the MMA can make trouble. Even if it sits in opposition, the MMA chief ministers of the North West Frontier Province and Balochistan will occupy two seats on the 13-member council. It could get more, through such offices as the speakership of parliament and the chairmanship of the Senate.

Most MPs from the tribal areas are MMA men who may, some analysts worry, provide havens for foes of Afghanistan's American-backed government. In Quetta, the capital of Balochistan, newspapers report that a dozen local Taliban were freed from the district jail on instructions from newly elected MMA representatives. This could be a taste of sabotage to come.

And what of those nukes? The prime minister will head the
National Command Authority but de facto control of the
weapons rests with the armed forces, says Hasan Askari Rizvi,
an expert on the Pakistani military. The army will not counte-
nance an extremist as prime minister; if he rashly ordered de-
ployment of nuclear weapons, says Mr Rizvi, the military would
disobey.

MMA Domestic Agenda

If the MMA's anti-American agenda is blocked, its domestic
wishlist may become more important. It has called for the implementation of sharia, Islamic law, which it says can be done
within the framework of the revived constitution. The party
wants to banish interest from bank lending. Its aversion extends
to the financial-aid programmes within Pakistan that are under-
written by the IMF [International Monetary Fund] and World
Bank. Whether the MMA sits in government or opposition, it is
hard to see a revival of a programme to modernise madrassas,
which General Musharraf had already put on a slow track. In the
North West Frontier Province and Balochistan state schools may
come to resemble madrassas rather than the other way around.
Pakistani liberals now fear a chilling effect that will close minds,
hinder reasonable expression and make women timid.

Prelude or interlude? Those who fret about fundamentalists
taking over used to be reassured by the religious parties' consistent failure to win more than a few seats in elections. That com-
fort is no longer available, but that does not mean that Pakistan is
succumbing to fundamentalism. The MMA's success arises in part
from a fleeting alignment of circumstances; the hobbling of the
mainstream parties, the Afghan war and the fragile alliance itself.
It won a tenth of the popular vote, not much more than religious
parties had won in previous elections. The difference was that this
time they pooled votes rather than splitting them.

The vote for the MMA is not a vote for beards, burqas, and jihad, wrote one columnist, but rather a vote against imperialism
and indignity. And against political fat-cats, some of whom
shifted from the mainstream parties to General Musharraf's
PML(Q). The new affection could be strengthened by war in
Iraq, or weakened by incompetent government, which would not
be surprising with so many newcomers in the assemblies. Black-
ing out cable stations could alienate people. People love to see

Indian movies, even in the villages, says Haji Muhammad Adeel, a candidate whose pro-American party was decimated by the MMA. After one or two years will everything return to normal? Not quite. General Musharraf has had three years to set Pakistan firmly on the road to modernisation. The elections confirm that he has failed.

CHRONOLOGY

3000s B.C.
Settlements emerge in the Indus Valley.

2800–2600 B.C.
The Indus Valley civilization begins.

ca. 1500–1200 B.C.
The Vedic Aryans immigrate to India.

ca. 563 B.C.
Buddhism is founded.

ca. 320–180 B.C.
Chandragupta Maurya establishes the Mauryan dynasty. Buddhism spreads throughout the subcontinent.

ca. 180 B.C.–A.D. 150
Saka dynasties rule the Indus Valley.

ca. A.D. 319–600
The Gupta Empire marks the classical Hindu Age in northern India.

610
According to the Muslim faith, the tenets of a new religion, Islam, are revealed to Muhammad the prophet on Mount Hira near Mecca.

711
Muhammad bin Qasim, an Arab general, conquers Sind and incorporates it into the Umayyad caliphate.

1001–1030
Mahmud of Ghazni raids the Indian subcontinent from Afghanistan.

1192
Muhammad of Ghor defeats the Rajputs.

1206–1526
The Delhi Sultanate reigns.

1398
Timur conquers Delhi.

1526
Babur defeats the last Lodhi sultan in the First Battle of Panipat, and heralds the arrival of the Mughal Empire.

1556
Akbar is victorious in the Second Battle of Panipat.

1556–1605
Akbar reigns as Mughal emperor.

1605–1627
Jahangir succeeds Akbar as emperor.

1612
The British East India Company establishes its first trading post.

1628–1658
Shah Jahan reigns and builds the Taj Mahal.

1658–1707
Aurangzeb, the last great Mughal emperor, reigns.

1707–1858
The Mughal Empire declines.

1757
At the Battle of Plassey the British defeat the Mughal forces in Bengal; the British period begins.

1830s
The British introduce English education and other social reform measures.

1857
Hindu and Muslim sepoys revolt in the Indian Mutiny.

1858

The British East India Company is replaced by direct rule by the British Crown. The British Raj is formally established.

1885

The Indian National Congress is formed.

1905

Bengal is partitioned into Hindu and Muslim electorates.

1906

The Muslim League is founded.

1909

The British Morley-Minto reforms establish separate electorates for Muslims.

1911

The partition of Bengal is annulled.

1916

The Congress–Muslim League Pact (also known as the Lucknow Pact) is signed.

1935

The British Government of India Act provides for the establishment of an autonomous Indian nation.

1940

The Muslim League adopts the Pakistan Resolution, demanding a separate nation for Muslims.

1946

The Muslim League declares August 16 "Direct Action Day." Widespread communal rioting spreads throughout India.

1947

The Republic of Pakistan is established on August 14. Mohammed Ali Jinnah becomes Pakistan's first governor-general and Liaquat Ali Khan becomes its first prime minister. India gains independence from Britain on August 15. The Kashmir conflict and undeclared war with Pakistan begins.

1948

Jinnah dies in September and Khwaja Nazimuddin becomes governor-general.

1949

The United Nations enforces a cease-fire, ending the first Indo-Pakistan war in January.

1951

Liaquat Ali Khan is assassinated; Nazimuddin becomes prime minister and Ghulam Mohammad is governor-general.

1956

The first constitution is adopted in March, and Iskander Mirza becomes president.

1958

Mirza abrogates the constitution and declares martial law in October. He is sent into exile and General Mohammad Ayub Khan becomes president.

1965

The second Indo-Pakistan war over Kashmir begins.

1969

Ayub Khan resigns and General Agha Mohammad Yahya Khan becomes president.

1970

In Pakistan's first general elections, the Awami League under Sheikh Mujibur Rahman (Mujib) gains a majority in the National Assembly, but the West Pakistan–dominated government declines to convene the assembly.

1971

East Pakistan attempts to secede and begins a civil war in March. In April, East Pakistan proclaims its independence. In December India invades East Pakistan, the Pakistan army surrenders to Indian armed forces, and East Pakistan secedes to form the new nation of Bangladesh. In West Pakistan, Yahya Khan resigns and Zulfikar Ali Bhutto becomes president.

1973

In August the new constitution of Pakistan goes into effect. Bhutto becomes prime minister.

1976

Pakistan establishes diplomatic relations with Bangladesh.

1977

Bhutto's Pakistan People's Party has a massive victory in the general elections held in March, which provokes protest riots. General Mohammad Zia-ul-Haq proclaims martial law in July and declares himself chief martial law administrator.

1978

Zia-ul-Haq becomes the nation's sixth president.

1979

Zia introduces the Islamic penal code. Bhutto is hanged in April. In December the Soviet Union moves troops into Afghanistan.

1980

Zia rejects America's offer of US$400 million in military aid as "peanuts."

1985

Non-Islamic banking is abolished, general elections are held for the National Assembly, and Zia invites Mohammad Khan Junejo to form a civilian government.

1986

The movement for the restoration of democracy launches its campaign against the government, demanding new general elections. Benazir Bhutto is arrested in Karachi.

1988

In May, Zia dismisses Junejo, dissolves the national and provincial assemblies, and orders new elections within ninety days. In August, Zia, the U.S. ambassador to Pakistan, and top army officers are killed in a plane crash. In November, the PPP wins 93 out of 207 contested seats. Benazir Bhutto is sworn in as the first female prime minister of a Muslim nation in December. Pakistan and India sign accords at the South Asian

Association for Regional Cooperation summit in Islamabad, agreeing not to attack each other's nuclear facilities.

1989

In February, the Soviet Union withdraws all troops from Afghanistan.

1990

Between May and June, ethnic troubles mount and rifts develop between the PPP and coalition parties. In August, President Ghulam Ishaq Khan dismisses Benazir Bhutto, her cabinet, and the National Assembly; orders general elections for October 24, 1990; and appoints Ghulam Mustafa Jatoi as caretaker prime minister. In October, U.S. president George Bush cuts off aid to Pakistan because of the country's nuclear weapons. Bhutto's PPP loses to right-wing parties. In November, Mian Nawaz Sharif is elected prime minister.

1991

Prime Minister Nawaz Sharif liberalizes the economy and announces policies to encourage foreign investment. The National Assembly adopts the Sharia bill. By July, the opposition parties call for dismissal of the government because of the declining law-and-order situation.

1992

Babri Mosque in Ajodhya, India, is destroyed by Hindu fundamentalists, provoking communal riots in India. Pakistan asks the Indian government to protect Indian Muslims.

1993

In April, President Ghulam Ishaq Khan dismisses Nawaz Sharif's government, citing corruption. The president and prime minister resign under pressure from the military in July. Moeen Qureshi, from the World Bank, becomes caretaker prime minister. India rejects Pakistan's proposal to sign a regional nuclear test ban treaty. In October, Benazir Bhutto's PPP forms a coalition government and is returned to office.

1994

Pakistan puts its troops on high alert along the Line of Control in Kashmir after India deploys two more army divisions.

1995

In March, a terrorist attack in Karachi kills two Americans and
draws international attention to the declining law-and-order
situation. In July, the United States alleges that Pakistan has
surreptitiously bought medium-range M-11 ballistic missiles
from China.

1996

President Farooq Ahmad Khan Leghari dismisses Benazir Bhutto's
government on charges of corruption and mismanagement.
Malik Meraj Khalid is appointed as caretaker prime minister
until national elections can be held in February 1997.

1997

Nawaz Sharif begins his second term in office based on a sound
victory in the national elections for his Muslim League Party.

1998

On the heels of nuclear tests in India, Pakistan conducts five nuclear explosions at a test site in Baluchistan on May 29.

1999

Benazir Bhutto and her husband are convicted of corruption
charges and sentenced to jail. They remain outside the country. Pakistan and India come to the brink of a third war over
Kashmir during a ten-week confrontation known as the
Kargil conflict. In October, Prime Minster Nawaz Sharif is
deposed in a military coup led by General Pervez Musharraf
that is widely condemned. Pakistan is suspended from the
Commonwealth.

2000

Nawaz Sharif is sentenced to life imprisonment on hijacking and
terrorism charges, but is pardoned by the military in December and goes into exile in Saudi Arabia.

2001

In June, Musharraf names himself president as well as head of
the army. After the September 11 terrorists attacks of the
World Trade Center and the Pentagon by Muslim terrorists,
Musharraf pledges support for the U.S. war on terrorism in
Afghanistan. Pakistan is implicated in a terrorist attack on the
Indian Parliament in Delhi. In December, India and Pakistan

mass troops along the common border in Kashmir amid mounting fears of war.

2002

On January 12, in a televised address to the nation, President Musharraf justifies Pakistan's cooperation in the U.S.-led war on terrorism and announces measures to curb religious extremism, including the Madaris Ordinance, which regulates *madrassahs* (religious schools). In February, Muslims firebomb a train of Hindus coming from Ajodhya, killing fifty-seven people. In April, President Musharraf wins five more years in office as president in a referendum criticized as unconstitutional. A terrorist attack in Jammu, Kashmir, in May, brings Pakistan and India to the brink of war. In August, Musharraf grants himself sweeping powers, including the right to dismiss an elected government. The first general elections since the 1999 coup are held on October 10 and yield inconclusive results, leading to jockeying by political parties to form a coalition government. The conservative religious parties do better than expected. In late November Zafrullah Khan Jamali, a tribal chieftain from Baluchistan, is elected by the National Assembly as prime minister of a Muslim League coalition government.

2003

In the February Senate elections, which President Musharraf calls the final stage of the country's "transition to democracy," the Muslim coalition government wins most seats in voting in the upper house. In March, Pakistan authorities arrest Khalid Shaikh Mohammad, a close aide to Osama bin Laden and the al-Qaeda suspect believed to have masterminded the September 11, 2001, attacks on the World Trade Center in New York, and hand him over to the United States for interrogation.

FOR FURTHER RESEARCH

General

Akbar S. Ahmed, *Discovering Islam: Making Sense of Muslim History and Society.* New York: Routledge, 2002.

Shahid Javed Burki, *Historical Dictionary of Pakistan.* Metuchen, NJ: Scarecrow Press, 1991.

John L. Esposito, ed., *The Oxford History of Islam.* New York: Oxford University Press, 1999.

Pre-1947

Larry Collins and Dominique Lapierre, *Freedom at Midnight.* New York: Simon and Schuster, 1975.

Bamber Gascoigne, *The Great Mughals.* London: Jonathon Cape, 1971.

Irfan Habib, *Akbar and His India.* Delhi, India: Oxford University Press, 1997.

Peter Hardy, *The Muslims of British India.* Cambridge, England: Cambridge University Press, 1972.

C.H. Philips, *The Partition of India: Policies and Perspectives, 1935–1947.* Cambridge, MA: MIT Press, 1970.

John F. Richards, *The New Cambridge History of India: The Mughal Empire.* Cambridge, England: Cambridge University Press, 1996.

Percival Spear, *Twilight of the Mughals.* Cambridge, England: Cambridge University Press, 1951.

Post-1947

Akbar S. Ahmed, *Jinnah, Pakistan, and Islamic Identity.* London: Routledge, 1997.

Mohammad Ayub Khan, *Friends Not Masters: A Political Autobiography.* New York: Oxford University Press, 1967.

Leonard Binder, *Religion and Politics in Pakistan.* Berkeley and Los Angeles: University of California Press, 1963.

S.M. Burke, *Pakistan's Foreign Policy: An Historical Analysis.* London: Oxford University Press, 1973.

Shahid Javed Burki, *Pakistan: A Nation in the Making.* Boulder, CO: Westview Press, 1986.

Shahid Javed Burki and Craig Baxter, *Pakistan Under the Military: Eleven Years of Zia ul-Haq.* Boulder, CO: Westview Press, 1991.

Stephen P. Cohen, *The Pakistan Army.* Berkeley and Los Angeles: University of California Press, 1984.

Ayesha Jalal, *The State of Martial Rule: The Origins of Pakistan's Political Economy of Defense.* New York: Cambridge University Press, 1990.

Alistair Lamb, *Kashmir: A Disputed Legacy, 1846–1990.* Karachi, Pakistan: Oxford University Press, 1992.

Hafeez Malik, *Moslem Nationalism in India and Pakistan.* Washington, DC: Public Affairs Press, 1963.

Hasan-Askari Rizvi, *The Military and Politics in Pakistan, 1947–86.* New Delhi, India: Konark, 1988.

———, *Pakistan and the Geo-Strategic Environment: A Study of Foreign Policy.* New York: St. Martin's Press, 1993.

Richard S. Wheeler, *The Politics of Pakistan: A Constitutional Quest.* Ithaca, NY: Cornell University Press, 1970.

Stanley Wolpert, *Jinnah of Pakistan.* New York: Oxford University Press, 1984.

Mohammad Zia-ul-Haq, *Introduction of Islamic Laws: Address to the Nation.* Islamabad, Pakistan: Pakistan Government Publication, 1979.

Lawrence Ziring, *The Ayub Khan Era: Politics in Pakistan, 1958–69.* Syracuse, NY: Syracuse University Press, 1971.

————, *Pakistan in the Twentieth Century*. Oxford, England: Oxford University Press, 1999.

Contemporary Pakistan

John L. Esposito and John O. Voll, *Islam and Democracy*. New York: Oxford University Press, 1996.

Christophe Jaffrelot, ed., *Pakistan: Nationalism Without a Nation?* New Delhi, India: Manchar, 2002.

Henry J. Korson, *Contemporary Problems of Pakistan*. Boulder, CO: Westview Press, 1993.

Christina Lamb, *Waiting for Allah: Pakistan's Struggle for Democracy*. New York: Viking, 1991.

Anita M. Weiss, *Walls Within Walls: Life Histories of Working Women in the Old City of Lahore*. Boulder, CO: Westview Press, 1992.

Websites

Center for Strategic and International Studies, www.csis.org. A research organization based in Washington, D.C., that provides in-depth analyses on South Asian politics in its *South Asia Monitor*, available online at this site.

Dawn, www.dawn.com. *Dawn* is the largest English-language daily newspaper published in Pakistan. It includes articles listed by subject from back issues to 1999.

Government of Pakistan, www.pak.gov.pk. Official website of the Pakistan government.

Guardian Internet Edition, www.guardian.co.uk. A British daily newspaper with good coverage on Pakistan.

Pakistan WWW Virtual Library, http://inic.utexas.edu/asnic/countries/pakistan. An electronic library of the University of Texas that includes reputable sources on Pakistan, with many useful links.

INDEX